MW00414716

To Jack,
This is wh.
when you go through
the Ouage Entity to a glome,
Best Wishes

STAR REBELS:

STORIES OF SPACE
EXPLORATION, ALIEN RACES
AND ADVENTURE

AUDREY FAYE • C. GOCKEL • CHRISTINE POPE
ANTHEA SHARP • D.L. DUNBAR • L.J. COHEN
PIPPA DACOSTA • LINDSAY BUROKER • PATTY JANSEN
JAMES R. WELLS • KENDRA C. HIGHLEY

STAR REBELS

ISBN-13: 978-1535430524
ISBN-10: 1535430524

CONTENTS

INTRODUCTION

We love anthologies like this—putting them together as much as reading them. There is such talent in the writer world right now, and so many people telling stories that are a little (or a lot!) outside the norm.

This collection is mostly prequel short stories to science fiction series. You likely picked up this anthology because there's a story in here by an author you love. Absolutely go read it—but also graze a little. Try a story from someone new to you. In the end, if this anthology doesn't help you discover new worlds, then we haven't done our job. However, given the number of new books on our Kindles, we're pretty sure that's not going to be a problem!

Thanks for reading!

—the Authors of *Star Rebels*

STAR REBELS

A TALE OF
TWO SHIPS

A KARMA CORP STORY

AUDREY FAYE

SHE WAS DEAD.

Sigrid Albrecht snatched her face off the console that had apparently turned into a pillow for her latest desperate catnap. Every damn alarm on the *Skrapp* was sounding, even a couple she knew hadn't worked for at least a decade.

All letting her know the obvious. Her old, leaky nav charts had been wrong. There weren't clear skies out this side of the Veridian ice fields—there was a fucking huge rock. And she had solar sails in full deployment.

Turning while deployed was suicide—it would rip the ship in half.

152 seconds until impact.

Her brain, suffering from traumatic lack of sleep, still had no problem doing that math. 2.5 minutes left to live.

Sigrid stabbed at buttons, ignoring the wailing behind her. Freja would just have to wait.

Freja.

Sigrid's heart clutched. Her precious baby girl. Everything else in her life had been mercilessly snatched away, and now it seemed the universe was coming for her tiny daughter too.

It hadn't even waited a week.

She banged her right hand on two different consoles, trying to quiet the damn alarms. Her left hand abused the sonar, radar, nav charts. Trying to find a way to take a crippled junker around a freaking huge asteroid.

One that wasn't supposed to be there.

131 seconds.

She should have bought better charts, but charts cost money, and there had been precious little of that lately. She'd needed the cash off this trip. Pickings had been good—not a lot of junkers collected in this sector. She had a cargo hold full of high-quality space trash.

It would form her burial mound.

117 seconds.

Freja's wailing pierced through the alarms. Sigrid glanced over at the tiny, mad arms flailing at the monstrous sounds that had invaded newborn sleep and felt her heart split in two. She'd never know now if her girl was going to have her momma's straight blonde hair or the curls of the man who had accidentally helped to make her.

Apparently black market fertility control wasn't any better than black market nav charts.

Sigrid looked back at her consoles. It was bleak. She could slow the *Skrapp* down a little. Enough to maybe leave their dead bodies intact instead of pulverized into ooze.

Long enough for the sky gods to find her tiny girl's soul.

101 seconds.

She'd always had a weakness for the gods. It wasn't reciprocal. They'd never noticed she existed.

Freja. Named for the Norse goddess of love and beauty—and of death. It had been the name that had come to Sigrid as she lay curled up on a pallet, exhausted and alone, after giving birth in the *Skrapp*'s cargo hold. The med bot had died right about the time her water had broken. Which was fine, because Sigrid had been about to strangle it anyhow. No damn bot got to tell her how to breathe.

82 seconds.

Breathing. Oxygen. The cargo hold had an evac pod. A junked one she'd scooped up in an asteroid field three days before Freja's birth—and hooked up to her systems long enough to verify its life support still worked.

Worth more that way.

Sigrid bolted for the port to her cargo hold. The evac pod wouldn't fly, and she didn't have a door to push it out of, but it was a tough, padded cylinder. One with oxygen.

The closest she could come to a womb on short notice.

No time.

She reversed herself back through the port hole and grabbed Freja, wrapped in a batik scarf and remnants of an old skinsuit. Poor kid. She'd had a weird life in her six days in the galaxy.

Fortunately, the med bot's single auto-diaper had still been functional.

61 seconds.

Sigrid kissed the top of her daughter's head and propelled them both into the cargo hold. She tucked Freja into the evac pod, batik scarf and all. And then, heart rending, touched one finger to her sweet girl's red, yowling cheek and slammed the door of the small capsule shut.

Two steps and she had both hands on the cargo hold console. It worked better than most on the ship, and it would let her spend the last 61 seconds of her life close enough to see her baby girl through the evac pod's tiny window.

Frantically she re-programmed the code, running shunts around the systems that were already broken and the ones unlikely to survive impact.

Impact. She couldn't think about that now.

46 seconds.

Sigrid's fingers flew, echoes of when she'd been one of the best programmers in the Federation's fleet. Before Antonio. Before the handsome man who had pulled her over to the dark side.

Before she'd sold her soul to try and save him.

Her luck with men had never changed—Brag had only been the latest. Named after the Viking god of music and poetry, and he'd been a master of both. His voice had seduced her in one long, slow evening over mugs of spiced mead in between sets at the bar on Heimili Station.

A bard with a golden voice. Maybe his daughter had inherited some of his fortune.

She would need it.

22 seconds.

Sigrid cursed and locked in the last two lines of code. All oxygen would route to the evac pod on impact.

Which would likely only mean that her beautiful, innocent, defenseless baby girl would die slowly and alone on the side of an unforgiving astral rock.

Sigrid's eyes filled with hot tears. She slashed them away with the back of her hand, knowing she had to be able to see. Had to time the execution of the code just right, or *Skrapp*'s sense of self-preservation would override the suicide script.

8 seconds.

She watched the view screen and the oncoming, rushing horror of the rock. Watched the evil numbers counting down, her finger hovering over the execute command. Looked one last time at the red, screaming face of her tiny girl, about to be birthed yet again into an unfriendly world.

And pushed the button.

✳

Eight Years Later…

"Hey, kiddo. Keep it under three gees, okay?"

Lakisha Drinkwater, eight and already one of the best pilots on Halkyn VII, rolled her eyes. "I can fly faster than that and you know it."

Her father ruffled her blonde, wavy hair. "I know. But the pressure hull can't handle it."

She sighed. "Is the patch failing again?" That meant they'd be grounded until they could borrow Tivi Malcolm's blow torch. Which, given how mad he was at the Drinkwaters right now, might be a while.

Everyone was kind of mad at the Drinkwaters. Her oldest brother Jingo was the newest full-fledged digger on the rock, and he'd been assigned the pile-of-crap shaft to mine. Or at least, that's what everyone had called it until he'd found the vein of iridium in the back right corner.

Iridium was the most valuable thing they mined in this sector, and a new vein would earn a hefty finder's bonus. Maybe Jingo could buy them a blow torch.

Whatever. Kish's mind swerved away from the boring issues of iridium and money and petty digger-rock politics and surveyed the horizon. It was a big treat to be out here, and she wasn't going to let anything distract her for a second. Even if she had to fly at the speed of a slow turtle.

She glanced over at the man in the co-pilot seat. Pops looked happy. There was no one better in the driver's seat of a flitter, but that wasn't the reason she'd been willing to get up before skybreak to come flying with him. Out here, he treated her like an equal—or at least like someone who might be worth his while one day. At home, she was just the smallest and scrappiest of eight kids, and if she got noticed, it was usually because she was in trouble. Again.

There were a lot of ways to get in trouble on a digger rock when your heart yearned to be somewhere else and there was nowhere else to go.

Kish looked out at the stars and wished, like she always did, that the clunky old tin can under her hands could carry her there.

"Don't be wishing for what you can't have." Her dad's voice was gruff, and a little impatient—they'd had this conversation before.

She could feel her lower lip popping out. "It doesn't hurt anything to look." But it did. She could see the small caldera coming over the horizon—the one that marked the spot where they'd found her DNA mother's ship.

The man who had rescued a squalling baby out of an evac pod and taken her home laid his hand on her shoulder. "Head right, kiddo. No time for sightseeing today. We need to run the lines. If we're not back by dinner, your mom will make us eat cold potato flakes."

That wasn't much worse than having to eat them warm. Payday for Pops was still four days away, and there would be a lot of potato flakes between now and then. And soy paste.

Kish scowled. She *hated* soy paste. She banked carefully to starboard—it wasn't a hard maneuver, but the left thruster had been acting up lately, and if she broke that, they'd definitely be grounded. She hummed a little to the flitter under her breath.

"Stop with yer singing already. It's a machine, not a baby."

Pops sounded annoyed. She glanced over at him, hoping he was just teasing.

He winked at her. "Think you can hold that patch on with a little ditty, do you?"

Not likely—but sometimes she thought her singing made Pops happier. Even when he scowled. Kish kept humming and swept her eyes over the instrument panel with a practiced gaze. Everything was good except for the auto-stabilizer, and that had been broken since she was three.

Fortunately, Kish had an iron stomach—so long as she didn't feed it soy paste.

She jumped as the radio squawked and dumped out a bunch of gibberish.

"Damn." Pops leaned forward, tension in his voice. "I thought Jingo fixed this thing."

Kish gripped the yoke under her hands until her knuckles turned white. They always left the flitter radio on the emergency frequency. Chatter on that channel meant something had exploded or someone was dead.

Or both.

Pops jimmied with the radio controls, trying to get a better signal. The squawking got louder— and then suddenly cleared. "… the Federated Commonwealth of Planets trader ship *Ios*. We have crashed and need immediate assistance. Repeat— we have crashed and need immediate assistance."

Kish and her dad gaped at the radio.

"We caught their signal. We must be close." Pops yanked an ancient pair of binoculars out of the net above his head and jammed them against his eyes. "Take her up. Now. Fast and hard."

He wasn't Pops now. Those were the terse orders of one of Halkyn VII's finest first responders.

Kish's chest nearly blew up with pride. He was letting her fly. In an emergency. Only the best pilots got to do that. She pointed the flitter's nose almost straight up. Height first—Pops needed visibility. The old machine stuttered, but it went up. Kish pushed a little more, and started to sing.

The stutters evened out a little. She watched the rising coolant temperature—much higher, and they'd have impeller issues.

Pops still had his binoculars glued to the window. "Nothing. Swing right. Head past that caldera first—I want to see the far side."

Kish gulped and headed straight for the place where her DNA mother had died. No one ever went there. Ghosts. Bad juju. Darkside cold.

A flash out the left window caught her attention. "Pops. Over here."

He swung himself to the other side of the flitter in one quick motion. "Where? I don't see it."

She didn't either—not anymore. But something inside her knew where it had come from. "I know where to go." Kish wrenched at the controls, suddenly frantic. In an emergency, speed mattered. Seconds mattered. People died in seconds.

Pops said nothing. He just stared out the window.

Kish couldn't look—she had her hands full holding the flitter steady. But she could feel the right way to go. There was a rope now, reeling her in.

His harsh intake of breath confirmed what she already knew. "Over there, by the rift." He glanced at her, eyes grim, assessing. "Take us down."

Her chest puffed again, even as her heart pounded against her ribs. This was what it felt like to be important. This was what it felt like to matter.

✳

Amelie Descol blasted the single high, pure note into every nook and cranny of the devastated bridge—and knew she was fighting a losing battle.

She gathered her breath and pushed more power into the single frequency. Sustaining. Demanding. Trying to snatch victory from the jaws of defeat. Her Talent shrieked, protesting the abuse. This wasn't sustainable, even for one of KarmaCorp's very finest.

She knew what her Talent didn't. This was the end game, one way or the other. If she couldn't hold on until help arrived, this was her last Song.

And the likelihood of help arriving in time had narrowed down to one small blip. They had a signal-obliterating cosmic storm behind them and a MayDay beacon that had deked left when it should have gone right. Amelie watched the bridge's last functional view screen as the tiny ship they'd picked up on their sensors came into view.

Her heart lurched. It was a surface flitter, barely bigger than the b-pod her brother flew for a living. Not the kind of vehicle that carried hull-piercing tools or interstellar comms.

Slowly, not letting her note waver in the slightest, she moved to step in behind the ship's captain, keeping one eye on the screen and one on the only other two people on the *Ios* who were still alive. Both were unconscious, and mercifully so. It had been killing her to listen to their thready screams.

The captain's hands clutched the edges of the console that was keeping her upright. "Attempting to hail incoming vessel."

Vessel was a polite term for what Amelie saw onscreen. The flitter looked ancient, and more beat up than her favorite pair of land boots. The kind of transport that colonies way off the beaten track held together with shoelaces and instaglue.

She closed her eyes and felt the fatigue clogging her throat. They would keep doing all the right things because Fixers didn't give up, and neither did the very tough captain of this particular small trading ship.

But shoelaces and instaglue weren't going to fix this.

Kish's head felt all swimmy and weird. Her DNA mother's ship had probably looked just like that.

Broken. Alone.

It was calling to her. She shook her head, trying to fix the awful pictures it was making inside her skull. It wasn't the same. This ship was new and shiny, not like the junker she'd been born on. Pops said it was a wonder that one had ever flown at all.

This one was a sleek trader ship, one of the ones that carried people and news and expensive things to colonies that could afford that kind of thing. And she could see why they'd crashed. One of the solar arms had a nasty, melted part. "They got hit by something."

Pops nodded sharply. "Space debris. People who fly out there are idiots."

Folks said the same thing about diggers. "They must have got caught in the solar storm." It had been a surprise one, or at least that's what the SatNet weather people said. No one on Halkyn VII had been surprised. Mama Simkin's big toe had been acting up again, and that always meant solar flares.

The storm had been pretty. Streaking lights in the sky. Kish looked at the ship, crashed on the side of the caldera, and felt her chin wobble. Pretty things could be mean. Every miner knew that.

She circled, eyes sharp now, looking for the flattest place she could find to set down the flitter. Not below the ship—the hills were too steep.

"No." Pops spoke sharply, moving his hands on top of hers. "Don't land—we'll hail them from here."

Her hands froze on the flitter controls as she swiveled to look at him, gaping. "We have to go help."

His eyes were angry—and full of the futile helplessness she only saw there when people were going to die. "It's a spaceship, Lakisha. They need shuttles and a rescue ship, not a couple of people in a flitter."

He never called her Lakisha. She looked down at the broken ship in horror. Halkyn VII didn't have rescue shuttles. And they were in darkside rotation—their interstellar comm couldn't send a message for hours yet.

Not a useful one, anyhow.

He laid a hand on her shoulder. "Let's hail them. Maybe we can bring them something they need. Until the rescue shuttles get here."

Pop's voice had that fake sound that happened when adults were lying about really bad things. Kish's chin wobbled some more. "I'll hold the flitter steady."

His hand on her shoulder squeezed a little.

Amelie winced as the crackling view screen jarred against the note she was Singing. She was tired enough now that stabilizing the interference took noticeable amounts of effort.

Butterfly wings. Just like the space junk that had clipped them and the solar flare that had knocked out their proximity detector. And the guy in engineering who had hit his head at exactly the wrong time.

The screen resolved into two blurry figures—a man with more facial hair than Amelie had seen in cycles, and a small girl with huge blue eyes and a ghost-white face.

The Singer struggled not to react. She didn't want a child to see this.

The man's voice was brusque. "Trader ship *Ios*, what is your status?"

The captain's fingers clutched the console more tightly. "Hull breach. We've lost pressure in six of our eight sections. Five dead, two badly wounded. All of us still alive are on the bridge and trapped. One of our solar ribs was driven through the bridge doors."

Amelie had to respect that kind of capacity for understatement. There were two hundred tons of metal between them and escape. And that wasn't the worst of it.

The captain's breath rattled. "We're losing oxygen."

The man on the screen knew what that meant. Amelie could see the sad horror in his eyes and knew what *that* meant. Rescue wasn't in his power to deliver. She jerked ruthlessly on her control as her Song wobbled.

Not now. She could be weak later. If there was a later.

The captain nodded feebly at the woman behind her. "Amelie here is trying some heroics."

The man and the girl both stared, puzzled.

Amelie gulped for air in the waning oxygen supply. Earlier, she'd managed to move the solar rib enough to extract the first officer and their comms intern, for all the good it would likely do them. Now she was trying to use pure vibration to hold thousands of tiny leaks at bay.

The Singer version of shoelaces and instaglue.

The captain's head lolled to the side. Dammit, make that three survivors badly wounded. Amelie stopped singing and stepped forward. Singers weren't in the line of command on any space vessel—unless they were the only one left who could speak. "We'll need something capable of drilling a hole in the side of this ship."

The man was already shaking his head. "We have drills, but nothing big enough to get them here fast. It's going to take hours."

He sounded competent. And certain.

The little girl beside him looked ready to punch someone in the nose. "We have to help, Pops. They can disassemble the drills. We can fly the parts."

She wasn't as fragile as she looked. Amelie registered that one thought as she sucked breath to start Singing again. If she could block the leaks well enough, maybe she could buy those hours. She added volume to her note. Power. The kind of power that might save a ship.

And would almost certainly cost a Singer her life.

Amelie felt a trickle adding to hers.

Her eyes jerked to the screen. The little girl was standing now, hands fisted at her sides, face fiercely focused. Singing. Precisely matching resonance with Amelie's note.

The Singer felt her eyes bulge. Talent. Immense talent, out here in the middle of asteroid hell.

The child stiffened as her father motioned for silence. And Sang louder.

Amelie reached for the tablet in her pocket and, sustaining the note she knew would be her last, sent off a short, seminally important message to KarmaCorp HQ. If a rescue ship ever arrived, it might even get delivered.

She looked back up into the fiery blue eyes of the child who would one day have the kind of Talent that might save this ship.

The child who didn't have enough control or knowledge to try today without putting her life on the line too. And Amelie Descol couldn't let that happen. It violated every oath she'd ever taken, every rule in KarmaCorp's very substantial manual, and every shred of human decency a dying Fixer had left.

So she shifted her gaze to the man beside the girl, looked him straight in the eyes, and let him see the truth.

He met her gaze for a long moment. And then he gave one sharp nod of respect and reached for the controls of the flitter.

The child's keening wail as the transmission ended nearly broke Amelie's heart.

And it made her smile. That one wouldn't ever back down from a fight. The child with the blue eyes would make a fine Fixer one day. The one legacy of this final horror that she could be proud of.

Today, only one Singer would die.

Kish couldn't see the ship anymore. They were almost back to Halkyn VII's derelict landing pad now, and the broken body of the *Ios* had disappeared from view long ago.

But she could still hear it. The woman with the green eyes, begging the stars to help.

Because the girl from the digger rock couldn't.

✳

Amelie could still feel the child. Her anguish and her guilt, and the echoing resonances of a Talent that had tried to throw itself across a vacuum of space and do the impossible.

A child born to be a Fixer if she'd ever seen one.

If it please the fates, not a child destined to die as one.

Amelie took one last look around the battered bridge and then lifted her chin and blasted her high, pure note one more time out into the infinity of space. A final moment of defiance.

Then she bowed her head and changed her Song. To a lullaby. One that would send calm to the child still listening, and put everyone still alive on the ship to sleep. The gift of oblivion, as quickly as she could bring it.

Amelie felt the black coming. And Sang it welcome.

✳

Three Months Later...

Pops had stopped coming with her, and when Kish got back, he would look at her with that cross face that made his eyebrows join together and lines run up from his nose.

But her astrosuit was always charged and ready to go, every night. And even though it was battered and dinged and two sizes too big, someone had done some careful repairs on all the seams.

She had no idea why she had to be in a dumb suit out here in the cold. Singing sounded way nicer in one of the abandoned tunnels, especially if she managed to swipe her brother's heater mitts before she left. That's usually where she went to sing.

But this note—it insisted that it must be sung under the night sky.

Kish placed the carefully shaped rock that would hold the surface tube open until she returned, and stepped away from the sensors. They were rusty as hell and nobody ever bothered to look at their logs, but occasionally even beat-up old crap managed to work right, and she didn't want any more lines running up from Pop's nose.

She turned herself toward the northwest. Toward the caldera.

The broken ship wasn't there anymore. A rescue vessel had come. It had saved the captain with the sad face and the comms intern with the nice laugh and the first officer with the gruff voice and wrapped candies in his pocket.

But Kish had known they were too late for the lady with the voice of gold and the fierce, sad eyes.

She drew in a deep breath, remembering. And let the single, shattering note rise up from her ribs.

The sound reverberated inside her helmet like a space cat on synth-caf, but Kish barely noticed. She focused only on the beautiful, heartbreaking sound.

Just like always, it made tears run down her face. And just like always, her ribs felt like they might never breathe again. It had taken her two weeks to stop panicking and triple-checking the oxygen levels on her space suit.

The oxygen had always been fine.

Kish tipped her head back to the night sky and imagined her puny note rising up to the stars. She knew the stars would never hear her—she was just a girl from a digger rock, and a troublesome, skinny one at that. But she sang up to the sky anyway.

It was where the song wanted to go.

Note from Audrey: There are more exploding spaceships in this short story than in all my other books combined...no idea how that happened. :)

If you're curious about what happens to Kish when she grows up and follows in Amelie's footsteps, the book you're looking for is *Destiny's Song,* the start of my Fixers series. A lot has changed—but Kish still wants to punch someone in the nose on a fairly regular basis…. Learn more about it on my website: www.audreyfayewrites.com.

CARL SAGAN'S HUNT FOR INTELLIGENT LIFE IN THE UNIVERSE

AN ARCHANGEL PROJECT STORY

C. GOCKEL

What Little Werfles are Made of

"...*CELLS ARE MADE OF PROTEINS, PROTEINS ARE MADE OF molecules, molecules are made of atoms, atoms are made of particles... And do you remember what those are made of?*"

"*Waves, Third One!*"

"*Yes, you are waves manifest as matter. You can become waves again at any time.*"

Sliding down the embankment, his ten legs not able to lift him, Hsissh reprimanded himself, *Next body, no sleeping in a field frequented by lizzar.* He knew better, but the rock had been sunny and wonderfully warm. And then one of the clumsy, wave-ignorant oafs had whacked him with its tail. Now this body was beyond reasonable repair and he had to move on. Finding a dry spot, he curled into a ball. Tucking his nose to his tail, he closed his eyes and...hesitated. He blinked. He didn't want to let this form go...Shissh, his blood kin in her last life, had been urging him for years to give up this shell and the pain that was tied to it; to let his memories of their third parent become a dream.

"What's that?"

His ears perked. It was the vocal utterance of a wave-ignorant Newcomer. Ish, one of the more scholarly members of Hsissh's kind, had decoded most of the language and shared it in the waves. Hsissh hadn't thought the Newcomers had spread this far north. He wondered what they'd found.

A sharp pain in his side made his body uncoil with a startled squeak.

"Is it some sort of albino-mutant-ten-legged weasel?" There was another sharp pain, and Hsissh was flipped over. Helpless in his weakened state, he lay sprawled on his back, all ten limbs and tail wriggling. Through blurry eyes, he saw three Newcomers standing over him. They smelled strange, like alien vegetables and meats partially digested and burned. Their naked bodies, where they showed at the edges of the faux furs on their heads and forelimbs, were disgusting. They looked smaller than he'd been informed; yet, even their shorter forelimbs were longer than his entire body. They could kill him by merely stepping on him.

"It's a werfle," said another Newcomer, using the enormous deformed paw on a hind limb to prod Hsissh's limbs. "Their bites are poisonous. Don't touch it."

The poison oozing from Hsissh's fangs could kill them with a single bite, but his body wasn't responding to his mind's order to roll over. And the pain was disorientating; he couldn't focus enough to agitate the waves into starting a fire. A shadow moved. He felt a stinging in his chest and a soft squeal came from his lungs. His mind slowly processed that one of the Newcomers was jabbing him with a stick. Ish thought these beings were worthy of study… Obviously, Ish was an idiot. Hsissh felt rekindled determination to leave this body—when he was new and healthy again, he'd join the faction that was pushing to have the Newcomers wiped off The Planet.

"Huh, looks almost dead," said the one with the stick. He poked Hsissh again, and pain shot from every root of fur on his body.

"My mom says they're really soft and we should make them into coats," said another, prodding Hsissh's side so hard it sent him rolling. When Hsissh came to a stop, he tried to squirm, but pain shot from his tail as one of them stepped on it, and he clawed helplessly at the dirt.

"Too small to make a coat. Maybe a muffler?" said the one that had kicked him.

Hsissh closed all ten of his claws and reminded himself he was a wave. He just had to focus…

"Leave him alone!"

The pain in his tail vanished. He shot forward and was able to feel the waves that coursed through his body. Grabbing hold, he let them carry him up and out, changing the electrical impulses in his body and mind to a pattern of particles in the waves. Bit by bit, memories from every shell he'd ever worn and his current thoughts were encoded. He felt Shissh's consciousness in the wave, and *felt* her speak. "Finally! You should have left that hide ages ago."

Not wanting to encourage her nagging, Hsissh did not answer. As the pattern that was Hsissh expanded out and upward, he was able to *feel* the scene in every direction. Above him, the Newcomer's time gate hung like a ring-shaped moon, visible even though it was nearly midday. He could just barely make out the ships that were slipping into the gate and then disappearing, primitively transported in their physical forms across the Milky Way to their home planet "Earth" and nearly a dozen

other colony worlds. Below him, much closer to his
rapidly dying body, a smaller Newcomer was standing at the top of the embankment, fists clasped at
its sides. It looked different from the others. The
fur on top of its head was nearly black and pulled
back in a way that exposed a flat metal circle at the
side of its skull. Its eyes were nearly as dark, and
its skin was a deep brown. The others looked more
like what he'd gleaned from the collective consciousness of his kind, The One. They had hazel-to-
brown eyes, tan skin, and fur that flopped over the
peculiar metal ornamentation Newcomers wore in
the sides of their heads.

"Are you going to stop us, Noa?" one of Hsissh's
tormentors goaded.

Dipping its chin, the smaller one said, "Yeah!"

"Pfft! You're a girl."

One of the others whispered, "She wants to be
a pilot...she doesn't know the Luddeccean Guard
doesn't take girls!"

The one that must be Noa snarled, "I'm going
to be in the Galactic Fleet. It's better than the stupid
Guard, and they take girls!"

One of Hsissh's tormentors picked up a clump
of dirt and tossed it at her. His other friends followed

suit. Hsissh's would-be protector sensibly retreated into the forest that surrounded the embankment.

"Ooooo! The brave pilot retreats!" one of the tormentors hooted before turning back to Hsissh. They huffed air out in staccato bursts of sound. "What are we going to do with the werfle?" one of them asked, swinging a stick.

Resuming his slow, steady slip into the wave, Hsissh had a moment between panic and curiosity. If he was hit hard enough in the head, and life seeped slowly from his body, would he become waveless, like his third parent? Energy could not be created or destroyed. Perhaps the waveless like Third went some place...else?

His rumination was interrupted by a frenzied vocalization he did not understand. "Arrrrrggghhhhhh!"

In his in-between state, Hsissh *felt* the girl swinging a branch thicker than his girth and longer than her body above her head. Her lips were curled, and her flat white teeth were bared.

The boy with the stick danced over Hsissh's body and cried, "Are you crazy?" right before the branch connected with his jaw. In his bodyless state, Hsissh felt the Newcomer's pain. The shock sent a ripple through the wave, Hsissh lost his concentration, and he found himself back in his body, staring up at the Newcomer known as Noa. She was panting, holding the branch in front of her chest with two hands. His body, perhaps trying to avoid its inevitable passing, slipped into unconsciousness.

A Nice Nest

Hsissh awoke next to a wall of immense, deadly, roaring flames. He might have immediately bolted, but he hurt too much; his body felt tight and alien. It was definitely time to leave.

Closing his eyes, Hsissh slipped from his body. Floating away, carried on the waves again, he saw that his shell had been wrapped up in some sort of plant fiber, and was cradled by a soft square of a similar fiber. He abruptly slipped back into his "werfle" form with a shocking realization. They'd made him a nest. He sniffed. More accurately, Noa had made him a nest. He smelled her all over it.

Ever so gently, he flexed his claws. It was a nice nest, he could tell that, despite his pain. It was almost as soft as the one made by Third of ptery scales and her belly fluff. The fire was a nice touch; bigger than he would ever light on a cold night, but he supposed that the nearly naked Newcomers might need more to ward off the chill. And now that he studied it, he realized it was well contained.

"He's awake!"

He heard a rush of footsteps and looked up to see Noa, his rescuer, leaning over him, forelimb outstretched. He drew back and another Newcomer said, "Be careful, Noa." This Newcomer was larger than Noa, and tan like most Newcomers, with black hair and golden eyes. By smell, Hsissh identified her as a female member of the dual-sexed species, probably Noa's mother. In spite of himself, he felt sympathy for her. How difficult would it be to raise a litter with only two adults? How would Third ever have managed without First and Second to hunt and protect her, Hsissh, Shissh, and their brothers and sisters?

"But the veterinarian milked his venom, Mom."

Whiskers trembling in alarm, Hsissh slipped his tongue beneath the sharp tips of his fangs and gently pressed. There was no swell of poison. He hunched into the nest, feeling violated.

"Yes, the veterinarian did," said Mom, and Hsissh entertained visions of killing Veterinarian once his venom returned.

"... but the veterinarian also said that it would take a while for his ribs to heal. You have to be gentle, Noa."

Heal ribs? Whatever for? It was easier to leave a shell and find the body of an unclaimed member of one of The One's host species. He blinked. But of course, the Newcomers were wave-ignorant—like Third had been at the end. They couldn't slip out of their shells and so had become resilient to injury and disease. They'd overcome the three plagues The One had let loose among them with "nanos" and "antibiotics." And he'd heard that, even when they lost limbs or organs, they replaced them with mechanical parts. Those who had such parts were called "augments."

Noa, who Hsissh was beginning to suspect was an adolescent among her kind, gently touched Hsissh's head. He thought of delivering a non-venomous bite out of spite for letting Veterinarian milk his venom; but her touch wasn't unpleasant, and he was too exhausted to bother. And then she scratched him behind his ears, and he couldn't help purring.

"Can we keep him as a pet?" Noa asked.

Hsissh's eyes snapped open at the unfamiliar word and the implications of "keep." Something to be eaten later?

Another voice, deeper than even Mom's, rumbled, "You know that we shouldn't do that." Hsissh's nose twitched. A male of the species, also tan skin with dark brown hair, who smelled like Noa, but not like Mom. Perhaps the other parent?

"But why, Dad?" said Noa.

"Because he is a wild animal," Mom said. The round metal plate in the side of her skull glinted dully in the light. At the center of it was an opening...and then darkness. Hsissh could smell no blood, bone, or other gore from the gaping hole. "And it wouldn't be fair," Mom continued. "You heard what the veterinarian said. These creatures die in cages; it would be wrong to keep him."

Maybe he wouldn't kill Veterinarian...but what was this "keeping" business? They didn't seem to want to eat him.

Mom continued, "We don't know why they die in captivity, but we do know they are intelligent, and social. They probably need to be with their own kind to remain healthy."

Hsissh's nose twitched. He'd become rather solitary since Third died the true death. He could go months without contact with his kind. Still, even a non-claimed member of The One's favorite host species, the "werfles," would leave its shell, too, if caught in a cage out of sheer humiliation. But it was a well-considered hypothesis.

"And they help us kill rats!" Noa interjected.

The deep-voiced one, Dad, muttered, "Damn rats, invading this pristine ecosystem." Hsissh's mind tripped over the word "damn," but he had the impression that Dad was angry. Whatever for?

Noa stroked Hsissh's head and the two adult Newcomers walked away. Another smaller, though still enormous, Newcomer came over and gazed down at Hsissh. He smelled like Noa, Mom, and Dad—a blood kin. His skin was tan, with dark brown fur on top of his head, like Mom and Dad, and his eyes were light in color.

"I wonder if he has a name, Kenji?" Noa whispered, scratching Hsissh behind the ears and under his chin, evoking a helpless purr.

"There are three sexes among werfles; I don't think it is a 'him,'" Kenji said. He idly played with the metal disk in the side of his head with the long, slender appendage of a paw.

Hsissh's whiskers twitched. In point of fact the werfles had males, females, and females that had matured to Thirds, nursing adults who passed on genetic information through their milk. "Him" and "her" worked well enough for members of the species not in a breeding triad.

"I'm not calling him an 'it,'" Noa said, increasing the intensity of the ear scratching. The Newcomers had curiously ineffectual claws; they were short, stubby, and thin. However, Hsissh was discovering they were perfect for grooming without the worry of shedding blood.

"And he needs a name," she continued, lowering her head so Hsissh was able to look into her dark eyes. Maybe he was becoming fond of this Newcomer because he didn't find her general furlessness disturbing. Or maybe it was the color of her skin. It didn't look as though her fur had sloughed off from illness. It was the same rich brown as the bark of a healthy red nut tree, and twice as smooth.

"A name," Noa whispered. "He has to have one."

And he did. It was against the rules of The One to communicate with the Newcomers, lest they know they were being scrutinized. Like sub-atomic particles whose behavior changed when observed, research subjects behaved differently when they *knew* they were being watched. But suddenly he wanted her to know. He concentrated and tugged at the waves that coursed between Noa, Kenji, and himself. "Hsissh," he sent along the wave. "Hsissh, I am Hsissh."

"Hsissccchhh!" said Kenji, the sound erupting not just from his mouth but also his nose.

Hsissh squeaked in joy and wonder. He'd been told that the Newcomers were incapable of wave riding, but Ish had hypothesized that they were on the verge of it—and Ish was right! The Newcomers were truly an intelligent species!

"God bless you," Noa said, eyes set on Hsissh. She nodded. "Fluffy, I think I'll name him Fluffy."

Kenji wiped his nose with a forelimb and touched Hsissh's fur gingerly with the other. "That is a good name; he's very soft."

Or maybe they weren't quite so bright.

The Gathering Place

In the dark, cavernous space that was the human attic, Hsissh sighed with pleasure. His stomach was filled with fresh rat, and his mouth was still flavored with its blood. Exalting in the feeling of all being right with the world, he rolled onto his back...and all was not right anymore. The attic was made of wood slats that were hard and had splinters that poked through his fur. Rolling back over, he scanned the room. A "box" in the corner caught his eye. The box was filled with faux fur humans used for colder temperatures. Rats enjoyed nesting in it; perhaps he would, too?

Trundling over, he slid inside, kneaded the soft material with his claws, and curled into a ball. It was very comfortable and, as a plus, smelled like his favorite prey. He closed his eyes. Rain was pattering on the roof and the single attic window. Downstairs, he could hear the family eating, their "silverware" clinking on their "plates." He still didn't understand why they used "dinnerware," but the clinks were pleasant. The sounds, his full belly, and the warmth of the "fur" lulled him into a doze almost immediately. As sometimes happened, his mind slipped slightly from his body and he *felt* the rain, the cold air outside, and the children and their parents in the dining room below.

A loud clacking almost woke him. And then he realized the clacking was coming from the wave. More specifically, from an aquatic organism not as tall as Hsissh's shoulder, ovoid, with a brilliant green, luminescent exoskeleton to protect it from the pressure of the ice-crusted oceans of the moon it evolved on seventeen billion light years away. It was Shissh, snapping two pincers at the front of her carapace, sending her consciousness to interrupt his nap and heckle him for not slipping out of his body. He almost woke up just to spite her; but seeing her, even in this new form, caused his body to release a flood of bonding hormones. He purred with familial love. Did she still feel the bond in that hard, cold shell? Did she still think of Third—the only member of their three parents whose werfle body had been inhabited by The One?

Shissh spoke into his mind. "Are you coming to The Gathering...*Fluffy*?"

Betrayed by familial love. He never should have told her that name. "No, of course not. Go away and let me sleep." He tried to burrow deeper into the furs.

Shissh clicked her pincers and waved her eye stalks. "If you want to keep your warm human nest, you'd better come now. Misch is pushing for a fourth plague and—"

A vision of Noa's eyes dulled by death permeated Hsissh's dream. Hsissh sent his thoughts into The Gathering before Shissh had finished.

Shissh's crustacean dream-self emerged beside him, eye stalks pointed in his direction. "Mighty fast entrance, Hsissh."

"I've got a good thing going," Hsissh grumbled, looking out at The Gathering. It was held in a cavern with an opening directly above that let in the sparkle of the stars—but not the glow of the time gate or human satellites. The cavern had been destroyed thousands of cycles ago, and this was only the memory of a memory that The One all shared. It was crowded with dream versions of The One. Most were in the form of werfles, but there were exotic creatures from several dozen worlds scattered among them.

"I've been to Earth!" one of The One's consciousnesses roared. It was Misch. He wore the form of a "cat," one of the few species on the human home world that was a compatible host and could tolerate living in close quarters with humans. The One had tried to inhabit humans; it didn't work. Human bodies rebelled and were inevitably drugged for "schizophrenia" and often "institutionalized." But cats were easy enough to possess. Pacing on his four feet, Misch said, "The humans have no fur, no claws, no speed, and no natural armor. They can't see in the dark, and they are more ignorant of the waves than a cat…and I can tell you, cats are short on brains."

Hsissh's whiskers twitched. His host species, the werfle, weren't particularly "long on brains" either, but The One outsourced their big thinking to the collective consciousness of the waves.

Swishing his feline tail, Misch declared, "They have stripped and poisoned their home world of natural resources to make up for their inadequacies. Introduce the Fourth Plague before it happens here!"

Hsissh had seen the results of the Third Plague in holos with Noa. He had seen orphaned human children too weak to defend themselves from rats feasting on their flesh. Hsissh's two hearts beat faster as he stretched his mind out to all who were in The Gathering. "But they are wave aware!"

He felt the focus of the room shift to him.

"Impossible!"

Misch sat down and swished his tail. "Hsissh, what are you doing here?"

Someone else said, "Shouldn't you be napping?"

A member of The One, wearing the same species host as Hsissh, stood up on her hind legs. "We know the humans don't use waves."

Ish, wearing a werfle body, said, "They do."

There were hisses and grumbles among The One.

Hopping up and down with the excitement of his own recent epiphany, Hsissh explained. "The circular metal devices affixed to the sides of their skulls enable humans to talk mind-to-mind. Every human with the metal implant has nanos—tiny machines—in their brains. They are awakened in later adolescence." Noa was too young, but her "data port" and "neural interface" had been checked by a "physician" at her yearly "checkup." She'd taken Hsissh to the visit as a "security blanket." A bit of the memory of the enclosed doctor's exam room slipped into the wave and some of the werfles hissed in fear. Hsissh rushed on. "The nanos turn their thoughts to waves, and allow them to interface mind-to-mind via light beams, radio, and microwaves—they call it 'the ethernet.'"

Misch's mind hissed, "Primitive and barbaric! Even a lizzar can hear and see, and a "nano interface" is not much better!"

Hsissh's chest tightened, and he couldn't help thinking of rats feasting on Noa's flesh.

"But they are wave aware!" Ish said.

At Ish's opening, Hsissh said, "Yes, yes! They know that all matter is made of waves." Hsissh shared the memory of a lesson he'd studied with Noa, a history of physics from Isaac Newton to the current ethernet age. Humans were aware of the subatomic world, but they couldn't feel it and barely used it; they hadn't found a way to do so practically. "But they are on the verge!" Hsissh said, as his memory of the holo documentary ended. "Lizzars aren't wave aware! Nor were the creatures we eradicated at the end of the last Epoch."

Shissh clacked, "Interesting..." very slowly, the way she did when Hsissh had said something stupid.

There was a collective silence from The One.

And then a thought, so soft he almost missed it, entered his consciousness. "Hsissh's Third died the true death ten cycles ago, it's left him addled."

From the collective consciousness rose an unmistakable feeling of pity. In Noa's attic, his physical body shivered...he'd failed.

Ish stood on his back four hind limbs and waved his paws. "The humans, as they call themselves, are wave aware—in the truest sense of the word!"

Thoughts rose in The Gathering like swirling mist.

Misch swished his tail. "I know nothing of this!"

"Because you haven't been to their places of worship," Ish said. "It is my understanding that on their home world the practice is all but forgotten; it was one of the reasons we have humans on our planet. The ones here were seeking enlightenment and to escape the material, non-wave focused cultures of Earth."

"Worship?" the question rose from Hsissh and all in attendance.

Ish clasped his top two claw pairs behind his back and strode through the Gathering Place on his back four legs. His middle pair of paws waved. "They enter states of profound meditation in group settings."

Misch hissed. "They don't feel the waves!"

Ish bowed his head, and said, "They feel closer to 'God' in their meditative state, a being they believe is responsible for all creation and is all powerful. That is the waves from which all matter is derived, obviously." Stopping his pacing, he raised his head and faced the crowd. "They have a concept of the oneness of everything."

There were soft noises of awe from around the cavern.

"Humans brought the rats," someone else thought. "They're everywhere."

Nearly everyone in attendance licked their lips; even Misch's feline form did. "We should reward them for that," said another werfle.

Clacking her pincers, Shissh drew the audience's attention. "If they could join the waves, they could become useful allies."

"Allies against whom?" Misch cried.

"You know it is only a matter of time!" Shissh snapped.

Misch's cat form's fur rose.

A member of The Gathering wearing a werfle host said, "In all probability, we will discover an enemy—or they will discover us. The universe is predator and prey."

"And symbiosis!" Shissh declared.

"Humans—the Newcomers—believe in symbiosis," Hsissh said, hopping up onto his back two pairs of paws. "They don't eat all the species they meet or even the ones they keep!"

Misch's cat-eyes narrowed to slits and he hissed. "But they do neuter them—"

Before Hsissh could inquire of the meaning of "neuter," the crowd erupted, and for a moment his mind was a whirl with so many thoughts he could scarcely hear his own.

At last, the tide began to subside, and a chorus rose in the cavern. "We will give the Newcomers one hundred cycles to join The One in the waves."

Hsissh felt his physical body relax and uncoil from the knot he'd tied himself in. The One were of one mind after the chorus…One hundred cycles around the sun…certainly in that time humans would evolve to feel waves, if they were already on the verge?

One by one, all the consciousnesses began slipping away into other dreams, and Hsissh found himself alone with Ish, Misch, and Shissh.

Licking a paw, Misch said, "They haven't found a way to ride the waves in the last four million years. They won't figure it out in a hundred years more."

"What has you in a snit?" said Shissh.

"Hmpf," said Ish, "You only say that because you've studied the ones on Earth. They are debauched and lazy."

Flattening his ears and hissing, Misch faded from view. Ish turned to Hsissh. "Next time, let me do the talking," the scholar said, and then he disappeared, too. Only Hsissh and his luminescent, crustacean once-kin were left. He felt a lump in his stomach; at the same time, he felt a warmth in his hearts. Shissh had chosen the crustacean form because it was not social, and did not mourn the departure of others of its kind. Still, because she had stayed, Hsissh felt that she must still care about him.

Combing his whiskers with his claws, Hsissh asked, "Do you really think we might become prey to something else?" It was difficult to imagine the "else." The One could mutate the genomes of viruses, bacteria, and fungi by exciting the waves within them. Whenever they had a species that became too problematic, it was easy enough to cull or eradicate them with a specially mutated pathogen. They'd culled the humans—and debated whether or not to cull the rats—but their primary hosts preferred to keep the rats plentiful, fat, and delicious.

Shissh's eye stalks swept toward him. "The species I inhabit now—they are like the cats of Earth—they can play host to wave riding beings, but they haven't learned to leave their bodies…not yet."

Hsissh smoothed his whiskers meditatively. Shissh had told him this much before.

Shissh continued, "There are rumors among this species ... stories of dark waters spreading on distant moons, wiping out all the creatures in the oceans and the land. Since the species I inhabit does not travel, I think there may have been other wave riding species that have brought their stories with them."

Hsissh's thoughts drifted to Noa. She dreamed aloud of traveling to distant moons when she snuggled with Hsissh at night...He looked through the opening in the ceiling. It was close to her bedtime now.

Shissh clicked softly, "I believe the humans might make a good ally, Hsissh...but I worry about you living among them. You should have left your body and its grief over Third's death. Living with humans, you're just setting yourself up for more pain." Her pincers clicked so fast they became a song. "You're much too sentimental to become attached to creatures that die."

Hsissh felt his frame tighten. "I just stay with them for their beds," he replied.

"Liar," said Shissh.

Hsissh's consciousness snapped back into his body. He found himself shivering despite the faux furs and bolted from the box. Shissh was right, he was too attached to Noa and her family. He had originally stayed for the rats in the attic, the beds, and out of curiosity; but he liked them, and they would die. His consciousness was over a thousand years old...Noa might live to be three hundred; but if a Fourth Plague came, even the humans' nanos and antibiotics wouldn't save them.

The sound of rain on the roof became louder, as though it were a command, "Run, Hsissh, run ..." Hsissh obeyed. Instead of darting down the trapdoor that led to the hallway, he skittered over to the window. He wasn't strong enough by the laws of Newtonian physics to move the latch, but he focused the waves inside his body to give his muscles more power. The latch gave, the window opened, and he slithered out into the rainy night. Sliding down the slope of the roof, he swung over the edge and jumped into the ivy that grew up the side of the house. He was halfway down when he heard a creak of a window opening. Noa's voice rose above the raindrops. "Fluffy!"

Hsissh hesitated, but then, shaking himself, leaped down into the garden. He slunk into the low, alien vegetation around the home that was lit by electric spotlights. Noa's voice rose in pitch. "Fluffy!"

He drew to a halt, his two hearts constricting, his claws sinking into the mud. He heard Mom say, "Noa, it's time for bed," and Noa respond, "But Mom—"

Mom said, "No buts!" and then Hsissh heard the window bang shut. Bowing his head, Hsissh wove through the plants toward the forest beyond. He'd gone only a few hundred body lengths when he heard the window creak and then bang closed. He increased his speed. He'd just traded the spotlights for the shade of the forest when he heard Noa's voice again, this time as soft as her paws in his fur. "Fluffy?"

He stopped. The bipedal steps hesitated. "Fluffy, are you lost?" From the sound of her voice, he could tell she was not ten body lengths behind. He heard a sound like branches clacking and realized it was Noa's teeth snapping together. The cold mud beneath him seemed to wrap around his claws and hold him immobilized. An enormous drop of frigid water fell from a tree and landed squarely on his nose. The rest of him was well protected, but Noa ...

"Fluffy?" Noa cried.

Hsissh turned around and slid through the underbrush. He found Noa at the trees' edge in a pair of "slippers" and thin "pajamas." Soaked and shivering, she was hugging her body. She should have gone home, but instead she was crying his name.

Noa was trying to save him—again. It was foolish. She could suffer hypothermia, or get lost and injured. Her parents might not even be aware she'd gone missing until dawn; then, it might be too late. He crawled out of the undergrowth. Noa's eyes widened at the sight of him, and she smiled as he hopped forward. Scooping him up, she touched her nose to his. "Fluffy, I found you!" Clutching him to her chest, she dashed back toward the house. "I climbed out the window, but it's too high to get back in," she whispered. Instead, she went through the front door, into the foyer, and then into the front room where her parents were reading.

Dad's voice boomed through the house with such force that the floorboards reverberated. "Noa Sato, were you outside?"

"What were you doing out there?" Mom exclaimed. "You'll catch your death of cold!"

Hsissh stiffened in Noa's arms, but she didn't seem to notice. Holding him up for her parents' inspection, she said, "I found Fluffy!"

"I'm getting a towel," Mom said. A few moments later, she wrapped one around Noa's shoulders, but Noa pulled it off and wrapped it around Hsissh instead.

"The towel was for you!" said Mom.

"He's wet and cold," said Noa, gently drying Hsissh's fur with the warm, absorbent fabric.

"Do not do that again, Noa!" Dad roared.

But Noa didn't seem to hear either of them. Teeth still clacking, she carried Hsissh back to her room and set him down on her bed. As she slipped into dry pajamas, Hsissh made a show of prowling under the covers for rats. His protector wasn't afraid of foes who were bigger or outnumbered her, or catching her death of cold, but she was terrified of the tasty little rodents.

He stuck his nose out of the blankets and gave the 'all clear' squeak and Noa bounded under the covers with a laugh. Her body was still trembling, and she pulled him close. Hsissh curled himself into a ball. Noa's fingers traced the line of his spine, and then scratched him behind his ears. Her touch was as gentle as Third's had been when Hsissh was just a hatchling. Her body was around his, much like how Third had coiled around Hsissh and Shissh as hatchlings and then kits. The down cover and mattress were as soft and warm as Third's fur. The way Noa's night light shone through the covering made everything soft and gilt around the edges, like a memory.

"Don't do that again, Fluffy," Noa whispered. "Please."

She drifted off to sleep. Hsissh heard Mom's footsteps by her door, and then Mom's voice. "Oh, child, don't do that to me again." He could hear the tears in her voice; they were, he had learned, a symptom of mourning.

There was something about Mom's plea that touched him. Noa was prone to misadventures, and Hsissh could see that begging her to be safe was like screaming into the void. It made him think of being with Third after her mind had been stripped by the wasting disease. Hsissh had begged her to slip into the wave, to stay with him. He kept pleading even after all hope was lost. Afterward, he'd admonished himself. He should have checked on her more frequently, in the waves and in the flesh. In the end, he found himself wishing for just a few more breaths of time to be with her, even just to have her nuzzle him in her wave-ignorant, mind-degenerated state. The memories of his pain, of Noa calling him in the dark, and Mom's plea to her headstrong daughter…Hsissh knew why he stayed with the humans. It was because he couldn't bring himself to leave.

Take Me to Church

"What the hell!" Dad yelled, and lifted his feet out of Hsissh's way. The "all-terrain vehicle" swerved and hit a bump. For a moment, they were airborne, and Hsissh braced his achy muscles for the inevitable reunion with the ground.

"George!" Mom exclaimed, using her own pet name for Dad.

"That damn werfle just crawled under my feet!" Dad roared, bringing the vehicle under control.

"Fluffy, come here!" said Noa, and Hsissh slunk past Mom and Dad to the back of the vehicle and the relative safety of Noa's lap. She stroked his sore back with warm, gentle hands, and he gingerly curled into a ball. His old rib injury hurt, and this body was getting old, period.

Noa's cousin John threw up his hands, as did her little sister Masako. "Fluffy is going to church with us again!" they cried in unison. It was Hsissh's tenth such visit in the three cycles of the sun since he'd joined the family. "Yay!" shouted Noa, Masako, and John. Kenji was quiet, his eyes focused on the window.

"He stays in the car!" said Dad.

"It's too hot in the car, George," Mom said and Dad grumbled.

Noa drew her hand down Hsissh's back. Ish had mapped human brain activity, what areas were energized by different patterns in speech, sight and hearing. Hsissh, if he concentrated, could use the waves to feel what areas were excited and read Noa's thoughts. She was so quiet, he did so now. He saw his body through her eyes. His spine was visible through his thinning fur, as were the joints of his limbs. He felt her feelings, too. She was afraid of losing him. Death wasn't eternal for him, like it would be for her. He could speak into her mind, and tell her so—and he had—but she discounted the voice in her head. It hadn't come from the active nanos that now let her talk to her grandparents, and new friends, solar systems away with only a thought. Her nanos told her it was "her imagination."

"He's getting so skinny," said Masako.

"He's getting old," said Noa, and Hsissh could hear the hitch in her voice. He couldn't hang onto this body for much longer, which was one of the reasons why he was going to church today. He wasn't sure how much time he had left, and he wanted to be with her as much as possible. This body had long ago decided that her family was his family, and he got the same rush of bonding hormones being with them that he did being with Shissh. When the time would come to change this body for another, those hormones would disappear. Intellectually, he knew it was for the best. Emotionally...he felt his hearts sink into a space near his gullet.

"Why do we have to go to church?" Noa said, her hand pausing its path. "You don't believe in The Three Books!" She didn't want to go. In her mind she was imagining zipping through the forest on her bicycle with Hsissh in a padded basket at the front, nose lifted to the wind.

"Because it's our community," Dad rumbled.

"It's stupid," Noa grumbled.

Hsissh wouldn't call it stupid, he'd call it hopeless. Humans were doomed. He was glad Noa was leaving, joining the Galactic Fleet and leaving this planet behind.

"If God were really all-powerful and didn't want us to eat the stupid apple, He wouldn't have let the snake into the garden," Noa muttered.

No one answered. Hsissh agreed that it was implausible; all the stories from the Three Books seemed so to him. It was odd that the implausible stories tied them, though ever so slightly, to the waves. Maybe it was because the waves were beyond what was plausible in observable Newtonian physics and the stories put believers in the correct mindset?

"And if He didn't want me to be a pilot, why would He make me want it so much?" Noa whispered. Hsissh lifted his nose toward hers and wiggled his whiskers. Noa's parents didn't discourage her from leaving the planet, but among the people of The Three Books, she was considered odd at best, a "dangerous little girl" at worst.

Seeing his whiskers quirking, Noa smiled and Hsissh felt her mood lift.

"There is a crash," said Kenji out of nowhere, in a toneless voice.

Dad slowed the vehicle, and Noa's eyes went to the window. Hsissh struggled to lift his protesting muscles. Outside, he saw a peculiar car protruding from a ditch. It had no wheels and lay flat on the ground. A family was standing around it, fanning themselves with their Three Books.

Noa touched the neural port at the side of her head. It had been activated a cycle ago. For a moment, her eyes became glazed. "It's a LX0001 hover craft," Noa said, gleaning the information from the "ethernet." "The new model's antigrav was formulated to handle Luddeccea's gravity."

Luddeccea was the name the humans had given to this planet. Hsissh had heard of the antigrav vehicles. They were powered by the same technology that powered the time gates, albeit on a much smaller scale. They created a "bubble" in time that allowed the vehicles to counteract gravity and float over rocky terrain, and even above treetops. As Hsissh understood it, hovers were very common on Earth. However, the antigrav had to be calibrated for each planet. Local gravity, the relative position of the planet in its solar system, and the solar system's position relative to the galactic core all had to be taken into account.

Dad sighed heavily and brought the car to a halt beside the immobile vehicle. "New tech...always buggy."

"Kids, into the back; make room for the Benjamins!" Mom said, and Hsissh was hoisted by Noa as she scrambled over the seat. He knew she tried to make the move as comfortable as possible for him, but his joints hurt, and his body squeaked in protest. "Sorry, Fluffy," Noa murmured, cradling him closer.

A few breaths later, the Benjamins were in the vehicle and Mom and Dad were occupied with making "small talk." Hsissh settled onto Noa's lap in the flat back portion of the vehicle. She was sitting cross-legged in her "Sunday finest." Hsissh glanced up at her. Her eyes were on the Benjamin's son, Sergei, sitting in the backseat. You didn't have to use telepathy or even be human to know she was attracted to him, or that it was one-sided. The sight made the fur on the back of his neck prickle, and he couldn't say why.

The sun was bright above the front lawn of the Church of Three Books. The adults were off talking in the shade of the steeple. Hsissh was draped over

Noa's neck. She was hanging around some boys, of whom Sergei was one.

"You only think you want to be a pilot," Jacob, one of Hsissh's former tormentors, was saying.

"What is that supposed to mean?" Noa demanded, hands going to her hips.

Jacob shrugged. "You'll fall for some boy and you won't want to be a pilot anymore. My dad says so."

And suddenly Hsissh knew what was bothering him about Noa's eyes on Sergei. She wouldn't be the first member of any species to be distracted by thoughts of procreation—Hsissh had often been, in this form and others. But she couldn't afford to be.

The church doors opened, and the congregation began moving into the building. Spinning on her heels, Noa muttered, "I will be a pilot." Stroking Hsissh's tail, she added, "Watch me."

Hsissh forced a long purr out of his chest. Her eyes slid to him and she smiled. As they moved into the shady interior and Noa took a seat at the pew, Hsissh desperately hoped that he would be able to see her achieve her dream.

As soon as everyone was seated, the church leaders—all male, and one for each of the books—raised their arms. "We will open with a prayer."

Noa bowed her head and silence swept through the church.

"Hsissh!"

The whisper on the waves made his ears perk—the source was very close—as was the smell of fresh rat blood. Peering down the aisle, Hsissh's nose twitched. He saw an unfamiliar young werfle on its hind legs waving at him. "Isn't it amazing!" the werfle whispered across the waves. Hsissh blinked and was able to identify the consciousness in the new body. It was Ish. What was he doing here, so far from the human "capital" of Prime?

Ish put his two middle pairs of paws behind his back, and gestured with the top pair for Hsissh to join him. Hsissh didn't really want to get up...but some deep social instinct within compelled him, as did the smell of fresh rat blood. He stiffly slid down to Noa's lap, and before she could react, skittered to the floor and down the aisle. "Fluffy!" she whispered.

"Shhhhh..." said Mom. "He'll be fine."

One of the church leaders cleared his throat. Noa settled and bowed her head. There was no sound except for Hsissh's and Ish's claws on the wooden floor. Ish's claws were much louder because his young body was hopping up and down.

"Do you feel it? Do you feel their conscious-ness rising?" Ish said, spinning in a circle. Ish was older, wiser, and more prone to reflection and study than Hsissh—who was mostly prone to eating and sleeping—but the body Ish inhabited was young and vigorous. It made Hsissh tired just watching his excitement.

Hsissh didn't respond. The first few times Hsissh had come to church he'd been excited, too. He'd felt some of the congregation's minds touch the wave and experienced the same elation he'd felt when his first blind hatchlings had cracked through their shells. But his hatchlings had soon opened their eyes; the humans never left their bodies.

"No, they're not," Hsissh said. "They've been doing this for all of their recorded history." He'd learned that through Noa's history lessons.

"Don't be such a pessimist," Ish said. He deli-cately touched his nose to Hsissh's, but his hind legs continued to hop. "We're witnessing evolution!"

Hsissh didn't agree. Noa had to become a pilot, so she could get off Hsissh's world and live. He didn't have Shissh's worries about spreading black waters, or Ish's scientific enthusiasm, Hsissh cared only about the human girl who had twice endan-gered her life trying to save him. He looked at her now, her eyes darting down the aisle to check on him as though he were the kit, not her, and he felt the same rush of feelings he'd felt for his blind hatchlings.

"Does it matter that they can't touch the wave?" Hsissh said to Ish. "They are telepathic in their own way."

Ish sniffed derisively. "If their satellites go down, or their time gates go offline, they are trapped in their own minds. Light beams, radio, and micro-waves...they are as primitive as their speech. Their ethernet is a trap, distracting them from true oneness."

Hsissh thought of the minds across the galaxy Noa spoke to. She'd joined a Reserve Fleet Training Corps. It was a group for adolescents who dreamed of joining the Fleet; through them she'd found support for her ambitions and discovered that although her dreams weren't *average* for a young girl, they weren't *weird,* and she wasn't a deviant.

He bowed his head. She had confessed to her friends that the only thing she was worried about was leaving her "pet Fluffy." His hearts beat pain-fully at the thought. "Does it matter though?" he whispered. "Maybe they aren't wave aware, maybe they will never be...but they feel as much as we do." Even though they'd evolved light years away from one another. Even though they weren't wave-aware.

Perhaps it was because they were creatures that had to raise helpless young communally, too?

Ish lowered his head and narrowed his eyes at Hsissh, his hindquarters' furious hopping abruptly coming to a stop. "Are you crazy, Hsissh? Rats have feelings, too…even lizzar do!"

"But it's not the same," Hsissh said. "Rats don't grieve their dead for decades." *Like I do,* he almost said.

Ish raised his head and put a paw through his whiskers. "Rats don't live long enough, Hsissh."

Hsissh's body hunched. "We could communicate with the humans if we wanted to, we could even discuss the wave with them; they see its existence—"

"Through the primitive mirror of their mathematics," said Ish. "Until they feel it, they can't know it."

"They could still be useful!" Hsissh protested. "They have opposable thumbs and fighting machines!"

Ish's whiskers twitched. "Are you worried about Shissh's dark waters?" He poked Hsissh's chest with a sharp claw. "I can feel you are not, Hsissh. You've become too close to your humans, or that old body of yours has. We cannot announce ourselves to the humans. Announce ourselves, and we would, at least temporarily, lose the upper hand. It would be very inconvenient if they tried to wipe out our host species."

"We're thinking of wiping them out," Hsissh countered.

Ish got very still. "Only on this planet, Hsissh. They will still have their sanctuaries on other worlds." Ish's eyes bored into Hsissh's, and then his consciousness did as well. Probing Hsissh's memories, Ish found the ones where Hsissh tried to talk telepathically to Noa—and succeeded—and then failed due to her mind's rationalizations.

"You're lucky you didn't succeed in that," Ish said, the wave crackling with malevolence. "It would ruin my observations and their natural evolution—and you'd be ostracized, if not condemned to have your pattern dissolved."

Hsissh swished his tail. "I never tried to tell her I was sentient...I just tried to let her feel that she doesn't have to worry about me."

Ish's frame relaxed. "You're young—well, not your body, you look terrible—and I see you didn't successfully break any rules." He put a claw through a whisker. "They're your 'pets,'" he said, using the human word. "And you're worried. But don't be. They'll evolve; you'll see."

Hsissh knew he wasn't going to get anywhere with Ish, and if he pressed too much, The One might separate him from Noa. He'd lose his chance to see her escape this world. He sniffed, and changed the subject. "I smell fresh rat blood."

Ish's hindquarters began hopping again. "This place is crawling with them! I killed three before the service—silly, really, I can only eat one at a time. Would you like to come finish off the rest with me?"

If he had any poison, it would have pooled on his tongue. "Does a bear shit in the woods?" Hsissh replied, using an expression Dad used from time to time.

"What?" said Ish, head drawing back.

"Never mind," said Hsissh. "Lead me to those rats."

"With pleasure," said Ish. Pivoting on his fore-quarters, Ish darted for the back of the church. Hsissh followed, muscles and joints protesting all the way. He was vaguely aware of Jacob whispering as he slipped after Ish through a door just barely ajar.

Hsissh followed his fellow werfle up a stairwell, and then another to the attic of the church. There were two dead rats laid out in a sunbeam, like a scene from a dream.

An hour and a half later, after a delicious snack, the creaking of floorboards awoke Hsissh. Eyes blinking open to a blur, he heard Jacob say, "There you are, rat!"

For a moment, Hsissh was confused. The rats were long gone; he and Ish had gorged themselves quite completely. But then he was caught in a crushing grip, he felt his ribs fracture, and the world went dark. It took him a moment of frantic sniffing to realize he'd been dumped in a burlap sack. His hearts' beating increased in speed exponentially. "Let's see what happens to Noa when you don't come back!"

Intellectually Hsissh knew he might be able to claw his way out, or gnaw a hole. But his werfle body couldn't abide confinement and just... stopped. He didn't have to concentrate to leave his shell; the patterns that made him himself scattered onto the waves almost too quickly. As he collected them, he felt Shissh's consciousness. "It's about time! Now you can leave that debilitating sentimentality behind."

And he had already. The deep emotional pull he felt to Noa and her family was gone, as was all the pain of his previous body. He saw Ish cowering in a corner as the boy lugged the sack across the room. Ish called out through the waves, "I'm sorry, Hsissh.

My body's calling for revenge, but this is the most perfect research opportunity."

"It's fine," Hsissh said, thought, and felt; they were all the same here.

He hovered a bit. He saw Noa racing up the stairs. "Hey, I've got your werfle," Jacob taunted. "What are you going—"

Jacob was interrupted by a lightning fast kick to the stomach that sent him stumbling backward into the wall, dropping the sack in the process.

Noa bolted toward the sack Hsissh's old body was in. Falling to her knees, she gently pulled out Hsissh's body. "Fluffy?" she cried. And then she screamed, "Fluffy!" and fell to her knees, her entire body wracked with sobs.

"Ha, ha, made you cry!" Jacob said. "You'll never be a pilot!"

And Hsissh had to leave. Not because he felt a pull to Noa, but because he didn't.

Luminous Creatures

"It's great to have you here." Shissh opened and closed her pincers; they didn't clack so much underwater. "You'll get over Third in this form."

Hsissh's pincers drooped. No mention of needing to forget Noa or her family.

Waving her eye stalks, Shissh continued, "It's too bad about the humans—I talked to Chisssh about tweaking their DNA to make them wave aware, but they reproduce too slowly…it would take ten hundred cycles at the least." She pointed with a pincer down the reef. "The elders of these hosts meet every three cycles of the moon. I'll see you then; we'll ask them to tell us the stories of the dark waters. In the meantime—my side of the reef is over there." She waved with her pincers and eye stalks. "Stay away."

On that cheery note, she crawled away. Not that Hsissh minded. This particular species wasn't sociable.

He skittered down his side of the reef, cracking open tiny mollusks and sucking them into his primary orifice. The waters weren't dark, even though the sun was a distant dream, cut off from them by meters of ice. The seas of this moon were alive with bio-luminescent organisms that drew their life's energy from the heat that poured through the vents to the moon's raging magma core.

Food was plentiful. Shissh had already taken care of all potential predators. Company was available if he wanted it. But he didn't. It was the perfect place to explore, live, and not hurt.

He lasted only three rotations of the moon.

✳

"You're an idiot," Shissh said.

Hsissh flexed the claws of the new werfle hatchling's body he'd acquired. "Probably," he agreed. Shissh's consciousness floated away. He didn't say goodbye. Blinking awake from his nap, he got up and resumed tunneling through the underbrush. He was barely weaned from this body's third. None of this body's three parents had been host to a member of The One. They were sweet, kind, and boring. Hsissh would miss them, the third especially; but he remembered Noa kicking Jacob across the room, and then sobbing for a creature that wasn't her species. He missed Noa more—the tightening in his hearts was unmistakable. As he hopped toward the Sato family, he felt elation in his sorrow. It felt so good to feel again.

Hearts pumping, he increased his speed. Time on the crustacean moon had passed more slowly, due to a difference in gravity. Noa was several cycles older and would be taking exams soon. He had to reach her, and be there to sit on her shoulder and her lap while she studied to offer moral support. He had to snuggle with her at night so she wouldn't be afraid of rats and could get enough sleep. He had to see her get off this planet before his kind unleashed the Fourth Plague—more and more humans were arriving every day, and many of The One were pushing to advance the date.

Hsissh had chosen his hatchling's body for its proximity to the Sato's homestead. He was at the edge of the trees, dirt stained and exhausted, just past sunset. He came to an abrupt halt before he entered the garden. There were boys outside of Noa's window. He felt venom pool on his tongue. Were they there because of some human "elopement" ritual?

A voice rose among the boys—it sounded like Jacob's, but deeper. "You're not going to race your brother's new antigrav bike?"

Noa was silhouetted by light and he couldn't read her facial expressions. But through the wave he felt her fury. "I've already beaten your ass twice, Jacob. Now I've got to study."

"Waste of time," said Jacob.

"If you're only interested in being in the Luddeccean Guard, sure," Noa hissed.

"Nothing wrong with joining the Guard," said another voice…again, familiar but deeper. Hsissh sniffed. It was Sergei! He'd grown since Hsissh had been gone. Noa's silhouette turned to Sergei and Hsissh could feel the war within her. He rushed through the garden, all ten legs pumping.

"She's lost her edge," said Jacob. "Let's go."

The boys turned away.

"Wait!" said Noa, her eyes on Sergei.

Hsissh leaped into the ivy on the side of the house and began climbing the vines.

"Noa?" Sergei said.

"I heard something!" Noa said, and Hsissh could feel her concentration had left the boy.

"A wild werfle!" Jacob cried, "Kill it!"

Noa shouted, "Stay away from him or I'll kill you!" Before Hsissh could blink or think, she was soaring through the window above his head and landing lightly on the ground.

"It's your funeral if he bites!" Jacob said.

Dad's voice roared through the night. "Who's there!"

Hsissh took the opportunity to sneak in the window and leap onto Noa's bed. He heard Sergei say, "It's her dad, run!"

Inside the house, there was the sound of Mom's footsteps running toward Noa's room. Hsissh dived behind the pillows on Noa's bed just before Mom burst in. Outside, he heard the boys' retreating footsteps, Dad's thunderous approach and booming voice. "Noa, what was going on?"

"They wanted to go racing," she said. "And then Jacob tried to attack a wild werfle." He could hear her rifling through the ivy.

Hsissh watched Mom go to the window, peer out, and then turn to shoo Masako and John from the room.

In the garden, Dad said, "Go back inside."

"But the werfle …" Noa said.

"Will be fine," said Dad. "You go inside …"

There was the sound of soft, quick steps and then a thump against the house. A moment later, Noa was climbing through the window, a few pieces of ivy clinging to her fingers.

"That wasn't what I meant!" Dad shouted.

"I have to get back to studying!" Noa said, landing lightly on her feet and immediately going to her hologlobe. The device was larger than the one she used to have—this one was as large in diameter as two grown werfles. Hsissh felt her concentrate. The globe glowed and within it appeared a scene of Fleet ships below a time gate.

Noa's paws balled at her side. "The Guard won't take me …" she muttered. Shaking her head, she focused … and then her mind was alight with the thoughts of members of the Reserve Fleet Training Corp.

"Hey, Noa, you're back!" said a boy Hsissh didn't recognize.

"You weren't kidnapped by crazy fundies and forced into marriage with a man five times your age," said a girl who looked to be about Noa's age.

"Ha, ha, you're hilarious," Noa said aloud. The words were picked up by the nanos in her mind and sent across the galaxy to her friends. Noa punched the air. "Let's get back to the Battle of Time Gate Five. What would we have done in Captain Malik's position? I was thinking…"

Hsissh dropped from her consciousness. He was warm between the pillows, but an uncomfortable feeling was coming over him. Noa didn't really need his help. She was going to leave. She had to, not because of any plague, but because she didn't belong here. Maybe he didn't, either.

It wasn't until she was putting on her pajamas that Hsissh slunk from his hiding place. Her back was to him, and he was pondering quietly leaving…but then she turned suddenly. Her eyes grew wide at the sight of him—and he reared on his hind legs at the sight of her. She'd grown in the time he was gone, and developed the secondary sexual characteristics of her kind, but she was still lean, her skin was still a beautiful rich brown, and her eyes that deep almost-black.

"Fluffy?" Noa said, reaching out hesitantly. In the waves he heard her thoughts. *It's not really Fluffy, but so much like him, he'd stand just like that…*

With a strike of inspiration, Hsissh dived beneath the covers and did his circuit. Coming up for air, he gave the squeak of 'all clear.' He tugged at the waves, and tried to reassure her, *I won't bite.*

Noa fell onto the bed and scooped him up into her arms. She scratched him behind the ears, the way he'd liked in his old body and still liked in this one. He purred unabashedly and she wept into his fur.

Later, with a belly full of leftovers Noa had sneaked from the kitchen, he curled up with her under the covers. Noa didn't need him to escape Luddeccea…and he didn't need to love her. But life without love was like a rat that had been dead for a few days. You could eat it, but it wasn't as delicious.

Releasing Pets into the Wild

Hsissh's body was old again. If he moved, his joints would ache, and his fur was thinning. But he wasn't moving, the chair beneath him was soft and comfortable, and he was warmed by a sunbeam.

"Looks like you've stolen my seat, Sir," said Tim. Hsissh blinked his eyes. Tim was Noa's husband. His appearance was as striking as Noa's. Instead of tan skin, his was as pale as a shaved werfle. His eyes were an eerie sky blue, and his hair was the color of dead grass.

Hsissh raised his head. "Oh, don't get up on my account," Tim said, scratching Hsissh gingerly behind the ears.

Not that Hsissh would dream of it, even though he liked Tim, despite his disturbing appearance. Tim was an engineer in the Fleet and served on the same "space ship" that Noa did. They were stationed light years from Luddeccea. Noa would be safe when the plague came; just as important …

Noa's voice echoed from the kitchen. "You're moving back to Earth?"

Dad answered, "Luddeccea is becoming too fundamentalist."

The turn in conversation drew Tim to the kitchen. Hsissh watched him go. As far as he understood these things, Tim was a fine specimen of the masculine gender of Noa's species. Broad-shouldered and tall. But more important, Noa and Tim were happy when they were together— the waves buzzed with their feelings. Hsissh was pleased. Humans, from the werfles' observation, were mostly polygamous in their youth, but then settled into monogamous relationships as they aged. It seemed to correspond with stability and happiness.

"We just don't feel comfortable staying here," Mom said.

Hsissh felt a warm glow in the pit of his stomach and put a proud paw through his whiskers. He couldn't speak into Mom's and Dad's minds, but he'd discovered he could tug at the waves in a way that sparked emotional reactions. Whenever a news report came on the hologlobe about The Three Book's growing influence in civic affairs, or a riot against new settlers occurred in the city of Prime, he'd pulled hard on the waves and made their natural unease greater. When Dad had gotten a job offer on Earth, Hsissh had augmented his elation. When Mom contemplated moving her own consulting business, Hsissh had increased her optimism.

"We'll *all* be off world ..." said Noa.

Hsissh kneaded his claws. He'd nudged Masako to go there to further her studies—and she'd stayed! John had always wanted to leave; his parents had died in the Third Plague before Mom and Dad had immigrated to the planet. John himself had augmented kidneys because the Third Plague had destroyed his; Dad had taken him to Earth for several operations as he aged so that his "plastic kidney beans" could be replaced with larger ones for his growing body. John blamed the "Luddeccean crazy-late acceptance of nano cures" for his parents' deaths and the augments that had cost him painful operations. Hsissh had only needed to strengthen John's resolve to leave the planet.

Mom sighed. "Kenji is very upset about us selling the house."

Hsissh's ears twitched. Kenji had been the only member of the family he hadn't been able to influence. Whenever Hsissh pulled on the waves coursing through his mind, Kenji had heard voices… much as the humans The One had tried to inhabit had. Perhaps it was because Kenji's mind had special nano augments to make up for a congenital syndrome he had? Hsissh wasn't sure, but the "voices" had worried Mom and Dad tremendously. Hsissh had to give up his attempts to guide Kenji, but in the end, the boy had left on his own, drawn by the promise of a better education on Earth.

"What will happen to Fluffy?" Noa said, and Hsissh's body grew rigid.

"Sarah Benjamin has offered to take him in," said Mom.

"She and Sergei know having an old werfle sleeping in the house is better than no werfle," Dad said. "Rats hate them."

"I wish we could take him aboard the fighter carrier," Tim said. "We have a rat problem."

Noa said what Hsissh was thinking. "He'd never survive the Fleet quarantine, even if he were younger."

Mom sighed. "Sergei and Sarah, they're kind people...they'll treat the old man right."

Hsissh's whiskers twitched. They wouldn't treat Hsissh at all. He'd be leaving this old body soon. In the kitchen, he heard Noa and Tim discuss their ship's upcoming voyage. Mom and Dad discussed their upcoming move off-world.

Hsissh blinked. The sunlight felt especially warm, and made bits of dust sparkle in its beam like distant stars and brilliant expectations...He'd done it, he'd seen that his humans would leave this world and make it to safety. It didn't feel a little like seeing hatchlings leave the nest; it felt *exactly* like that.

Carl Sagan Discovers Intelligent Life

Hsissh was in the body of a male werfle in his prime. He was watching as his latest hatchlings, now grown adults, set off through the undergrowth. Beside him the second in his parental triad squeaked. She wasn't inhabited by The One and was simple, but Dich, the "other female" in the group, and the third in this triad was. It had made Hsissh's time as First more interesting. Dich touched her nose to Second fondly, and Hsissh did the same. Second wiggled, sniffed the air, and set off on her own through the undergrowth.

"Well, that was well done," Dich said into the wave. "We made great parents."

Hsissh agreed and felt the warmth of satisfaction in his chest.

"I'm going to curl up and join The Gathering," Dich said. "Will you be coming?"

Hsissh's tail flicked, a dark mood settling upon him. He didn't relish going over plans for the Fourth Plague.

"Suit yourself," said Dich, and she hopped over to the tree log they used as a den.

Lifting his nose to the breeze, Hsissh detected the scent of a rat. He licked his lips. He could eat all of his kill for the first time in cycles! He slunk off, and an hour later he was rolling over on his back in a bright patch of sunlight, a rat carcass partially consumed beside him. He was utterly content. And then a wave-dream apparition appeared beside him. Hsissh blinked. The apparition was in the form of a cat. Before Hsissh could ask, the cat flattened its ears. "It's me, Shissh!"

Hsissh blinked. "You're a cat now?"

"I wanted to hitch a ride on one of the humans' space ships," Shissh said.

"How interesting," said Hsissh, not particularly interested in anything but enjoying his current sunbeam and full belly.

"It's Noa's space ship," Shissh said.

Hsissh sat up with a start. "Really, how is she?"

Shissh swished her tail. "I don't know."

"You don't—"

"Pay attention," hissed Shissh. "It may be the maternal hormones from the litter of kittens I just bore, but I've become fond of your human. She saved me from being thrown out of an airlock."

Hsissh put a claw to his chest that was swelling with pride. "Well, of course she—"

Shissh hissed again. "She went to visit her brother on Luddeccea."

"Kenji is here?"

"He's been back for years. Haven't you been paying attention?"

"Years?" said Hsissh.

"Listen," Shissh growled. "Luddeccea's time gate has gone offline and Noa is on the planet. If you want her to get off that self-righteous fundamentalist rock—"

Hsissh blinked.

Shissh licked a paw. "The attitude toward Luddeccea around here is influencing me." She swished her tail. "You've got to find her and get her off the planet."

"Is she alone—or is Tim with her?" Hsissh asked, rising to his hind legs.

For a moment, Shissh said nothing. She just sat, swishing her tail and glaring at him. And then she *snarled,* "Tim has been dead for several Earth years now."

Hsissh sank to all ten paws. "What?" He'd been distracted by hatchlings and kits for a long time... he hadn't realized how long. Or maybe he hadn't wanted to follow Noa too closely, afraid to know what he wouldn't be able to influence.

"None of that matters," Shissh said. "Find Noa!"

Hsissh launched himself into the waves, spreading himself as thin as he could... and encountered Ish's consciousness in Prime. Ish was in werfle form, dancing in a home that had a ceiling that was a hundred werfle lengths high. "Isn't it wonderful, Hsissh! The time gate is closed. No more ships from Earth, the humans here will be able to focus on enlightenment; they'll evolve!"

Hsissh thought frantically, "Have you seen Noa?"

Ish put a paw through a whisker, and Hsissh felt his disapproval. "Your human is somewhere in the capital...she is wanted by the Central Authority. She is involved in some horrible new 'technological experiment.' But never fear, we'll catch—"

Hsissh cut away from the conversation, feeling a bubbling wrath in his stomach—the same he'd felt when a rat had tried to attack one of his hatchlings. He tore himself completely away from his body, leaving behind just a werfle bewildered at finding itself stuffed with a delicious rat in a field. Letting his pattern flow through the waves, Hsissh found a werfle host not inhabited by a member of The One in Prime and slipped in.

Blinking his new eyes, he was assailed by the overwhelming smell of human. Instead of sod, underneath his feet was pavement.

He'd never been to Prime, but this werfle host had lived here all its life and Hsissh had all its memories. He wore a collar—once this werfle had lived with humans. He recognized the "alley" he stood in. It was behind a tall, slender "town home" where he'd resided with two adults and a little boy. But recently, the "boy" was only a technological imitation of the man and woman's child who'd died of a lung infection. Outwardly it was almost perfect, but it smelled wrong. And when the adults were not in the room, it became nothing but a piece of furniture, its mind simple and unchanging. It never cried, and it never yelled at the parents. The real boy had chased the werfle with such enthusiasm that they sometimes knocked over furniture and he'd screamed when the werfle had been separated from him. The machine boy never played chase. The memory of the strangeness of the artificial boy sent a cocktail of depressive hormones to Hsiss's mind, and he cried into the waves at the lie that was the machine. Shissh must have been paying attention, because she heard. Hsissh *felt* Shissh reply, "Ah, yes, Noa's spoken of those... Some humans use robots to replace their dead—but they don't have the computing power to be like real humans. Something about Moore's Law banging into Moore's Wall... Human innovation has been stalled for the past few hundred years. To have a robot as smart as a human, you'd need a machine with the brain the size of a small moon and a nuclear plant to power it."

Shaking his head to clear it of Shissh's gibberish, Hsissh stood up on his hind limbs and looked to the home. He knew without going in that it was empty. He was assailed by a painful memory of Luddeccean Guards coming into the house, dismembering the machine boy, and taking the parents away. This werfle—not intelligent like the one inhabited by The One—had attacked one of the Guards and had been kicked across the room. Hsissh took a deep breath. His "new" ribs still hurt from the experience. He patted his body. It was amazing he hadn't been killed…that had been months ago. This body hadn't eaten well since then, even though he had fresh venom on his tongue.

Hsissh pivoted on his back hind legs and caught a glimpse of blue sky between the tall town homes on either side of him. He paused, struck by another memory. That ribbon of blue should have been filled with space ships traveling up to the time gate, but it was empty of everything but clouds. He craned his neck to see the time gate. A bright spark flashed beside the gate's ring and then streaked toward the planet like a falling star. A meteor? He searched his mind, and the mind of The One…and all the thoughts of all The One on Luddeccea collided with his. He knew what the explosion was; it was a space ship. Worse, he knew where the two parents of the machine boy had been taken. He saw it through the eyes of another werfle somewhere so far north the snow had already fallen: a huge camp where humans were dying like they'd been afflicted by another plague. He felt in the collective consciousness of The One that these humans were "augmented" or had been owners of imitation robots. They had been rounded up and made to work until they dropped because of it. It wasn't plague, but hunger that made them slump into the snow…Humans were starving their own kind to death.

His claws fell to his sides and he had an uncomfortable feeling in his gut. Perhaps The One need not exterminate the humans on this planet…they were doing the job themselves. Hsissh dropped down to all ten paws.

The sound of two human children behind him made him turn. They were thin, and he noticed with a start that they didn't have the usual metal circle in the sides of their heads.

"Is that a rat?" one of the children said, raising a slingshot, a projectile device Noa had used on occasion as a child. Hsissh's body reacted on its own. He dashed into a hole at the side of the "street" before he'd even thought about it. A moment later, he was in the darkness of the "sewer." The hunger this body carried made the short dash exhausting. He curled into a ball and tried to seek out Noa's consciousness. He searched until the light coming through the sewer "grate" had dimmed. But there were literally millions of humans in Prime and he had to gently probe each one at a time. After a while, his exhaustion broke down his concentration and carried his body into fitful sleep.

Shissh's feline apparition found his dreams. "Have you found Noa? The Captain's talking of having me spayed!"

"What is that?" Hsissh asked.

Swishing her tail, Shissh said, "Never mind! Where is Noa?"

"Ish told me she's here in Prime," Hsissh replied. "She's being hunted by the Luddeccean Guard for her part in some sort of undesirable technological innovation."

Sitting down, Shissh's ears perked. "That's odd, I know nothing of that."

Hsissh wiped a nervous paw through his whiskers. "There are so many humans here, Shissh. Trying to find her is like—"

"Finding a needle in a haystack," Shissh said. "That means—"

"I know what it means!" said Hsissh. "Do you have any ideas?"

Shissh's tail swished. "Doesn't she have an aunt in Prime? Aunt Eliza?"

Hsissh sat up, or his dream self did. "Yes…do you think Noa would go there?"

Shissh nervously licked her paw. "I don't know …"

Hsissh thought of a tiny Noa barreling toward his tormentors so long ago. "I have to try and find her...I remember a map to the aunt's home. I will go."

Shissh's cat ears perked again. "You're going to do it ..." And Hsissh felt her wonder. His whiskers twitched at the insult. She purred and kneaded her paws. "You've never been a werfle of action...it looks good on you. That means—"

"I have to go now," he said. He tore himself from the dream, forced his body up from the ground, and began the journey through the sewers to Eliza's house. The map in his memory was of streets above ground, but he knew his relative location from this body's memories, and his body was sensitive to the magnetic pull of the planet's pole. He would make it even in the dark, if the tunnels were clear, if he didn't encounter any human "maintenance" workers, or children with slingshots.

He didn't account for his body's state of near starvation. After half a day cycle he collapsed.

*

He dreamed of Noa. She was arguing about stealing a space ship with...was that a member of The One in human form?

"Noa," the maybe-member of The One said. "I need to know what your plan is. If I don't know what the plan is, I can't calculate the odds of its success."

"Calculate the odds of success?" Noa said. "Some things are worth more than any odds."

They continued to argue, and then Noa shouted, "If that's what you believe, then go!" And then a real shout made Hsissh awaken. "Go!"

Blinking his eyes in the dim light of the sewer, Hsissh saw two humans not sixty hops away. One looked like Noa.

Hope giving him strength, he skittered to his feet and hopped as fast as he could toward the pair. A blast of air sent the slighter human's scent toward him…and it was Noa! His exhausting trek toward Aunt Eliza's domicile had paid off! His sense of victory was dampened by the smell of disease and hunger about her. A worried cheeping came from his chest. Noa turned, and he stood up on his hind-most legs, just as he'd done that first time he'd come back to her. His hearts slid toward the ground… She'd become so thin…

Taking off her outer upper garment, Noa sat down on her heels and held it out like a hammock. Hsissh approached cautiously, remembering her trepidation the first time he'd come back.

"They're venomous!" the other human said.

Hsissh felt the waves...not a member of The One. But not quite *right* either.

Noa snorted. "Did you notice he's wearing a collar? His venom has already been milked." Not that Hsissh suspected she'd care...she'd managed to keep him from being milked when he was in his second body so he could "have some protection from the Jacobs of the world." He slid into her garment and rolled onto his back.

"Someone's pet," Noa murmured, looking down at him. "But he's in bad shape."

Hsissh gave a cry of confirmation.

"I know you're hungry, little one." She sighed. "You lost your family, didn't you? And there aren't any more rats in the sewers." She wrapped him in the fabric so only his head was exposed, and ran a finger down his chin.

Another soft cry escaped Hsissh against his volition. The other human hesitatingly proffered a "soybean." Hsissh was too hungry to reject the offering. His nose twitched as he ate. The other human smelled like steel and synthetics. His host's memories shot through him. The man smelled a lot like the imitation boy! His nose twitched again... but no, that wasn't quite right; the other human also smelled like a human male, and blood. Also, he was much too disagreeable to be an "imitation."

He'd argued with Noa quite infuriatingly. So much plastic, metal, and steel though…a human who had been excessively augmented? Hadn't the werfles near the snow camps said that the humans trapped there were augmented?

"What are you still doing here?" Noa said. For a moment Hsissh thought she was talking to him, but then she resumed the argument she'd been having with the man. After a few minutes Noa said, "Fine, let's go," and started walking in the direction of the aunt's house.

In her arms, Hsissh trembled. Could he really help Noa? He had poison fangs and a worn out body. She was sick. The other human was prone to arguing. Hsissh blinked at the other human; his slightly mollified hunger had cleared his eyes a bit. The other human looked a lot like Tim, taller though, more muscular, but did not radiate happiness in Noa's presence. He did have a neural interface for the ethernet, unlike the two boys in the alley. Hsissh sniffed the air. The other human didn't smell like Tim…he smelled, oddly, opposite of Noa. Hsissh couldn't quite explain it, but as the two of them continued to converse, the fur on his back rose.

Perhaps sensing his tension, Noa ran a finger over Hsissh's belly. Despite his hunger, and all his apprehensions, he purred.

"I think I'll name him Fluffy," Noa said, and Hsissh whispered into her mind, "Yes! Yes! Yes!"

"He isn't fluffy, his fur is short. That name doesn't even make sense," the man said. Hsissh went stiff in Noa's arms. He felt a trembling in the waves, as though someone were using it for communication.

"They are fluffy when they're kits," Noa said. "We named our werfles Fluffy back on our farm."

"You named more than one werfle Fluffy? How is that even practical? They wouldn't know which one you were calling," the man said.

"Not at the same time!" Noa replied. "After the first died, we named the second werfle Fluffy. That way we didn't slip up and call werfle number two Fluffy, when his name was actually Rex, or Spot or something. Calling him by a dead werfle's name would have been rude and weird." And in the wave Hsissh felt her think, And they were so similar…I felt like they were the same being.

"But technically, you were calling him by the dead werfle's name," the maybe-human protested. "Fluffy was the dead werfle's name even if it was also werfle number two's name."

Noa huffed. "Fine, if you don't like Fluffy, choose another name."

The man looked down at Hsissh, and Hsissh felt it again, a tiny disruption in the waves that came with communication across time and space. "I wouldn't even think you'd like werfles. They look like rats," the man said.

Hsissh's ears flattened like a cat's. He tried to send disapproval into the man's mind, but…the wave felt different in the other human.

Noa's eyes went wide and she gasped. "They look nothing like rats. Their noses aren't long and pointy, their eyes aren't small and beady, they're clean—well, when they have access to clean water, they're clean. Their tails aren't naked, and they don't eat people." She lifted Hsissh to her nose. "They eat rats. They're cute, they're friendly, and they're intelligent—smartest creature on Luddeccea—at least as smart as ravens as far as anyone can tell."

Hsissh could see the irritation flaring in the other human as Noa touched her nose to his. Hsissh purred with the new beginnings of familial love…

…but then a rush of *alien* waves sparked through his mind. "Fine, call it Carl Sagan if it's so smart," the man snapped.

Hsissh's whiskers trembled, and it all came together. He understood. The other human was extremely augmented, not just in his body, but in his brain—like Kenji! Hsissh hadn't been able to touch Kenji mentally either, not effectively anyway. The different "augmentation" in the man's brain allowed him to use the waves. Humans had achieved wave manipulation through their technology! If he'd had more energy, he might have wiggled out of Noa's grasp in excitement. Ish had been wrong thinking humans would achieve oneness through their prayers—maybe that had shown them the way—but they were inadequate creatures in fur, claw, and mind. Like every other inadequacy, they'd made up for their weakness with their machines. He took a deep breath...would the other werfles accept it? He exhaled. Not fast enough. They still had to leave before the next plague—but maybe someday...

"Carl Sagan?" said Noa.

"Twentieth-century scientist," the man muttered, looking away from Hsissh. "He theorized that there was intelligent life in the universe, just that it hadn't visited us."

Hsissh purred. The One had neglected the quadrant of the galaxy that was home to humans—it had been a complete fluke that the humans had found The One's home planet first and not the other way around. To think a human named Carl Sagan had theorized that was possible... His purr halted. The One thought that there was no other intelligence in the universe but their own, and so had humans, though they'd been under one another's noses for a few centuries now. Their concepts of "intelligence" were just too different to allow them to see one another. A purr rose in his chest again. But their sense of love, it was the same. Hsissh tried to send a rush of admiration and validation to the other human. The man didn't respond. Hsissh almost got mad, but then realized that maybe the human hadn't felt it. What had Dad said? "New technology, always buggy"?

"Carl Sagan," said Noa. "I like it."

Hsissh purred. He liked it, too.

If you enjoyed this story and would enjoy reading another story in this universe, check out C. Gockel's *Archangel Down*. Learn more at her website: www. cgockelwrites.com/archangel.

BLOOD TIES

A GAIAN CONSORTIUM STORY

CHRISTINE POPE

Author's note: This story takes place approximately six months before the beginning of *Blood Will Tell,* the first book in the Gaian Consortium series.

✳

EVEN THROUGH THE CLOSED DOOR OF HER BEDROOM, MIALA Fels could hear the deep voices of the men who'd gathered in the main room of the flat she shared with Lestan Fels, her father. She hated the sound, since she knew those voices signaled yet another opportunity for Lestan to get himself into trouble.

He never intended to cause trouble, of course. All he wanted was to provide a more stable life for his daughter. Unfortunately, his particular skill set was one Iradia's crime lords found valuable. And since they could pay far more than any legitimate employer....

She'd been sitting in front of her computer, staring at the old-fashioned flat display—they were too poor to afford the heads-up style—when the men arrived. Her father had given her the order to hide herself in her bedroom well before the time the visitors were due to arrive. Well, it wasn't really an order; giving orders wasn't Lestan's style. But he'd made the suggestion, casting a nervous eye toward the front door of their flat, and she hadn't argued. Right around the time she'd turned seventeen and had begun to leave a somewhat awkward adolescence behind, she'd begun to attract the kind of attention she really didn't want from the men who did business with her father, men who cast flat, leering glances at her and even started to suggest that Lestan might make more money by loaning her out rather than setting up their security systems or hacking their rivals' computers.

After deflecting those outrageous suggestions on two or three occasions, Lestan and Miala had mutually decided it was better that she not be present at these meetings, even though he'd been training her ever since she was eight years old, and she knew almost as much about computers and making them impervious to outside attack as her father did. Too risky for her to be anywhere near those men, he'd said, and she knew he was right. According to Gaian laws, she had still been under-age at that point, more than three years ago now, but the Consortium's laws didn't mean a hell of a lot out here in a backwater like Iradia.

Miala abandoned the project she'd been work-ing on—setting up a secure payment system for Nala, who owned the coffee house down the street, and who had been hit by hackers several times during the last few months, draining her meager profits—and headed over to the door of her bed-room. She didn't even need to press her ear against it to hear what the men were saying.

"...sure you can do it?" one of them asked.

They hadn't given their names, but she'd seen the two men around town more than once while she was out running errands. Aldis Nova was one of Iradia's larger settlements, but even so, it was small enough that you got to know who was a resident and who wasn't, even if you'd never exchanged a single word. One of the men was tall and well-dressed, with faintly lavender skin that spoke of Eridani her-itage a generation or two back. The other one was shorter and heavier, with dull dark eyes that had made a shiver go down Miala's back the one time she'd made the mistake of making eye contact with him on the street. Somehow, her bedroom door seemed like a flimsy barrier when she considered that it was the only thing standing between her and the black-eyed stranger.

"Of course," Lestan replied. His voice sounded calm…on the surface. Beneath that apparent composure, however, Miala could hear an underlying tension. He needed this job. He'd delivered on the last one, but the man he'd done the work for had gotten himself shot up in a dispute with one of his fellow "silk merchants"—all right, smugglers—and the work had never been paid for. That financial blow had been enough to wipe out their meager savings, and they now had only enough left to buy food for another week or so. Paying the rent on their dingy little flat would be impossible without a fresh infusion of funds.

"What about the girl?" the shorter man asked, and Miala held her breath. Of course he couldn't know she was there listening, since she hadn't made a sound, but still….

Right then, she wished her door had a lock that worked.

"What about her?" Lestan replied.

"Heard she was doing some work for you. If she is, I think she should be in on this discussion, don't you?"

Oh, hell no, she thought. But she didn't move. The last thing she wanted was for them to know that she was right there on the other side of her door.

"I've had her perform a few simple tasks, debug a few routines." Lestan was doing a decent job of sounding casual and unconcerned, but Miala didn't know if that would be enough to move the conversation in a safer direction. "But I'd never trust her with something this important."

"Good thing," said the other man, the one who looked part Eridani. "This commission is far too important to be entrusted to a child."

"She didn't look like a child the last time I saw her," the shorter man retorted. Again Miala had to force herself not to react, although right then she felt sick to her stomach.

"My daughter is a decent programmer," Lestan said. "In five years, maybe she'll be in a place where she could take on something like this. Right now, though, she won't be involved at all."

"She home?" the unpleasant one asked. "Maybe I'd like to ask her myself."

"I'm afraid not," Lestan replied, and this time he seemed unable to hide the edge to his voice. Normally, Miala liked hearing him speak, because he had the smooth, cultured accent of his home world of Gaia, rather than the flatter timbres of those who'd been born out here on the fringes. In that moment, however, she feared that his tone only betrayed the nervousness and fear he was trying so desperately to hide.

"Leave the daughter out of it," the part-Eridani man cut in, sounding annoyed. "As her father pointed out, she's not capable of handling this commission. But you, Fels," he went on, words becoming brisk, "what do you think your timeline will be for the project?"

"Shouldn't take more than a week," Lestan said, and Miala experienced a sinking sensation somewhere in her midsection. Her father was always being far too optimistic about when he thought he could deliver a project, a trait that inevitably resulted in both him and his daughter having to work around the clock to meet his employers' unrealistic deadlines.

"A week?" the man echoed, sounding impressed despite himself. "Well, it sounds as if we've come to the right person. Then let's move forward. Two thousand as a deposit, and the rest upon completion."

His words were followed by a faint metallic clink, and Miala guessed he'd deposited the promised units on the shabby plastic table in the dining area. The vast majority of financial transactions in the galaxy took place electronically, but on Iradia, people preferred cold, hard cash. It was a hell of a lot harder to trace.

"Thank you, Mor—" her father began, then stopped himself. Clearly, he'd been about to say the man's name, and cut the word short before Miala could overhear. She might be included in her father's programming work when necessary, but he did everything in his power to keep the identities of his employers from her.

"We'll check in three days from now, see how the work is going," the part-Iradian said. Then he added, the words carrying an ominous weight of their own, "We expect great things, Master Fels."

"You won't be disappointed," Lestan promised.

No reply, but Miala could hear movement, followed by the tired whoosh of the front door. Its hydraulics had needed servicing forever.

She hurried back to her chair and sat down, then returned her attention to the display in front of her. The subterfuge probably wouldn't fool her father, but she figured she might as well pretend that she hadn't been eavesdropping. Besides, he would wait a little bit before coming into her room, just to make sure the men were truly gone. That would give her some time to ease back into her work, even though this particular bit of coding was so simple, she could have done it four or five years ago. She'd only taken on the job because Nala had asked for help, and the elderly coffee house owner had slipped Miala free drinks on enough occasions that she figured helping out was the least she could do.

As she'd thought, her father entered the room not quite five standard minutes later. Since there was no place else to sit down, he took a seat on the bed.

"I suppose you heard all that."

She didn't see the point in lying. For too long, it had been just Lestan and her. They didn't keep a lot of secrets from each other...except the ones that might get them into trouble. "I did. They sounded like a couple of choice specimens."

"The one isn't too bad." Lestan paused there, as if he knew there wasn't a single thing he could say to defend the shorter of his two visitors.

"I suppose." Miala swiveled her chair partway so she could face her father. He looked back at her with a sort of tired acceptance, and it seemed to hit her then. Lestan had always been there, the one fixed object in her universe, but for the first time she really noticed the gray in his hair, which had long ago overtaken the original dark brown, and the worry lines around his eyes. Sometime during the past few years he'd slipped into middle age, and only now was she beginning to realize what a toll living on this world had taken on him. Because he looked so weary, she bit back what she'd been about to say, that he needed to be more discriminating in his choice of commissions, no matter what their financial situation.

He truly believed they had no other choice.

Tempering her own dismay, Miala went on, "At least it's just a standard data security setup, right?"

Her father let out a sigh, then ran a hand through his hair. It needed cutting, and stuck out in all directions. The effect wasn't comical, though, but instead only served to intensify the aura of weariness that surrounded him. "Not exactly."

Despite herself, Miala's voice sharpened. "Not exactly how?"

"There's more than one facility involved. And the person paying for the commission wants a layered system."

Of course he did. Not that these crime lords didn't have a lot to hide, but still. Building the sort of electronic fortress they all seemed to require took time, and time was the one thing Miala and Lestan didn't have, thanks to his overly optimistic assessment of how long this would all take.

Well, she'd pulled all-nighters before. And they did have two thousands units of actual cash sitting there in the flat with them, which meant the rent would be paid and the refrigeration unit could be stocked again. She hadn't really been looking forward to yet another evening meal of leth, a cheap grain-based dish usually relegated to breakfast fare and the only thing they'd been able to afford for the past few days.

"All right," Miala told her father. "Then I suppose we'd better get to work."

✳

Thank God she actually had inherited her father's facility with computers. Sometimes Miala wondered what Lestan would have done if it turned out that she'd gotten more from her mother genetically than just her red hair, and didn't have the skill to replicate her father's efforts. Would he have kept on trying to teach her the tricks of his trade, whether or not she had the talent for it?

As with so many other topics that skirted her parents' past, Miala had never worked up the nerve to ask her father that question. He never spoke of her mother; the few tidbits Miala had gleaned over the years were due entirely to listening to neighborhood gossip. Apparently, even in as jaded a town as Aldis Nova, it was something to take all your husband's money and disappear off-world, leaving him with an infant daughter.

But since Miala had never known her mother, she couldn't really miss her. Occasionally she'd wonder if there was anything about her own looks or speech or mannerisms that might be similar, besides her hair, but again, she knew better than to ask. Lestan Fels was a mild man, but prying into his past was one of the surest ways to arouse his slow-burning anger.

The job was just that, a job. Harder than some, not as tricky as others. If they'd been given a full two weeks to work on it, or, even better, an actual standard month, Miala might have said she even found the task enjoyable. Numbers and code were a lot easier to deal with than people, after all. You knew how they were going to react. Plug this formula in here, get that result over there. Oh, occasionally something would blow up, but again, tracing the problem back to the original input would usually give you a solution.

Too bad real life was a whole lot messier.

Its current messiness was a direct result of not having enough time. She knew better than to reproach her father for that, though. They'd had this argument several times in the past, and his response was always the same: "You don't know these people the way I do."

It was a truth she had to acknowledge, although she didn't like it very much. Maybe if she hadn't lately been engaged in the mildest of flirtations with young Captain Malick, who'd recently been posted to the Gaian Defense Fleet's station here in Aldis Nova, Miala might have felt differently about the corruption that powered the place…and the way she'd gotten sucked into it because of her father's activities.

Her father didn't like her connection with Captain Malick, tenuous as it might have been. Of course he wouldn't; Lestan Fels had dealings with some very questionable individuals. He justified the work and the people who paid him by saying all he did was write programs. It wasn't as if he was hired muscle, paid to break heads in alleyways or take out business rivals with a well-timed pulse bolt. Miala still thought the services he performed inhabited a very gray area, but since she didn't have the freedom to leave, she mostly kept her protests to herself.

Still, she couldn't help but experience a sinking sensation as she built their unknown client's system piece by piece and wondered how they could possibly get it all done on time. She'd stay up tonight,

and tomorrow as well, but any more sleep depriva-
tion than that, and she had a feeling that she'd end
up with her face planted right into her keyboard.

It was very quiet. Their neighborhood was
shabby, but still one of the more peaceful sections
of the city. Its inhabitants worked at the town's bars
and restaurants, or in the warehouses and factories
that stored and processed the precious moon-moth
silk which brought Iradia most of its income. At
this time of night, if people weren't at work, then
they were sleeping, trying to store up their energy
for another day laboring away in the desert world's
blistering heat.

For some reason, though, Miala could feel the
skin on the back of her neck crawl. A shiver went
over her. Stupid, because her room was uncomfortably warm, even at just past midnight. Their land-
lord kept promising to service the cooling system,
but he never did, so mostly what blew through the
vents was barely processed hot air.

The numbers on the screen in front of her
blurred, and she blinked. Maybe it was time to take
a break. A cold glass of water from the refrigeration unit might help to combat the heat, which was
something she couldn't seem to get used to, even
though she'd never experienced anything else,
had no idea what a world whose average daytime

temperatures were below forty degrees Celsius would even feel like.

Miala pushed her chair away from the worktable where she sat, then got up and headed to the kitchen. It wasn't much, just the refrigeration unit, the dish sanitizer, and a tired old convective oven, all bordered by plastic countertops that had begun to delaminate years ago. Despite the dilapidated surroundings, the hum of the fridge calmed her a little. Silly, she knew. She wasn't the type to jump at shadows. There were far too many of those on Iradia.

She glanced over at the door to her father's room. Shut, of course. He claimed that any noise distracted him, so Miala was used to tiptoeing around when he worked, and forget about knocking if she needed something. Long ago she'd learned to fend for herself unless it was a dire emergency.

The water soothed her dry throat. She'd read about worlds that were mostly water, had seen holos of them, but even so, she couldn't quite imagine what that would be like to see water stretching out free and blue on every side, for the air to be thick with its moisture, instead of so dry that it made your skin feel as if it had been stretched across your bones like the hide on a drum.

Maybe one day, she thought. *With the balance of what's due us, and if Lestan can get another commission that pays as well—*

She cut herself off there. Now she was starting to sound just like her father. It was always the next score, the next job. One day the payoff would come that would get them away from Iradia and the long, hot, desperate days.

Problem was, that day never did seem to come.

From behind her, Miala heard the faint *whoosh* of the front door opening. She startled slightly, then realized it had to be her father coming back into the flat. Sometimes Lestan Fels would walk the neighborhood at night to clear his head, to enjoy a brief few moments when the temperatures dipped to something more tolerable. No one ever bothered him because he had nothing worth stealing.

She turned, about to ask if he wanted a glass of water after his walk. Only that wasn't her father advancing toward her, but the short, swarthy man who'd come to visit earlier that morning. The overhead light in the kitchen was just bright enough to reveal the glitter in his close-set dark eyes.

Her first impulse was to scream, but what would that do? They didn't own any weapons, unless you counted the dull knives in the kitchen drawer. And while her father could hold his own against any programmer she'd ever heard of, she knew his skills didn't extend to hand-to-hand combat, so she doubted he would be of much help. Right then she could only thank God or whatever power guided the universe that she'd been working and was still dressed, rather than wearing the light knit shorts and sleeveless top that was her usual sleeping attire.

Willing herself to remain calm, she crossed her arms and stared at the intruder. "It's a little late for a business call, don't you think?"

The question seemed to puzzle him. He looked at her, taken aback for a second or two, before he recovered himself and said, "I just wanted to talk."

"'Talk'?" she repeated. "Kind of a strange hour of the night to talk."

The man grinned at her. He did have good teeth, straight and white, but even that asset wasn't enough to make him remotely attractive. "It's nice and cool outside. Why don't we take a walk?"

Her pulse began to accelerate, but Miala forced in a breath and told herself not to panic. At least he was talking, instead of coming for her and dragging her outside by brute force. She couldn't allow herself to glance at the door to her father's room, because she worried if he tried to interfere, he'd end up hurt or worse. All the same, she was surprised he hadn't come out to investigate, considering the smallest noise was usually enough to make him tell her she needed to be quiet while he worked.

"I'd better stay," she said carefully. While her father had lied and said she wouldn't be doing any of the programming on this particular job, Miala didn't see a problem with trying to make it sound as if she was indispensable in her own way. "My father usually asks me to bring him something to drink or make him a snack when he's working. What if he comes looking for me and I'm not here? It'll break his concentration—and that'll put him behind. I'm sure your boss wouldn't like that."

The stranger regarded her for a moment with narrowed eyes, clearly weighing what she'd just told him. Then his shoulders lifted. "We won't be gone long. He'll never notice."

"But—"

Her protest was cut off as he crossed the meter or so that separated them and took her by the arm. His whisper came harsh in her ear. "You wouldn't want to do something that would disturb him, would you?"

That was just the problem. Even the conversation they'd just shared, spoken as it was in more or less hushed tones, should have been enough to bring him out to the living room, complaining that they were making an unholy racket. Getting interrupted while he worked was about the only thing that could make him angry—well, that and asking about her mother. That he hadn't emerged already worried Miala more than she wanted to admit.

Worse, fear of the stranger thrummed along her veins. She wasn't naïve enough to pretend she didn't know what he wanted. Aldis Nova had plenty of dark alleys, quiet corners where anything could happen. About the most she could hope for was that he wouldn't kill her afterward.

Something hard and cold pressed into her side. She swallowed.

"You just come with me, and he won't have to know anything. No one will have to know anything. You play nice, I'll play nice. Okay?"

Since she didn't trust herself to speak, she could only nod. The stranger dragged her toward the door, pistol grinding into her waist the entire way. Maybe she should have screamed. It was remotely possible that her father could have done something to defend her. What, exactly, she didn't know, but wasn't that what fathers were supposed to do?

Go along for now, she told herself. *This guy obviously isn't all that smart—maybe you can get away while he's distracted or something.*

Right.

But since having a pulse pistol blast a hole in
her stomach sounded even worse than letting this
man do as he willed, she kept quiet as he pulled her
outside. The night breeze now felt pleasantly warm,
rather than oppressively hot, but Miala was in no
position to enjoy it. If only this part of town had
a pub or restaurant—anything that might still be
open at this hour. That way, it was possible someone might see her. But the streets were deserted,
illuminated faintly by the light of a single moon,
with not even a glimpse of the scavenger reptiles
that usually flicked their way from sheltered spot to
sheltered spot as they looked for food.

The stranger was quiet as well, guiding her
along with an inexorable pressure on her arm.
Miala had no idea what his destination might be.
Some seedy hostel where no one would bother to
see why she was screaming? Or would he not even
make the effort to go that far, but instead find an
isolated corner that suited him, and take her there?

I will scream, she thought then. *I'll scream and
scream, even if no one is around to hear me, and I'll
knee him so hard he won't be able to piss for a week.
And then I'll run.*

Brave words. Whether she'd have the courage
to do such a thing when the time came, she had no
idea.

Miala had her answer soon enough, because after being hauled along for several blocks or so, the pistol in her side the entire time, the stranger pulled her into an alley where even the dim moonlight couldn't reach. In a way, maybe that was good. Maybe this would be easier if she couldn't see his face.

She could feel him, though, his hot breath against her neck, moving to her mouth. Her throat spasmed, and she wondered if she was going to be sick then and there, and what he would do if she did vomit.

"That's it," he whispered, lifting his lips from hers for a second. "Nice and quiet."

Oh, no. Not even if he did blast a hole in her side. She'd rather be dead than—than —

Despite her earlier vow, she didn't scream. Almost without thinking, she brought her knee up into his groin with as much strength as she possessed. He let out a piercing howl, jerking the gun, which fired harmlessly into the wall instead of straight into her gut. She kicked him, too, for good measure, this time driving her booted foot into his side. He doubled over, breaths coming in tearing gasps, and she realized now was her best chance to escape.

If she'd had more experience with that sort of thing, she might have tried to get the gun away from him, but Miala decided it was better for her to use her knowledge of the streets to flee, running at top speed down the opposite way from where they'd originally come. She didn't dare go home— he was sure to follow her there—but she could head straight to the local garrison offices. Captain Malick wouldn't be on duty, not at this hour, but most of the soldiers posted to this district of Aldis Nova knew her by sight if nothing else.

She hadn't gotten more than a block, however, when she saw a tall figure standing in the street, and skidded to a halt as she realized who this new stranger was.

The tall, lavender-skinned man who had accompanied her would-be rapist to that meeting with her father.

Shit. Miala looked frantically to her right and left, hoping that an alley would offer itself as a viable means of escape. But this street was lined with warehouses, blank-faced and unfriendly.

Then his cool gaze seemed to move past her, to a spot somewhere behind her, and she risked a quick glance over her shoulder to see what he was looking at. Despite the warm night, ice flooded her veins. Because there was the lavender-skinned man's partner, limping toward her with fury in his eyes.

Before she could do anything, could decide which one was the lesser of two evils when it came to trying to get past them, the lavender-skinned man lifted the pulse pistol he held and fired. Miala's entire body clenched.

The pale blue pulse bolt lit up the dingy street as it flew past her and struck her erstwhile attacker in the chest. He fell onto the sandy ground, blank eyes staring lifelessly at her.

"Well, then," said the lavender-skinned man. "Let's get you back to your father, Miala."

She walked next to him in silence. What the hell was she supposed to say? "Thank you" seemed woefully inadequate. He didn't seem inclined to talk, either, only accompanied her back to the flat she shared with her father, then waited politely while she opened the door and went inside. The biometric lock had been shorted out, obviously by the man who'd assaulted her, but the door mechanism seemed to be working more or less normally. She supposed they'd have to find the money to fix the lock as well.

The lavender-skinned man followed her. Strangely, she didn't detect any menace from him. At least, none that was directed at her.

"Lestan!" she called out. He'd never wanted her to call him "Dad" or "Father" or anything except his given name, and she'd never asked why. And after everything she'd just been through, she wasn't about to scruple at interrupting him, no matter how involved he might be in his work.

No reply. Despite herself, Miala couldn't help darting a quick, worried look at the part-Eridani stranger. He waited in the living room, impassive, his elegant dark suit and fine-boned face strangely at odds with the shabby surroundings.

The hell with it. She hurried to her father's combination bedroom/office, and pushed the button to open the door. Once upon a time, it had a working lock, but that had failed years ago, just like so many other items in their flat.

At least the door itself still functioned. It slid into the wall, wobbling slightly, and she ran into the room, then stopped dead.

Her father was slumped over his keyboard, face pressed against the flat plastic in much the same way she'd envisaged herself an hour or so earlier, when she knew she had to get up or fall asleep. But his face was gray, almost as lacking in color as his hair.

Oh, my God.

She hurried to his side, then reached for his wrist. She wouldn't let herself think about what she'd do if she couldn't find a pulse.

It was there, though. Weak, and erratic, but some faint life still moved through his veins.

A slight rustle made Miala turn her head. The lavender-skinned man stood in the doorway, that same unreadable expression on his face.

He'd helped her before, but would he help her now?

"I think he's had a heart attack," she said, marveling a little at how calmly the words came out. "Can you call a med transport?"

"I think you had better do that," the man replied. "You are his daughter."

"But—"

"You know I cannot be connected to him." This statement was made simply, as if Miala should have thought of such a thing.

She didn't have time for arguments. Lord knows how long her father had been passed out like that, and time only kept slipping by. Without speaking, she pushed past the stranger and went to the comm unit in the kitchen. At least there was a one-button push for emergency services—although those services came at a price. Nothing on Iradia was free.

The voice answering her call was so flat and monotone, it could have belonged to a mech. Not that she much cared. At least someone was there to get the details of her situation, to tell her that a medi-transport would be there soon, and to have her credit voucher ready.

Damn. That request sent a stab of panic through her, until she remembered that her father had put some of the deposit money for their current job in their credit account, and so there should be enough to pay for the transport. As for the rest of his hospital stay....

The lavender-skinned man was watching her carefully. "It's a good thing this is a lucrative contract, isn't it?"

She blinked at him. "Excuse me?"

A faint smile touched his thin lips. "Your father told me that you would not be working on the project, but we all know the truth there, don't we?"

"I—"

He came closer, and Miala flinched. Not again. She didn't have the energy to fight or run. She couldn't run, not with her father lying near death in the next room and the medi-trans on the way.

But the part-Eridani man only lifted his elegant shoulders and said, "Why do you think I killed Nilson? Your person means little to me, but your mind—that is important. The contract is important. So don't linger too long at the hospital, Miala Fels. You have work to do."

With that parting shot, he turned and headed out the front door, even as the night began to be lit up with flashing orange lights, and the harsh sound of a siren rapidly approached the flat. And Miala could only stand there and watch him go, and wonder what the hell she was supposed to do now.

✳

First to the hospital, where the medi-mechs worked on Lestan and got him stabilized. He even recovered enough to blink up at her and ask weakly, "What happened?"

And then stared at her in puzzlement as she began to laugh and laugh.

She couldn't stay long—just enough to see her father slip into sleep, real sleep, not anything brought on by drugs, and then she knew she had to go home and get to work. The lavender-skinned man hadn't precisely threatened her, but she knew what the price of failure would probably be.

Her father's computer had automatically locked itself down, of course. Luckily, she knew the codes and got in without too much trouble. She couldn't allow herself to feel relieved, though, not when she looked at the volume of work still left to be done. It had been daunting enough when she'd thought she and Lestan would be sharing the burden of the project. Now, though….

His face came to her, pale and strained, wires and leads attached to his arm, his heart, his temples, mussing his already tousled gray hair. When had he gotten so gray, anyway? It seemed as if it had only been a few days ago when his hair was dark as the nighttime sky.

Tears pricked at her eyes, but she wouldn't allow them to fall. If she started to cry now, she feared she would never stop. She had to focus. Her father couldn't do the work, but he'd been training her for this moment ever since she was old enough to set up her own passphrases. There was no reason in the world why she couldn't handle this particular task. It wasn't intrinsically difficult, only complicated. True, there was that little matter of getting some rest. She'd have to go back to the hospital to check on Lestan at some point, which meant choosing between catching a few precious hours of sleep or seeing her father.

No contest, really.

Sleep is highly overrated, she told herself.

Miala had seen too many people combat the drudgery of life on Iradia with drugs—and lose themselves in the process—to be tempted to use illegal stimulants to keep herself awake. Nala, after hearing a carefully edited story of what had happened to Lestan, promised to provide Miala with as much free coffee as she needed, and sent home carafes of her strongest brew.

Even so, by the end of the sixth day of working on the project, Miala's eyelids felt so sore and irritated, she might as well have scooped up handfuls of her home world's fine white sand and rubbed them all over her eyes. She'd caught snatches of sleep here and there, just enough to keep herself from completely losing her mind. But she knew she couldn't stop; the lavender-skinned man was expecting a completed product to be delivered at the end of the week.

Besides, there was the hospital bill to consider. The deposit for the project had been enough to cover the transport to the hospital and Lestan's first night there, but they'd expect payment in full before they released him. And because he'd seem to stabilize, and then lose heart rhythm again, they wouldn't let him come home before a full week had passed. There was even talk of implanting an artificial heart. Miala prayed it wouldn't come to that, because there was no way she could afford that kind of surgery. She'd have to get three more projects just like the one she was currently working on to even begin to afford it. And then there was the physical therapy afterward....

With an effort she could actually feel, Miala pushed those thoughts far to the back of her mind where they couldn't interfere with the self-replicating algorithm that was her current focus. She couldn't make her father's heart magically heal itself, but she could make sure this damn code did what she needed it to do.

It seemed to compile correctly, so she sent it over to her test server and ran the routine that would simulate its real-world installation on multiple workstations, each with their own separate logins and security protocols. She hadn't questioned why the lavender-skinned man's boss needed something so sophisticated. Asking questions only got you into trouble. Besides, there were only a few men on Iradia with the sort of organization that would require this level of complexity, and she now had a fairly good idea of who she was working for. Gared Tomas, a man who'd never met a backroom deal he didn't like. She'd never say the name out loud, though. The only good thing about the whole situation was that at least Tomas had a reputation for paying his debts, rather than killing off his service providers once he no longer needed them.

As the automation churned away in the background, Miala got up from the chair at her father's workstation and went to pour herself yet another cup of coffee. Cold coffee that had been sitting in the refrigeration unit, since it was now midday and the flat was as stifling as the inside of an oven.

The bitter liquid made her want to gag, but she forced it down anyway. To think she used to like the stuff.

But a flicker of triumph went over her as she went back to the computer in her father's room—that machine was far more powerful than her own, and so she'd decided it was better to do the work there—and saw that the simulation had run through its processes and hadn't thrown up any error codes.

However, it was far too soon to organize any victory parades. She ran another simulation with a different set of parameters, and then another. Fifteen in all, and as dusk finally began to approach, bringing with it some relief from the relentless heat of the daylight hours, Miala stared at the computer screen and blinked. The work was done. As far as she could tell, the program worked exactly as it should. She'd thrown everything at it that she could dream up, and it had performed flawlessly. For some reason, though, all she could think of was how tired she felt.

With a small groan, she got up from the chair where she'd been sitting for the last four or five hours, and went to the kitchen again. Not for coffee this time. No, tonight she might finally be able to get some real sleep, and more coffee would only make her jittery and restless. But a long drink of cold water, which refreshed her in a way the coffee couldn't.

And then to pick up her handheld and type in the code she'd found buried in her father's notes. It seemed clear that the lavender-skinned man had been watching her, or he wouldn't have come to her rescue a few days earlier, but walking out the door, waving her arms, and shouting, "I'm done!" didn't seem very subtle. Better to enter the code, then see the word "ready" pop up on her screen. She typed "done," and then hit "enter."

The precious code had been transferred to a portable drive not much bigger than her thumbnail. That drive now rested in the pocket of her tunic, giving no sign of what it contained.

Miala didn't know how long it would take for the lavender-skinned man to appear, but she figured she had enough time to run to the bathroom, brush her hair, and splash some cold water on her face, all the while doing her best not to look at her reflection. Her previous glimpses had told her the days of no sleep had already taken their toll—features pale and pinched, shadows showing like black bruises under her eyes.

Not that Gared Tomas' lieutenant probably gave a crap about those sorts of things. He certainly hadn't shown any interest in her, beyond her coding abilities.

And thank God for that, she thought as the front door buzzer sounded and she hurried to answer it. *It's refreshing when a man actually wants to keep it in his pants.*

He stood outside, looking calm and cool. Miala wondered how he managed to pull that off. Yes, the sun had finally set, but it would take hours for the temperature outside to be even remotely comfortable. Was Eridani a hot world? She couldn't remember.

She moved out of the way so he could enter the flat, then quickly pushed the button for the door. Yes, he probably had been seen, but she didn't see the point in letting him stand on her front step for any longer than necessary.

"You have it?" he asked.

"Yes." She reached into her pocket and wrapped her fingers around the drive, but she didn't pull it out. Now that the moment had come, her stomach began to twist with nervousness. What if he'd decided not to pay her? After all, there was very little she could do if he decided to reach out and tear the drive from her pocket...except hope he wouldn't hurt her in the process.

Gared Tomas isn't like that, she told herself. *He pays his people. He can afford to.*

But still she hesitated.

"Is it this what you wanted to see first?" the lavender-skinned man asked softly. Violet-blue eyes fixed on hers, he dipped his hand into an interior pocket of his jacket and withdrew a dark pouch that jingled faintly.

"Yes," she replied, then cleared her throat. That single syllable had come out sounding awfully shaky. "Yes, I need to make sure it's all there."

"Be my guest."

Miala took the pouch from him and went over to the table in the dining area so she could pour out the money. It glistened in the reflection of the light fixture overhead.

All there, every last unit.

She turned back toward the lavender-skinned man and pulled the drive from her pocket. "I tested it fifteen ways from Sunday. It works."

"I have no doubt of that. Otherwise, you would have waited to call."

The intimation being that the program had better perform as advertised, or she'd be hearing from him in the very near future.

"If you run into any problems—" she began, but he held up a hand.

"No worries, Ms. Fels. I know where to find you."

He slipped the sliver drive into the same pocket that had held the money, then went to the door and let himself out. Miala stood in the middle of the living room for a long moment, not sure if she could allow herself to breathe. What if he changed his mind, decided that he could return and take the money from her, since there wasn't a damn thing she could do about it?

But the minutes stretched on, and the night turned empty and quiet. She was safe…for now at least.

Even then she couldn't allow herself to relax.

✳

Her father's color had improved. He was still pale, but there was a proud glint in his eyes and the faintest flush along his cheekbones as he looked up at Miala.

"I can't believe you did it. And Gar—that is, the payment came through all right?"

"Everything's just fine," she told him. "And I've settled up your bill here. You really can come home tomorrow?"

"That's what they're telling me." He looked down at the tube in his arm with some disgust. "Not a moment too soon."

That was for sure. Paying for this one last night would wipe out almost everything they had left. There'd be enough for food for a few days, and Nala had said that Miala could come work at the coffee house and earn a little extra, since Nala's daughter, who usually performed such duties, was going to a friend's wedding in the next settlement and would be gone over the weekend. That was something, but it wouldn't be enough.

It was never enough.

From somewhere, Miala summoned an encouraging smile. "The important thing is that you're going home. I think our client is happy, so maybe there'll be more work soon."

Her father nodded. "I have no doubt of it. Word always gets around. And that'll be the commission to finally do the trick."

Suddenly, her smile hurt her cheeks. Miala patted her father on the hand and then went to the window, making a show of closing the antiquated blinds, which were still open. Really, though, all she'd wanted was to catch a glimpse outside, to see the stars blinking down from Iradia's perpetually clear skies the way they always did.

One day. God, she was tired of telling herself that.

This time, though, she could almost feel the resolve forming in her, hardening like clay baking under the midday sun. She'd shown that she could do this on her own. No, she would never abandon her father, because he'd watched over her all these years, but she could damn well pull her own weight. And his, if it came to that.

One day, we will get out of here. One day, I'm going to leave and never look back.

No matter what it takes.

You can read more of Miala's adventures in *Blood Will Tell*, Book 1 of the Gaian Consortium series. To find out more about Christine Pope and all her books, go to www.christinepope.com.

PASSAGE OUT

A VICTORIA
ETERNAL STORY

ANTHEA SHARP

Author's note: Steampunk with a twist! Enter a
fantastical world filled with alien spacecraft and
Victorian sensibilities, ball gowns and travel to the
stars. "Passage Out" is one of several stories set in
the alt-history universe of Victoria Eternal; a world
where a constantly cloned Queen Victoria rules for
centuries over a British Empire spanning the stars.

✳

THE ROAR AND SHAKE OF SPACECRAFT BLASTING OFF FROM
Southampton had long since ceased to wake Diana
Smythe from her ragged slumber. The door alcove
she called home was scant shelter from the elements,
but she'd learned to catch what rest she could. A
stealthy approach or a whisper of malice, however,

would bring her awake in an instant, hand tight around the hilt of her makeshift dagger.

She'd had a gun, once, a light-pistol that could slice a man's arm off, or put a smoking hole in his chest at fifty paces.

Long gone, now, along with the rest of the remnants of her former life. Diana didn't even have a gold locket with her parent's picture, or a pocket watch with a loving inscription, or any of the tokens common to novels about abandoned girls seeking their long lost homes and families.

Her life was not a storyvid. She knew well enough that parents didn't miraculously come back to life after a flaming carriage crash, and lost fortunes never magically re-appeared.

And the dream of the spaceport had long since become a grimy reality, measured in take-offs and landings, in the ebb and flow of her small store of coins. Not enough. Never enough to buy passage out, not even a berth to the moon.

"Di, get up."

A toe in her ribs made her roll away and open her eyes. Dawn feathered the sky in blue and pink, and made the grungy corner she called home almost pretty. Silhouetted against the sky stood a young boy with matted brown hair and a chipped-tooth smile.

"Go away, Tipper."

"Can't." The boy squatted down next to her and poked her shoulder with a grimy finger. "Found something."

That woke her up. Diana sat, her holey woolen blanket wrapped tight around her shoulders. The nights were still chilly, but at least spring had finally come. She'd made it through another winter on the streets.

"What did—" She broke off, waited for the roar of the blast-off to fade.

Both she and Tipper looked up. From the sound of that lift, it was one of the bigger ships; a Fauntleroy 220, she guessed. The gleaming silver shape arced overhead, catching the light that hadn't yet reached the alleyways and streets. It was a Fauntleroy, just as she'd guessed. A year after she'd arrived in Southampton, hopeful and starving, she'd found she had a talent for identifying the ships, scanning the arc of their flights in a heartbeat, gauging velocity and lift, and guessing at their destinations.

If she couldn't get to the stars, she could image others traveling there, and watch them go.

Tipper stared at the ship, the longing on his face so clear Diana had to look away. Sure, she probably had the same look in her eyes, but she'd had a few extra years to hide it. Tipper was still a kid, for all his cockiness. Still dreaming the child's dream of space—the blackness full of stars and possibility. A million futures to choose from.

Diana swallowed and ignored the tight clutch of hunger in her belly. When the sky was empty, she asked again.

"What did you find?"

Tipper darted a glance down the alley, then shook his head and motioned her to follow.

"If this is some kind of joke…" She gave him her best hard-eyed stare as she rolled up her blanket and shoved it into the satchel holding her possessions. The ones that mattered, anyway.

"Isn't," he said.

"Tally-ho, then."

She brushed off her trousers, scooped up her bag, and grabbed the parasol she'd nicked from a highborn chit. It was battered and stained, but if she held it just right, wore her salvaged satin skirt, and did her hair up in style (fastened with string and bits of charred metal, not that anyone would get close enough to notice), she could pass for gentry. For a brief time, anyway.

Her accent helped, of course. At least, when she was in the better part of the city. Down here, in the rookeries by the spaceport, she pulled a covering of Cockney over the smoothly articulated syllables she'd grown up speaking.

Darting like a mongoose, Tipper led her through the twists of the alleys, through derelict buildings, and at last to the sheer, shiny wall of the spaceport itself. It rose a dozen meters into the air, silvery and impermeable, and so clean.

Diana went and laid her hand against the surface, the alien material faintly cool against her palm. There was no need for a stun current—the Yxleti-made wall was impervious to any human effort. No knife or gun, laser or explosive could even mar it, let alone break through.

There were only two ways into the oval-shaped spaceport district. Passengers and those with official business used the front entrance at one end of the oval. Cargo and employees went through the Spaceport Authority processing area on the other end. Between the two, nothing but sheer walls.

"Psst." Tipper waved at her from a shadowy ruin ahead.

When Diana joined him beside the crumbling wall, he gave her a grin full of mischief.

"Lookit this." He nudged a crumbling piece of pressboard aside with his foot to reveal a dark shaft disappearing into the ground.

She leaned over and peered into the blackness. The edges were perfectly straight, the hole just big enough to admit a body. Provided that a person was not afraid of closed-in, dark places. She shivered.

"Where does it go?"

"I waited for you, to find out."

Diana shot Tipper a look. It wasn't just the rough fondness of the streets that had made him wait, but the sense of self-preservation every alley rat needed to survive. It would be sheer foolishness to disappear down that black shaft without anyone knowing where you'd gone, or waiting up above to pull you back up if necessary.

"You've got a rope?" She glanced around the ruin, the two partially-standing walls not providing nearly enough cover for what they were about to do.

"Sure. And lights. And water and some brat bars, just in case."

He went to the corner and rummaged beneath a piss-scented tarp, emerging with the described items.

"Here." He handed one of the foil-wrapped bars to her.

"I don't want that."

B-rations, brats for short, were the lowest-level foodstuffs. Even at her hungriest, she could barely choke down a mouthful of the gluey substance.

"Toff," Tipper said.

"Ain't."

Despite hazy memories of silky dresses and mathematics lessons and a pony of her own. That was half a lifetime ago, or more. It didn't matter now. She tucked the brat bar into her trouser pocket, planning to give it back to Tipper after they... well. After they found whatever it was they were going to find down there.

"Probably just leads to the sewers," she said, taking a sniff of the air over the shaft.

It wasn't as foul as she expected. Dry, not rank, with a whiff of fuel. A jagged shard of hope sawed at her. Could this possibly be a tunnel into the spaceport?

Rumor was the Yxleti had used a network of tunnels when constructing the port. But they had all been filled up again. Even if this was a former passage to the spaceport, it surely ended in an impassable wall of rubble.

Still, her heartbeat pumped up with possibility.

She helped Tipper secure the rope to the sturdiest beam they could find. He wrapped it around his chest and under his arms, then donned a pair of stained leather gloves two sizes too big.

"Are you sure you want to go first?" She glanced into the hole. "It looks deep."

"I found it, I get to explore it. And I dropped a lightstick down there yesterday. Bottom's not too far."

He grinned at her. She had the feeling "not too far" had a different meaning, once you were dangling at the end of a rope.

"Speaking of light…" He held a battered lightstick out to her, then tucked a second one into a makeshift headband and settled it over his filthy hair.

Before she could wish him luck, he scrambled over the edge of the shaft and let himself down.

Diana knelt and watched him go down. The shaft was small enough that he could brace his legs and back on opposite sides and control his descent. Once, he slipped, and she swallowed back a cry of dismay as he slid a full meter down the hole before catching himself.

Sooner than she would have liked, all she could see was the lightstick attached to his head. It bobbed up and down, sparking dull reflections from the sides of the shaft. After a while, the light stopped, and the rope jiggled wildly.

"Tipper?" She leaned over the hole, fear clenching her gut.

Something was down there, and had eaten him. The rope went slack.

Dammit. Without com devices—which no alley rat could ever afford—she had to guess at what was happening.

Hands shaking, she pulled the rope back up and inspected the end. No blood, no fraying.

"Di." Tipper's voice echoed softly up.

She blew the stale air of fear out of her lungs. "Now what?" she hissed down into the hole.

"Going to explore. Sit tight."

The roar of lift washed over the silvery spaceport walls. Diana glanced up as the Volux V-class freighter lumbered up into the lower atmosphere. Bound in-system, she'd guess; one of the outlying Jupiterean moons, or maybe just Mars.

"Tipper?" She leaned forward at the flicker of light from below.

"Di! Come down—it's a passage through."

She didn't believe it, though Tipper had never been a practical joker like some of the other alley rats.

"Who'll guard the rope?"

"I don't care." His voice was jubilant. "Hurry."

She pulled the rope back up, and tied it around herself. Unlike Tipper, she hadn't brought gloves to protect her hands. It wasn't so far down that she'd burn her hands terribly—unless she fell.

Diana gave the rope a couple tugs, testing the beam. Solid enough. Gritting her teeth, she lowered herself into the shaft. The coarse rope bit her palms, and the metal wall was cool against her back. Slowly, she inched down, the pale blue sky overhead becoming a smaller rectangle as the dark swallowed her. Only knowing that Tipper was waiting for her with his lightstick made it bearable.

At last she saw the glow from below.

"The shaft ends," Tipper said. "There's a drop of a few meters to the floor."

Jaw aching from clenching her teeth, Diana's feet hit empty air. She kicked out, the rope slipping too quickly between her hands, and landed painfully on the hard surface below.

"All right?" Tipper gave her a hand up.

"Well enough."

She straightened and gave an experimental stretch. Other than what would probably be a spectacular bruise on her tailbone, and the rope burns on her palms, she was uninjured. She pulled the extra lightstick out of her pocket and flicked it on.

The straight, dim corridor was nothing special—except for the immense possibility it represented. Feeling a smile stretch her face, she nodded at Tipper.

"Lead on, sir."

They walked quickly, excitement pushing their steps. They reached the spot that Diana calculated corresponded to the boundary wall of the spaceport overhead.

"Wait." She held out her hand. "Did you come this far, earlier?"

"No." Tipper stopped. "Just far enough to see the passage was open."

She studied the corridor ahead. It appeared safe, but stun currents were invisible until triggered. No alley rat traveled without an assortment of useful items in their pockets. Never knew when one might need a bit of string or graphite piece. Or, in this case, a pebble.

Diana tossed the stone a few meters ahead of them. It passed the potential hazard point and kept going to clatter down on the floor. Nothing flared or buzzed.

"Safe enough." She hoped.

"Milady." Tipper swept out his hand in a move worthy of a gentleman.

"Coward," she murmured as she strode past him, winking to show she didn't truly mean it. He'd been first down into the darkness, after all.

She flinched, just a little, as she passed the place the boundary wall stood, but like the pebble, she passed through untouched. Tipper came up behind her, and their twin lightsticks reflected eerily off the silvery walls, the pale yellow glow barely pushing back the blackness. They walked ten paces beyond the wall, then twenty.

"Why do you think they built this tunnel?" Tipper whispered.

She shrugged. Who knew why the enigmatic Yxleti did anything? A hundred years earlier they had appeared from the sky, crowned Victoria *Queen Eternal,* then stood back. They had allowed humans to use their strange technology to reach the stars, and they never interfered—only watched.

"Well." Tipper held his light up, illuminating the sheer wall in front of them, blocking their way. "Now what?"

"Go back for the rope?" She leaned back, lifting her lightstick high. "I think there's a trapdoor overhead."

"That won't work. There must be a way to access the hatches. Hidden ladders or something."

Made sense. The workers who used this tunnel in the past wouldn't want to be carrying around ladders as they went about their business.

"Take that side." She nodded to the left, then moved to the right and started running her hands over the smooth wall. Soon, her fingers found an irregularity—a long seam running vertically up from the floor.

"Here," she said, pulling out her blade.

Tipper hurried to her side, and together they pried and pulled at the metal. Diana levered it up, then Tipper wedged his gloved hand in the space and yanked. Finally, with a loud creak, the seam parted to reveal a ladder built against the wall.

She jumped back, dropping her lightstick, but Tipper just stood there, grinning.

She made him go first, then followed. As they neared the ceiling of the corridor, strange, thumping vibrations filled the air. At first she thought it was drums, but the rhythm was too uneven.

"Footsteps." She tapped Tipper on the leg. "I think this opens onto a walkway."

That complicated matters. Spaceport travelers would not stand idly by as two alley rats clambered from a shaft in the floor. Especially not two individuals as soiled and dirt-stained as herself and Tipper. She hadn't bathed in at least a month. He'd gone twice that long, judging by his rank boy-sweat and matted hair.

"Let's get closer," he said. "I think I see a bolt across."

Despite her doubts that the hatch was secured by anything so mundane as a bolt, Tipper was right. She gripped the metal rungs of the ladder tightly as he slid the bolt back in slow, screeching increments. Hopefully the people tromping above would pay little mind to the noise, or think it just another bit of spaceport ambiance.

Tipper braced his palms against the trapdoor.

She tugged his ragged trouser leg. "Wait. Not yet."

She'd been counting the steps, the ebb and flow, the pattern swirling in her head in elliptical shapes. A rise, a smoothening, a dip as the traffic diminished. Soon, soon.

"Now," she said. "Quick!"

Tipper heaved the hatch open and flung himself out. She was right behind him. The door banged against the floor, and the three people in evidence turned, staring. One, a woman in a long, ruffled gown, began to scream.

Moving in accord, Diana and Tipper flipped the hatch closed and raced away, deeper into the spaceport. The woman's shrieks echoed behind them.

Unlike the alleys of Southampton's rookery, there were no side passages, no dark places to duck into. Just flat, straight walls. Diana's breath burned in her chest, her eyes darting from side to side, barely registering the looks of shock as she and Tipper dashed past.

They had to find a hiding place. Behind them, she could hear the rough commands of Port Security, ordering people out of the way. Her blood iced as she considered the very real possibility that she and Tipper might get shot.

"Stop!" a deep voice bellowed. "Stop those two!"

Diana sidestepped a man in a bowler hat, then wrenched out of an older lady's grasp. The wild exhilaration of breaching the spaceport had curdled to panic. She and Tipper were in trouble deep.

"Hey!" Tipper yelped.

She whirled to see him caught, arms pinned against his side by a tall man wearing tweed.

"Tip!"

Could she pull him from his captor's grasp?

That moment of hesitation cost her freedom. Before she could dash away, a woman in the blue uniform of Spaceport Security grabbed her wrist and slapped a shackle on it. The man holding Tipper thrust him into another guard's custody, and their mad adventure came to an end.

"It's over," the policewoman said. "Come quietly."

Diana pulled in a deep breath. At least she'd seen the inside of the spaceport—however briefly. She didn't try to pull away. Though she'd never been in stun shackles before, she knew how they worked, and had no desire to feel that current race through her.

Tipper shuffled his feet and hung his head low, but Diana looked everywhere, soaking in the sights and sounds. The officers led them down the hallway. Ahead, doors whooshed open and closed, the brighter light of day spilling through.

The security guards took them outside, onto a partially enclosed walkway, and Diana nearly forgot she was a captive. On the right-hand side of the walkway, ships spread in a half-circle in their berths. She slowed, staring, cataloguing. There—a Xeros Two-thousand, sleek as an arrow. Beside it, the crablike shell of an older hauler bound for the asteroid mining belt.

On the far left, another freighter rose, engines wheezing, but holding. Overloaded, by the way it listed slightly in the air, and not with legal goods she'd wager. She frowned. Couldn't the authorities tell when smugglers freighted contraband out right under their noses?

At the midpoint of the freighter's arc, a Class A Cruzline ship began ignition. The fore engines fired, and then the aft. Slowly, the ship rose, gleaming and no doubt full of important and moneyed passengers.

Diana halted. Something was wrong.

"Keep moving," the policewoman said. Her name badge simply read *Nails.*

"Wait... wait." Diana leaned forward, listening, watching, calculating the arc of the Cruzline as it began its ascent.

"Stop that ship!" She lifted her shackled wrist and pointed at the gleaming passenger ship.

The policewoman's hand fell to the stun unit. "Don't make me use this."

"They're going to crash!" Diana strained forward. "Contact the control center—it's a direct collision course in... twenty seconds."

The policewoman narrowed her eyes, but the edge of panic in Diana's voice must have convinced her. Her gaze went unfocused as she activated her nano-comm and spoke hurriedly, using lots of acronyms and letters.

Twelve seconds.

Diana half-listened, her attention fixed on the gruesome calculation unfolding overhead. It sounded like the policewoman was getting through.

The bright ship tried to veer, but it was going too fast. Too fast. Eight seconds. Seven. Six.

The Cruzline's engines stalled, and Diana sucked in her breath. Three. Two.

The edge of the Cruzline nicked the freighter, then spun out, but beautifully slowly. The pilot was good enough to control the move, steering his craft into a shining silver loop. The freighter wobbled, the collision barley nudging the massive ship off-course.

Diana watched, heartbeat bumping back to normal as the Cruzline steadied and returned to its berth. A security bugship, lights flashing, buzzed the freighter, leading it back to the customs screening pad.

She glanced up at the cloud-specked blue overhead. In a different universe, the air would be full of fire and death and a hundred personal tragedies. But not this world. Not this day.

Diana lifted her hand to rub the back of her neck, the motion cut short by the cuff on her wrist. With a resigned slump of her shoulders, she turned back to the security guard.

"Right away, sir," Nails said. Her gaze cleared and she looked at Diana. "Taking you upstairs."

"What about my friend?" Diana nodded to Tipper, who stood uncharacteristically silent. "He comes, too."

The security guard hesitated.

"I mean it." Diana put the steel of truth in her voice.

Whatever was going on—and she suspected it had to do with the averted crash—she and Tipper were in it together.

"Very well—the both of you. Don't try anything." This last was directed at Tipper, with a narrow-eyed glare.

He put on his wounded face, and Diana hid her smile. His expression wouldn't get him anywhere with Nails, but at least the two of them wouldn't be separated.

Nails and the other security guard led them through a paneled door that took a special key code, and then to a grav lift tucked in a corner.

They stepped inside, and Diana tried not to show the jittery nerves pulsing through her. But this was posh—the marble floor and polished wooden walls of the lift far above the normal trappings of the Spaceport. The smooth, fast rise left her courage sinking to her feet. Tipper shot her a look that showed too much eye, clearly as nervous as she about wherever they were going.

The lift slowed and halted, the doors slid open, and Diana blinked at the view. She barely noticed the plush burgundy carpeting and wingback chairs, the wide desk or the gray-haired man sitting behind it. Her eyes were drawn inexorably to the huge bank of windows on the wall opposite the lift.

They were at the very top of the Spaceport. Ships dived and flew, and she could see the near neighborhoods of Southampton spread out beyond the silvery wall. The rookery, of course, was behind them—a view no one wanted to contemplate.

"And so." The man behind the desk stood, revealing a portly figure dressed in well-tailored clothing. "Our heroine of the hour. Come, come."

He gestured to her, and Diana took a step forward.

"Wait." He held up a hand. "Remove her cuffs, Nails, if you please. I would like to shake this young woman's hand without fear of a shock."

He laughed, and the security guards guffawed along with him.

"Apologies, Director." Nails quickly took the cuff off, with a warning look at Diana. Her hand grazed the lightpistol holstered at her side, the message clear.

The luxurious surroundings made Diana acutely aware of her own grime and stink. She lifted her chin. If this director fellow wanted to talk to her, he'd have to take her as she was.

Somewhat to her surprise, he stepped forward and took her hand, giving it a firm shake.

"What is your name?" he asked.

"Diana." She didn't think he'd like her street name of Diver. "Diana Smythe."

"The spaceport owes you a debt of thanks, Miss Smythe. Are you aware that a very important delegation was aboard that Cruzline vessel?"

She shook her head, but it didn't surprise her. Who else but the toff gentry would book passage on that kind of ship?

"Without your acute observational skills, a very messy incident would have occurred. Tell me—how did you know the ships were on a collision course?"

"It was clear as glass, least to me," she said. "The liftoff arcs intersected, and the freighter's smuggling something. They were too slow to clear the line of flight."

Nails prodded her in the back, and she added a belated, "sir."

"And you could tell all that at a glance?" He did not sound dubious, just curious.

"Yes."

"She's always been good at such things, sir," Tipper said. "Knowing how a mark moves through a crowd, or the fall of dice, or—"

He broke off as Diana elbowed him in the ribs.

"I notice suchlike," she said.

"Hm." The Director gave her a keen look. "Join me at the window, if you would."

Diana followed him to the expanse, and couldn't help smiling once more at the view. The whole port spread out below her feet. All those lives and dreams and arrows to the stars, shot right from here—the busiest port in England, the center of Empire— into the heart of the stars.

"What do you see?" he asked. "Describe the ships to me as they come and go."

It was a test, though she wasn't sure what the penalty for failure might be. She narrowed her eyes and rolled forward on the balls of her feet, focusing on the geometry, the arcs and parabolas forming and re-forming outside the window.

"That ship—the Tellium X class, just landing. They're coming in a little too fast. Bet they get a warning. And the Aristo there needs a tune-up. They should have better lift, especially a later model like that."

She continued to scan the spaceport, point-ing out holes where ships were too slow or too fast, speculating aloud on destinations and cargo, flagging possible smugglers and lazy pilots. All the while, the Director nodded and, judging by his slightly unfocused stare, accessed his data.

Ten minutes passed, then twenty. Diana's throat tightened from talking so much. Behind her, she could hear Tipper fidgeting and coughing, and finally, the Director spoke.

"Impressive," he said. "You have quite a gift, Miss Smythe. Along the lines of a mathematical genius. What would you say to putting it to official use?"

She took a step back, her torn boots sinking into the plush carpet. Did they mean to barter— no jail time for her and Tipper, in exchange for her servitude here?

"What do you mean?"

The Director must have seen the suspicion on her face, for he let out another hearty laugh.

"No, no, it's not what you think. You and your friend's misdemeanors have already been dismissed. A bit of a youthful lark, what?"

Diana heard Tipper let out a theatrical sigh of relief, but she kept her gaze focused on the man before her. Distrust warred with hope, churning together uneasily in her belly.

"On behalf of Spaceport Authority, I would like to offer you employment, Miss Smythe. What would you say to that?"

"What would I need to do?"

"Exactly what you just demonstrated. Watch the ships, calculate the trajectories and arcs. Help us all achieve the stars to the best of our ability, and put your rare skills in the service of the greater cause of humanity."

It was a pompous speech, but it stirred her all the same. There was a glint of truth in the Director's eye that swayed her, even more than the grand words.

"How much?"

"Ever practical, aren't you?" He named a sum that stilled her heart for a moment.

But only a moment.

"A month?" she asked, half in jest.

This time it was the Director's turn to blink. Then he laughed again.

"And why not? Do we have an agreement?"

She pulled in a breath and glanced once more at the spinning arcs and sines weaving outside the window. The sum she had named would keep her in grand style. Even better, it would send Tipper, and any other alley rat who wanted out, a ticket to the stars. In style.

Slowly, she gazed up, past the blue, to where the stars gleamed and shone. The stars were a wonderful dream. But not, as it transpired, the best dream of all.

She extended a grimy hand to the director, and smiled when he took it without hesitation.

"Yes," she said. "We surely do."

Want to read more Victorian Spacepunk? Scoop up the STARS & STEAM collection for more tales set in the universe of Victoria Eternal!

A *USA Today* bestselling author, Anthea writes Victorian-set romantic adventure under the pen name Anthea Lawson and Science Fantasy featuring cyber-punk elements and treacherous faeries as Anthea Sharp.

Learn more at Anthea's website: antheasharp. com.

ARCTURUS 5

A TWENTY SECTORS STORY

D.L. DUNBAR

EVERYONE TRAVELED MULTI-SECTOR DISTANCES BY THE Fold, but Xella wished for once she could take the longer, more scenic route to the Andromeda Galaxy. The endless passage of white stars in a cold, black background was soothing, a reminder that there were things far more vast than their daily concerns—far more important in the cosmic scheme of things than a squabble over helium collector transport and the restriction of space in key shipping lanes.

But Mother had decided that involvement in this dispute was key to their future in this sector. And one more sector under the influence of the Graha-Es was a good thing—for the Graha-Es as well as these other races who seemed only to care about short-term gain and personal wealth.

Of course when some species measured life in a few hundred orbits of a planet around a sun, they were bound to have such a narrow view of the future. And these short lives were the reason she was traveling by The Fold rather than take the two-thousand light year scenic route.

"Ready, Tovenaressa Xella?"

Xella turned to her little sister, Pey. The girl was so excited—her first trip to this sector and her first time experiencing The Fold. Pey had assisted other Tovenaressa in diplomatic missions over the last century as part of her training, but this tense arbitration would be yet another first.

With one of her long forearms, Xella reached out to touch the decorative gem embedded in her sister's pebbled skin, giving it a reassuring pat. "Ready."

The girl keyed in the sequence to begin The Fold and edged the ship into the transport window. There was a feeling of intense pressure. G-forces immobilized them against the seats. Stars blurred outside the viewer, then there was nothing on the screen besides a dark, empty space. Most races needed personal pressurization containers when using The Fold, a few even needed to enter stasis or travel in a cryogenic state. The Graha-Es were thankfully able to withstand great G-force as well as a variety of atmospheric conditions, even if they were somewhat limited in the temperature ranges in which they could function.

Not as limited as some. Xella had heard of creatures who could only survive within a two hundred degree temperature range. How difficult those races must find space travel.

"We're here," she said as a red streak burst into view on the screen, then froze. Their speed abruptly dropped, and the blur of red became a planet.

"Oh!" Pey extended a midarm to touch the viewer, as if she could hardly believe her eyes.

"Pretty, isn't it?" Xella reached out again to stroke Pey's gem-studded skin. How wonderful to have a companion along for this negotiation. So many times she was making these journeys alone. Graha-Es should not be alone. Ammita, in all her wisdom, had not created them to be solitary creatures.

But she *was* alone, even with Pey right next to her. Xella's warm feeling faded as she contemplated how very alone she was. At eight thousand orbits, she was far too old to still be alone. All the other Graha-Es sisters had been gifted with their soul mates before four thousand. Even Pey at a young two-thousand orbits had just been joined.

Envy was a disgraceful emotion, and self-pity not much better. Mother would eventually find her the perfect match, and then she would never be lonely again. Calm acceptance, attention to duty, and diligent work toward the betterment of the Graha-Es was what she should be contemplating, not how much she wished Mother would hurry up and find her someone.

It was embarrassing, though. She knew there were whispers. She knew the others wondered why Mother had denied her a soul mate. Was she not worthy? Had she done something wrong and fallen into disfavor?

Xella straightened her torso, lifting her head. It didn't matter what others thought. Mother had sent *her* on this mission. Her work here would prove her loyalty and her worth. And then maybe she would eventually be gifted with a match.

The planet grew larger as they approached until nearly the entire viewer was encompassed by its pretty twisting lines of red. Arcturus 5 was the fifth planet out from the star, and home to the warehouse and transfer outpost of the Mol for this particular part of their business. The first two planets had been engulfed by the red giant when it had expanded, the second two were boiling masses of liquid rock and violent volcanic activity. Arcturus

5 wasn't much in terms of an ideal outpost, but helium collection required a site close enough to the star to easily retrieve the units for shipment, yet far enough away that a biosphere and shipping was feasible. This fifth planet barely met the requirements. Its temperature varied 1100 degrees from day to night, and the scant atmosphere meant it was constantly buffeted by solar winds. Thankfully the planet rotated slowly, meaning the biosphere "walked", shifting locations in time with the rotation, keeping it constantly in the twilight zone.

"Why is their outpost on the surface?" Pey asked, her black eyes riveted to the screen. "If they're just storing and transferring collection containers to a freighter, why not run an orbital site? Or a midspace one?"

Xella was secretly thrilled to play the role of teacher, to impart what knowledge she could to Pey. Although she would be a terrible teacher if she just told and didn't push the girl to think through these things herself.

"If the Graha-Es were to run an orbiting site, what environmental controls as well as health and safety procedures would be needed for the workers?"

The girl tapped the long curved hook at the end of a forearm on the monitor. "Artificial gravity and mandatory weight-bearing sessions for workers with internal skeletons. Although if we used Capire or Arach workers, we could minimize that. No, maybe not. They'd need a high nitrogen atmosphere and the costs of that might outweigh the AG units."

Xella deployed the breaks to slow the ship as it entered the atmosphere and listened to Pey continue to think through the engineering and financial scenarios out loud. If the girl wasn't suitable for diplomatic missions, she'd definitely recommend her as a project manager. Although that wouldn't be as coveted a job since it would force her to work day-to-day with the Mezadu. The worker males of the Graha-Es were enthusiastic and loyal, but didn't exactly provide stimulating conversation.

Descending below the wispy layer of pink clouds, the Mol transport and storage facility appeared on the horizon. It was ugly, like a squat, misshapen gray beast. The tallest portions were docking bays for shuttles and small ships. Atmospheric and worker concerns aside, Xella would never have chosen to place such a facility surface-side. The helium collectors were close to the red giant star that occupied the lower quarter of the sky. Small ships grabbed the full containers, replacing them with empty ones, then brought them to the surface for storage here only to haul them back up to the massive freighter once a month. That was a whole lot of fuel, and a whole lot of little ships when an orbiting facility could load directly onto the freighter.

It wasn't her business how the Mol ran their operations. She was here to arbitrate a dispute, not judge them on cost-effectiveness and operational efficiency.

Xella took control of the ship, using the guided assist from the landing bay to enter the bay doors and gently touch down. The doors shut behind them. Mechanical collars locked the ship's landing devices to the floor and the whoosh of decompression began.

This was an expensive outpost in a tight-margin business. She'd been briefed that the Mol kept environmental controls to a minimum. The workers ate nutrient sticks and received fluids on a schedule, as conditions even inside the biosphere weren't suitable for growing food or for producing more than the minimal necessary water. Only species who could tolerate the six hundred degree temperature of the biosphere were allowed to work here. It would be far too costly to fight the planet's heat and cool the domed area to accommodate more temperature sensitive workers. The Mol weren't particularly sympathetic to complaints. Xella had been here forty orbits ago to settle a labor dispute. There had been changes in feeding and shift schedules, and some turnover of workers who probably weren't suited for this type of employment, but the Mol were the Mol.

Yes. An orbital warehousing structure would have been wiser. Idiots. But thankfully she wasn't here this time on a labor dispute. The Dark had begun cutting through the Bootes constellation as part of their salvage operations, passing near Arcturus 5. Their presence had made the Mol uneasy. The Dark were an opportunistic race. What they called salvage was often what another species called momentarily unattended, or perhaps insufficiently guarded.

The Mol fears weren't unfounded. Two hundred orbits ago the Dark had seized one of their freighters. It had been completely dismantled and sold as scrap along with its cargo by the time the Mol had tracked it down. The Dark had claimed they'd found it drifting near Gamma Crucis, no crew aboard and severely damaged. They blamed raiders.

Of course they did. Clearly the Dark were the luckiest of anyone in the twenty sectors because they always managed to come upon ships that had been attacked by raiders and left behind with a wealth of cargo and equipment. Amazing how often that seemed to happen.

The Mol lodged a protest but didn't pursue any action. Bringing the Dark to justice had proved an expensive and deadly endeavor for many species. There hadn't been any other provable infractions against Mol ships until this past month, when a cargo ship had disappeared right outside the Arcturus system.

Rather than accuse the Dark outright and risk an international incident, the Mol claimed domain of the system and the shipping lanes around it as part of their operations. If they prevailed, the Dark wouldn't be able to come close enough to find a "salvage" ship without a fleet of Graha-Es destroyers on their tails.

The few female Graha-Es, the Tovenaressa to which Xella and Pey belonged, were known for civilized diplomacy and cultured negotiation. The sterile male Graha-Es, the Mezadu, were gifted with extra chromosomes, making them best suited for battle—and they were *fierce*. They lived to serve, and if Mother told a group to protect the shipping lanes, there would be no further complaints from the Mol about Dark raiders.

The Mezadu were what solidified the Graha-Es position in the twenty sectors, and why the Dark kept as far away from them as possible. The fact they'd agreed to this arbitration was a surprise. A Dark at the table was unusual enough; a Dark agreeing to abide by a decision by a Graha-Es Tovenaressa if a compromise was not reached was unheard of. It made Xella nervous. All races were predictable to a certain extent. This behavior shift worried her greatly.

But she wasn't about to show uncertainty in front of Pey. Tovenaressa were sisters, daughters of the Mother, but there were no guarantees that Pey wouldn't let slip a few stories of her weaknesses if things went bad. Increasingly, Xella worried about things going bad. Her assignments had become more challenging over the last dozen orbits—so challenging that she feared it would be only a matter of time until she failed. And failure was something that the Mother did not forgive.

"Welcome, Tovenaressa Xella, welcome." The Mol escort greeted them enthusiastically the moment the bay door opened, bobbing his gelatinous head.

Xella adjusted the voicebox she'd attached to the port on the side of her neck, ensuring that the frequency was compatible with Mol vocal communication. "Greetings to you, also. May I know your name?"

The Mol's body shifted color to a lavender hue, indicating how flattered he was to be asked. Polite creatures with clear lines of societal structure, all but the most important of Mol were used to remaining anonymous figures. It was much the same among the Graha-Es, but Xella had learned early that personal attention went a long way in securing loyalty. And if things went as badly at this negotiation as she feared, she'd want every Mol possible on her side.

"T434, thank you for asking Tovenaressa Xella."

She nodded. "This is Tovenaressa Pey who will be observing and assisting me."

The Mol blinked at her turning a pale golden color. "We were expecting only one."

Mother did like to surprise. Xella tilted her head in what passed for a smile among the Mol. "We can share accommodations. That would be no insult to us as we frequently do so at home."

T434 bobbed his semi-liquid upper half and motioned for them to follow, their footsteps echoing loudly in the empty landing bay.

Empty. How odd. There should have been crates of boxed storage containers ready to shuttle up to the freighter parked in the upper atmosphere. It couldn't have been full or it would have left by now. Unless the Mol were holding shipment until negotiations were complete to ensure no interference from the Dark. Still…it seemed oddly empty for such a large landing bay.

T434 led them through a giant set of doors large enough to accommodate pallets and to the left into a narrower hallway. The biosphere was sparse, the temperature cool to Graha-Es standards. Not cool enough to cause either of them to be lethargic, and certainly not cool enough to send them into stasis, but cool enough that Xella felt mildly uncomfortable. From the liquid the Mol leading them was dripping onto the floor, she assumed he must be fairly new here. Their home world was quite a bit cooler, this being near the upper limits of temperature that Mol could comfortably tolerate. No wonder they used other races in thermal collection and processing. A Mol exerting himself physically at this temperature wouldn't be conscious for long.

But where were those other races? They'd encountered no one on their long walk through the facility—no Mol or anyone who might possibly be a worker. It was as if they were all hiding as far from the Graha-Es visitors as possible.

T434 opened a door and waved a round white arm at the room—their resting quarters, a space barely big enough for them to lay side-by-side. It was luxurious compared to what the workers had the last time she was here. Pey entered first, then T434 pressed a button on the wall and Xella saw how honored they'd been to receive this space. As private as the room was, the entire thing had a clear view of the planet outside the biosphere. It must have been right on the edge of the dome to have such a view.

Pey gasped and pressed her fore and midarms against the barrier, drinking in the landscape. Xella longed to do the same, struggling to appear professional and not like a young, untested sister rarely off her home planet.

Arcturus 5 was stunning. The prevalence of iron on the planet colored everything in shades of red. The ever-setting sun filtered through the thin atmosphere, tinging the jagged cliffs in the distance a bright gold. The magnetic storms that slammed into the planet created the dancing streaks of white and green far off on the horizon.

In all her orbits, Xella had yet to become jaded to the beauty around her. And she was absolutely aware of the fleeting nature of such beauty. In a few million orbits this red giant star would have depleted all of its helium and collapse upon itself, leaving Arcturus 5 a cold rock in an empty sky.

It would still be beautiful, but it would be the beauty of death.

T434 touched another button on the wall and a blue line appeared. "Will one tick be sufficient to rest, Tovenaressa Xella? The Donnar Mol is eager to begin."

She nodded. "I too am eager to begin."

He bowed out of the room. "Then I will return to escort you when the blue line is exhausted."

As soon as he was gone, Xella allowed herself a moment to feel her exhaustion. Even with The Fold, travel was tiring, and she needed to be constantly alert from the moment she arrived. It all mattered—the landing bay, the corridors, the room they'd received, T434's gestures and words. There were so many variables in a negotiation, and what was said at the table was often the least important.

"What did you notice, Pey?"

The younger Graha-Es tapped her midarms against the barrier that separated them from the planet surface. "We encountered no other lifeforms beyond our escort. I would have expected a high-level delegation to meet us at the docking bay, given the influence of Graha-Es in this sector. It's either an insult, or the Donnar had an unexpected emergency. If the latter, he clearly didn't want us to know about it, as no excuses were given for his absence."

"Excellent, Pey. What else?"

She nodded in thought. "We encountered no one else on the way here, so it's possible the emergency is requiring all the workers to assist. I also noticed that based on the biosphere layout I studied, the Mol escort appeared to take us on a circuitous route to reach our quarters."

"Which bypassed…?"

Lids blinked horizontally across Pey's black eyes in a rapid motion. "The…the product storage areas! The cargo bay where we landed was empty— no thermal cells, no helium collectors, nothing. Is the emergency in the product storage area?"

"It's a plausible theory." Xella nodded in approval. "The Mol would hardly have sent out every last bit of their cargo with the Dark still traveling their shipping lanes. They would have waited until after the negotiation to ensure safe passage for their cargo. They have taken great pains to move heavy cargo away from the bay area, cargo which might be why the Donnar and all the workers are elsewhere. They're shifting cargo to another location."

Pey again blinked. "But why hide cargo? The emissary from the Dark is not likely to steal directly from their outpost. And we have no interest in thermal cells or helium collectors."

Xella again looked out the window at the color-ful polar lights. The atmosphere on Arcturus 5 was thin, and there was hardly any magnetosphere to speak of. "Pretty, aren't they?"

The younger Graha-Es twisted her forelimbs together in agitation, realizing there was something in all of this that she was missing. Xella watched her with affection. Pey was still young—young enough to learn.

"We will rest, Pey, and as we do you are to think on what could possibly be accelerating those charged particles and causing such a spectacular display."

Pey pressed her antennae against the barrier, blinking so rapidly her eyes appeared light gray. "It's the solar wind. Arcturus throws forth a strong solar wind."

"Hush." Xella reached out again to touch the line of red stones decorating the younger's skin. "You know as much about this planet and its sun as I do. You have read the briefings on both the Mol and the Dark with their histories. Let your mind wander through the facts. Sometimes rest brings about greater insight."

Pey sighed, ending the noise with a series of clicks that showed both frustration and impa-tience. But knowledge given was not as valuable as knowledge discovered on one's own, so the elder Tovenaressa kept silent and curled up tight against her younger sibling on the bedding slab. If the answer hadn't come to Pey in the one tick they had, then perhaps this sort of work wasn't in her future.

✳

There wasn't much time left before the blue line was gone and T434 would return to escort them to the negotiation table. Xella carefully extricated herself from her sister's many arms and studied the doorway.

It wasn't locked, but the sensing device that opened and closed it would send an alert somewhere when activated. It wasn't uncommon for hosts to have this on their guest room doors.

Which is why Xella had purchased a bypass wire many orbits ago from those crafty Dwall who knew how to get around any system, mechanical or electrical. A small amount of saliva on the wire carefully placed in the sensor and the door slid open just wide enough for her to squeeze through.

The light still blinked as if she remained curled up next to Pey with the door firmly shut. With a quick prayer of thanks to Ammita for giving the Dwall such ingenuity, Xella made her way down the hall and through the corridors.

It would be foolish to step foot on any outpost without a firm knowledge of the layout. Running as quickly as her legs could carry her, she was at the doors to the sections that T434 had carefully skirted while escorting them to their quarters. Again, she'd encountered no one on her journey. No one. It was as if they were the only ones in the outpost.

In a few breaths, she'd raced through the skirted sections and stood before the areas that had been labeled on her map as long term storage. Unfortunately the doors to the rooms were locked, and Xella had used her only wire on the door to their room. She blinked in frustration, wondering how long she'd have until discovery if she forced her way in.

She was Graha-Es, a Tovenaressa. Their word was law in the twenty sectors. In theory there would be no punishment, no retribution for entering any part of this facility. The Mol had invited them here, and thus had opened their outpost to such scrutiny as she deemed necessary. This was the bargain they'd made when they'd agreed to the arbitration.

But still, she hesitated. They were in a remote sector. There was no guarantee the power of her race would protect her. Normally she would have been confident that every Mezadu would be sent to assist, or to avenge, but lately... She hadn't been mated. She was still a solitary soul in a race that valued diplomatic ties and expansion of power through joining. Perhaps she would disappear and Mother would accept whatever reasons the Mol gave for it.

With a tentative stretch of her forearms, she placed them against the door and jerked them back at the feel of cold. Bone and exoskeleton aching cold. The temperature in the biosphere was so warm she hadn't noticed until she'd gotten her arms right next to the door.

By the grace of Ammita, how cold *was* it in that room? And why would the Mol spend a fortune chilling that space when they were cheaper than a two coin Fustain when it came to other environmental controls of this facility?

Xella tried two more storage areas, both locked, before she headed back to her room. There was no need for such security on thermal cells or helium collectors. None. They were not particularly valuable, which was why the Mol kept production costs so low on this outpost and why they were so concerned that each shipment made it to its destination. In such a low margin business, the loss of one freighter would take nearly a full orbit of sales to recover. Not that the Dark would be interested in such products, it would be the freighter itself, chopped up and sold as parts, that would motivate them. There was simply nothing here worth the bother of locking.

There was no way to steal enough product from this outpost to make it worth the effort. There had to be something else behind the locked doors, and Xella had an idea of what it might be. Something the Mol did not want a representative of the Graha-Es to see. Something they feared the Dark might discover in a stolen freighter. If she was right, then it had been terribly risky of them to invite her into their outpost.

Risky. But if they could secure the protection of the Graha-Es through their Mezadu, then it would be worth the risk. Mezadu weren't especially intelligent. They did their job with great enthusiasm and commitment, but anything outside their narrow duties might as well have never happened. If the Mol were doing something illegal, they just needed to hide it until she ruled in their favor and left. Then they'd have the protection they needed to continue without any chance of discovery from the focused and somewhat "nearsighted" Graha-Es warrior/worker class.

And with these locked doors, it was impossible for her to accuse them. A theory based on what she'd observed wouldn't be enough. She couldn't act on theory and suspicion.

The blue line was nearly gone as Xella snuck back into the room, closing the door and removing the wire. Pey was still at rest, a somewhat pink glow tinging her fingertips. It was time. She reached down to wake her little sister, once again praying to Ammita for clear sight and a mind focused on logic and a just ruling.

The Donnar of the outpost was introduced by his title. The emissary from the Dark was introduced as such. There were three other Mol in the room standing behind the Donnar, their gelatinous forms remarkably still. The Dark emissary had another with him to the left. None of these others were introduced. Two beings with titles. It was so ridiculous given that both she and Pey had given their names.

"I can't tell them apart," Pey whispered.

Neither could Xella. The only way to differentiate the Dark emissary from the other was by position, and the same was true of the group of Mol. She assumed if she spent sufficient time with them, little differences would become evident, but right now the four Mol in the room looked exactly like T434.

"It's always evident who to address," she assured her sister. "These are formal meetings. If we were in a social situation, I'd be in just as much trouble as you."

Pey stifled the involuntary click of amusement, covering up the sound with one of her forearms. It *was* amusing. As skilled as she was in diplomacy, Xella knew her weaknesses. Eventually her knowledge of all the differing races in the twenty sectors would grow, but she'd never be good at socializing and random small talk.

It was the sort of defect the perfect mate could remedy. But she was done thinking about that.

"First I need to confirm that both of you understand that although we are here in hopes of reaching compromise through negotiation, if none is reached you both agree to uphold the decision made by me, Tovenaressa Xella of the Graha-Es. This is to be considered a binding arbitration."

Both parties signified their agreement, but it wasn't yet time to relax. "Good. I have heard the Mol complaint as part of the original request for arbitration, and I will allow them to restate it along with supporting detail, but first I wish to hear what the Dark emissary has to say."

Donnar Mol quivered with indignation, but remained silent.

The Dark emissary shifted position, his shiny metallic face turning toward Xella. "We claim rights of passage through common space. The Mol do not own the Arcturus system or the Bootes constellation. Shipping lanes are not there for their private use. We merely wish to continue traveling through such common space in search of abandoned ships and space junk to salvage."

Xella wished she could read the emissary. His bipedal form was like smooth silver, as if he were a statue cast from heated metal. The face held no expression, the body did not move except to pivot about to speak in her direction. The other Dark behind him was equally unhelpful. They didn't breathe, they didn't appear to have muscles to move. There was nothing in their physical form to indicate what might lie behind their words.

She had nothing to go on but history. The Dark were brutal. They'd been accused repeatedly of raider activities hidden under the legal guise of salvage. No crew ever remained alive to dispute their claims. Bodies were never recovered. Still, as distasteful as she found them, as suspect as their business interests were, she could find no fault in their claim to what were common routes, open to all races of the twenty sectors.

The Donnar Mol, as well as his contingent, were not so stoic. Xella deliberately waited a moment before asking them to speak, watching as their quivering increased. It was somewhat hypnotic, the sway of their gelatinous forms.

"These *are* private shipping lanes," the Donnar announced. "No other race has outposts or mining operations in the Arcturus system. There is no need for them to be searching for salvage or junk where *we* are the only occupants. If there is a disabled ship in this system, it is ours to take care of, not the Dark."

True, but their initial complaint had stated they wanted sole use of far more than the Arcturus system.

"But what are your reasons for claiming private use of the entire Bootes constellation?"

The Donnar stilled his shaking, gold tinging his form. "No one else uses it. The Dark has no reason to be there."

The Dark representative made a slash motion with one hand. "Just because no one is currently using it beyond the Mol doesn't mean there are not items of interest from many orbits ago. There is also the possibility that a junked vessel may drift into the shipping lanes. Are we to hinder our business operations just because the Mol have a prejudicial fear of us?"

The Donnar glared. "There is a universe full of shipping lanes to search for salvage. We only ask this one to be off limits."

In the big scheme of things it wasn't a request that would grossly hinder the Dark. This was a remote sector, and the Bootes constellation shouldn't have anything worthy of the Dark's attentions. Were they doing this to harass the Mol? To make them pay a protection fee? Why did the Dark care about this tiny system in the middle of nowhere that only served to transport items of little to no value?

That was a series of questions that must be answered, but in the meantime, as inconsequential as the Bootes constellation was, Xella didn't want to set a precedent for this sort of thing. If the Mol received their exclusive use, then others would want the same.

It would be unfair to other races who shouldn't be restricted to only a handful of shipping lanes. And it would anger the Dark, who would retaliate in a sneaky and violent fashion. War. The kind of war where the attackers claimed innocence and struck in the dark of night, vanishing without a clue as to who they were. It would be a diplomatic nightmare.

Xella tapped one of her mid-limbs on the table. "Would it be acceptable if the Dark were to notify the Mol of any salvage they come across that relates to their shipping and mining operations? Would the Dark agree not to board or remove anything from the ship without consent from the Mol?"

As expected, both parties exploded in speech, protesting the proposal. Finders keepers was the philosophy of the Dark, and the Mol were also unwilling to budge.

Xella faced Donnar Mol. "You haven't complained about Dwall or Human ships in this space. Why do you object specifically about the Dark presence here? Do you have proof that they will do your ships harm? Do you have proof that they have done so in the past?"

Of course not. The Dark would never be so foolish as to leave anything behind that could possibly implicate them in murder or a piratical raid. This was a no-win situation. Xella knew the Dark illegally seized ships, and she also suspected the Mol of illegal operations on Arcturus 5. What to do when both parties were in the wrong? How she longed to slap them like naughty children and send them off to stasis on a cold slab as punishment.

The Donnar Mol turned a darker shade of gold, but before he could speak, an explosion rocked the biosphere.

There was silence as everyone in the room looked at each other. Xella felt one of Pey's midarms touch her side.

"What was that?" It seemed silly to ask. The collection of thermals and helium was a safe operation. Helium was inert, and none of the storage containers should have enough pressure to create a risk of explosion.

The Mol were neon yellow at this point. The Donnar nervously fingered a button on the table.

"Yes, what was that?" The Dark emissary seemed amused, although Xella wasn't sure how she could tell with their lack of facial expression.

Another explosion rocked the room. Then another. Then a series of violent blasts that sent both Xella and Pey to the ground. Something cracked, and with a sound of shattering glass, the biosphere broke.

It hadn't been a small breach. Emergency lights flashed and sirens wailed. The Donnar Mol pushed the button on the table and a set of containment suits shot from the floor to cover the Mol.

How convenient, Xella thought as she struggled upright. The temperature in the room doubled. She could feel the radiation against her skin, sparking and burning.

It wouldn't kill her—or Pey. It *would* have killed the Mol. It might have already killed the Dark. They'd liquefied at the breach, becoming puddles of mercury on the cracked floor.

"Biosphere breach. No doubt an attempt by the Dark to sabotage negotiations." Donnar Mol glared at the pools of silver, his voice system muffled by the containment suit.

Xella hid her frustration. Given the state of the Dark emissary as well as the direction their negotiations were heading, it was ridiculous to lay the blame for this on them. Especially given what she suspected the Mol were doing at this facility.

"This is clearly an assassination attempt, a deliberate act of terrorism against our facility," Donnar Mol continued, staring intently at the two Graha-Es. He seemed to be hoping for something and Xella got the feeling it was her death. Well, he'd have to wait a while. This radiation hurt. Prolonged exposure might mean she'd need to molt, putting her in stasis for a few orbits. She'd be vulnerable, but *that* level of physical damage was hours away.

"Is there an evacuation procedure?" Xella calmly asked. Pey was practically clinging to her. The two Dark were sloshing around the floor, giving her hope that they were still alive. The Mol just stood, wide-eyed and bright yellow.

The door burst open and in came a suited Mol. It was T434. Xella felt a sense of pride that she'd been able to recognize him. Perhaps they didn't all look exactly alike after all, although she wasn't sure what difference she'd noticed that caused her to recognize the escort.

"Donnar Mol! Storage eight and ten have exploded. We're holding atmosphere in the northern bay until we can isolate the damaged sections."

"Please take us there," Xella instructed T434.

The Mol turned to her and Pey, his eyes protruding even farther from the semi-solid head. "I… you…"

"Yes, we are unharmed. I'm not sure how long those containment suits will hold out the radiation, though. The Donnar and the other Mol should go to a safe area right away." Xella looked down at the Dark. "And I guess we need a bucket?"

The two puddles rolled along the floor, causing the Mol to jump out of the way. Xella watched with amusement. "No. Evidently a bucket is not needed. Let's proceed."

T434 recovered his composure enough to lead the way.

"You go ahead. I'll catch up later." Xella pushed Pey forward to follow with the group of Mol while she took up the rear just behind the silvery liquid of the Dark. The radiation burned its way along her joints, where skin and hardened plates came together. This wasn't good. Pey definitely needed shelter because with this level of radiation, they had far less than a few hours before their bodies were irreparably damaged.

The thought of molting and being at the mercy of the Mol scared her, but Xella had a job to do, and may Ammita smite her down if she returned home to the Mother without completing her task. With a quick look at the suited backs of the Mol ahead, she ducked down an adjoining corridor and made her way back to the storage areas, thankful that she'd always memorized the layout of every facility before journeying there.

Xella's fears were confirmed before she even saw the burned, twisted walls of the corridor and the blackened debris of the storage room. There was an unmistakable pull, something deep inside her that homed in on a strong magnetic field as if it were a beacon.

This planet shouldn't have had polar lights. And nothing mined from the surface or resulting from the legal operations of the Mol should have generated this strong a magnetic field.

Detrium. Highly explosive in its raw form and illegal to both mine and refine, the mineral could be made into weapons that had been banned in all twenty sectors. But banned didn't mean there wasn't a lucrative black market for the substance. No wonder the Mol had hidden the mined ore in lead-lined rooms, artificially cooled to the point where the lead had acted as a superconductor and shielded the magnetic fields. No wonder they hadn't wanted the Dark sniffing around their transport freighters. No wonder they had built their outpost on the planet instead of constructing an orbiting facility instead. There must be an underground mining facility to the north, where the entrances allowed enough of a magnetic field to escape and collide with the charged particles in the solar winds which cause the lights.

She'd suspected the possibility of surface collection, but Xella was now convinced this operation was far larger.

Another blast rocked the facility and Xella instinctively ducked. Bits of shielded polyglass bounced like hail off her pebbled skin. Following the pull of the magnetic field, she ran down a maze of corridors and came upon a locked door.

Detection was no longer a concern at this point, so she grabbed a nearby safety pole and slammed it full force into the door's electronics. They sparked, twisting enough voltage up the metal rod to send her flying backward against the wall. It hurt. Combined with the heat, the excess gravity, and the radiation battering her exterior, it *really* hurt. But the door was open and the proof was right in front of her.

Clear cylinders glowed light green as they stood upright in metal support units. Hazy white and green swirled around them in arcs like a dance of lightning. They were leaking. And with the breach of the biosphere, the charged atmosphere was reacting with the Detrium. Xella had no idea what had caused the initial explosions, but once environmental safeguards had been breached, there had been a chain reaction.

The floor shook again with a series of three blasts, cracks opening up from the far side of the room across the hallway. Part of a corridor wall collapsed in a spray of dust and polyfiber.

Xella ran, dropping down to gallop along on legs and forearms in an inelegant method of locomotion that would have drawn scorn back home. Scorn was better than dead, and at this point all she was concerned about was getting to Pey and then getting to their ship.

Another blast knocked her sideways into a wall. If she'd been upright, she would have fallen, but being on four legs like a cursed animal gave her the agility to kick off the wall and keep her forward momentum. The whole place was going to go up. And even if she and Pey managed to survive the detonations, they'd soon be in molt and stasis from the radiation. They'd be helpless, and there would be a good chance no one would find them for hundreds of orbits, if ever.

Leave. Now. Xella ran, fighting the urge to head straight to the docking bay where their ship sat. Thank Ammita the Mol had moved all the Detrium from those areas because there was a chance their ship was still in one piece. But first she had to get Pey. There was no way she was leaving her sister behind. She'd never leave without Pey.

Xella skidded around a corner, leaping to jump the two foot crack that crossed the floor. This was where she'd snuck off from the group, but where had they gone from here? She racked her brain, trying to think of where in the schematics of the outpost the Mol would have put an emergency shelter.

Pey might be safe inside a shelter, but Xella was less than an hour away from molt. And as bad as that would be for her, she was terrified to think that inexperienced Pey would be in the hands of these criminals. Only two thousand orbits old. Newly mated with her second soul.

No, Xella would allow herself to die before she succumbed to molt and the protective stasis. She just needed to find the shelter. Hopefully the outpost would hold until she could stabilize her bios, then she and Pey could get out of here.

And any others who wanted to, even the Mol and the liquefied Dark, because the Graha-Es weren't monsters.

The blueprints of the facility came up in her mind as if the hologram was before her. She'd lectured Pey numerous times on engineering and safety protocols. If this were her responsibility, where would she designate for emergency shelter?

There. Xella narrowed her eyes as she looked down the hallway. Centrally located away from the edges of the biosphere, but with a direct path to the landing bays. It had appropriate shielding, a supply of breathing apparatus along with pressure and temperature control suits. And behind the room was a space that appeared to have emergency evacuation bags—what any Mol would need to survive enough rotations on this planet until help could come from outside the system.

Xella headed toward the room, still loping along on all fours and grimacing at the explosions that were now a steady beat, cracking walls and separating sections of floor. Her skin burned. Her internal fluids felt ready to boil. She felt the separation of muscle and plate that signified an approaching molt. Oh no. This couldn't happen now, now when Pey was among unsympathetic strangers and their futures hung by a thread.

There. She rose to her legs and beat on the door with her forearms. The moment she'd touched the door she realized how futile those actions were. They were on lockdown in an emergency refuge. They wouldn't open the door, so she'd need to open it for them.

The wire. A bit of saliva. And the kick of a very powerful leg. The door slid open with a creak and a whine. A chorus of screams met her ears. Xella dove through the doorway and swept the room, frantically searching the suited Mol for the one six-limbed form in the room. And she found her.

"Xella! Oh, thank Ammita you're okay. I think we're going to die."

Xella felt the leathered skin that covered her mandibles peel back, exposing her pointed double-row of fangs. "We are not going to die."

Pey ran to her and she turned, one forearm linking with her younger sister's. "Oh. And if any of you wish to leave, I'd suggest you head to any available shuttles. We have room for any who wish to subject themselves to Graha-Es ruling."

There was a profound silence that followed her speech, and as the pair left the room, a notable lack of footsteps following them. A scant three feet down the corridor and Xella heard the door close and lock once more behind her. Fine. They'd made their sleeping mat, now it was time for them to rest on it.

"Where are we going?" Pey whimpered, clinging to one of her midarms. "I think I'm going to molt. Xella, I've only molted once before. I'm not sure... I'm scared."

Xella felt everything inside her twist with anxiety. Pey was so young. She'd only molted once. By all Ammita held holy, of course the girl was scared.

"Our ship," Xella announced with a confidence she was far from feeling. "I have little hope this place will survive the chain reaction of Detrium explosions."

"Detrium?" Pey's voice was a few octaves higher than usual. "Of course! How could I have been so blind? The polar lights on a planet with no

magnetosphere. The unusually intense environmental controls around the secret storage units."

Xella risked falling to shoot her younger sister
an incredulous glance.

"What?" The girl twitched her lower jaw in
amusement. "I snuck out while you were resting to
check. You're not the only one who memorized the
outpost schematics. And you're not the only one
who bribed the Dwall for a bypass wire."

Maybe Pey'd make a decent diplomat after all.
Or if she proved especially skilled, a double agent.
Her youth, her wide-eyed innocence. Yes, Pey had
quite the future ahead of her.

The biosphere shook violently as they neared
the docking bay. Xella felt her sister's fear, felt
the ground shift like quicksand under her feet.
Dropping again to all fours, she yanked Pey with
her midarm. "Run!"

The ship was in sight, shimmering and dancing
with the violent quakes that shook the ground. It
wasn't just the explosions of Detrium at this point,
it was the surface itself, plate tectonics shifting from
the explosions. Xella had no idea how much of the
volatile substance lay below the surface, but there
was a good chance that the blasts in the biosphere
had destabilized the Detrium below the planetary
crust.

It wasn't just the environmental controls that were jeopardized, it was the entire planet.

"Run!" Xella screamed again, dropping Pey's hand to allow the girl to use all six limbs. Running like a crass beast, she launched herself toward the ship, scrabbling up the ladders to the interior.

The ship listed to the side. It would have been knocked off its landing gear onto its side if the cruiser hadn't been locked into place with bay-floor clamps.

Oh, mighty Ammita. The floor clamps.

Pey latched herself into the pilot seat, still whimpering. Xella threw herself into the operations area, firing the launchers and setting up the navigations. Not that any of this would do any good. The bay doors were still closed and the thrusters could never overcome the reinforced metal of the floor clamps.

Their ship rocked from side to side. "Xella! Tovenaressa Xella, I can't...the bay doors."

"I know."

Xella grabbed a flare spot welder and raced down the ladder. It was hard to remain upright at this point as the whole facility was shimmying side to side as if a continuous terra quake were in action. Crawling on all sixes, she made her way to the landing gear and fired up the welder, concentrating the blue flame on the clamps.

There was a rumble in the distance. She ignored it, figuring that she could only deal with one crisis at a time. The clamp softened under the intense flare of the welder, separating as the upward force of the ship overpowered the weakening metal.

One free. Xella scampered to the other landing gear, focusing the blue flame on the other clamp. Nothing made sense anymore. The vibrating world around her seemed oddly normal. The intense heat...it was becoming cold. She was molting. If she could just get this clamp free and manage to force the bay doors open, Pey could get the ship out and off the planet. She'd be free. She'd be safe.

Let her live a long and glorious life. Let her learn and serve the Mother and the Graha-Es with all her considerable knowledge and skill. Let her live.

The second clamp snapped free. Xella stumbled over to the shimmering electronics on the far wall, wondering why they seemed like dancing stars in a far off galaxy. Something grabbed her waist with smooth and flexible metallic arms, dragging her backward and upward. She blinked, seeing Pey at the controls at an odd angle and realized she was on her side on the shuttle floor.

"Doors. Bay doors." It felt way too cold for eight hundred degrees. Xella shivered. It slowly dawned on her that the atmosphere and temperature within

the shuttle were fast approaching normal levels…
and that they were moving.

"He opened them," Pey announced, her four
arms rapid at the controls. "Can you strap in? We're
getting out of here as fast as this ship can move."

Xella struggled to her feet, gripping the back of
the chair for balance as the shuttle rocked from side
to side. Sure enough, the viewer showed the bay
doors wide open, chunks of the biosphere dome
falling. One hit the ship with a bang, and Xella
threw herself into the seat. "Go! Go!"

Pey punched the accelerator and they rocketed
through the doors. Only when they'd cleared the
planet's thin atmosphere did Xella think to wonder about the "he" who'd opened the bay doors.
Looking behind her with a sense of dread she saw
not one, but two Dark.

The Dark had saved them. Maybe. They had an
unproven reputation for piracy. It would be easy
for them to take the ship, dispose of her and Pey.
No one would be the wiser. But of all the things of
value, this small ship wasn't worth much. Hopefully
not worth discovery and the war an attack on a
Graha-Es arbitrator would bring.

"Gentlemen," she nodded to the pair. "Where
shall we take you?"

Xella could have sworn the one smiled. "We would be most appreciative, Tovenaressa Xella, if you would take us to our ship behind the fifth planet's moon."

She hesitated, realizing their vulnerability if they docked on a Dark Wrecker.

Again, there was an odd glint of metal on the Dark's face that seemed like a smile. "From there, we would be honored to escort you through The Fold to your home planet. We hope for a long, mutually beneficial relationship with the Graha-Es, and ensuring their arbitrator and her assistant arrive safely is the least we can do to prove our intent."

"Thank you," she replied. "Tovenaressa Pey and I accept your offer."

The planet spun out of view behind them, a red rock with the dance of polar lights now visible even from space. The Dark and the Graha-Es. Stranger alliances had occurred in the history of the twenty sectors. Xella had a premonition theirs would be the shortest of friendships, but *that* was a matter for Ammita, for the future, to decide.

✳

"Arcturus 5" is a prequel to the Twenty Sectors series. Book 1, *Two-Souls*, will be releasing in Fall of 2016.

For information on this as well as Debra's Urban Fantasy novels—which include the Imp series and the Templar series—please visit debradunbar.com.

TREASON'S COURSE

A HALCYONE SPACE STORY

LJ COHEN

THE GUARD SHE'D LEFT AT THE ENTRANCE TO THE LAB HAD disappeared, leaving Dr. Dauber unsupervised. Had it been long enough for him to have committed treason? Emma took a deep breath and pushed on the door.

It didn't budge.

She withdrew her sidearm and knocked.

Silence answered her.

Emma checked the settings on her weapon—narrow beam, non-lethal was the Commonwealth standard for close quarters where there was a high probability of civilian engagement. She shifted the pulse width to a fatter beam. At this range, pinpoint accuracy was less of an issue than coverage if something turned sideways.

And something always turned sideways.

With the safety disengaged, Emma targeted the lock. The beam from her weapon traced a small, perfect circle in the metal door. Heat radiated outward to warm her before the entire lock mechanism dropped into the lab with a loud crash. She figured Dauber had heard that.

Her sidearm sat comfortably in her left hand. With her right, she pushed the door open and called the doctor's name. A deep boom that she felt more than heard rumbled through the corridor. The door blew outwards. A twisted shard of hot metal embedded itself in her right shoulder. The stink of explosives and burned flesh filled the air.

Emma staggered back, swearing, but didn't fall. Her right hand dangled limply by her side. Pain lit up the nerve pathways from her shoulder down to her fingertips. Shock slowed her thoughts. She glanced down at the weapon still clutched in her left hand as if it had betrayed her. Several additional explosions rattled the corridor. The lab filled with thick smoke. It billowed through the open doorway.

Dauber. Fuck. Dr. Dauber was in there.

Any of her squad-mates in the 24th would have killed for a position like this. Emma was sure she would die of tedium, if not irritation, before she got reassigned. All of her training and two tours aboard a dreadnought should never have landed her here, playing nanny to a pair of scientists who didn't understand the concepts of security or discipline. But the Commonwealth of Planets, in its infinite wisdom, had pulled her six weeks ago, just as her squad was getting ready to deploy back to the colonies again.

She strode through the hallways of what had once been a busy research facility on the campus of the University of Calgary. Now, instead of academics and their students, it was peopled with armed soldiers in Commonwealth silver and gray who guarded every intersection and doorway. All for scientists who, if Charles Dauber and Adiana May were any indication, spent all their waking hours playing with sims and thinking deep thoughts. Emma could see the wisdom in moving them to the orbital facility. No matter how much security the Commonwealth brought in, the university was a civilian enterprise and inevitably full of holes.

The brains had better be worth all the resources, time, and energy, as well as the potential lives lost while she and her fellow soldiers kept them safe.

She saluted and stood at attention just inside the doorway to command. "Corporal Gutierrez, reporting as ordered, sir."

Commander Brent turned and faced her. His uniform was as crisp as ever. A large man, he dwarfed even Emma's height and carried himself like someone used to wearing a pressure suit and armor. Not for the first time, she wondered what he had done to deserve a spot warming a chair planet-side.

He pinched the bridge of his nose and took a deep breath. "I've had nothing but good reports about you, Gutierrez."

"Yes, sir." What did he mean by that? Her service record was exemplary. It was one of the main reasons she couldn't understand why she'd been sent here.

"You are not happy with this assignment."

"Sir?" Emma nearly fell out of her controlled stance. "Permission to speak freely?"

"Granted."

"My place is with the twenty-fourth. In combat. This isn't what I was trained for. The blockade—"

"I appreciate your frustration," he said, leaning against the edge of his desk.

Being Earth-bound couldn't have been any more pleasant for him.

"But orders are orders. I suspect you know that." She nodded.

"I have an assignment for you. A sensitive assignment."

Her heart raced but she waited. It was one of the first things you learned as a recruit. To wait. To relinquish any expectation of explanations. Life in the military wasn't all that much different from growing up in the settlements in that regard: someone else always had more authority and rank.

"We have reason to believe that our security has been breached."

That was no real surprise. It just confirmed why they were relocating to the orbital lab.

"Dr. Dauber may have been compromised."

Emma stiffened. A serious accusation. The man was annoying, but there was no denying he was driven. He and May barely slept, barely left their main lab and their computer.

"The relocation order has spooked him and we believe he's delaying in order to smuggle his data out before the move."

Commander Brent studied her but she wasn't sure what kind of reaction he was looking for. "What are my orders, sir?"

He let out his breath in the smallest of exhales. "Dauber and May's project is vital to the Commonwealth. It may very well be the turning point in this war."

Her head snapped up. There were rumors about the blockade. About rebel colonists and suicide missions. About heavy losses on both sides.

Pushing away from his desk, Commander Brent walked toward her until he stood uncomfortably close. It took all of her discipline not to step back.

"Yes, your work here is more important than you know." He lowered his voice as if they could be overheard through the sound-masking walls. "These next twelve hours are especially critical. I need you to watch Dauber. You should be able to stay close. The two of them trust you." The commander quirked his lips into a brief smile. "At least they've stopped sending daily memos complaining about their babysitters, so you and Ensign Odachi must have done something right."

They were not the first team to be their primary guards. She wondered what had happened to the prior pair. The rest of their detail rotated in from the commander's security ranks, but she and Odachi were never assigned anywhere other than to the lab and to Dauber and May, supervising twelve hour shifts, which were wearying and wearing.

"Will I be coordinating with Ensign Odachi?"

"No."

That made no sense. He was her commanding officer. "Then who? Will I report directly to you?"

Brent resumed his pacing. "Because of the nature of Dauber and May's work, we can't trust the security of any communications outside of this room. Once you leave here, you're cleared to act on your own authority. Understand, what they're working on cannot fall into enemy hands. If you obtain evidence of his treason, or detect any compromise in the lab's security you must take action."

Emma's mouth dried. She did stumble out of her stance, then. As Brent watched silently, she wiped her clammy hands on her trousers.

"This is war, soldier, and you have been authorized to use deadly force. Do you understand?"

She swallowed hard. "Yes, sir."

"Dismissed."

Emma bent down, gasping when her right arm swung away from her body. There was no time to bind it. The smoke from the lab would travel fast and poison all the oxygen in the room.

A high-pitched frantic voice screamed from behind her. "Chaz! Chaz! No!"

Emma glanced back. Dr. May was twisting wildly trying to break Ensign Odachi's hold. She was clutching a to-go box from the commissary. There was no one else. Where were the guards on duty? Why weren't there building-wide alarms? The fire suppression should have been activated by now.

Brent's orders tumbled through her thoughts: *cleared to act, evidence of treason, deadly force.* Someone had acted, but who? And under who's authority?

Her mind seemed to have taken a wormhole trip without her body. Time expanded and sped up simultaneously, but the smoke that continued to billow out into the hallway followed its own deadly trajectory.

Emma ducked into the lab and slammed into the wall of boxes she had helped Dauber stack less than an hour before. The impact jarred her injured arm. Pain burst through her like afterimages of the detonation in the room.

Burning polymers turned the smoke thick and oily. Emma took small sips of air through the cloth of her left sleeve. "Dauber!" Her call ended in a cough that pulled more smoke into her lungs and set her eyes watering.

Against her better judgment and all her instincts, she moved further into the lab, crawling with her left arm, her right dragging along the floor in passive agony. There was still some cooler air down there, but it wouldn't last much longer.

Get in. Find Dauber. Pull him out. She only had a few minutes. Maybe less. Visibility was almost nil, but she knew the room. The roughly rectangular shape sketched itself out in her head. Dauber's desk was about a meter directly in front of her. If he were there, she stood a chance of rescuing him. If not, and she stayed any longer, they would both be dead.

Was that the point? Brent had given her an impossible job to do in an impossible time frame. And without the resources she needed. Why?

Not why the orders. If there was a security breach, it had to be sealed. But why her? Emma knew she was competent. Her weapons ratings were the highest in her company. She'd received several commendations for her leadership ability, but competent or not, she was only an enlisted soldier. Replaceable mass in anyone's jump calculation.

No one would open an investigation if she vanished. She had no family. Her death benefit was set to get added to a widows' and orphans' fund for the families of deceased soldiers. And her spot was already filled in the 24th.

Brent had chosen her. And it didn't make sense. Nothing about this made sense.

Each time she lurched forward, Emma paused and swept her left hand in an arc in front of her. Nothing. The stainless floor was getting warm beneath her. Time was running out. She hitched closer to Dauber's desk and this time when she reached her arm out, it connected with its metal leg. And a shoe. The smoke coated her nose and lungs with a caustic heat. Taking a full breath was impossible. Her head swam as if she had been spaced without air. Even that would be a more merciful death than this.

She yanked hard on the foot. Dauber's body slid a few centimeters from under his desk. Grunting with the effort, she pulled him closer. There was no time to assess his condition. They had to get out. Now.

Her right arm was less than useless. Her left hand kept slipping off Dauber's leg. She went to wipe her hand dry and blood sheeted off it. Dauber's blood. His leg was slick with it and it spilled onto the floor in a pulsating flow that diminished to a trickle as she watched.

Arterial flow. And then nothing. Emma gasped, choking on thickening smoke. She pulled with increased urgency, but something had trapped him and she couldn't get him free of the desk.

*

Dauber and May must be something if all this force and infrastructure existed to safeguard their work. Emma stopped short in the hallway. A pair of patrolling corporals bumped into her. She shook out of her thoughts, apologized, and headed to the lab.

Dauber was yelling at Odachi when she stepped in.

"… can't just unplug it all and carry it away. Some of these machines were built in this room." He ran his hands through his thick, curly hair. "Do you have any idea how hard taking an AI off line and recalibrating it will be?" Dauber didn't wait for Odachi's response. "Of course you don't. Why do I even bother?"

Of their two charges, Dauber was the animated one. The passionate one. May had the steadier temperament. They did seem to make a good team. Emma paused at the door and frowned. Was the woman under suspicion, too?

Dauber kept talking into Odachi's silence. "Be reasonable. This is a university research facility. You and Gutierrez can't just field strip my equipment and move on."

Emma jerked her head up at hearing her name. Through Dauber's harangue, Odachi stood calmly, his narrow face expressionless. Normally, that would de-escalate a situation, let the angry party burn through their emotion, but Dauber's cheeks remained as red as a warning light and he strode through his lab sweeping papers and the remnants of a food tray from a deeply pitted metal desk. Resin bowls and dishes clattered to the ground.

"Dr. Dauber?" She kept her voice soft and low. The papers settled like dried leaves. "Perhaps we all need to take a step back."

The two men turned to her.

"We all get how vital your work is. What resources do you need to make this move happen?"

Odachi looked like he wanted to reprimand her, but there was also curiosity in his gaze. Then he nodded, content to let her continue playing her version of 'good cop.' If only he knew what had just taken place in Brent's office. If only she knew what he knew.

"This is for your own safety. We're under orders, Dr. Dauber," Odachi said.

"Yes. I know. There's always some order or another, some more urgent command."

Dauber thundered across the room and loomed over the much smaller ensign. Odachi stood his ground, his stance balanced, his right hand resting near his sidearm.

What would Dauber do if he thought they were going to dismantle his lab here and now? She needed proof and she wouldn't get it in the middle of a tantrum, real or fabricated. Keeping pressure on him was important, but so was having the time to assess the authenticity of any threat he might pose. She caught Odachi's eye and shook her head to signal him before stepping in close to Dauber.

"Show me what needs to be done." She made a point of turning to Odachi. "Sir? I suggest we reconvene here in four hours." That would be enough time for the ensign to get some rest and for her to get a better sense of Dauber's motives in delaying the move.

Both men nodded and backed off from one another. Dauber strode across the room to his computer array. Odachi studied her, his gray eyes narrowed, before he left the lab. The ensign was always hard to read, but there was no mistaking the anger in his percussive footfalls and the slammed door. Figuring out what her immediate supervisor knew was going to be a challenge, but Dauber was her main mission.

"How can I help, Dr. Dauber?"

He turned and studied her. "You do know the work Ada and I are doing here is highly classified," Dauber said. "I could explain it to you, but then I'd have to kill you."

It was hard to tell if the glint in his eye was from genuine humor or manipulation.

"I don't need to know the nature of your project to assist in moving your gear." She watched him carefully. "This isn't up for negotiation. You're here by order of the Commonwealth, just as I am. Just as Ensign Odachi is." She waved her arm in the direction of the door. "No matter what your position was outside these walls, here you're part of a chain of command, whether you like it or not. So how do we begin?"

Dauber twisted his lips as if he'd tasted something bitter, but it was no less true for being unpleasant. Just as the Commonwealth supported Emma's training, it funded his research, and there were strings attached. There were always strings attached. The real question was how much was Dauber pulling back?

He rubbed his eyes and collapsed into his desk chair. "Fine. This isn't your fault."

Emma stood at parade rest, waiting for him to continue.

Leaning forward, he slid open a desk drawer and pulled out a slim tablet. "Most of my notes are in this, but I'm going to need all of those papers, too. If you can start on those shelves over there, I can do today's backup. Then when Ada's ready, she can help me with Mnemosyne."

Their computer. Emma tried not to smirk. There were soldiers she knew who named their weapons, but ascribing a kind of identity to a tool seemed terribly precious. And somewhat out of character for two brilliant scientists.

She might not know a lot about sophisticated computers, but Emma understood people and what drove them. Dauber put in long hours in the lab, getting here before Dr. May and leaving later, night after night. Was it passion? Or was he masking treason through his devotion to the project?

"Have you had dinner yet?" Emma crouched down to gather the rogue papers. They were filled with precise notes in an impeccable hand. Tiny drawings in multiple colors made her think of photos she'd seen of ancient illuminated manuscripts. Dauber's controlled writing was definitely at odds with his temper.

"That was lunch. I think." He waved in the direction of his upended tray. "I can eat later."

They worked in silence; Emma packing the papers and journals in a series of lidded cartons, Dauber hunched over his desk furiously scribbling across the surface of his tablet. She thought of the notes again. They were probably May's.

As if Emma's thoughts had summoned her, Dr. May walked into the lab.

"Sorry I'm late, Chaz. I was . . ." The small woman paused and nodded at Emma. May's cheeks were flushed and her piercing blue eyes took in the room with one quick glance. "Good evening, Corporal Gutierrez."

"Evening, doc."

"No luck with our minders?" Dauber asked.

As May shook her head, Dauber slammed the open desk drawer. The sound reverberated through the lab. May came up behind him and rested her hand on his shoulder. Leaning forward, she spoke too quietly for Emma to hear.

Emma stacked the last box on top of the others. So Dr. May had tried to intercede with command. Did that mean she was compromised, too? Shit. She hated covert crap. Give her a target and a weapon any day.

Right now, her mission was Dauber. She had yet to decide if he was a target as well.

"I know. We have to finish what we started." Dauber sighed before pushing away from the desk and standing.

"Chaz, are you sure her systems are fully isolated?"

Dauber glanced over at the rack of computer components. "I've walled her off from the testing rig. She should be okay even if the program spills over the sandbox." He glared toward where Emma stood by the stack of boxes. "Brent is an idiot. This whole project is a mistake. Moving it now?" He shook his head. His round face was red again, clear up to his hairline.

Was his anger sufficient motivation for treason? Emma and her squad-mates bitched about command all the time. That didn't make them traitors. And when it came time to carry out orders, there was no second guessing or hesitation. So what was Dauber going to do?

Emma didn't know enough about the tech they worked with to catch him in the act of sabotage. Communications were on lockdown, so there should have been no way to get the data out. At least not virtually. And not physically either, unless he had an accomplice here at the University. It would have to be someone with security clearance to get out of the lab building. Even she didn't have that.

Only officers did. And then only on a case by case basis. She wished she could get a list from Brent, but he had essentially forbidden her from contacting him. All Emma could do was keep Dauber under surveillance until they moved the lab. Once in orbit, it would be easier to make sure the two scientists were truly isolated.

This was the mission's most vulnerable time. They would need to bring in personnel to move the boxes and computer gear and any of them could be a conduit, even an unwitting one.

She flexed her left hand and brushed it against her firearm—a habitual gesture that was nearly unconscious.

Choking, Emma scrabbled backwards until she reached the door and the blessedly cooler air of the corridor. She struggled to her feet, her chest heaving, her eyes streaming. Smoke engulfed the entire lab. Even if Dauber had been alive when she first found him, he was certainly dead now. "Keep moving," she gasped. "Bring her."

Dr. May was still holding the food container in a white-knuckled grip. "Chaz?"

Emma shook her head. "The transport." She coughed and couldn't catch her breath for a long moment. "We have to get her out of here."

Odachi narrowed his eyes and looked down the hallway. Then he nodded. He must have come to the same conclusion as she had: someone had blown up the lab, disabled fire suppression, and pulled security. It didn't matter who that someone was. What mattered was they hadn't gotten to May. Yet.

And for now, the safest place for her was off planet and isolated.

The three of them raced to the loading dock. They hadn't passed a single soldier on the way. At the security scan, Odachi slipped free of Emma's right side. She cried out as he jostled her injured arm. The fingerprint and retinal checks seemed to take forever. Had their clearance been revoked?

Nothing made sense. Why kill Dauber and blow up the lab? It wasn't what the rebels wanted and it wasn't what the Commonwealth wanted, either, was it?

The loading dock door swung open silently. They hustled a dazed Dr. May through the storage area and into the tiny cockpit of the small military transport.

"I hope you can fly this thing solo." Emma heard her own thin voice as if it were coming from very far away.

"Strap her in!" That was Odachi.

Gentle hands pressed her into one of the flight chairs and fumbled for the buckles. Emma wanted to apologize for not being able to help, but couldn't find the words.

"I have a pilot's rating." May's voice cut in and out like a military radio on a faint frequency.

"Go. Just go," Emma said. Or tried to say. Or imagined she'd said.

Then even the small sounds of the engines spinning faded down some distant corridor in her mind until everything was heavy and still.

✳

Emma followed May to the woman's quarters. Like her own small room, it had once been an office. There was barely room for the two women to squeeze in beside the single bed frame and a storage locker.

"Everything I need is in there," May said, gesturing to the trunk on the bed.

Crouching over it, Emma tested the weight. Not too bad. She grabbed the handles, prepared to hoist it, when May interrupted.

"I'm not useless," she said.

Emma tried to wrestle the side of the trunk from May, but the woman's grip was steady. "Suit yourself."

They walked in silence carrying the trunk toward where the building's loading dock had been converted into a makeshift hanger and launching pad. Normally, there would be a full shift on duty, but tonight the halls were silent. A ruse to see if Dauber would act? She was sure they were under surveillance, which meant command would know if anyone tried to access the transport. Or if May were to say anything incriminating.

So far the woman had said little. Not just tonight, but for the entire six weeks Emma had been assigned here. Maybe it would help if she knew more about the scientist. Maybe she would reveal something about Dauber that would help Emma assess just how much of a threat he posed.

They set the trunk down at the security lock that had been installed on the loading dock entrance. Emma had to input her fingerprints and submit to a retinal scan. When she stood up from the scanner, May was watching her, smiling.

"What?"

May shrugged.

Emma paused, her hand hesitating at the enter screen. "Tell me."

"You really want to know?"

After clearing both scans, Emma folded her arms across her chest.

May sighed. "Fine. It's not really secure." She gestured at the control panel with its input screens and lights. "Chaz and I offered to upgrade the defenses but Brent turned us down. You'd think he didn't trust us, or something."

"How do you know it's not secure?"

"You really don't know anything about what we do, do you." It wasn't a question.

"Above my clearance." And not the kind of problem she was trained to solve.

The petite scientist sat down on the trunk. "We design and create Artificial Intelligences and the human interfaces that interact with them." She pointed up at the lock device. "That's an isolated system. A simple input device that cross checks the patterns in your fingerprints and retinal scan against a known database. If it were connected to a true AI, the security protocols and pattern recognition algorithms would be close to infallible. I can think of at least a dozen ways to defeat your system that Mnemosyne would not be susceptible to."

"Are we in any danger?"

"From what?" May sprang up from the trunk and shoved it with her foot. "We're in a building swarming with armed soldiers."

Emma brushed her left hand across the cool surface of her firearm.

"I don't think anyone wants my clothes and my kit bag, do you?"

"The contents of your trunk aren't classified." It was the closest Emma could come to asking her about the work May and Dauber were doing.

"No. It's the contents of our minds that's the problem." May sighed again. "Lets get this stowed so I can help Chaz finish in the lab. Your commander has made it abundantly clear that what doesn't make it on the transport doesn't come with us."

With one last glance at the scientist, Emma went through the security protocols again and waited for the doors to unlock. The transport's storage bay was still mostly empty. She hoisted the trunk by herself and secured it against the wall in free-fall netting.

The locks engaged as she stepped back into the building side of the loading dock. For as much good as they would do, if May were right.

As they headed back to the lab, May paused at the entrance to the commissary. "I'd better bring up some food. He forgets to eat and then he gets cranky."

Emma smirked. How could you tell? "Fine. I'll meet you there." Her orders were clear: observe and assess Dauber. Besides, aside from the security restrictions, the scientists weren't officially prisoners and she and Odachi weren't technically jailers. Though, to be honest, the line between security and incarceration was a thin one. Especially now.

"Can I bring you anything?" May asked.

"No." Emma was surprised by the offer. "No, thank you," she said, softening her tone.

Was Commander Brent just being especially paranoid? There wasn't a lot of official news from the blockade, but she'd been a soldier long enough to be able to fill in the star chart. If Brent had had definitive proof, he would have acted instead of sending her on this close recon.

Emma woke to silence and the high shine of bright lights on stainless steel. Her right arm was a numb weight against her side. She turned her head, stared at her distant fingers, and willed them to move. They twitched slightly before stilling again.

A chair scraped against the floor beside her.

"Welcome back." Dr. May's voice echoed in the small room.

"What happened?" Emma's voice cracked.

May handed her a sealed water container with a straw. She drank it down without stopping and immediately started coughing.

"I was hoping you could tell me that." Her piercing blue eyes seemed to concentrate and then reflect all the light in the room.

She coughed up what tasted like smoke from the lab—metallic and oily. "I guess we made it to the orbital lab."

May nodded. "Odachi put us on communications blackout as soon as we got here."

"How long?" Her voice was hoarse and speaking hurt. She handed May back the cup and the woman refilled it without a word.

"Not long. Just a few hours. I don't think the staff Odachi herded off the station in the transport were very happy, but they left." May's lips twitched into a brief smile. "Of course, he did threaten to shoot them all."

Well, that was something. "So we're alone up here."

Odachi stood in the doorway. "For now."

Emma nodded. "My arm?"

"We pumped you full of fluids and pain meds. The good doctor removed a fifteen centimeter hunk of shrapnel from your shoulder and filled the wound with emergency glue."

"It's just a temporary fix. You're going to need to see a surgeon. Probably sooner rather than later."

The meds explained the vaguely floaty feeling she had. "I didn't think you were that kind of doctor."

"I'm not." She lowered her eyes and her hands trembled. "Chaz was. Biomedical engineering and cybernetics. Please. What happened in there?"

"I don't know." Emma wiped her left hand on the sheet covering her, remembering the blood. It still stained the skin on her palms and around her nail beds. She looked up at May and winced at the pain in the woman's face. "Any word from Brent?"

"Command knows we're here," Odachi said, shrugging. "But there's been nothing. No word on the condition of the research building or if there were any other casualties. No intelligence or forensics on the explosives used in the lab. Aside from the three of us and whoever the Commander has officially informed, I suspect no one knows that Dr. Dauber is dead."

"Now what?"

"I have to go back to work." May blinked back tears.

✳

"I can't believe he's gone," May said. "Thank you. For trying to pull him out."

"I was doing my job." Uncomfortable with the woman's grief and gratitude, Emma turned away. If May only knew that her job included orders to kill Dauber if necessary, they would be having a very different conversation.

"He was a good man."

A good man that command believed had turned traitor.

May fell silent for several minutes. "Odachi. Can he be trusted?"

Emma jerked her head to face the woman.

"I need to know. Is he a good man?"

The question troubled Emma more than she wanted to admit. Was Odachi a good man? Who was she to judge? "We're soldiers, ma'am."

✳

Brent sent them no new orders. He did, however, send up the security detail that had been slated to fly with them to the station, before their precipitous departure. The first thing they did was lock down comms except for the progress reports May had to give twice a day.

Over the next week, Emma quickly fell back into the rhythm of twelve-hour shifts, supervising May. The woman never seemed to sleep. Odachi barely spoke with her other than to urge her to return planet-side to get her arm assessed. But it wasn't an order and she insisted on staying. She wasn't exactly sure why.

Was Odachi a good man? Emma turned May's question over and over in her mind. Did she trust him?

Odachi sat on a tall stool opposite the table May was using as her desk. With each of them overlapping only twice a day and for just a few moments, it was hard for Emma to get a sense of the man. Certainly ever since the events in the lab at the university, he'd been keeping May under his close watch. And she knew he'd been practicing with the target sims, including under full battlefield conditions.

"She's all yours," Odachi said, yawning.

They could do twelves for a bit longer, but they were tough, especially when there wasn't anyone to give them a shift off. They hadn't spoken about it, but neither of them suggested adding any of Brent's guards to their rotation.

Emma watched him as he strode out of the lab. She turned back to May. "Can I get you anything?"

The woman shook her head. Except for when May had changed Emma's dressings, she had turned grimly silent since they had gotten here. It was different from the reserve that had always seemed to surround her. Sometimes, Emma would find her staring out one of the port windows blinking back tears. Then she would catch herself and work furiously, moving back and forth between precise handwritten notes and her tablet.

She muttered something Emma didn't catch. "Ma'am?"

"I need Chaz." Her voice cracked and she leaned back from the desk, pressing the heels of her hands against her eyes. "He always checked my equations." She lowered her hands and pressed them against the desk. "I've done the best I could. I can transmit this ground-side during the next comms window."

"And then?" Emma hadn't meant to ask that aloud.

May looked up at her. There was a terrible sadness in her gaze. "Does it matter?"

Emma woke to the emergency siren and bolted out of the narrow bunk. Grabbing her holster, she buckled it over the light pants and shirt she slept in and slid into her half-boots. Her right arm was at least functional enough that she didn't need to keep it immobilized anymore, not that it was going to be useful for much in an emergency.

She listened for the alarm's pattern. If it had been a hull breach, the klaxons would have sounded in urgent, short bursts, but this one was for weapon's fire.

Shit. Emma raced from her quarters toward May's lab and nearly stumbled on a body in the corridor. One of their new security contingent and he'd been neatly shot in the exact center of his forehead with a tight beam at close range. She drew her sidearm.

The alarm continued to wail, accompanied by a red strobe. It would cover the sound of her approach, but also render her deaf to any enemies.

A second body lay crumpled on the floor, executed in exactly the same manner as her fellow soldier. Emma couldn't tell which of them was shot first, but it didn't matter.

Was Odachi a good man? He was definitely a good shot.

She ran faster.

The lab was empty except for a third body and the smell of recent weapons fire. May's notes and tablet were gone. There was no sign of Odachi.

Emma tore through the station, heading to the docking bay. There was no other place they could be. May and Odachi. The only question was if May was a prisoner or a willing accomplice.

Just outside the docking bay, she passed a fourth body. And a blood trail leading toward the door. That meant only two more guards, unless they were dead in their bunks. And either May or Odachi had been hit.

Why was Emma alive? If Odachi was planning on going AWOL, he should have killed her, too. He had to have known she'd be honor bound to stop him.

She burst into the docking bay, her weapon steady in her hand, the slight hum of its powerpack a comforting menace. The smell of burnt flesh hit her before she saw Odachi pulling a limping Dr.

May toward the airlock. Her left ankle was wrapped in a clumsy bandage. The wound left a smear of blood across the room.

"Stop!" Emma ordered. She aimed her sidearm in the center of Odachi's chest. At this distance, there was little chance she could miss.

He turned. The right side of his face was a ruin of blistered skin.

"Let her go, Odachi!"

May yanked him closer to the lock. It only took a fraction of a second for Emma to understand that she was not his prisoner.

Odachi lifted his weapon.

Emma tightened her finger on the trigger.

"Enough!" May shoved Odachi hard and the two of them stumbled as the arc of Emma's blast hit the wall behind them.

"Corporal Gutierrez, please," May said. "Just turn around and leave. We've all been betrayed and I'm trying to make things right."

Emma took a new aim at Odachi. "Ensign, I've counted four bodies so far. Care to explain?"

He winced and she wasn't sure if it was from the pain or her question.

"You think you're the only one with secret orders?" His quiet voice filled the docking area.

"Please," May repeated. "You don't want answers to these questions." Her wound was still weeping blood and the drip drip drip of it on the floor was an urgent ticking of a clock.

"Yes I do." Emma was breathing fast, as if she'd just run kilometers instead of walking across an open room.

Odachi stared at her with a steady, unblinking gaze as if he hadn't noticed that half of his face had gotten seared. "Someone didn't want to wait for whatever proof you could find. My orders were activated. When you went to help May pack, I relieved the guard you called, incapacitated Dauber, and rigged the lab to blow."

She stared between May and Odachi. He just admitted to killing Dauber. How could she stand by him so calmly?

"I was told to destroy the AI, isolate May and keep her working. You weren't supposed to be here. The blast at the door was supposed to take care of you."

"You should have killed me this time."

"She asked me not to."

"Give me one good reason not to kill you both."

"I can give you ten thousand," Odachi said softly.

"I don't understand."

"Marast 3. That's how many civilians live on the colony there. Did you know I was born on Marast 3?"

"What are you talking about?" He was a Commonwealth soldier. It didn't matter where the hell he was born. Besides, not every colony was on the side of the independence movement. And not all the indies supported the rebels. Officially Marast 3 was one of the neutral ones.

May patted his arm. "Let me. It's okay." She limped towards Emma keeping her hands open in front of her. "The work we were doing." She swallowed hard. "Chaz and I. We were tasked with creating a virus to disable an AI. We thought the threat of it would help end the war. Bring the Commonwealth and the rebels to the negotiating table. Stop this insane hemorrhage of lives and resources. We were so sure they wouldn't risk deploying it.

"We were wrong. Chaz found out they were planning to target civilian populations and blame the independence movement." She trailed off and winced as if in pain. "It's not just rebel ships. AIs control everything on the colonies, too, from basic life support to the power station to mine infrastructure."

Emma didn't have to work too hard to imagine the catastrophic consequences. "Where's your proof?"

"Chaz hid it on Mnemosyne."

Which Odachi had blown up along with the scientist. "Convenient."

"Do you really believe that?"

Emma didn't know what to believe anymore.

"Chaz had a temper. He threatened to go public on the net." Dr. May smiled ruefully. "I think he knew he wouldn't survive past the completion of our work, but he tried to shield me. Told them I didn't know anything. That I hadn't finished the error correction and testing.

"We just hadn't counted on them acting so quickly. Or ordering the destruction of the lab. We thought we'd have more time." May's breath caught in a sob. "I thought I'd have a chance to say goodbye."

"But you finished the program," Emma said, barely breathing. "You transmitted it this morning."

"A crippled version. Along with the supposed anti-virus protection for Commonwealth-based AIs."

"Supposed?"

"Yes. If they're stupid enough to deploy it, it will not discriminate."

May stumbled and it took all of Emma's self-control not to help her. The gun remained steady in her left hand, targeting Odachi.

"And now what? You head off and contact the rebels? Sell them your services?"

"No. I disappear. So no one can use me as a weapon anymore."

"Why did you choose him?" She gestured at Odachi. "He killed Dr. Dauber. Obliterated your proof. Assassinated Commonwealth soldiers. What makes you think he won't kill you?"

"He was supposed to. Once I completed the virus. And honestly? Oblivion would be a blessing. A lot of people are going to die because of the work Chaz and I did. But maybe, just maybe it will end the war." May met Emma's gaze with a direct stare. "I needed a pilot with two functioning arms. You were injured. I didn't have a lot to choose from. As for Taro here, he signed his own fate with the blood of his fellows. We both have to live with the consequences of our choices."

May limped a little closer. Not close enough to be a threat, but close enough that she and Odachi presented two divergent targets.

"And now you have a choice, Emmaline Gutierrez. You can kill us and this ends here. A lot of people on both sides of the war get hurt. Or you can let us vanish. Let me work to leave something other than mass death and destruction as my legacy."

Emma had no direct orders. At the very least, her superior officer was guilty of murder and dereliction of duty. He'd killed Dauber and nearly killed her under orders. But those orders were illegal by any interpretation of the rules of war.

"Taro," May said softly.

Odachi nodded and lowered his weapon, leaving himself open and unguarded. She could kill them both in the span of a few heartbeats, report in, and be a war hero. Move up in the ranks. Maybe even end up an officer.

A tiny sound startled her. Just a small scrape from the station side of the docking bay door. By the time she recognized it, the manual release had triggered and a wounded soldier lurched through, dragging his leg behind him.

Before Emma could react, he fired his weapon. Odachi crumpled to the floor. The smell of cooking meat and burned polymer filled the room. May cried out and it broke Emma's momentary stasis. In a smooth movement, she whirled and fired. The injured soldier's eyes widened before he fell. A ten centimeter hole smoked in the center of his chest.

Her hands shaking, Emma stepped over to where Odachi lay and pressed the hot barrel of her gun into his temple, growling incoherently. He didn't move.

"Emmaline." May's soft voice penetrated the buzzing in her ears. "Is this your choice?"

"Can you do it?" Emma asked, not taking her gaze from Odachi.

"Do what?"

"End the war. Save civilian lives."

May took a deep breath. "Yes."

She pulled the muzzle of her gun away, leaving a perfect circle of red behind and kicked Odachi in the leg. "Get up. Get up now."

He groaned and his eyes fluttered several times before he could focus them. The security officer had hit him in the left arm. The material of his uniform shirt was melted into the wound. So much for a pilot with two good arms.

"Go. Get the hell out of here."

May limped over to the fallen Odachi and helped him to his feet. "Thank you."

"Don't. Just don't. I didn't do this for you." Emma looked back at the soldier she had just killed. He could have been any of her squad-mates in the 24th. Someone she was sworn to protect and fight beside.

No longer.

She was no better than Odachi. There was no honor in this. In any of it. Not in a Commonwealth that killed its own. Not in a war that targeted civilians. And now she, too, was guilty of treason. She stood up and aimed the gun at her own temple. At least she couldn't be court martialled if she were dead.

May reached up, covered Emma's left hand with her own, and pushed it down. "No. There's been enough death on my account."

Emma blinked back tears. The doctor's earlier words filled her mind. *So no one can use me as a weapon anymore.*

That's all any of them ever were. Weapons. Tools to be manipulated and scrapped when no longer useful. Scientist, soldier, flitter, gun. It was all the same.

She slipped the gun into her right hand. Her injured hand. It shook slightly. "No," she echoed, but she was responding to a different imperative. As May exhaled and relaxed, Emma lifted the gun. And she shot her own left arm at point blank range.

Heat seared through her and the pain followed. Her anguished howl filled the docking bay. The room slid sideways and she stared up at May, confused. When had the scientist gotten so tall?

"Why?" May's voice was a horrified whisper. She knelt at Emma's side, her hands fluttering uselessly in the air beside her.

"Hey, look, no blood." Emma stared at the burned ruin of what had been her shoulder and upper arm.

"Why?" May insisted.

There were tears rolling down her face. The doctor was crying for her. For her.

Odachi looked down at her. "I'm sorry." He turned to Dr. May. "We have to go. Now. Or never."

"We can't leave her!"

"Trash the docking bay," Emma said. "Drag me out of here and set charges." Her voice seemed to come from someplace very far away. "Do it!" Everything made sense now. They had to leave. Make it look like they'd blown themselves up in the process. She had to stay. Stay to cover their tracks. And with her gun hand ruined, she would never be just a weapon again.

There was a strange logic to her thoughts. She stared at Odachi. "Get her out. Don't waste this." The nerves in her left arm were screaming and it was getting harder and harder to focus her vision. "If I ever see you again, you're a dead man."

May squeezed her right hand and everything went black.

✳

An insistent beeping interrupted the silence. Emma tried to lift her arm to swat the noise away, but her arm didn't listen to her.

"Welcome back, Corporal."

She blinked her eyes open. Bright lights nearly blinded her.

"I'm sorry. We couldn't save it."

That's why she didn't feel any pain. It was okay. Being alive was a surprise. She just wasn't sure it was a welcome one.

"Are you up for a visitor?"

She wasn't sure she was ready to stay awake either, much less talk to anyone.

Voices slid past her and she let them. It had nothing to do with her. A chair scraped along the floor.

"Corporal, how are you feeling?"

The voice was familiar, but it was shrouded in haze and she couldn't identify it.

"Can she hear me?" the man asked.

"Yes, Commander."

Commander. Commander Brent. Emma's thoughts sharpened to a knife's edge. Brent. And it all came flooding back. Dauber. The dead soldiers. Odachi. May. Treason. Treason and lies. She glanced back at where her left arm should have been. It was an empty place covered by a thin sheet.

"Corporal?"

"Yes, sir."

"What the hell happened up there? The salvage team is still combing through the wreckage."

She closed her eyes again. Good. No one would know what she had done. "Odachi killed them. The security detail." The man Emma had hit was so clear in her mind. His expression of surprised betrayal would be with her forever. Her own heart ached with an echo of her kill shot.

"What about Doctor May?"

Emma sighed. "Dead."

"Tell me."

She drifted off again and started at a rough touch on her right arm.

"Corporal?"

He wasn't going to leave her alone until she gave him some kind of answer. May's voice echoed in her mind. *Emmaline, is this your choice?*

She had made a choice. It may have been her first real choice in a lifetime of obeying orders. "Odachi thought I was dead. I trapped them in the docking bay. Set my powerpack to overload."

"What happened to Dr. May, Corporal?" Brent's voice was as insistent as the station's alarm had been.

May's earnest gaze shone in her memory. There were so many dead. Too many. What were two more in the official record?

"Dead," Emma repeated softly. "She's dead."

LJ Cohen is a novelist, poet, blogger, ceramics artist, and relentless optimist. After almost twenty-five years as a physical therapist, LJ now uses her anatomical knowledge and myriad clinical skills to injure characters in her science fiction and fantasy novels.

The events of this story take place approximately forty years before the start of *Derelict: Halcyone Space* book 1, available now.

Learn more at LJ's website www.ljcohen.net.

FALLING

A GIRL FROM ABOVE STORY

PIPPA DaCOSTA

Do you know what the biggest lie in the nine systems is? It can't get any worse. It can always get worse. Unless you're dead. I wasn't dead, yet. But I'd soon wish I was.

"This is your fault, Captain." Francisca's voice bounced around the empty silo's innards. She tugged again on the rope knotted around our wrists, yanking my arms and bumping her back against mine. She'd said, "Captain," but what she'd really meant to say was, "Asshole." It would have been a step up from the names she'd been calling me since we'd officially met a few hours previously, right before we'd been thrown inside a water-storage silo.

Shafts of rust-orange light pierced the dark, spilling in through what looked like phase-bullet holes. At least we wouldn't suffocate. Sweat beaded at my hairline and crawled down my cheek. "I'm not sure how this is my fault when you're the one who told Jin exactly where he could shove his rig."

She muttered something that sounded distinctly Spanish and fidgeted, elbowing me in the ribs. This close, she smelled like lavender soap—that cheap brand fleet used. Much of fleet's used stock found its way to the out-of-orbit recycling rigs—scrappers, like this one in the Jotunheim system. All the crap in the nine washed up here.

A smile pulled at the corner of my mouth. If she'd just relaxed, I could've slipped the ties, but she hadn't sat still since Jin's guys had dumped us in the silo. If she kept wriggling, my thoughts would soon start a'wandering. It wasn't every day I was tied to a woman, even under duress. For her, anyway.

"You're supposed to be some kind of criminal mastermind, right? Jin's paying you for a reason. How are you going to get us out of this?" She twisted her head, glaring over her shoulder.

She must have been thinking of another Caleb Shepperd. "Criminal, yes. Mastermind, not so much." I was a fixer. Jin had paid me to fix her. The old man didn't like new and unknown folk in his backwater corner of the nine. She'd been taking the prime smuggling runs from his tight cadre of usual guys by undercutting and outflying them.

Making waves, Jin had called it. Exactly why the old guy wanted her gone didn't matter. I'd do anything for credits, but after I caught up with her on Ganymede and shadowed her runs between there and the Jotunheim system, it became pretty clear Jin shouldn't have been hiring assholes to kill her. He should have been recruiting her.

Fran lifted her head, bumped it against mine and growled out a curse.

"Sit still," I grumbled, digging my fingers into the ties to test their strength.

I'd seen her flare up in front of Jin like she owned the rig, not the other way around. She had to be outright nuts or stupid to rattle him. Maybe both. Although seeing Old Man Jin lose his sedate cool was almost worth the trip to his silo.

She was wriggling again. "I'll die of old age before you get to the rescuing," she said. Her hands twitched, and the ties fell away.

Tingling rippled up my arms. I rolled my shoulders, working out the stiffness. Fran was already on her feet, tapping the point of her dagger against her thigh. Dark shadows crowded her face, hollowing her cheeks and pooling in her eyes. In the light, her features—when not snarling—were an alluring combination of Spanish elegance, full lips, and sharp cheekbones. Soft and hard. But in the silo's smothering dark, the only pretty thing about her was the sly spark in her eyes. I'd seen that spark in her sideways glances when she'd unleashed a verbal tirade. It was there now, like she knew she was better than me in every way and I was something she'd like to scrape from her boot. She was probably right.

"You had a knife the whole time?" I asked, massaging my arms through my flight-suit sleeves, trying to work some feeling back in to the muscles.

She'd been frisked. Which meant she'd had the blade in her boots, or somewhere real close and personal.

"I'm always armed, Captain." She held out her hand. "Unlike you, I haven't survived in the black by looks alone."

Something told me if I took her hand, I'd be in for more trouble, not less. I should kill her. Keep it simple. Get away clean. It'd be a whole lot easier that way. Her tank top revealed enough muscle to show she'd put up a decent fight, and she was quick too. She'd proven that when clocking one of Jin's heavies in the face. But she wasn't a brawler. Jin's guys had kicked her legs out from under her and manhandled her under control in seconds. Her tongue was clearly sharp though—and her wits too.

I took her hand and let her yank me to my feet. Soft hands, smooth skin. That lean figure of hers was trained, not earned through manual labor. She still had the dagger out. I'd run a check on her dataprint when tracking her, and there was nothing in her past to suggest she'd use the weapon on me. Still, life in the black changed people.

Running a hand through my hair dislodged bits of grit. I wiped the sheen of sweat from my face and considered all the questions I needed answers to. Things hadn't exactly gone to plan. "What's a girl like you doing smuggling for scrappers?"

She made a dismissive pfft sound. "What's an ex-fleet captain doing hiding out in Jotunheim?"

I turned away and scratched at the back of my neck, pretending to examine the silo while hiding my face. So she knew I wasn't just the captain of a tugship. She knew who I was—who I'd once been. If I told her why I was keeping a low profile, she wouldn't believe me. Or she would. And then I'd have half of fleet's armada bearing down on my ass. I'd kept off their radar this long. Some backwater smart-ass bitch wasn't going to change that.

Expression back under control, I smiled—my default response when challenged. "Get me drunk when we get off this stinking rig and maybe I'll tell you."

"When we get out this silo I'm leaving your worthless ass and this godforsaken corner of the nine behind." She tucked her dagger back inside her boot and straightened. Her smile was a slippery thing, and when combined with her sly glances and her down-the-nose looks, it made it quite clear she had me pegged. She couldn't be much older than me. Maybe mid-twenties, but by the way she carried herself, chin up, shoulders back, she was a woman used to being right.

"Youngest fleet captain to earn his stripes?" She huffed a laugh when all she got from me was a scowl. "Don't look so worried. Doesn't matter who you are out here." She looked up and examined the silo's cap. "Boost me."

She wasn't getting out of here without my "worthless ass," but I wasn't escaping anytime soon without hers either. The silo cap would push off easily enough. But what was to stop her leaving me once she'd climbed out? She already knew I was ex-fleet and Jin's fixer. She'd probably already decided she knew my type. Shit, even I'd leave me behind. If she suspected I was being paid to kill her, she'd have already tried to stick me with her dagger.

"I don't think so." I scratched at my chin. "I'm stronger than you. Boost me, and I'll lift you out."

In the gloom I could just make out how one of her dark eyebrows lifted. "And I'm supposed to trust you?"

"Do you see anyone else here? I sure as shit ain't trusting you, honey."

"Why did Jin put you in here?" She started circling the silo, and me, kicking at the desiccated garbage strewn about the floor.

I swallowed, or tried to. Machine dust tainted the air, lacing my tongue with a metallic aftertaste. "Because I'm the asshole who tracked you through three systems and two jump gates, watching you profit from his loss. By the time I told him what I knew, he'd decided he didn't need me no more. Jin likes to make inconvenient people—like you—disappear." There were a dozen silos like ours in the scrappers yard, and I'd bet credits on some of them harboring more of Jin's enemies. Couple that with all the heavy crushing and metal-harvesting machinery, and it was almost too easy to grind human body parts to dust and scatter them in the black. I'd seen the old bastard smile while doing it.

She stopped her walk and faced me, closer this time.

"You can glare at me all day," I said. "But the longer you do, the more time Jin has to strip both our ships clean and think up new and exciting ways of dealing with nuisance smugglers." Rolling up each sleeve, I checked I had the cap directly above. "Boost me, honey."

Her eyes narrowed.

"C'mon." I beckoned her forward with a curl of my fingers, enjoying the way her scowl touched me in all the right places. "I don't bite. Unless you want me to."

She sauntered close and cupped her hands between us. "*Pinche* idiota."

I didn't speak a word of Spanish, but I sure liked how it sounded on her lips. "Ready?" I settled my hands on her shoulders, surprised at her softness. I'd expected her to feel as hard as steel, just like her words.

She rolled her shoulders beneath my grip. "As I'll ever be."

I barred a smile from my lips. She wasn't going to give an inch in anything. Stuck in a silo with an asshole smuggler, and so far she'd taken it like it was just another day in the black. Most folks would be having a hard time battling panic. Not her. She had to know Jin had her number punched. So what was she afraid of?

I planted my boot in her hands and bounced off my back foot, reaching up to shove the silo cap free. It clattered down the sloped sides of the silo and landed with a clang on the platform outside. Fran boosted me again. I gripped the rim and heaved myself through.

The cavernous insides of Scrappers Rig 19 resembled a vast engine. The hungry rig gobbled up decommissioned ships, devoured anything of worth, and then melted down their remains. From my perch on top of the silo I could see three ships on the decom belt: a dilapidated warbird that looked as though it had been around since before the Blackout, the skeletal remains of a fleet freighter, and Fran's Pelican-class smuggling ship. I winced. Its guts had been torn out. Welders sparked, and metal clanged and chimed. That bird wasn't flying again. I could just make out Jin's orange-jumpsuit-clad guys picking through the remains like vultures back on old Earth. We were far enough away, clad in dark enough clothing, and surrounded by enough machine noise not to be noticed.

"Shepperd?" Fran's enquiring tone rang up from inside the silo, not quite concerned, but close.

I could leave her behind, find my ship before Jin gutted it, and be back in black in no time. I'd lose the last fifty percent of my paycheck but could make the first payment last a few cycles, if I skimped on luxuries.

But if I left, Fran would likely die in that silo. Or Jin would pass the time by running her through one of his compacters. Fleet didn't patrol Jotunheim. Nobody was going to come by and save her. I'd seen her skirt fleet's patrols during her smuggling runs. She'd outmaneuvered patrols like she piloted a warbird, not the heap of junk Jin's guys had stripped. She was too good a pilot to die in a Jotunheim scrappers rig.

I leaned over the hole and smiled down at her. Anger had tightened her features—now bathed in light—and pulled her lips into a thin line. The heat in the silo had loosened strands of her dark hair from her braid. They clung to her flushed cheeks. But man, those eyes were all wildcat fury. "Say, 'please.'"

"Besa mi culo."

I was fairly certain that wasn't "please," but it did sound delicious. I braced myself over the opening and reached down. She clasped my hand and I heaved her out through the hole. Steadying herself on the silo's sloped edges, she brushed her hands together and admired the view.

"That's my ship. Son of a bitch!"

"Say it any louder and they'll hear you on old Earth." Crouched low, I maneuvered my way off the silo and climbed down a ladder to the platform below. We were out of the silo, but that was the easy part. Getting off Rig 19 would be a whole lot harder.

She hissed a few more colorful Spanish phrases and joined me on the platform. "That ship was all I had. There are procedures. Formalities. They can't just steal what they like."

I might have laughed had we not been out in the open. Clearly she hadn't been in the black for long. "Ain't nobody all the way out here to stop them."

Bathed in the rig's orange work lights, she somehow managed to look both fierce and vulnerable. She brushed grit from her clothes, her strokes short and sharp. The anger was still there—I was beginning to think it never left her—but her shoulders sagged. She'd lost her ride. That was no small thing. I wouldn't wish being grounded in Jotunheim on my worst enemies, and I had a few contenders.

"Maybe I'll give you a ride out of here."

She eyed me sideways and brushed a few stray locks of hair out of her eyes. "And what do you want in exchange?"

Heavy equipment clanged and groaned in the belly of the recycling rig.

I pushed back against the wall, eager to get out of sight, and spied a nearby personnel door. "I'm sure we can agree on something, once we're back in black."

We made our way from the catwalks into narrow corridors and the guts of the rig. Pipes groaned and the occasional hiss of released steam blasted from pressure valves. Inside my flight suit my tank clung to my skin and rode up my waist. I wiped sweat from the back of my neck and steered my thoughts toward anything besides how close the walls were and how the air seemed to clog my lungs.

I took a right and climbed a ladder. Fran followed, her boots scuffing the floor. The rig layouts were all the same, so I figured the control room had to be a few levels up, and close. If we could get inside, I could locate my ship's dock and slip away unnoticed.

"Was Jin going to kill us?" Fran asked. Her voice carried into the steam-filled corridor ahead of us.

I stomped on, listening to the distant clang of metal against metal. "Jin's a ship short of a flotilla—he ain't all there. Never leaves this rig. That kinda life? Trapped in this place? There's not much reason left in his head. He'll kill us both—eventually."

"How do you know that?"

"I make it my business to know folks who owe me credits—know what makes them tick, should they ever try and screw me over." Her hot gaze crawled up my back as we strode on.

"Why is ex-Fleet Captain Caleb Shepperd hiding out in Jotunheim?" she asked.

"Same reason a merchant's daughter is," I threw back. I'd dug around her dataprint. Her past was peppered with the usual life junk—college, finances, pilots license—but clean. No offenses.

"You think I'm hiding?" A hint of disgust snagged her voice. From what I'd seen of her so far, hiding wasn't her way. And the thought clearly didn't sit well with her.

I checked over my shoulder. "You think I'm hiding?"

"I know you are." She smiled a playful smile and fell into step beside me.

So damn confident. I wanted to see her rattled, find out who she really was underneath all that swagger. "I didn't tell you why before. What makes you think I'm going to tell you now?"

"I spotted your ship." She lifted a shoulder in a half shrug, like it was no big deal, when we both knew I'd gone to great lengths to stay off her proximity sensors. "It took a bit of digging, but I tracked your ship's outdated ID and your name showed up on an old purchase order. There's a whole load of interesting things about a Caleb Shepperd in the cloud. Aren't you supposed to be in Asgard, Captain?"

Just mention of that godforsaken prison twisted my gut. Most folks didn't survive Asgard. Some days I wished I hadn't. I swallowed hard enough to clear the hitch in my throat. "Keep talking and I'll be leaving you here for Jin. He's too old to get it up, but he has his own unique way of getting his kicks. It's probably been a while since he last had a woman visit." I unzipped the upper half of my flight suit and shrugged it off my shoulders, letting it hang about my waist in the hope the air would cool me off. It didn't.

"Are you always such an asshole?"

"You bring out the best in me, honey."

"Shit, what are you like on a bad day?"

"Drunk, mostly." I picked up my pace. She matched it.

"Just when I think I've seen the worst the black can throw at me, I meet some lowlife piece of shit who lowers the bar for the rest of 'em."

"That's some high horse you're riding." I stopped dead and squared up to her. "Did daddy buy it for you? This lowlife is your only route off this rig."

If her dry, haughty look was meant to demean me, she'd have to try a whole lot harder. "You'd still be in that silo without me."

"You—honey—were the reason I was in the silo."

She shrugged and canted her head. "Maybe I'd rather take my chances with Jin than with a hired criminal like you."

"Be my guest. I don't take live cargo, anyhow."

The clang of a door slamming and the thud of boots reverberated down the corridor. Fran shoved me in the shoulder, shunting me deep between tightly packed pipes, then pushed in after me. A scalding-hot vent burned against my shoulder and a U-bend dug into my leg, but that wasn't the worst of it. When she eased back against my chest, her ass nudged me in the all the right places. She reached up to brace herself. I got an eyeful of the black dragon tattoo coiled around her biceps and squeezed my eyes shut. Breathe. This might have been easier if my heart had quit trying to hammer its way out of my chest. The heat, the hole. Shit, I needed air. I needed off this fucking rig. And whiskey to wash away the taste of confinement. Fran's shoulder nudged me in the chest. I huffed out a grunt. She shifted her hips and my thoughts veered toward more-familiar territory. The distraction of her pushed against me would do just fine. I gripped a pipe above my head and allowed my thoughts to dive deep, chasing the fantasy.

Boots stomped nearer.

If she screwed with the same anger she lived by, I needed to get myself a piece of that. I bowed my head and whispered close to her ear, "Just so you know, this is pressing all the right buttons. If you could maybe move a bit more, that'd be grand."

She turned her head slightly and smiled a shark-ish smile. "Make it last, Captain," she whispered. "This is as close as you'll ever get."

That didn't stop me from hoarding the feel of her pressed against me, for later use.

One of Jin's guys stomped by. I listened to the sounds of him descending a ladder, and then Fran was out and moving—the wrong way.

"Hey," I called, staggering out of the gap.

She raised a middle-finger salute over her shoulder and sauntered back the way we'd come.

I admired the sway of her hips. If she was going to walk away, I was going to watch.

Shit, it had been a while, but I had more important things to focus on than her ass, such as saving my ass. Suck it up, Shepperd. If she wanted to get lost on the rig rather than let me help her, that was her mistake. She had a dagger and could clearly look after herself—if she kept that sharp tongue clipped.

I made my way toward the control room. Jin and his crew wouldn't be too difficult to slip. The rig was vast, and manned by just a handful. If it was my lucky day, I'd be black bound and looking for my next job before Jin noticed I was gone.

Lady Luck and me have never really gotten along.

∗

Piles of junk cluttered an otherwise-empty control room. I made my way through mounds of spare parts, scrap metal, and shit I didn't even want to identify and stopped in front of the live-feed monitors. Maintenance used them to pinpoint any problems with the machinery. I scanned the screens, searching for the distinctive shape of my tugship. If Jin had laid his hands on her, I'd run him through one of his machines and scatter his remains throughout the nine systems.

"Well?" Jin asked, jolting my heart into my throat. He moved about his rig like a damned ghost.

I didn't turn. There was little point. He either had a pistol on me or didn't.

"She's capable." I continued to scan the screens for my ship, fighting the urge to bolt. "Maybe even privately trained. Old Earth, or she's spent long enough there to pick up a trace of the accent. Dataprint says she's the only daughter of a merchant running supplies from the original system to Lyra. She was all set to inherit daddy's business, and she must have figured she'd take off. There's a lot of black to get lost in. She doesn't quite know yet how things work out here. Hardly a threat."

"Then why's she sniffing around my business?" Distrust snarled through his words. "Why her? Why now? This is all mine. I won't let it go."

Now I turned. Slowly, like everything was perfectly fine and I hadn't been about to hightail it off his rig without upholding my end of the deal. His hunched frame blocked the doorway. I'd compared his crew to vultures, and with his long nose and narrow face, Jin sure looked like one. He had a pistol tucked into a makeshift holster, within easy reach of his filthy clawed hands. His skin was the color of rancid meat, his hair a stark white. He should have died years before, but the stubborn bastard was hoarding his remaining time like he hoarded scrap metal.

"As far as I can tell, she's out here for the credits." Same as me, I added silently. I sure wasn't on Jin's rig for the scenery. "She's not interested in you personally. Just easy money." *Just trying to get by in the black.* Weren't we all? I didn't know what Jin's paranoia had him all excited over, and I didn't care. He'd paid me half up front to get answers, and half would follow when I killed her. Or so he thought. The first half would do me just fine. I'd killed for money, but I wouldn't this time. Not for this old man and his mountains of metal.

"That's all you got out of her?"

"Whoever searched her did a piss-poor job. She had a knife. Cut herself free in the silo. The plan doesn't work if she escapes before I can talk her 'round."

"Clearly," the old man grunted. His hooked fingers drifted over his pistol. "Nobody worth their weight in iron comes out here without a good reason. She wants something." Jin darted his tongue across his bloodless lips and then rolled them together. "What about you, Shepperd?"

"Me?"

He moved through the cluttered room slowly, like a wounded animal, but the old-bastard routine was all for show. I'd seen him slap down one of his crew and put a bullet between his eyes in the time it took him to lament the loss of the good ol' days.

"What are you doin' out my way?" His gaze shifted, never really settling on anything long enough for his watery eyes to focus.

"I needed a change of scenery when your call came in." Why were we talking about me? We'd already had this conversation when I'd taken the job. "There's only so many jumps I can do before my routes get flagged for suspicious activity. I

gotta shake things up, make it look authentic-like."
I turned my back on him, hoping to give him the
impression all was well, and scanned the screens
again. Where had the old guy put my ship? Boots
thudded behind me. I turned, projecting noncha-
lance until one of Jin's heavies ushered Fran into
the room. She screwed her nose up at the stench of
machine grease but seemed unharmed and unruf-
fled. My gut sank.

"She—" Jin thumbed over his shoulder at Fran,
"—says you're fleet."

Shit. "Fleet?" I spluttered a laugh. "What? I'm
not fleet." My heartbeat drummed in my ears. I had
a hostile audience, and in the middle was Fran with
her crazy-ass smile. "She's lying."

Jin's shrewd eyes narrowed. "Shepperd, I hired
you on recommendation. I don't put much weight
in a man's past. You don't get by in the black without tough choices. I reckon it's the choices we make
today which matter. Can't change the past, right?
But after we caught this 'ere woman breaking into
your ship, and she starts bleating about a fleet captain on my rig, I had one of my guys do some more
digging." He sucked in air between his few remaining teeth. "I don't like them fleet fuckers, which
means I don't like you, Shepperd."

They caught her breaking into my ship? Oh, Fran was good. When had she figured out I was playing her for intel? From the first word, probably. So what was her angle? Turn all eyes on me so she could slip away? I mirrored her smile. "C'mon, Jin. I might have been fleet. Once. A long time ago—"

"Two years."

"Okay, two years ago." A goddamned lifetime for me. I did not want to be explaining my short fleet career and subsequent prison stay to Jin, and I scraped a hand across my chin. "You're right about the past. Doesn't mean shit right here and now. We had a deal. Just you an' me."

"Yes, we did. She also says you were planning to depart without notifying me. Our deal isn't done. Is it, boy?"

My shallow smile grew. I opened my mouth to explain, or lie, or bluff, but the tangle of words lodged in my throat.

The old man's hand rested over his pistol. He'd shoot me down and grind my remains to dust for entertainment. His crewmember stood quiet, face blank, but his eyes were hungry for violence. A very real smile curled Fran's lips.

Jin's shrewd, unblinking glare pinned me still. Outnumbered and outgunned, I had limited options. "Jin." I lifted my hands, palms out. "I hate fleet as much as you do. Probably more."

"Or maybe they sent you out here to spy on me?"

I snorted, tossed my gaze around the room, and sighed. "Your rig, your mountains of crap—there ain't nothing here worth their time."

His watery eyes widened and his gun hand twitched.

"Fleet don't give a shit about Jotunheim, and couldn't care less about some crazy rig owner stripping ships and not paying his dues." I inched forward. Only crazy folks reasoned with crazy folks. Talk wasn't going to save me. Fran reached down and slipped her fingers inside her boot. She'd obviously reached the same conclusion. I swallowed, licked my dry lips, and continued, "Why do you think I'm all the way out here?" I laughed a little and stole another step forward. "It certainly ain't for the hospitality. The pay's good, but the alcohol's like thinners and the women all look like you. Stop worrying about me and start worrying about her—"

Jin drew his pistol. I lunged. The gun fired too fucking loud in the cramped room. Fire blasted through my right arm, but I was already moving. I plowed shoulder first into Jin's gut, slamming him into the wall. It wouldn't be enough. Pain throbbed up my arm and radiated through my shoulder. Jin smacked his forehead into my face. The inside of my cheek split, spilling blood across my tongue. I wrangled with his wrist and arm, trying to pin him down—Damnit. He's a whole lot stronger than he looks—but he bucked like a mule. I brought a knee up, and it impacted hard with his gut. But all that did was double him over so he could shove his face in mine and try and bite a chunk out of me. His hot breath smelled like wet metal, and those crazy eyes rolled back. But I had him, if I could just—

Arms grabbed ahold of me from behind. A sharp blow to the back of my skull jolted down my neck, then a rapid silence and numbing dark rushed in.

Shit can always get worse. Unless you're dead.

I hurt too much to be dead.

Cracking open my eyes, I winced as needles of pain jabbed me in the back of the skull. I should never have agreed to this job. I could have been on Ganymede, running drugs, getting drunk in Tink's bar and forgetting.

I dangled by wrist ties hooked into a pulley system, arms stretched high. And I wasn't the only one. At first, I couldn't wrap my head around why

Jin would have a butchered animal carcass hanging around his storage rooms. And then the stink hit me. The slab of flesh hanging from a pulley system like mine was human. Jolting out of my daze, I twisted, scuffing my boots against the floor. Pain beat hot and hard down my arm and into my shoulder while sickness rolled up my throat. I swallowed excess saliva and wet my lips, praying I didn't throw my guts up. Jin could have killed me while I was out, but that wasn't his way. The crazy bastard liked to have his own brand of special fun first. By the time he was done with me, I was gonna wish he'd been a better shot.

I craned my neck to get a look at the six-foot machine looming just behind me, its wide nozzle pointed at my back. A sandblaster; lovely. My brother had once told me I'd die in some alley somewhere if I didn't get my shit together. The joke was on him: Caleb Shepperd—sandblasted by a compulsive hoarder in Jotunheim. A manic chuckle bubbled up my throat.

Jin leaned on one of many curved metal panels strewn about the windowless room. "You're more crazy 'an me, Shepperd."

A sense of humor was about the only thing I had left. That, and my ship.

Fran sat against a panel near the back of the room, her tied wrists resting over her drawn-up knees, guarded by the guy who'd clocked me over the head. My laughter cut off at the sight of Fran's bleak face. She'd die when Jin was done with me.

"How about we do a deal?" I asked Jin, pointing my toes down to stop myself from swinging. "There must be something you want. I'll carry any cargo. Let me go an' I'll get whatever your withered heart desires."

"I already have your ship. I'll strip her of anything valuable. That's all I need from you, Fleet Captain Shepperd."

My smile died. "You could go anywhere, do anything. There's a whole lotta black out there. But you'd rather stay in this stinking rig? You can hardly move for all the scrap. Haven't you stolen enough?"

"It will never be enough." Jin's glassy eyes hardened. "If the jump gates fail and the nine systems collapse again, I'll be prepared."

He really was nuts, and old enough to remember the last years of the Blackout. "You've been out here too long, Jin. Jotunheim's fucking with your head. Let me go and I'll take you to Lyra, show you a city made of stars. Drink and girls aplenty. Guys too. Whatever floats your boat. You'd love it."

The old man's top lip curled. "It's a lie, Shepperd, fed to you by fleet."

I knew that better than most, better than him. I blinked sweat or maybe blood out of my eyes. "Everything in the nine is a lie, Jin, but that doesn't mean we can't enjoy it. C'mon, you don't wanna live out the rest of your days here."

A flicker of fear darted across his gaunt face. What was he afraid of? Unless Jin couldn't leave. This rig, these broken bits of ship... They occupied his every day, his every thought, his entire life. He couldn't—wouldn't see a way out. My heart galloped harder and panic clawed at my thoughts. "All these ships, huh? And all you do is dismantle them. You're afraid to fly them. Afraid to leave." Afraid of freedom. Afraid of the black. He feared the very thing I lived for. He'd never leave, and he'd never change; some upstart ex-fleet captain wasn't going to alter a perspective buried under a lifetime's worth of junk. Shit, I was really gonna die here.

Fran's pale face confirmed it. She'd worked her fingers into her boot. The knife. Her guard watched me, assuming his quarry was beaten. Fran had better hurry up with the rescuing; the old guy wasn't going to let either of us go. I swallowed and darted my gaze back to Jin as he pushed himself off the panel and brandished the slim sandblaster control pad.

"I'm fleet," I blurted. "And you're right. It's all a long con. Why do you think I left?"

Jin tilted his head, his eyes flat and unerring. "Dismissed for misconduct, so says your data."

"I saw things. The lies you mentioned. It could happen again. The Blackout. Starvation—the wars an' riots. I can help you get ready. You need me, Jin. I can bring you more scrap, all kinds of shit people will need when the gates fail again." I'd agree the sky was purple and the nine systems were flat if he'd let me go.

Behind Jin, Fran had the blade out and hidden behind her hand. I gave my ties a tug, rattling the pulley wheels, keeping the dull-eyed guard's attention all on me.

The old man's thumb hovered over the control pad. Was it doubt delaying him? He didn't look doubtful, just pensive—like he might be committing my final moments to memory. How do you reason with insanity? There was nothing I could say, nothing I could do. No escape. Jin jabbed the controller. I flinched away, hiding my face for all the good it'd do me. The machine's generator coughed to life. The next press would kill me.

I twisted and bucked, trying to dig my toes into the floor. Nothing worked. This couldn't be it. I couldn't die here. There had to be…more. Mouth dry, I scratched around my head for any information I could dredge up from my past that might help now. "Killing me is a waste. I have connections—"

He'd moved closer while I'd fought with my ties. Was his gnarled, liver-spotted face the last thing I'd ever see?

"If I let you go," he calmly said, "you'll bring fleet here and they'll change everything."

"No." My voice cracked. "I'll work for you. They won't come."

He smiled, but it was a thin wisp of smile, barely skimming his lips. So flat, so cold. Old Man Jin was already dead inside. "You can run from your past, kid," he said. "But I reckon it's like running from your shadow. Fleet will come for you."

"Then…not like this." Any second now sand would pressure-blast my skin. My racing thoughts imagined it would feel like fire, like being burned alive. It wouldn't be quick. "Please, not like this."

The old man's face softened, and a flicker of hope skittered through my heart. *C'mon, you old bastard. Feel something…anything. Don't do this.*

"You're trouble, Shepperd. There ain't no place for trouble on my rig."

The guard's ragged cry whipped Jin around. Fran came for him, blocked a wayward swing with her forearm and plunged the dagger deep into his gut, then clutched his shoulder and pulled him into an embrace. She slowly whispered something into Jin's ear, her lips brushing his skin, and all the while she looked at me—through me—then she prized the control pad from his gnarled grip and let him go. He crumpled at her feet.

That fire in her eyes, the way she was smiling; was she about to finish what Jin had started?

"Wait—"

She jabbed the controller. I flinched, turning my head away, but the pain didn't come. Instead, the generator died and the machine powered down. My thoughts swirled, my head light and my body numb.

Fran reached up to cut me free. "You owe me, Caleb Shepperd."

The ties snapped. I fell to my knees, bracing myself against the floor while battling with waves of hot nausea and cold relief. The guard she'd taken out writhed and groaned, clutching at his bleeding ankles. Jin didn't move. His wheezing breaths sawed through the quiet. He'd die here, trapped by fear on the fringes of nowhere. Nobody would come. Nobody would care. *Fuck obscurity.* I was getting off this rig, and now.

"You know where my ship is?" I asked Fran, my voice rough and broken.

"Sure do." Fran wiped her dagger on her thigh and offered her free hand.

I closed my hand around hers without a single doubt. "Let's get black bound."

We made it one level before the yellow work lights flared bright white, chasing away the shadows. Alarms beat through the corridors. Fran ran hard, swung herself around ladders, and dropped down hatches so damn fast I had a hard time keeping up with her. After so many twists and turns, I lost track of where we were until we emerged near the rig's mouth—a jutting dock, currently sealed and sheltering my ship among a line of other vessels waiting to be stripped.

I pounded up the ramp only to find the locking panel hanging loose. Fran's handiwork. "Couldn't get in, huh?" I said dryly. I expected the lock to be intact, but at my trembling touch, the doors clunked and opened.

"Maybe I could, but had second thoughts about leaving your worthless ass behind?" She brushed by me, nudging my bleeding arm, and sauntered into the ship's hold. Her perpetual smile still threatened to break out, but didn't quite settle on her face.

"Women like you are the reason men die earlier in marriages," I muttered.

Shouts ricocheted behind me. A phase bullet smacked into the ramp somewhere near my feet. I ducked inside and sealed the door, wincing every time a bullet skipped off the ship's exterior. The bullets wouldn't penetrate, but that didn't stop them from hurting. I knew every wound on this ship like I knew my own scars. We'd gained a few more on this job.

"Get to the bridge."

Fran appraised the cargo hold with a less-than-impressed frown. "This bucket is an antique. We should have stolen the hawk next door. It'd be faster, and in better condition."

"Welcome to *Starscream*. She'll fly us straight, but keep talking like that and I'll leave you here. Go. Bridge. Now." My threat was an empty one. I owed her.

"You can't take off, you realize that?"

Man, she just knew it all, didn't she? I ignored her and left the hold, striding along the familiar catwalks, running my shaking hands along the rails. It was good to be home, even if we weren't yet free.

Fran fell quiet when we arrived at the bridge.

"Not so shabby now, huh?" *Starscream's* unusually pristine bridge was the only outward hint she wasn't all she appeared to be. I dropped into my flight chair and booted up her initial sequences, watching the rudimentary display blink a quick succession of system-check lights.

Fran gripped the back of the chair next to mine and peered out of the obs window. "They're never going to release us."

A quick glance out of the obs window and I counted half a dozen of Jin's guys waiting to see what we did. "I don't need them to."

Fran's fingers tightened on the back of the chair. "You can't fly manually in a pressurized bay. It's insane."

"Insane is coming to Jotunheim. This system is more fucked up than I am. Sit down," I said. "And strap in."

She moved the antique romance novel from the co-pilot's chair and to her credit didn't say a word, but the look she shot me was enough to summon a grin. *Yeah, honey. You think you know me. You don't.*

Starscream's engine noise quivered through the ship, and a similar thrill spilled through me, kicking my husk of a heart up a beat.

"What's the plan?"

"Plan?" I flicked the atmosphere engines to manual and gripped the flight controls in my grease-caked hands. A sharp twinge sparked down my arm, numbing my fingers. "Brute force and ignorance?"

"You're just going to take off? What about the umbilical? The clamps? The thrust alone will tear the ship apart."

I threw her look of disbelief right back at her. "Tugship. She'll pull this whole fucking rig before she breaks apart."

"The pressure door? You just going to fly right through that and expect to live, huh?"

"The bay will depressurize and the door will open on approach."

"And if it doesn't? If you try and punch through it, the blast will twist—"

"Ssh."

"But—"

This was the first time I'd seen her rattled. I liked it. "Do you trust me, Francisca?" A loaded question, designed to rile her.

"I trust you're an idiot."

At least she was honest. "'I trust you're an idiot, Captain.'"

She gripped the arms of her flight chair and muttered a string of Spanish.

"Close your eyes, if you think it'll help." I flexed my fingers on the grips, trying to clear the numbness. My arm continued to throb. If I didn't get out of the rig soon so I could go find the med kit, we wouldn't be going anywhere. I pulled back on the controls, turning the four atmosphere engines ninety degrees, ready to heave off the dock. *Starscream* responded in every way I knew she would. The rumble of the engines, the strum of the thrusters vibrating through her hull, even the damned flicker of the gyro light that I'd been meaning to fix for countless cycles. I knew it all, and could fly her in my sleep.

"You can't do this."

"You already said that. Any other last words?"

"No, Captain—you can't do this. You're wounded and you're not good enough. But I am."

She might have been right. She seemed to be right about a lot of things. It was starting to piss me off. I could fly in the open, but in a cramped bay like this one? I'd never officially tried it—definitely not with a rear-heavy tugship. Shuttles, yes. I could fly one of those through a canyon. But despite *Starscream*'s many upgrades, she was still a tug, and a bitch to handle at low altitude, in artificial gravity or tight spots, or in-atmosphere. Anywhere that wasn't the wide-open black.

"This is a mark-two independent tug." Fran's tone had taken on a hard, no-bullshit edge. "About the same age as you. She's all power and no finesse. Has a nasty bite at low atmo. Given her age, I reckon she's had, what? Three recalls to rectify the blow-back from her RR engines. Am I right?"

"Two recalls. I never got around to the last one, what with bein' a smuggler an' all."

Her frown scolded. "What's the first rule of the black, Shepperd? Look after your ship, and she'll look after you. Switch control to me."

"I thought the first rule was *expect to get screwed?*" I wasn't switching control to her. I barely knew her.

"How's the arm? Losing sensation yet?"

"Fine."

"You were out a good while, and bleeding all that time. And when Jin's guard cracked you over the head…" She winced. "Must hurt, huh? Those twinges, they're bitches. If one of those hits while you're flying in this cramped dock—" She sucked in air through her teeth. "Could kill us both."

I cast her a side-on unappreciative glare. She smiled.

"What are you afraid of, Captain? That I'm better than you?"

She wasn't going to shut up until I let her have control, and given how half my attention was already focused on not passing out, she was completely right to do so. "Okay." I sighed and flicked the master-control switch over to her. "But take her easy."

Fran immediately tapped out a few new inputs on the flight dash and wrapped her fingers around the controls.

"She pulls starboard, made worse when—"

"Shepperd. I have her." I must have broadcast fear all over my face, because she glanced my way and her smile softened. "Trust me."

She eased back on the controls and Starscream's engine whine dropped toward a growl. We pulled away from the dock with a godawful sound of grinding metal.

"The clamps will give," I said. "They always do." I may or may not have made some quick getaways from similar docks before.

The handful of orange-jumpsuit clad guys along the dockside quickly realized we weren't hanging around and fled the dock, sealing the pressure doors behind them. If shit went sideways, and we crashed and burned, those doors would keep the rig's internals intact. Unlike their boss, they weren't dying today.

Starscream jolted. Her port side dropped, and Fran wrestled with the controls. "I got her... We're good. One more clamp to go." More groaning rolled through the ship. The remaining clamp released. *Starscream*'s nose veered upward, hauling her ass away from the dock until the umbilical snagged. The ship twitched one way, then another, and all the while Fran corrected, keeping the ship from flipping stern over bow and taking a dive into the dock.

"More thrust," I suggested, gripping the flight chair.

"Thrust isn't everything, Captain. Sometimes you gotta go slow."

She was clearly enjoying my discomfort. "Too slow and you'll burn out—"

"Ssh. She's right where I want her to be. Are you sure the doors will open?"

"The proximity sensors will pick us up." I hoped.

The umbilical snapped, lashing across the dock, taking out much of the equipment in its path. Starscream bucked, but Fran had her. I sat in silence the whole time, while Fran piloted my tugship like she'd always been behind the controls. She turned the ship at the dock without an inch to spare, her hands working fast to correct Starscream's many

fluctuations. She'd been in the flight chair minutes and flew my ship better than I did. One of the
benefits of growing up the daughter of a shipping
merchant.

The pressure doors opened, and with a blast
of air, we left Rig 19 behind and punched into the
black.

When Jin had summoned me to his rig with
a job to track and kill a nuisance smuggler, I'd
expected someone like me. Fran wasn't like me. She
wasn't like anyone I'd met in the black. Instincts
told me to drop her at the next port.

"I did him a favor," she said, once we were well
enough away to relax. "He was rotting away on that
rig." She kicked back in the flight chair like it was
her own. "I put him out of his misery."

Jin might have disagreed with that assessment,
but I couldn't say I wasn't happy Francisca had my
back.

I needed to get my ass to the rec bay, so I could
fix up my wound, but that meant trusting her to
fly us straight. That thought had unease twisting
through my gut.

"Are you afraid of anything, Fran?" I asked.
Know a man's fears, know the man. Or so my father
had once told me. I didn't listen to much of his BS,
but he had a few gems worth holding on to.

Fran considered my words for a few moments. The background din of the engines cocooned the bridge in a comfortable quiet.

"Falling." When she flicked her gaze to me, a challenge burned in her eyes.

A half smile lifted the corner of my lips. "Plot a course for Ganymede."

✳

You couldn't move in Tink's bar without nudging some asshole with a bounty on his head. Ganymede's notorious hangout was exactly the kind of a place someone could keep their head down and hide in plain sight.

I was doing just that, while nursing a whiskey and watching Fran sweet talk a guy at the bar. Somehow she fit right in here, chatting with the dealers and outlaws like she'd always belonged.

She laughed at something her mark said, even threw in a little touch of his hand. Poor bastard didn't stand a chance. The crowd spilled in and blocked my view, interrupting thoughts of how I wouldn't mind her playing me. I soon scrubbed that fantasy clean. A woman like her was trouble. Maybe the kind of trouble that just might be worth it.

"You're going to offer me a job," she said, tugging me out of my thoughts. She dropped herself into a chair and sipped from a dirty glass. The drink had to have been paid for by her mark, given that everything she owned was back on her dismantled ship.

"I am?"

"Payback for saving you from getting sand in all those hard-to-reach places."

I smiled into my drink. She was right. Again. I had considered offering her a job as my second-in-command. A second meant *Starscream* could make non-stop runs. I'd double my profits even after her share. I'd had seconds before, but they didn't last. Most quit. The rest I'd fired before they could quit. I'd gotten used to flying solo.

"What did you whisper to Jin when you stabbed him?" I asked. The fact she'd filled Jin's last seconds with her words seemed important, and I'd been mulling it over in my mind. Whatever she'd said, I'd seen the look in her eyes, she'd made sure of that. Those words meant something.

Her dark lashes fluttered, the only outward sign she felt anything about killing a man. "*Cuando en medio de lobos, hay que aullar,*" she replied, her voice softer than before. The smooth roll of her foreign words licked pleasure way down low and had me shifting in my seat. It'd be worth riling her just so she dusted off the Spanish and I got a cheap thrill.

"Which means?" I cleared my throat.

She rapped her fingernails on the tabletop and skipped her gaze away too quickly for me to read. "'When among wolves, we must howl.'"

I could assume she meant that when trapped, she had to do what was necessary to escape—a parting explanation for the poor bastard she'd just stabbed in the gut. Or a reflection on her joining the ranks of predatory assholes, like me? Both, maybe. I'd sworn off curiosity, but in her case, I was having a hard time ignoring its siren call. I'd never know merchant-daughter-turned-smuggler Fran if I left her on Ganymede. My gut told me that was probably for the best. *Keep it simple. Get away clean.*

"My ship. My rules." She'd have a hard time following orders, but she'd tell it to me straight. Maybe that was what I needed. Someone not afraid of the truth. Speaking of the truth… "Exactly why were you smuggling in Jotunheim?"

She smiled and looked at me as though she already knew she'd gotten the job. "Easy credits. I fly faster, harder, and better than anyone else. Jotunheim's rep doesn't frighten me."

Leaning in closer, I said quietly, "What is it you're flying faster and harder from?"

She wet her lips. "A lot of things, Captain. Some you'd understand. Some you wouldn't."

"Try me."

"Mistakes, for one."

Now that I could understand. We all had our secrets. She'd scratched at some of mine. What I couldn't figure out was why she'd want to run with me. Ganymede's port was riddled with folks she could hitch a ride with.

"I'm a fixer." I relaxed back in my seat. "Pay me enough and I'll fix anything, from running illegal weapons to making someone disappear. If you wanna fly with me, check your morals at the airlock."

She sipped at her drink, eyeing me in a way that had me wondering who should be warning who off.

"Why me? Why not some other asshole? Ganymede is full of 'em. Your skills? You could get a sweet deal running legit cargo."

"You need me."

"Right." She had an ego bigger than mine. Impressive. I tipped my drink to salute her. "There are a lot of things I need, honey. A mouthy second on my back in the black ain't one of them."

Her know-it-all smile was back. She twisted in her seat, draped an arm over its back and nodded at the bar. "The guy I was talking with? Someone tipped him off there's a Captain Shepperd frequents Tink's. Apparently, Shepperd is a wanted man in Niflheim and there's a rich sum offered for his capture. I guess you wouldn't know anything about that?"

I frowned and checked the bar, but her mark had gone. "Where is he?"

"Took him out back for a bit of R 'n' R."

Shit, had she killed him?

"Not that." She grinned, easily deciphering the fear on my face. "He'll come around with one hell of a hangover." She leaned forward, bringing her close enough to whisper. "You might also like to know I heard on intra-system chatter that some hotshot ex-fleet captain should be in Asgard. Fancy that. Maybe fleet will come looking, maybe they won't. Maybe you need me, maybe you don't. I'm not afraid to fly with you, Shepperd. But you are afraid to fly with me." She leaned back. "Or are you just afraid of falling?"

Well, double shit. Tink's bar just took on a whole new sinister edge. When was Fran ever not right? If I stopped running—stopped flying, even just for a little while—I'd fall. And she knew it. She'd probably known it since the silo. I downed my drink and peered over the rim at Fran—the best damn pilot in the nine systems. "Welcome aboard *Starscream*."

✳

Read more from Caleb and Fran in the Girl From Above series, the space opera adventure readers are comparing to *Firefly* and *Ex Machina!* Available now at all good online retailers.

About the Author: Born in Tonbridge, Kent, in 1979, Pippa's family moved to the South West of England where she grew up among the dramatic moorland and sweeping coastlands of Devon & Cornwall. With a family history brimming with intrigue, complete with Gypsy angst on one side and Jewish survivors on the other, she draws from a patchwork of ancestry and uses it as the inspiration for her writing. Happily married and the mother of two little girls, she resides on the Devon & Cornwall border. Learn more at Pippa DaCosta's website: www.pippadacosta.com.

STARFALL STATION

A FALLEN EMPIRE STORY

LINDSAY BUROKER

Foreword: Thank you for checking out "Starfall Station," a fun side adventure in my Fallen Empire series (all right, it may not have been much fun for the heroes, but I enjoyed writing it!). It takes place between Books 2 and 3, but I've designed it to work as a standalone. If you're a new reader, I hope you will be intrigued by this introduction to my two main characters and that you might even want to check out the rest of the books. Thanks, and enjoy the adventure!

✳

HIERONYMUS "LEONIDAS" ADLER WAITED UNTIL LATE IN THE space station's day cycle to walk down the ramp of the *Star Nomad,* his hover case of damaged combat armor floating behind him. He could have carried the two-hundred-pound case easily, but he was a wanted man—a wanted cyborg—and he did not wish to call attention to himself by displaying inhuman abilities. Not here, not on a space station controlled by the self-proclaimed Tri-Sun Alliance.

His mouth twisted with bitterness. Almost everything was controlled by the Alliance now. When the empire had maintained order over the dozens of planets and moons in their vast trinary star system, Leonidas would have walked proudly onto the station, his head high as he wore his Cyborg Corps military uniform. He wouldn't have waited until the lights dimmed for night to skulk into the concourse on his errand.

Alert for trouble, Leonidas spotted Alisa Marchenko, the captain and pilot of the Star Nomad, when she was still hundreds of meters down the concourse. This did not take enhanced vision since she was leading a train of hoverboards, each piled more than ten feet high with crates. Her security officer, Tommy Beck, also walked at her side, his white combat armor bright and undamaged. Why wouldn't it be? He had spent most of their last battle hiding under the console in the navigation cabin.

Leonidas waited at the base of the ramp for them to approach in case they bore news that could affect him. Such as that squadrons of police officers or Alliance army soldiers were roaming the station, looking for stray cyborgs.

"Evening, mech," Beck called to him as they approached, his expression more wary than the cheerful tone would have implied. "Are you waiting to help us load these boxes into the cargo hold?"

"No," Leonidas said, his own tone flat. He would help if Marchenko asked him to, but was a passenger, not crew. Besides, he had little interest in assisting the security officer, a man who had served in the Alliance army during the war and who preferred to call him mech rather than use his name.

"Going to get your armor fixed, Leonidas?" Captain Marchenko asked, giving him a warm smile and waving at his case.

Alisa, he reminded himself. She had asked him a couple of times to use her first name, though he found the familiarity difficult. She, too, had been in the Alliance army, and she'd referred to him simply as "cyborg" for the first week after they had met. Still, they had been through a lot since then, and she had fought to keep the Alliance from capturing him during the Perun battle. She'd said that he had paid his fare for a ride on her freighter and that was that, but she had risked her life, doing far more than most civilian captains would do to protect a passenger. For that, he could certainly address her by her first name.

"I am," Leonidas said. "I made a late-night appointment with an excellent tech smith in Refinery Row."

"Better watch out for yourself, mech," Beck said, lingering instead of leading the train of cargo into the hold. "When we were out, looking for cargo-hauling deals, I saw lots of sleazy villains and opportunists skulking in the back alleys. And the not-so-back alleys. This station is rougher than it was the last time I came through here."

Leonidas was tempted to point out that the empire had likely ruled the last time Beck had visited. Of course the station had been safer and more orderly. The Alliance had been so busy overthrowing the throne that it hadn't worried about how well it could govern the system once it achieved its objective. But he didn't want to engage in a conversation with the security officer, so all he said was, "I've heard."

"I could go with you," Alisa said, still smiling at Leonidas.

He blinked slowly, perplexed as to why she made the offer. Something to do with his warrant?

"For my safety?" he asked.

She chuckled. "Yes, with my prodigious muscles and state-of-the-art weaponry—" she patted the bullet-slinging Etcher pistol in its holster under her jacket, "—I'll be your bodyguard."

"There's an image," Beck muttered. "Your head only comes up to his shoulders. Do you even weigh half as much as he does?"

Leonidas wanted to order Beck to trot up the ramp to unload the hoverboards and to butt out of his conversation with Alisa, but he wasn't a colonel anymore. Once, he had commanded a battalion and undertaken special missions for the emperor. Not anymore. He was nobody now. Except a man wanted for information he didn't have.

"I don't know," Alisa said. "We haven't jumped on a scale together and made comparisons. Why don't you get Mica to help load our cargo, Beck? She's got a hand tractor in engineering."

"Sure, Captain." He saluted, an Alliance army salute that came naturally to him, reminding Leonidas of what Beck and Alisa had been in the war, a noncommissioned officer and an officer. Alisa didn't act much like an officer, preferring flippancy and irreverence to stately shows of decorum and authority, so he could forget sometimes that she had been a captain and had flown ships against his people. Perhaps even against him.

"I just meant that I'd keep you company if you want it," Alisa told Leonidas as Beck ambled up the ramp, the hoverboards of crates barely fitting through the wide hatchway at the top. "You'll have to wait several hours while the smith repairs your armor, won't you? We could grab some dinner."

"I ate on board," Leonidas said before it occurred to him that she was making an offer of camaraderie rather than one of necessity.

In his youth, he would have caught that sooner, navigating the relationships between men and women without any more trouble than the average teenager, but twenty years with cyborg implants, in addition to the physical and biological changes the army had made to him, had left him a stranger to male-female relationships. He hoped to change that one day, perhaps even to have a family, but his quest to find an appropriate cybernetics specialist had been waylaid.

"Ah," Alisa said, her smile faltering. She turned to head past him and up the ramp.

"Coffee, perhaps?" Leonidas suggested.

"If I get a mocha this late at night, I'll be swinging from the catwalk," Alisa said, waving toward the elevated walkway in the cargo bay. Despite the words, she returned to his side and nodded toward the concourse. "Perhaps a decaf. Also, did you know that there's a shop in there that specializes in nothing but chocolate?" Her eyes gleamed. "It's open around the clock."

Leonidas didn't share her obsession with the sweet stuff, but he burned a lot of calories even when inactive, so he wasn't opposed to the occasional carbohydrate bomb. He subvocally ordered the case of armor to follow them as they left the ship. The earstar that hugged his lobe, awaiting his commands, relayed the order to the smart interface on the case, and it hummed along behind them.

The concourse was quieter than it had been during the day cycle when they had first landed, but the people they passed seemed more disreputable than the ones he'd observed then. Many wore hats and hoods that shadowed their faces, with few efforts made to conceal the BlazTeck firearms that they carried. Weapons had been illegal for civilians to carry, especially on ships and space stations, when the empire had maintained order.

More than one of those armed men eyed his armor case, but nobody approached him openly. A good set of combat armor was worth thousands, and even damaged, his would fetch a high price. But it had been issued by the imperial army, the crimson color of the case matching that of the armor inside, a color used predominantly by the men in the Cyborg Corps. Those who had served in the military, both imperial and Alliance, knew the meaning of that color, and many who hadn't knew it too. He doubted anyone here would be foolish enough to assault him.

Alisa cast a wistful look toward the restaurants and shops in the kitschy Castle Arcade, a wide walk-way lined with faux cobblestones, the buildings to either side and on the levels above ensconced in gray brick. If any castles on Old Earth had flash-ing cloud lights in obnoxious colors such as these, it would be news to the historians. Leonidas sup-posed the chocolate shop was down there.

Presuming she would be fine with waiting to visit until after he dropped off his armor, he guided her to one of the floating bridges that created tun-nels between the two massive cylinders that marked the different halves of the station, separating the shopping and entertainment region from the refin-ery that this station had first been built to house. The tech smith's shop was on that side.

The number of shoppers and passersby dwin-dled significantly as they stepped off the bridge and into a night-dimmed corridor. His ears, sharper than those of any unmodified human, caught the whisper of clothing rubbing together from around a corner at an intersection ahead. That wouldn't necessarily have alarmed him, but then he heard the snap of a battery pack being secured in a blazer rifle.

He shifted from walking beside Alisa to walking in front of her.

"Does this mean you're not open to hand-holding?" she asked.

He lifted a hand, hoping the gesture would be quelling. Her sense of humor came out at the oddest and most inappropriate times. Granted, she didn't have his hearing and likely did not sense the possible threat ahead.

Feet shuffled around the corner. The ceiling lamp over the intersection, already dimmed for night, flickered and went out. Suspicious timing.

Leonidas rested his hand on the butt of his destroyer, a deadly weapon some referred to as a hand cannon. It wasn't useful in stealth situations, but he had a feeling that making a statement might be ideal if muggers waited around the corner.

By the time he reached the intersection, his senses had informed him of three people waiting, two on one side, one on the other. The single person had light footfalls and sounded like someone small, perhaps a woman or a child. Leonidas drew his destroyer and with his left hand, removed a fluidwrap from his pocket. He wasn't as well-armed as he would be for going into battle, but with the warrant the Alliance had out for him, he had assumed he might run into trouble.

Before entering their line of sight, he glanced back at Alisa, this time lifting his palm in a stay-there gesture. Inappropriate humor or not, she had drawn her Etcher and appeared ready for a confrontation. That was good, but he had no desire for her to risk herself in some minor squabble.

Not making a sound, he burst around the corner. He threw the fluidwrap across the intersection at the smaller person while sprinting for the other two. He was tempted to shoot them, but they hadn't yet committed a crime. Also, he doubted the punishment for mugging was death on this station, and even if it was, he no longer had the authority to help enforce the laws.

Two big, fat tattooed men with long hair bound with beads scrambled back, their eyes widening. One carried an old shotgun more appropriate for hunting Arkadian ducks than men. The other had the blazer rifle Leonidas had heard being loaded.

He surged across the five meters between them and bowled the first man over, even as he registered that the second was lifting his arm to throw a fluidwrap of his own. Leonidas ducked as he hurled his first adversary aside, the ball-shaped projectile flying over his head, its energy netting unfurling too late. The shotgun clunked to the floor as the first man struck the wall so hard that he might have cracked his skull.

Leonidas realized he had used too much force, a constant problem for a cyborg capable of bending steel bars with his hands, but he did not feel much regret in this case. Realizing his net had missed, and perhaps what he was up against, the other man dropped his blazer and tried to back up, to flee.

He did not scurry away quickly enough to outrun a cyborg. Leonidas caught him around the neck and lifted him in the air, his feet dangling six inches above the floor. The man gasped and gurgled even though Leonidas was careful not to completely cut off his airway. His foe kicked futilely, the efforts so puny that Leonidas did not bother blocking them. His torso and thighs, enhanced with subcutaneous implants as well as ridges of hard muscle, could take a lot of abuse.

As he glanced toward the intersection to make sure his fluidwrap had, indeed, caught the third person—it had—the dangling man reached for a pistol holstered at his belt. Leonidas reacted instantly, tearing away the belt as well as the trousers it held up. He wouldn't normally rip off an opponent's pants, but he didn't want to hurt these people more than he already had and thought humiliation might do as much to end the fight as brutality.

"Are you done resisting?" Leonidas asked the man, chilling his voice to ice, an art he had mastered as an officer commanding hundreds of young, strong idiots.

His adversary's eyes grew round at the realization that his hairy legs were dangling, exposed to the alley and its occupants. Or maybe he realized that he was the only one capable of responding. His nearest ally was unconscious, and the young man on the other side of the intersection lay pinned by a net. The mugger's own net had flown uselessly wide and now plastered the wall, lighting it with electric blue tendrils that crackled and zapped. They would deliver a stun charge to a trapped person, but they had no effect on the wall.

"Leonidas?" Alisa asked from the corner, an odd note to her tone.

He looked to her, worried that she had spotted some other trouble. Her head and her firearm stuck around the corner, her gaze turned toward him.

"Am I disturbing you?" she asked, a smile quirking the corners of her lips. "I can leave you two alone if you want to take more of his clothes off."

Leonidas gave her a sour look. Of course she would make a joke. He should have known.

"I'm... done... resisting," his captured thug wheezed, Leonidas still using his throat as a handle by which to hold him up.

As he lowered the mugger to his feet, Alisa strode over to the one flattened on his back by the net. His features were hard to make out under the crackling blue energy of the net, but he looked young, fifteen or sixteen perhaps with an attempt at facial hair tufting his chin.

"What was the plan?" she asked him, tapping him on the chin with the muzzle of her Etcher. "Rob anyone who came this way?"

"Slavers are around," the boy said.

"On Starfall Station? Really? This used to be a respectable place."

"Always around," the boy mumbled, "and paying good right now."

"For cyborgs?" Alisa looked at Leonidas.

Leonidas barely glanced at them. He was searching his captive and removed a small pistol from his jacket pocket—amazing how a man with no belt or trousers could still be armed.

"For women," the boy said.

Surprise blossomed on Alisa's face.

"We were just going to shoot the cyborg." The boy's gaze slid toward Leonidas. "And take his armor."

"You'd just kill him? For no reason? Why, because he's not human?" Her tone had turned impressively frosty.

Leonidas watched her indignation with some bemusement since just a few weeks earlier, she'd been calling him cyborg and hadn't seemed to believe he was fully human. He did appreciate that once someone shifted from enemy to ally for her, she was loyal to that person. He hadn't experienced a lot of that from those outside of his unit, those who weren't cyborgs and didn't understand what it was like to be human, but different. Mostly, he encountered fear and uneasiness, even from men he had worked beside for years.

"Uh, because he had big guns," the boy said, wilting under her glower. He looked toward Leonidas, his expression hopeful, as if he might help him. Hardly.

Leonidas had been debating whether to let his captive go since the muggers hadn't actually managed to do anything to them, but that comment, along with the fact that they had wanted to sell Alisa to slavers, hardened his heart. He ripped off the man's shirt, drawing another look of surprise from Alisa, and tore it into strips. He used them to tie the mugger's ankles and wrists together, then moved onto the unconscious man to give him the same treatment.

"I suppose you'd find it unseemly if I made a joke about how you like to strip your captives and then tie them up."

"Yes." He didn't even know what she was implying. Something sexual, he had no doubt, but most such jokes went over his head.

"You're good to have along for a fight—or a mugging—but we need to work on your sense of humor."

"We?" After tying the first two men, Leonidas started for the third, but something on the ceiling behind the light fixture caught his eye. He berated himself for not noticing it earlier, but the fixture nearly blocked it.

"I'll help," Alisa said. "I like projects. In truth, I just want to see you laugh now and then."

"I laugh. When it's appropriate."

"You haven't laughed since I met you."

"We've been fighting enemies and fleeing for our lives since you met me."

"What about after we escaped from the pirates? Remember? Beck barbecued that bear meat. We were relaxing, chatting, and drinking Yumi's fermented tea since that was the closest thing we had to alcohol. Everyone was enjoying themselves, and Beck told jokes while he grilled."

"Beck isn't funny."

Alisa squinted at him.

Three suns, she didn't think Beck was a comedian, did she? Please.

"I laugh," Leonidas repeated sturdily.

"I don't believe you. Unless you do it alone in your cabin at night. Which I doubt, because I've heard you thumping around in there, presumably having nightmares."

He'd had an argument poised on his lips, a suggestion that maybe he did laugh when he was by himself in his cabin, but it froze before coming out. He hadn't realized that he made noise when he slept. That he had nightmares was no surprise— he remembered them well when he woke up with a jolt, memories of battles gone wrong and lost comrades and guilt rearing into his mind. But he felt chagrined to learn that others were also aware he had them.

Not knowing what to say, and certainly not wanting to linger on this topic, he returned his attention to the light fixture. He stood on tiptoes to pull an item down from the ceiling.

"What's that?" Alisa asked, thankfully changing the topic.

He flipped it to her. "A small mirror."

She caught it easily, perhaps not with a cyborg's enhanced reflexes but certainly with a pilot's reflexes. He'd seen her fly a few times when it counted, such as when they were being chased through asteroid belts, and she was good at her job.

"Low tech way to see who's coming, eh?" Alisa tossed it onto the boy's chest, shaking her head as she looked down at him. "Slavery. I'm not sure whether to be horrified or flattered. I would have thought I was too old to attract slavers."

Leonidas raised his eyebrows. He knew she had an eight-year-old daughter and guessed her to be in her early thirties. Since he was edging up on forty, he would hardly call someone in her thirties old. The muggers—slavers—probably hadn't looked beyond her face and the curve of her hips when determining her potential as a slave. While she wasn't gorgeous, she was attractive and had an appealing smile. Too bad she was usually mouthing off when she made that smile. The Alliance had probably encouraged mouthiness, considering it a promising trait in someone signing on to help overthrow the government.

"You're supposed to say something like, 'You look fabulous, Alisa, and you're not too old to attract slavers.'"

"You want to attract slavers?"

"No, that's not my point. Never mind. Are you collecting your net?"

"Yes." Leonidas stepped past her and found the casing for the ball, which had split open into several segments to release its electric cargo. He deactivated the energy aspect, then tugged the slender tendrils of the net off the supine figure. The boy leaped up and tried to dart off. Leonidas caught him by the collar of his shirt. As he proceeded to tie the kid up, he asked Alisa, "If I call the police, what are the odds that they'll get here before someone comes by and mugs our muggers?"

"If you call the police, someone will probably come for you, wanting to collect—" She cut herself off, glancing at the boy, who was listening. "They'll probably come for you," she finished.

He appreciated that she hadn't mentioned the warrant. Even if these three weren't a threat, who knew who they knew?

"I can call them," she said, slipping a comm unit off her belt. She never wore an earstar comm-computer, as was common. "No idea on the mugging the muggers part. Beck was right. The station seems rougher than the last time I was through here."

"I'll wager that the last time you were here, the empire controlled the station and maintained order." He hadn't brought it up with Beck, but he couldn't help himself this time. He supposed he wanted Alisa to see reality, to realize that she'd fought on the wrong side, that her people had made the system a worse place, not a better one.

Alisa grimaced. "Yes, the empire was excellent at maintaining order."

"That order meant you wouldn't be mugged on the way to a coffee shop."

"We're not on the way to a coffee shop. We're on the way to some smithy located on the dubious side of the station. Besides, under the old regime, I would have been arrested for walking around after curfew, and my gun would have had to stay on my ship, a ship that has no weapons of its own because the empire forbade civilians to be armed, even if they were lugging freight through pirate-infested space. Even you have to admit it's been inconvenient that we haven't had a way to defend ourselves this past month."

"Pirate-infested space was rare when the empire ruled, unless you were way out near the border worlds."

"People on those border worlds like freight delivered to them too. My mom and I had more than our share of run-ins when I was growing up on the Nomad."

"That was your mother's choice to go somewhere unsafe, to take a child somewhere unsafe." Leonidas couldn't stifle the distaste in his voice, though it was directed more toward his resentment that the Alliance had destroyed the empire without having anything sufficient to instate in its place. If the war had created a better universe, perhaps he could have accepted being on the losing side more easily, but it hadn't.

"My mother," Alisa said coolly, "flew freight because she couldn't stand the stifling rules of living on an imperial planet, which was all of them in the last century. She should have been allowed to defend herself out in the system."

"Rules exist for a reason. They keep people safe."

"Safe." Her lip curled, and she said it as if it were a curse. "You can get arrested, be thrown in a jail cell, and be safe as a bramisar in its den, but you'll never see the stars again. People love to give up their freedoms for safety. Pretty soon, you can't walk where you want, when you want, and you might as well be a dog instead of a human being." She issued a disgusted noise somewhere between a grunt and a growl, then stalked down the corridor in the direction they had been headed before the attempted ambush.

"The Alliance is overflowing with freedom-seeking idealists," Leonidas called after her, though he doubted she was listening. "It takes a few pragmatists to run a government. You'll see. When the entire system collapses and your government is replaced by chaos, you'll see."

Alisa did not look back. Leonidas glared down at the tied-up muggers.

"You sure you don't want to let us go so we can catch her and sell her to slavers?" the boy asked.

Leonidas grunted and walked away, hoping Alisa would remember to comm the police to pick them up. If police even existed on Starfall Station anymore. Star fall, indeed.

Leonidas put out a hand to stop Alisa. They were in the wide corridor leading to the smithy—it was more like a street with buildings to either side, a high ceiling arching about thirty feet overhead. The area was very quiet, considering how many of the shops kept night hours. To their left, a window display showed all manner of netdiscs and personal comm assistants, and floating holosigns promised inexpensive repair rates. Two buildings ahead, the roll-up door of the smithy was closed, though a glowing sign shed light from the window beside it.

A faint odor reached Leonidas's nostrils, that of a butcher shop—or a battlefield.

"More muggers?" Alisa looked down at his hand.

"Perhaps," he said, scanning the buildings more intently than he had when they first turned onto the street.

"You've accused me of being someone whom trouble always finds, but I think it's even more likely to find you."

"I believe I said you're someone who makes trouble wherever she goes. You're quick to mouth off to people, even those it's unwise to be mouthy with."

"Like cranky cyborgs?" She smiled, her irritation from ten minutes earlier apparently forgotten.

After years of outranking most of his peers and having them defer to him, he was never quite sure how to handle her irreverence. This time, he said, "I'm not cranky," and regretted that it sounded petulant rather than authoritative.

Her smile only widened.

He sighed and walked down a maintenance passage between the computer repair building and the next structure, checking to see if the shops had back doors. He couldn't yet tell where that smell was coming from, but striding through the front entrance of the smithy might be unwise.

A waist-high, bug-shaped trash robot rolled through the alley that ran parallel to the street, sucking debris into its proboscis, incinerating it in its carapace, and shifting the ashes to a bin in the rear. It reminded him of the chase that he'd been on with Alisa and Dr. Dominguez in the sewers below the university library on Perun. They had temporarily escaped pursuit by catching a ride on an automated sewer-cleaning vehicle. He and Alisa had sat side by side in the cargo bed, their shoulders touching. It hadn't exactly been pleasant since they'd both stunk of the sewers, but she hadn't been mouthy then, perhaps being too tired to make quips. For some reason, the image came to mind now with a feeling of fondness. Odd.

His memories faded as he turned into the alley and saw the robot trundling toward a charred box lying on the floor. A hole burned in the side displayed destroyed interior circuit boards and wires.

"That's an imperial spy box, isn't it?" Alisa asked, stopping beside him.

His armor case stopped, too, just shy of bumping into his back.

Leonidas nodded. "Yes."

The boxes were usually floating through the air when one saw them, built-in cameras observing from above and sending the feed to police monitors.

"Guess the Alliance decided they didn't want to use them when they took over," Alisa said.

"No." Leonidas shook his head as the trash robot widened its nozzle and sucked the box in, the same way it had the other debris. "That was shot down today, not months ago when the Alliance took this station."

"Good point," she said quietly, looking up and down the dim alley. "Someone was doing something they didn't want observed, eh?"

"So it would seem."

Leonidas waited for the trash robot to incinerate the box and continue down the alley, then walked to the back door of the smithy. Unlike the vehicle-sized, roll-up door in the front, this was a simple door for humans. There were no windows on the back of the building, so he couldn't see inside, but he caught that butcher-shop scent again.

He paused, looking down at Alisa. "You may wish to wait outside."

"Oh?" Judging by the curiosity in her eyes, waiting outside wasn't what she had in mind.

Even though he had served with some female soldiers and knew they could be tough, his instinct was to protect women from gruesome experiences.

"I don't think my armor case will fit through this narrow doorway," he said. "Perhaps you could watch it for me."

"Afraid the trash bot will come along and suck it up? I don't think it'll fit inside its maw."

"Nevertheless, I'll purchase your chocolate beverage later if you wait here."

He thought that might draw an agreeable smile from her, but her eyes closed to suspicious slits. Still, she leaned her shoulder against the wall and nodded for him to go inside.

The door was locked with an old latch-and-bolt system, rather than with electronics. He gave a quick tug on the handle, snapping the mechanism. If he was wrong and nothing had happened inside, he would pay the smith for the damage.

The area he stepped into was dark, but his eyesight was better than human, and he could make out most of his surroundings. An aisle ran the length of the back wall, with tools, crates, and unidentifiable clutter rising over his head and blocking the view of most of the building. All manner of machinery towered at one end, a mix of modern and computerized with old-fashioned and antiquated. At the other end, laser smelting equipment dangled from a ceiling beam, the tip resting against an anvil and a rack of mallets of various sizes. Heat radiated from a furnace behind the equipment.

Leonidas stood quietly and listened before venturing away from the door. The scent of blood was stronger inside.

When he did not hear anything, he walked down the aisle and turned toward the front of the building. The holosign glowing in the window, proclaiming the business open, shed some extra light. To his eyes, it clearly illuminated the prone person lying on an open stretch of floor near a front counter and payment machine. It was a man, blood pooling on the floor next to him, a rivulet of it leading to a drain nearby. It had dried, but only partially. This hadn't happened long ago.

Though he shouldn't have disturbed a crime scene, curiosity drove him forward. He knelt, careful to avoid the blood, and rolled the body over. With his keen night sight, he easily saw the hole in the man's clothes. Something—most likely a knife—had punctured deep into his flesh, slipping between his ribs and piercing his heart. It had only taken one stab to kill him. Someone had either gotten lucky or had known exactly what he was doing.

A draft stirred the hair on the back of Leonidas's neck, the door he had used opening. He sniffed, then sighed as he caught Alisa's scent, a mix of simple, warm feminine skin and the lavender hand soap in the lav on the ship. She bumped against something in the dark, but otherwise moved quietly as she maneuvered through the shop toward the front of the building.

He turned to face her, his nose and ears having already determined that they were alone in the shop, aside from the dead man. Whoever had stabbed him had since left.

The holosign must have provided enough light for Alisa to see his outline in the front of the room, because she lifted a hand toward him. "Turns out your armor case fits through the door fine if you tilt it on its side."

"Ah." He stepped toward her, thinking she might not notice the body, the shadows being thicker along the floor. Maybe he could usher her away from it. But her gaze fell upon it before he reached her.

"Uh, not your work, I assume?"

She didn't appear overly squeamish about the body. He supposed he shouldn't be surprised. If she'd fought in the war, she must have seen plenty of death, even as a pilot.

"No," he said. "I believe this is Master Tech Camden Meliarakis, the owner of the smithy."

"The one who was going to fix your armor?"

"Yes. I spoke directly to him about six hours ago and made the nocturnal appointment." Leonidas lowered his voice to murmur just for his earstar, "Time?"

It responded by speaking a soft, "Twenty-three twenty-seven, Starfall Station time," into his ear.

"I'm three minutes early for my appointment," Leonidas told Alisa.

"Very punctual of you." Alisa frowned as the armor case floated to a stop beside her, almost bumping her arm, as if it wanted attention. Or maybe it wanted to know when the armor inside would be repaired.

Leonidas started to wonder who else he could contact for the job, but that made him feel self-ish—and guilty. So he walked around the shop, thinking he might figure out what had happened. It wouldn't matter to the dead smith, but it would make Leonidas feel better about thinking of his own needs first. Besides, it was hard to forget that he'd had a hand in keeping the peace for a long time. It was hard to shed that responsibility. Granted, he'd been more of an interplanetary peacekeeper than a police officer, but he'd always fought to protect civilians.

"Shall I call the police again?" Alisa asked. "Or should we just disappear without touching anything? Reporting a mugging was one thing, but I'd hate to be detained because we were suspects in a murder. You, especially, shouldn't be caught here."

"No," Leonidas murmured, peering at the closed roll-up door. Since the lock in the back had been intact, he presumed the murderer had come in through the front. Given the shop's around-the-clock hours, the door had likely been unlocked at the time.

He confirmed that it was still open without touching anything. Leaving fingerprints behind wouldn't be a good idea for exactly the reason Alisa had alluded to. He did not need the Alliance adding civilian murders to the list of reasons they wanted him arrested.

"Unlocked," he said. "The murderer may have come in, pretending to be a customer. The smith was stabbed in the front, so he might have even known the person. At the least, I bet he didn't expect trouble."

As Leonidas moved away from the door for a closer look around the premises and the counter, he was aware of Alisa watching him.

"Are you going to attempt to solve the crime?" she asked.

"You don't approve?"

"Well, I don't mean to belittle this man's death, but you investigating it won't get your armor fixed, and I'm worried that if we're found here, you'll be in a lot of trouble." She walked to the window and peered out into the street, her gaze flicking upward, as if to look for spy boxes.

Leonidas could now guess why the one in the back had been shot down. Had the murderer gone out that way? So as not to be seen? Locking the door as he went?

"You don't think you'll be in trouble too?" he asked.

"Oh, I reckon my mouth could also get me into trouble—" Alisa flashed him a quick smile, though it appeared more distracted than heartfelt, "—but you're the one my people want."

"Your people."

"The Alliance people." She shrugged. "The ones with two hundred thousand tindarks on your... not your head, exactly, because they want you alive. That's one boon for you. I can't imagine less than an army taking you in alive. Even that army would need some tanks and armor-piercing rounds."

Cyborgs were not quite as invincible as that, but Leonidas did not correct her. No need to educate her on the various poisons and chemicals that could act on his unique mecho-biology. And it wasn't as if he was impervious to blazer bolts or bullets. In his armor, he nearly was, but that armor was in shambles now. He needed to get it fixed, one way or another. Was it selfish to hope the smith had an apprentice that he might contact? He leaned around the clerk's counter to eye the shelves and display screens.

"Hm, what is this?" Leonidas mused, pulling a large case out from behind the counter. The case was familiar, since one very similar to it floated in the middle of the room. This one was resting on the floor rather than hovering, but it was the same size as his.

"Combat armor?" Alisa asked.

"Red combat armor."

"You mean crimson," she said quietly. "And only cyborgs have that, right?"

"The color isn't—wasn't—forbidden in the private quarter, but it's somewhat infamous, yes, since it was issued to soldiers in the Cyborg Corps."

The case was unlocked, so Leonidas opened it, wondering if he would know the owner. He also wondered what had brought one of his people here after the war ended and the imperial army largely dissolved. He supposed Starfall Station was as likely a place as any to move on and look for work. He'd heard rumors that some of his cyborg colleagues had become mercenaries, others bodyguards and heads of security for wealthy civilians. It seemed demeaning employment after working for the empire for so many years, maintaining order and keeping the people safe. Though it was not as demeaning as piracy—he'd already run into one of his people engaged in that, planning to carve out an empire of his own in territory no longer being patrolled.

"Sergeant Lancer," Leonidas read off the plate fastened to the inside of the lid.

An image of a big farmer turned soldier came to mind. Sandy blond hair and freckles, a boyish look even after more than ten years in the army. Yes, Leonidas remembered him, and a twinge of excitement ran through him at the idea of reconnecting with someone from the unit. Even if Lancer had been along for many of the battles that were the fodder for Leonidas's nightmares, he still wanted to see the man. He hadn't had a chance to say a proper goodbye to anyone when the empire had lost and the unit had been disbanded. He had been too busy on a last mission for the emperor.

"Anyone you know?" Alisa asked.

"Yes, I remember him. We fought together on many occasions." Leonidas found a receipt on the top of the set of armor and read it. "This was just finished. He's scheduled to pick it up at midnight station time."

"That's not far off, but I'm not sure waiting here for him would be wise." Alisa leaned closer to the windowpane. "Someone's coming."

"Someone who looks like he might need the services of a smith? Or someone who might be a smith?" Leonidas hoped it would be the apprentice, though it might not help him if it was. The man would be too distraught over his master's death to fix armor tonight. Besides, Leonidas twitched at the idea of an apprentice handling his most prized possession—and one of the few possessions he had left. He would have to do some research to find out if anyone else on the station was qualified.

"Someone who looks like she might be here to investigate the death of a smith," Alisa said. "It's a woman, and she's wearing a police uniform."

"We better leave then." Leonidas nodded toward the back door.

"Don't forget your box."

"Never," he murmured.

The armor case floated after him as he moved away from the counter. He stepped past the body, experiencing a twinge of regret at leaving the smith's killer at large without trying to help, but it wasn't his responsibility to enforce order here, and he doubted the police would appreciate his assistance. Besides, if a patroller was on the way, she would be more useful here than he.

Leonidas held the back door open for Alisa and his case to exit. He heard someone lifting the roll-up door. He slipped outside, shutting the back door softly, noticing his bare hand on the knob. He should have taken more care not to leave fingerprints, but maybe it didn't matter. The Alliance was already after him. He'd probably be on the run for years to come. If they didn't catch him first.

Alisa did not make any jokes as they retraced their steps through the alley, and for that he was glad. He wasn't in a good mood and didn't want to make the effort to be good company. Uncranky company. His helplessness here on the station—in the system as a whole—grated on him more than it had in the previous months.

As Alisa turned up an alley heading toward the street, Leonidas paused, a ladder catching his eye. It led up the side of a warehouse to a third-story rooftop.

"Alisa," he said softly, waving for her to come back. He gave a subvocal command for the case to stay put by the side of the building, then told her, "Side trip."

"Oh? Somewhere exotic?" She arched an eyebrow toward the ladder.

"It depends on how exotic you consider rooftops."

"Not very," she said as he started up.

"Then this side trip may disappoint."

As he climbed, Leonidas listened for noises back at the smithy or out in the street. He did not hear anyone walking or talking, but if the policewoman had verified the existence of a body, a violently murdered body at that, she might have called for backup. He wondered how she had learned of the smith's death, since he hadn't seen a flashing alarm or anything of that nature.

Once he reached the top of the warehouse, he had to drop to his belly to crawl across it. The arched ceiling that had seemed high when down in the street, had its beginning at the wall behind the buildings, and it stretched only a few feet above the warehouse rooftop. Pipes and ducts rose in spots, too, further tightening the space as they disappeared into the station above. The hum of machinery reached his ears, reverberating through the rooftop. In spots, colorful graffiti adorned the ceiling.

He crawled to the far side of the warehouse so he could peer into the street. An inebriated couple crossed at an intersection several buildings away, leaning on each other and laughing too loudly. Targets for muggers, Leonidas supposed. He didn't yet see any other police, though he scanned the shadows closely in case others lurked in the recesses.

Alisa scooted up beside him, eyeing the white outline of a penis and balls graffitied above them. As a military officer, she had doubtlessly seen worse, but he found himself hoping that it was too dark for her normal human eyes to pick out the details.

"If I'd known you would bring me someplace so cozy, I would have brought a blanket and a picnic basket."

Apparently, she had better-than-average normal human eyes.

"Do you have one? A picnic basket?" He couldn't imagine her bare bones freighter possessing such comforts, not when it had been huddled in the back of a junkyard cavern a month earlier. The lavatories didn't even have towels, something that might have compensated for the fact that the body dryers only worked intermittently.

"Not presently, but for you, I would have bought one."

"I had no idea I rated special consideration."

"Yes, the specialness of braided wicker." She grinned at him, surprising him since he hadn't thought his comments that witty. "You're bantering with me. That's excellent. I have hope that you might one day laugh, after all."

He returned his attention to the street. With a man dead a few buildings down, Leonidas did not think this was the time for laughter. Or banter.

"Are we looking for anything in particular?" Alisa asked, not visibly chagrined by his lack of a response.

"Sergeant Lancer. His armor will be ready soon, and if it were me, I wouldn't be late to pick up such a precious item. He may have deliberately asked for a late-night pickup so he could avoid walking through the station during prime hours."

"Is there a warrant on his head too?"

"I don't know, but if he's toting a case of red armor around, people will know what he is. Most former imperial soldiers can change out of their uniforms and blend in. It's not so easy for cyborgs, even without the armor."

"You look completely human when you're not cut up with your implants showing." She waved to his arm, where he'd received such a cut a couple of weeks earlier. Dr. Dominguez had sealed it, leaving only the faintest of scars, one of many after so many years in the military. "An overly muscled human who spends four hours a day in the gym," she added, grinning again, "but a human."

"Overly?" He twitched an eyebrow.

Her grin widened. "Depends on your tastes, I suppose. I have a fondness for lanky scholars who appreciate my irreverent humor." Her grin faded, and he wondered if that described her late husband.

"Which is why you're on a rooftop, shoulder to shoulder with me," he said, thinking that responding to her banter might distract her from uncomfortable memories. The three gods knew he had his share of uncomfortable memories and understood about needing distractions.

To his surprise, her cheeks reddened. Someone else wouldn't have noticed in the shadows, but he had no trouble picking up the flush.

"I just wanted an excuse to go out for a mocha," she said, scooting closer to the edge of the building and peering into the street. "Will you be inviting your friend along if he shows up?"

That wasn't what he'd had in mind, though the image of Alisa walking arm-in-arm with a big, brawny cyborg on either side of her amused him for some reason. She wasn't that short of a woman, standing roughly five-foot-ten, but the top of her head only rose an inch over his shoulder, and he wasn't even that tall for a cyborg. The imperial army had enforced strict recruiting standards, picking men that had rated highly on athletic tests and had also already been physically imposing. They had been fussy about who they invested in for the expensive surgery necessary to turn a human into a cyborg—or killing machine, as Leonidas's recruiter had said all those years ago. He remembered being unimpressed by the rhetoric. Yet here he was.

"You wouldn't be intimidated by walking into a coffee shop with two cyborgs?" Leonidas asked, realizing she was looking at him and remembering that she had asked a question.

"Intimidated?" Her forehead crinkled.

He snorted. "Never mind. I forgot who I was talking to." He had yet to see her intimidated by anything, neither cyborgs turned pirates nor imperial warships on their tails. No matter who was after her, she was always ready to fling sarcasm like others flung bullets. "To answer your question, I want to keep him from walking in on a murder investigation where he might be turned into a suspect and held."

"Ah."

Alisa looked past him and toward the front of the smithy. "Is the policewoman still in there? I wonder how she knew to come looking. That body didn't report itself."

"She may have been sent to investigate the broken spy box," Leonidas said, though he thought it was interesting that Alisa, too, had noted that there hadn't been any alarms triggered.

"It was behind the building, not in it. She strode straight to the front door, didn't she?"

"You sound like you want to go peek in the window."

She raised a finger, looking interested in the idea, but then lowered it and shook her head. "No, I don't need to go looking for trouble any more than you do. We'll just wait for your friend and—" Alisa frowned. "There's not a possibility your friend is responsible for this, is there? What if he already came by, and the smith tried to gouge him for some reason? Because he was a cyborg, and the smith's loyalties were with the Alliance maybe."

Leonidas was shaking his head before she finished speaking. "First off, if he had come already, he wouldn't have left his armor behind. Second, a cyborg wouldn't have bothered with a knife when he could simply break a man's neck."

Alisa frowned down at his hand where it rested next to the lip of the rooftop. "Thanks for putting that image in my mind."

He regretted making the comment, not wanting her to feel uncomfortable around him. He had two brothers who'd never gotten over the fact that he'd given himself to the army, mind and body, twenty years earlier. After their mother died, he'd stopped going home. Family gatherings were awkward enough when everyone was... fully human.

A faint whir reached Leonidas's ears, and he squinted into the gloom at the back of the building. Something stirred in the shadows. He whipped out his destroyer, instantly locking onto the target. It wasn't a person—he would have seen that—but it took him a couple of seconds to figure out what the squarish thing bobbing along the far side of the roof was. A spy box. One that hadn't been shot. Yet.

Alisa probably wouldn't have heard or seen it if he hadn't been pointing his gun across the rooftop, but she followed his gaze and spotted it.

"You don't want to just break its neck?" She waved at his big handgun.

"If it had a neck, I'd be glad to do so," he murmured, keeping his voice low. The devices recorded audio as well as video. That had never bothered him when the imperial police had been monitoring the feeds, but it was different now.

After bobbing along the edge in the back, the spy box floated onto the rooftop, spinning slowly as it headed in their direction.

"They only deviate from their usual routes if they see something suspicious, right?" Alisa asked.

"That's my understanding. Apparently, we're being suspicious."

"We're just a couple looking for some privacy."

"On top of a warehouse?" Leonidas asked.

The cube floated closer, one of its lenses focusing on them.

"Don't get twitchy with those neck-breaking hands." Alisa scooted closer to him before he could ask her what that meant. She slung her arm across his shoulders and tossed a leg over his.

"What are you doing?" Leonidas whispered.

"We're canoodling," she murmured back. "And keeping it from getting a good look at our faces."

Leonidas decided that might, indeed, fool the spy box. It wasn't as if a sophisticated AI ran the devices. It had probably only come in this direction to investigate the missing unit in the fleet of spy boxes that patrolled the streets collecting footage.

He shifted onto his side, facing Alisa and resting a hand on her waist. It had been so long since he'd had sex—or even canoodled—that he found the intimacy awkward. Alisa ducked her chin to hide her face under her arm, and he did the same. Their foreheads brushed as she peeked under her sleeve to eye the spy box. He resisted the urge to pull back and put space between them. If he had met her eight months ago, he would have treated her as an enemy—and she surely would have done the same to him—but they were just people now, neither employed by their governments. Neither soldiers, not anymore. After all his years of service, that was hard to accept, but he forced himself to think of her as nothing more than the captain of the freighter he was riding on, a captain who had stuck up for him when the Alliance came looking for him, risking her own reputation—and her life—to help him escape. She deserved to be treated well, like a friend, or at least a fellow officer. Not that he'd made a practice of canoodling with the officers in his all-male cyborg unit. Fortunately, she smelled better than they did, that lavender scent teasing his nostrils.

The spy box floated to their side of the roof, pausing to hover just beyond Leonidas's feet.

"What's it doing?" Alisa muttered. "Watching to see if we take off our clothes?"

"Perhaps our ruse isn't fooling it."

"Perhaps it's a perv."

Alisa lifted her gaze to meet his and quirked her eyebrows. He wasn't sure if she wanted his opinion on the likelihood of robotic fetishes, or if she was checking to see if he appreciated her humor. Her suggestion that he didn't know how to laugh anymore trickled into his mind. If it was true, he knew it had nothing to do with his cyborg implants—he refused to believe those had altered his humanity in any way—and everything to do with the war. He'd once laughed with his comrades, not as often as some, perhaps, but he had laughed. Unfortunately, years of being on the losing side of a war, of having his people survive only to lose the frailer humans they had been protecting, had left him with guilt, regret, and the knowledge that he had failed. Humor did not tickle his inner spirit very often anymore, and he did not know how to fix that.

With a faint whirring sound, the box floated toward the rear of the rooftop. Leonidas lifted his head to watch it go while wondering if it had sent its footage to police headquarters and if the patroller investigating the smithy was even now being alerted to nearby spies. He still found it odd that only one person was poking around down there.

As the spy box drifted over the edge, Leonidas heard a click from the street, from the direction of the smithy. He whirled back to his stomach, shedding Alisa's arm. He was in time to see the top of a man's headful of short blond hair before the person disappeared inside, the rolling door dropping down behind him with a thud.

Cursing inwardly, Leonidas leaped over the edge of the roof. It might be too late to keep Sergeant Lancer from meeting the policewoman, but perhaps there was still time to help. The last thing he wanted was for one of his people to run afoul of the authorities here for no reason.

After sprinting to the smithy, Leonidas crouched to grab the latch on the bottom of the roll-up door, but he halted in shocked surprise as the faint odor of charred almonds reached his nose. He leaped back, crossing to the far side of the street, his instincts driving his reaction. He forced himself to stop, analyzing the ramifications and his options instead of sprinting several blocks to make sure he wouldn't inhale too much of that gas.

Tyranoadhuc gas.

At least two years had passed since anyone had used it against him, but he recognized the smell immediately. And he remembered being flat on his back in the middle of combat in a corridor on his ship, his mechanical implants frozen, even his eyes locked open, unable to blink as the gas affected every enhanced body part he owned. That day, his people had been caught unprepared, a secret betrayal turned into a surprise attack, and neither Leonidas nor his cyborg men had been able to take the time to don their combat armor, armor that would have filtered out the gas and protected them. He remembered the smug look of the female commander leading the Alliance troops as she had walked up to his side, looking down at him through the faceplate of her helmet, her left cheek and jaw shiny with an old burn she'd never had grafted. She'd pointed her rifle at his chest, and his instincts had screamed for him to move, but his body had refused to comply.

"Colonel Adler," she murmured. "We meet again." Instead of shooting, she had lifted her rifle to her shoulder, barely noticing the energy bolts flying past her, one even glancing off the shoulder of her dented green armor. "I think it will hurt you more to survive when your ship falls, when all of your people are killed. And I believe I shall tell you that one of your own officers was responsible for this betrayal. A Captain Morin. You know him, I'm certain. Cyborgs, it seems, are as amenable to bribes as human men."

She'd stalked past him without waiting for a response—not that he could have given one. It had taken nearly twenty minutes for that gas to wear off, an eternity in battle. Most of his people had been killed, including the senior command staff on the Excelsior, and he'd barely roused in time to grab his combat armor and make it to an escape pod.

"Leonidas?" Alisa asked softly from the corner of the building—she must have left the warehouse rooftop via that ladder and come around through the alley.

He shook the memories from his head and looked up and down the street, aware that they had consumed him so fully that he hadn't been paying attention to his surroundings. He could have been an easy target for someone with a grudge against cyborgs. Or for the person who had loosed that gas. The policewoman? She was probably a victim. Maybe someone else had slipped in while Leonidas had been distracted by the spy box? Or maybe he'd been mistaken about who had been entering the smithy? When he had spotted that blond hair, he had assumed it was Sergeant Lancer, but he hadn't seen the man's face.

"What's wrong?" Alisa whispered, jogging across the street.

Leonidas took a step toward the smithy, but halted and thrust his fingers through his hair in frustration. "I can't go in." He couldn't smell the gas from the middle of the street, but he knew his nose hadn't been mistaken. It wouldn't take much of a dose for him to be affected, and holding his breath wouldn't work. The potent stuff had such small molecules that it could enter the bloodstream through the skin. "Tyranoadhuc gas," he said, catching Alisa's puzzled expression.

"Ah." The puzzlement faded.

She recognized the name. He kept himself from asking if she had ever used the stuff, or piloted a team of soldiers who had used it, against his people. What was going on in that building now was more important than the past. If that had been Sergeant Lancer, he could be sprawled on the ground in there, helpless.

"It doesn't bother humans, right?" Alisa pulled out her Etcher. "I'll go in."

"No. This isn't your battle."

Her eyebrows rose. "I don't think it's your battle, either."

Not true. His unit might have been dissolved, but he would always consider the cyborgs who had served under his command as his people.

Explaining that would take too long. Instead, he lightly gripped her arm to keep her from crossing the street and said, "Stay here. I'll put my armor on."

He let go and sprinted for the case, tugging it into the alley so that he could dress with his back

to the wall. Whatever was going on, it wasn't anything innocuous. They didn't sell that gas at the
corner market. It could damage all computers and
machinery, not just cyborg implants, and it was
illegal for civilians to have it. Military supplies were
tightly controlled, or at least they had been when
the empire had been in charge.

Growling to himself, he stuffed his legs into the
greaves as quickly as possible. Usually, they flexed
and conformed around him automatically, fitting
precisely and comfortably about his limbs, but
every piece of his armor had taken damage during
his escape from the Alliance, and some of the ser-
vos whined and grumbled as he manipulated them.
Under the best circumstances, it took more than
five minutes to suit up. Unfortunately, he dared not
take any shortcuts. He needed the suit to be airtight
before venturing in to deal with that gas. As airtight
as it could be. Normally, it was spaceworthy, but he
well remembered the leak he had sprung during his
brief space walk on the way back to the freighter.
That small hole shouldn't let in enough gas to affect
him. He hoped.

Someone shouted, and a clatter arose inside the
building. Cursing, Leonidas tried to dress faster.
That had been a woman's voice. The police officer?
Something crashed to the floor inside. He wished

there were windows, but neither the side nor the back of the building had any, and getting his armor on was more important than running over half-dressed and peering through the front window. Or so he thought, until he heard the front door roll up quietly.

Alisa?

He lunged out of the alley, still fastening his torso armor around his body. "Don't go in," he barked.

It was too late. The street was empty.

It took another minute for Leonidas to get his helmet on and the rest of his charred and dented armor into place. An eternity. As soon as he could, he pulled up the roll-up door. He hadn't heard any more ominous noises from within—he'd heard nothing at all since Alisa disappeared inside. And that worried him.

He made himself open the door slowly, using all of his senses, as well as the ones augmented by the armor, to get a feel for what danger lay within. Whoever had set off that gas had come expecting to deal with cyborgs and would likely have more weapons that could affect him. Somehow, the person inside had anticipated that Leonidas would come. It must be some bounty hunter after him for the reward money—the gas would be perfect for someone who wanted to bring him in alive.

The faintest of footfalls came from the back of the smithy. Leonidas eased inside, putting his back to the wall. Data scrolled down the side of the glastica display of his faceplate, not interrupting his line of sight as it informed him that gas had been detected in the space. No kidding.

The same Open sign that had allowed Leonidas to see before was enough to glimpse the smith's body still on the floor near the counter, but there were too many crates and too much equipment in the way to see Alisa or whoever was making noise in the back. It might be she. But he was certain they weren't alone. He imagined the policewoman's body in an aisle somewhere while a powerful bounty hunter stalked Alisa, prepared to kill her for daring to intrude.

As he strode silently along the wall, Leonidas listened for sounds of distress—sounds of any kind at all. But the footfalls had halted.

The armor made his shoulders even broader than usual, so he had to pick his route carefully past machinery and tools. He did not want to bump or scrape against anything, nor knock anything over. Combat armor wasn't made for stealth, but he could step carefully, keeping his footfalls silent.

A gun cracked, black powder igniting. Alisa's Etcher. An instant later, a second weapon loosed a sizzling bolt of energy, the orange beam blasting out of the darkness at the rear of the building. It slammed into and through the wall it struck. Hand cannon.

Knowing Alisa didn't have such a weapon, Leonidas gave up stealth and sprang in the direction where the bolt had originated. He leaped over a fifteen-foot-high vat, hardly worrying if he landed on the ground or on something else.

As he dropped onto a stack of crates, he spotted Alisa and another woman. Alisa was charging, trying to bowl her opponent over before the hand cannon could fire again. Her foe leaped to the side while launching a kick. With surprising reflexes, Alisa reacted, dodging while grabbing the leg from the air. The other woman did something Leonidas couldn't see from his position, and they both tumbled to the ground, grappling with each other.

He crouched to spring over another stack of crates and to their aisle, but noticed something out of the corner of his eye and paused. A man lay on his back on the floor by the furnace. He wasn't moving. The face and blond hair were familiar. It was Sergeant Lancer. And he'd been shot in the chest with that hand cannon. He lay there bleeding, unable to even lift a hand to staunch the flow of blood.

The sound of a thump pulled Leonidas's attention back to the women. He jumped twenty feet to land in the aisle beside them. The woman—it was the one they had dismissed as a police officer earlier—had gained the advantage, rolling atop Alisa, her hand cannon clenched and ready to use.

She glanced toward Leonidas as he landed and shifted her aim. He reacted too quickly for her. He surged forward, grabbing her by the back of the uniform and hoisting her into the air. His knuckles brushed against something hard and skin-tight beneath her clothing—fitted body armor. It wasn't as tough as his combat armor, but it would deflect bullets and energy bolts from most hand weapons.

Furious about Sergeant Lancer, Leonidas hurled her across the room. Let the armor deflect that.

The woman hurtled toward a wall and should have crashed shoulder-first, but she twisted in the air with impressive agility. The soles of her feet struck the wall as she crouched deep to absorb the impact, and she sprang off before gravity dropped her to the ground. She landed lightly on her feet like a cat. A cat with a thief's set of impact boots.

"You're no police officer," Leonidas said, only pausing long enough to make sure Alisa wasn't gravely injured—she lifted her head and made a rude gesture toward their foe. Then he strode toward the woman.

"And you're the cyborg I'm after." She flicked a dismissive hand in Lancer's direction. "Why don't you take off your helmet and breathe deeply for me, Colonel?"

"Who are you?"

She grinned, not showing any sign of fear as he strode closer. "Someone who would love an extra two hundred thousand tindarks."

Instead of lifting her big hand cannon again, she flung a black ball at him, a fluidwrap. Leonidas fired one of the miniature blazers built into his armor. A beam of energy struck the ball just as it started to unfurl. The net never reached him, instead bursting into a tangled mess in the air.

Leonidas leaped toward the wall to avoid it and jumped off at an angle that took him straight toward her. She was already moving, dropping a pellet that exploded in smoke at her feet. As Leonidas landed, she dove to the side, rolling behind the furnace. He lost sight of her, the chemical-laced smoke interfering with his helmet's cameras and sensors as well as his eyes. Static burst across his helmet display.

It didn't matter. He anticipated her path, his ears telling him what his eyes could not. She was quiet, but not quiet enough. Her sleeve caught against the edge of the furnace, and he leaped, powerful legs taking him through the air faster than she could run. He landed behind her as she came out of the smoke, and grabbed her with both hands. Furious with the woman—the damned bounty hunter—for mistaking Lancer for him, Leonidas wrapped his hand around her neck even as she kicked backward, trying to fight him. He squeezed once, and bone snapped. She thrashed a few more times, then fell limp in his grip.

"The threat is gone," Leonidas said for Alisa's sake.

A soft groan came from the aisle behind him.

"Good." Alisa came into view as she staggered to her feet, grasping her ribs. "I nearly had her defeated, but a little help never hurts. Besides, I was holding back because I thought she really was a police—" She caught sight of the woman hanging from Leonidas's hand, and her humor evaporated, her face growing grim.

Leonidas did not respond. He dropped the woman and ran around the building, turning on all of the vent fans and opening the doors. As soon as he finished, he raced to Sergeant Lancer's side. His old comrade's eyes were open, his face scrunched with pain. He didn't seem to be able to turn his neck or move his hands yet, but his eyes were a window to his agony.

When Leonidas knelt beside him, Lancer smoothed his features, trying to hide the pain. His fingers twitched, as if in a salute. Saluting was the last thing he should be worrying about now. The hole in his chest was like a crater—that damned woman hadn't hesitated to fire, probably shooting him point blank as soon as the gas froze him in place. All he had been doing was coming to pick up his armor. He'd had no chance of defending himself.

Leonidas knew a fatal wound when he saw one, but he whispered, "Hospital," and a map with a flashing blip rose on his helmet's interior display. It was on the far side of the station from here. Leonidas growled and slipped his arms under Lancer's body, prepared to lift him up and carry him there.

Lancer winced and shook his head. "Too late for that, sir," he whispered, sadness and regret replacing the pain in his eyes. "Wasn't… alert. Didn't expect trouble here. Should have. Trouble everywhere. Not a good time… to be a cyborg." That regret seemed to deepen, as if he was talking about far more than his death, far more than this night.

"I know," Leonidas said, his voice thick. He was aware of all the blood on the floor, the blood still flowing from that wound. His sergeant was right. It was too late. Even if he sprinted to the hospital, they wouldn't make it in time. "I'm sorry, Sergeant. Todd," he corrected, remembering the man's first name from the personnel reports, even if he'd never used it. "She was after me, not you."

"Ah." Lancer's brows rose slightly. A mystery solved? "After she shot me... said I wasn't the... right one." His gaze flicked toward a hover pallet floating near the wall. The woman must have intended to roll Leonidas onto it to take him in. She'd just shot Lancer because—for no good reason, damn it. "Makes sense," Lancer added.

"Because I'm an ass that everyone wants to kill?" Leonidas asked, trying to smile, to make Lancer forget about his impending death, at least for a moment. He eased one of his hands out from under him and pulled off his helmet. To hells with the gas—he wanted his sergeant to see his eyes, not just the reflection of his own pained expression in the faceplate.

"Because you're important." Lancer managed the grin that Leonidas couldn't.

Leonidas snorted. "Hardly that. It's because the Alliance thinks I know where someone is, someone I haven't seen in six months." His throat closed up again, refusing to let him speak further. It was just as well. Lancer didn't need to know that his death had been for absolutely nothing. That the Alliance wanted Leonidas for information that was six months out of date and growing staler by the day.

"Sir?" Lancer whispered, his voice barely audible now. His fingers twitched again. "Will you—" He broke off and coughed, blood dripping from his mouth. His eyes closed, and Leonidas feared that was the end.

Leonidas clasped his hand. "What is it, Todd?"

His eyes did not open again, but Lancer's fingers wrapped around Leonidas's hand weakly. "Let my mother know I'm—let her know... what happened. Only make it sound heroic. At least... respectable."

Leonidas tried to swallow down the lump in his throat. "I will."

"Thank you, sir." Lancer managed another faint smile before taking his last breath, before dying in Leonidas's arms.

After a moment, Leonidas eased back, resting his man on the floor. He rose and stepped away, anger and frustration replacing his sorrow. He punched the wall, his armored fist knocking straight through it. He might have destroyed the whole place, but when he turned, thinking of kicking that hover pallet into pieces, he glimpsed Alisa standing near the front counter. She had risked herself to fight the bounty hunter, and none of his anger was for her, but he eyed her warily, anticipating some inappropriate display of humor.

"I think I understand now," she said quietly.

"What?"

"Why you don't laugh." She looked toward Lancer's body, then back to him, moisture glistening in her eyes. "Do you want me to wait outside?"

He groped for an answer. Did he? He needed to take care of the body, arrange to send Lancer home for a proper funeral if he could, and he still needed to find someone to fix his armor. This wasn't her mission. She'd just come along for a coffee.

Alisa walked over to him, eyeing him a little warily, then reached up and put her arms around his shoulders and leaned against his chest, not seeming to care that he was wearing his armor and covered in blood. He returned the hug, figuring he must look like he needed it. Maybe he did.

"I'm sorry," she said.

"Thank you."

She reached up, resting her hand against the back of his head, fingers lightly touching his hair. He'd never thought of himself as someone who needed comforting—he would go forward, dealing with the realities of being a soldier, as he always had—but he found himself appreciating having someone close. Having someone care. It almost startled him to realize that she did, considering what he was and especially considering he had pointed a gun at her chest the first time they met. She probably cared about a lot of things and just didn't let it show. Usually.

Alisa stepped back, resting the palm of her hand on his cheek before letting go. "I'll wait outside."

She looked over her shoulder at him, holding his gaze as she walked out the door. As he stood in the dark smithy, it slowly dawned on him that she had come along for reasons that had very little to do with coffee. He doubted he should encourage that, and didn't know how he felt about it, but he admitted that at least for now, it was good not to be alone.

Want to find out how these characters met? And see where they go from here? Please check out the rest of my Fallen Empire series. Book 1, *Star Nomad,* is available now. You learn more on my website at www.lindsayburoker.com.

LUMINESCENCE

AN ISF-ALLION
WORLD STORY

PATTY JANSEN

A BRIGHT FLASH TURNED THE ICE UNDER MY FEET INTO A sheet of white.

The inside of the inflatable dome blazed in X-ray vision as my visor's auto-polariser cut in, providing me with a skeleton-view of the flexible struts that held up the fabric.

A split second later, the murky orange hue of the Titanian atmosphere returned. Darker still inside our tent on the ice of Kraken Mare on Titan's south pole.

I depolarised my visor, heart thudding. Black spots danced in my vision. "Paul? Did you see that? Paul? Do you hear me?"

I stared at the entry hole in the ice in the middle of the tent. The black surface rippled.

"Paul!"

There was no reply.

The snaking hoses of the breathing apparatus and the heater were the only sign of Paul's presence in that blackness. Through my suit's helmet I couldn't even hear the humming of the air compressor in the shed.

Static crackled in my earphones. Paul's words garbled into unintelligible mush, laced with excitement.

"What is it? What do you see?"

"It's…beautiful. I can't begin to describe it, Hadie. There's colours and pictures and…it looks like a spider's web…. Holy fuck!"

The line went dead. I strode to the reception unit and pressed the reset with clumsy gloved hands. The roamer icon tracked over the screen and found . . .

Nothing.

Oh for fuck's sake. This lousy radio never worked when you needed it.

I waited. I told myself not to worry. Paul could take care of himself. The hoses still pulsed, and now—relief flooded me—the downrope was moving, a sign that he was climbing up the ladder.

Sure enough, ten minutes later Paul's helmet broke the surface, then his shoulders, followed by his be-suited arms. I hauled him up the last rungs of the ladder, the touch awkward through both our suits.

"You OK?" I asked.

Vapour rose from the suit, methane gas curling towards the roof of the tent, where it condensed against the fabric, ran down until it met the ice and froze in globby stalagmites.

Paul dropped his sampling canisters, which he'd taken to collect samples from bacterial patches we had found living under the ice. My helmet receiver remained silent; I couldn't see his face behind his visor. I cursed. This time when we got back to the habitat, I would complain to the Research Division—fuck the notes it would earn me against future promotion. It was one thing to let scientists work with substandard equipment when they worked in an environment where they could breathe the air and sit around waiting for a bail-out if things went wrong. We didn't have that luxury. Small things about the Titanian atmosphere, like the general lack of oxygen and temperatures that would freeze your butt off, meant that any equipment malfunction quickly turned serious with big fat capital letters. The tight-arses could at least give us receivers that fucking worked all the time, not just when they felt like it.

I guided him across the tent. His steps were stiff, that all-too-familiar feeling that leg muscles had frozen senseless, through the suit and layers of insulating clothing.

Into the air lock. I pulled shut the thick door and operated the panel. Waited. Just us in our suits, and a tiny light. Vapour rising off Paul's suit, curling up to the vent in the ceiling. I hated the silence.

Lights flashed; the inner door opened. I preceded Paul into the familiarity of the tiny lab of Research Station 5: a simple table and four straight-backed chairs, lab benches with stacks of sample tubes and an assortment of equipment parts: mostly spare parts for the dive gear, because the samples needed to be kept outside—too warm for them in here. A rack with protective clothing. Thermal under-suits.

Monitoring and comm screens blinked warnings against the back wall. *Initialisation sequence not detected.* Unease clawed at the back of my mind.

I flicked the heater up as far as it would go. Fans jolted into action. The pump hummed below the floor, sucking up methane from under the ice.

The light was warm in here, and when I wriggled off my suit's helmet, the air was heavy with the scent of synth-coffee. Empty cups still sat on the table.

Paul sank down in one of the chairs. He reached for his helmet and I helped him unclip it.

"Paul? What happened?"

He said nothing, his hazel eyes staring at the opposite wall like a blind man's.

"Paul!"

I swung one leg over his so I faced him. His expression remained blank. His skin looked marble-pale, his eyes wide open. Most of his curly hair lay plastered to his head, his lips dark with cold. Those lips I'd kissed before he went down.

"For fuck's sake, Paul, it's not funny!"

Still nothing.

What to do now?

Notify Emergency crews—was this an emergency?—notify base at the very least.

I went to the bank of computers against the back wall and hit the screen. This would normally take me to the Base Operations menu.

The screen said *connection not detected.*

Oh for crying out loud! Nothing worked, and there was not a single human being within at least another fifty-odd kilometres. I was beginning to feel some urgency about making that distance considerably smaller.

First: get Paul out of that fucking dive suit.

With a great deal of cursing, I unzipped the suit. Shit from the bottom always clogged the zip, some sort of bacterial goop that went crazy in areas of higher temperature, such as the relatively poorly insulated zipper recess. It was hard enough undoing the suit when you were the person wearing it; trying to undo someone else's was nigh impossible. But I managed to free his torso and his arms and then set about wriggling off his gloves.

His hands were covered in…mud.

That was impossible. That liquid down there didn't much look like water because it wasn't—it was liquid methane, all minus one hundred and seventy-three degrees of it. One did *not* touch it, no matter how briefly, without suffering a horrendous case of frostbite. Man, if his suit had leaked enough to let in this much mud, Paul should by rights be dead, because the suit would have depressurised, the methane would have evaporated, expanded inside the suit…ripped it… and left him snap-frozen like a mass-processed prawn. I shuddered.

I examined the suit's top which I'd tossed on the floor, but found no obvious flaws.

When I wrestled his legs out of the bottom half of the suit, something fell out and rolled under the table. I dived after it, retrieving a ball that fitted neatly in the palm of my hand, cool and heavy and completely transparent.

In Research Division's museum of collections from the Titanian surface, they had a number of these balls, although the ones I had seen were murky. There were a great deal of theories about how they had formed, but no one had a definite answer on what they were, apart from the fact that they consisted of silica, in other words, were a glass of some kind.

"Where did you get this?"

Paul shivered. The muscles on his stomach jerked in a spasm, letting out a wet burp. His eyes were wide open, crazy almost.

My sense of urgency increased. Somewhere in a hut on the methane ice of the Kraken Mare on Titan's South Pole was not a good place to be stuck with an emergency. I had the medvac module in the truck, but it was programmed only to deal with cuts and bruises, the odd case of concussion maybe. I bet it said nothing about *lightning strikes*. Hell, we didn't even know if there *was* lightning on Titan, let alone in about five metres of liquid methane— what the *fuck* had happened?

I needed to know—like, now.

No fucking radio.

The medbase in the Envio 2 habitat was half an hour away if I made good time. Transmission might pick up along the way, but I couldn't provide any treatment while I was driving the truck. The med-track on Earth was eight minutes via the relay, providing I had a datacaster strong enough to project my signal to the satellite. By the looks of the flashing screens on the walls, the one in here was at least temporarily dead, and I didn't think the dinosaur in the truck was up to that task.

Shit.

The truck back to Envio 2 it was, then.

I hauled Paul to his feet. He was much taller and heavier than me, but with the pathetic gravity, he almost hit his head on the low ceiling while I wriggled him into the thermal suit. Boy, it was awkward. His movements were jerky, uncontrolled; and where I held him, around the muscular part of his upper arm, he shivered as if he had a fever.

I got him into the suit, out of the station and through the tube into the truck seat, and belted him up as tightly as I could. Then I slid behind the controls, clipping on the headphones.

"Scout Hadie Kessler to Envio 2. I'm coming in with a medical emergency. Advise which tube to use."

Static crackled in my earphones.

Nothing, yet. Shit.

Not that reception became any better when the truck crested the ridge, tyres ploughing through knee-deep snow and sticky black tholins. The truck's compressors worked full time, making it roar and shudder with their jackhammer-like jolts to stop the crap sticking to the undercarriage.

At least I could see Envio 2 now, a shining bubble in the orange-yellow Titan plain, stark against the dusky yellow sky. Every time a ship of supplies landed, it brought more plasti-beads, which the small colony's extruders promptly fashioned into another section of Dome. Go forth and multiply. Since I had come here, the colony had grown by thousands. One would almost think humanity wanted to swap the green continents of Earth for this fucking ice plain.

The downward path was more of a slither-slide. Even the caterpillar wheels had little traction on the icy sand. The previously clear track dissolved in a series of scars made by vehicles slipping and sliding their way up or down.

I still had no reception, and that puzzled me. It could of course be that the entire habitat was off-line—outages did happen every so often—but I was becoming suspicious that something had been rigged in the comm systems of the truck. The same undersea flash that injured Paul?

He sat in the seat, mute and unresponsive, his eyes hollow. His throat worked, judging by his Adam's apple going up and down. He was going to spew, I was certain of that. I wanted to be in the medbase when that happened. For all I knew he had internal damage and was bleeding inside.

With the Dome now filling most of the front window, I still didn't know which tube to connect to.

My pocket comm beeped.

That was strange; pocket comms were only used for within-dome communication. As I wrestled it out of my back pocket, stopping the truck to do so, I thought that perhaps its range extended to just outside the Dome. I had simply never tried.

I answered, "Scout Kessler."

A warm female voice said, "Hadie, are you all right?" That was Shona. Inside the Dome, sure enough.

"No, I'm not all right. Paul is...behaving strangely and I'm not getting through to medbase. I requested med assistance, but I received no reply—" My voice choked. Paul was everything to me.

"I am medbase at the moment, and comm base and relay base. The habitat is out of the relay. All

off-world communications are cut." That figured.
The truck used the surface-to-air-to-surface relay.
The comm still worked because it relied on direct
transmission. One piece of the mystery solved.

"Look, Shona, can you open an airlock pronto?
Tell me which one to sucker onto."

"Is Paul in danger right now?"

"I don't think so, but whatever happened to
him creeps me out. I want to get him into the medbase as soon as I can."

"I understand." She did; she knew what I had
given up to be with Paul. "Use tube 31. Someone
will be there."

Thank heavens. Belatedly, I registered the
apprehension in her voice.

"Anything wrong in there?"

"We're rather stretched. The datacaster is down,
too. We're on manual." Her words were controlled;
her voice, however, told a different story.

The reason for Shona's apprehension became
apparent as soon as I opened the door of the truck.

Blaring sirens. Flashing lights.

No running or screaming or swearing, just people charging down the corridor, faces grim. I, for
one, had not the fuck of an idea what was going on.

Habitat Operations was not my field. This, however, looked like a major outage.

Just my luck. I had hoped for a satellite record of the light flash, with an analysis of light temperature, refraction and possible source; anything that might give me some answers—but it didn't look like that was going to happen.

Amidst the noise and goings-on, a common soldier in uniform helped me drag Paul down the tube into the body of the habitat. His gait was jerky, his knees locking with every step.

"You picked a time to have a medical emergency," the soldier said.

Not the smartest, was he? I glanced at his tag, which said Grimshaw 86, his construct batch. He glanced at mine, which said Kessler 129. Our eyes met and in his gaze, I saw a world I had forsaken by becoming involved with Paul. Somewhere in the barracks this man would have eight brothers and sisters with whom he had gone through programs ever since he had been awoken, with whom he'd share his private life and to whom he turned for emotional support.

I looked away, uneasy, trying hard not to think of Aphrodite, who had been my closest sister.

"How long has this been going on?"

"About half an hour. Apparently, an external computer malfunction sent a massive burst of data that locked up the system. Now it seems it caused a lot of software to disappear." He jerked his head at a new and louder siren. "That's the air composition alarm going off."

I *should* have looked at the computers at the Research Station. If this outage caused climate control to fail in the hut for any length of time, a lot of our equipment would be frozen into a very expensive heap of plastic and metal junk.

Not good enough, Hadie Kessler. You're supposed to be focused on the tech.

An emergency team was waiting for Paul at the medbase: two nurses and a doctor, all without construct tags.

"We'll take care of him now," a nurse said in a voice that meant, *You are no longer needed.*

"I'd like to stay. I want to know what's wrong with him."

She raised her eyebrows. "You can wait over there." She pointed to a couple of chairs in the corner of the room, next to the medical waste bins.

I so hated that condescending tone when Pristines used it on me, the tone that said they were better than me, the tone that people like the Grimshaw construct seemed to be happy to accept.

I sat. I waited.

A doctor asked Paul questions. He sat propped up on pillows, simply staring, blinking occasionally. Then they took him to a machine that scanned his brain—there was plenty of activity within. They took off his clothes, but found nothing except the traces of mud on his hands. They washed him, and put a hospital gown on him.

Then a young doctor came to me and asked me about Paul's medical details.

Spilling Paul's personal data felt like betrayal; he had only one set of them. As construct agent, I went through so many personality swaps that my biological form had become separated from my mind, one lot of data patched onto another, dumped into a body that felt right for my task. I and my sisters had been old, young, male, female, politically conservative and progressive. Name the vocation, condition or opinion, and it had been grafted onto me. There were backups in various places.

With that thought, I got an idea. "Could you kick-start his mind, reset his memory with a backup?" It was a chilling thought, too. Imagine pressing the delete command on the only copy of yourself and then not having a spare. That was as good as committing suicide.

Surely Paul had left a backup somewhere. Even Pristines couldn't be that stupid.

He gave me a wide-eyed stare. That was obviously out of the question. "That shouldn't be necessary. He's in no physical danger." He sounded like he'd just taken a mouth full of sand.

"But he's not even reacting to us." I raised my voice, too much. A passing nurse glanced over his shoulder, and met my eyes.

"He will be fine. I'm sure he'll recover on his own."

"He doesn't look fine to me." He didn't react to anything. His eyes remained unfocused, his face in that marble aristocratic mask. "Can I please talk to the senior doctor?"

"Sure, wait here."

I sat and waited. Nurses walked past, casting me glances.

Eventually, the doctor came, beckoned me aside in the corridor, away from beeping heart-rate monitors and Paul's unresponsive body into the beeping alarms of the habitat and its unresponsive systems. Medical personnel walked past, shouting at each other about resets and emergency generators. Power flickered.

"Look, Miss…"

"Hadie Kessler 129, Surface Exploration Branch."

The corners of his mouth twitched. "Miss Kessler, to be honest, I have no idea why he behaves like this. Apart from the occasional electrical shiver, his body functions normally. His brain shows a lot of activity, which is good. You say he came out from under the ice like that?"

"Yes." I dug in my pocket for the glass ball and held it out to him. "This fell out of his clothes. Do you think that could have anything to do with…?" I felt like a tether dangling in empty space, idle, hoping against hope that something would latch onto it.

"What? That?" He frowned at the ball, and looked at it from different sides. "I can't see how a marble could have anything to do with his condition."

I put the ball back in my pocket, feeling stupid. I knew the ball hadn't been there before. I knew that it couldn't have entered his suit while he was under the ice. But the doctor was going to think I was an idiot. "Is there anything you can do…to help him…?"

"Not at this stage. We will need to run a number of additional tests, but they are quite invasive and we will need to obtain his next-of-kin's approval to do them. Anyone we could contact?"

I shrugged, hugging myself. I didn't want them to do any more tests. They would find nothing. Paul's condition had something to do with the flash, and with the ball. "He grew up on Ganymede. He has two sisters there." I remembered the names: Lori and Anka. Obsessed with marrying well and the latest fashion, according to Paul's stories.

"Parents?"

"Still alive. Also on Ganymede." Distant, aloof, little interested in the pursuits of their academically-gifted youngest child.

"Do you have any means of contacting them?"

"I could find out." But the idea of doing that made me feel sick. Would they care? He had shamed his Old Earth family, after all. Since I moved in with him, I only remembered Lori having contacted her brother, and that was to gripe about how he should have made an effort to come to some family occasion.

"Any relatives locally?"

"No."

"All right, then I'll ask administration to get onto Ganymede. Thank you, Miss—" He turned back to the door.

"Wait."

He stopped, his hand on the door handle, frowning at me.

"He has me."

He gave me a sharp look and I glared back. Seriously, *everyone* in Envio 2 knew of our relationship. It had been splashed across the gossip columns and had even made it to other colonies. Mars Base didn't care; I heard constructs could marry there, but it was big news amongst the uppity Old Earth families on Ganymede. *Top Scientist announces engagement to construct agent.*

Shit, they all knew what it cost us both. Me—my sisters; Paul—a promotion out of this hellhole to Ganymede University, the most prestigious of prestige institutions. He would have gotten it, if only he'd walked away from me. But we were in love.

So yes, I would always be there for Paul. Because I had nowhere else to go. Because he had no one else.

"That, I think, might be slightly problematic."

What? Then it came to me. I said, in a low voice, "You suspect me of having attacked him, don't you?"

His face went blank. "At the moment, we cannot rule anything out."

So he did suspect me. And suddenly the reactions from the medical personnel made sense. "Do you? Tell me to my face, yes or no? I would never do anything like that, do you hear me? I love Paul, and you know that. No matter what happened with that construct who went berserk and killed his boss. That has nothing to do with me."

The doctor gave me a cold stare, and went back into the room, slamming the door behind him. I ran to the door, but it was locked. The panel said, *enter security code.*

Fuck it!

It had all been a ploy to get me out of the room.

Those Pristines thought our relationship was inappropriate and made every effort to pretend it wasn't happening. These people weren't helping Paul; they were only keeping him from me. They were more interested in keeping up appearances than in healing him.

A nurse came past and went up to the door, keyed a code into the pad—

I called out, "Excuse me. I need to get into that room."

She turned, raising her eyebrows at me. "Do you have authorisation to be in here?"

"My partner is in there."

She looked at my tag. The expression on her face said *not bloody likely.* "If no one has given you a code, go to the front desk and ask for one."

Palming me off elsewhere, as usual.

"Or you could just let me in."

"Sorry, you can't go in there without authorisation."

"Watch me." I shouldered her aside, and pushed into the room.

She shouted, "Hey! Stop!"

She must have pressed an alarm, because a siren started wailing, but it only added to the general din of various alarms that were already blaring.

I ran to the bed.

"Come, Paul!" I dragged him to his feet.

He was still clumsy, but a little more secure on his feet than previously, I thought. I draped his arm over my shoulder and moved towards the door, mumbling at him, "I'm taking you out of here. These clowns have no idea what's going on, and—"

"Miss Kessler, what do you think you're doing?" That was the doctor again.

"I'm taking him home. You don't know what's wrong with him, and you can't help him. I can see no point in keeping him here. He needs care from someone he loves—"

"You can't take him—"

"And watch you do nothing? You don't know what's wrong with him either. I'm taking him home. Once you get any idea of how to help him, you'll know where to find us."

"Take one step further and I'll call the guards."

I laughed into the shrill sound of various alarms blaring in the corridor. "Good luck with that. I think they have other priorities."

I pulled Paul into the corridor.

Fortunately, at least the air composition alarm had stopped blaring. I hoped the trouble had been sorted out.

✳

Walking Paul down the corridors of the habitat wasn't easy. More than before, his muscles seemed to go rigid with the little spasms of pain. We constructs knew these things without spoken words or facial expressions. The ability unnerved Pristines sometimes, but it came with being only a segment, a partition of a larger whole, one of many people connected in mind but not in body. We learned to see feelings in a way our creators had not envisaged, and right now I saw Paul's pain. It was orange. Never mind what the doctor said, whatever had got hold of him was tormenting him.

Paul's unit was one of the executive apartments on the ground floor of the residential wing. Here, with lush green plants and moist warm air, it was almost possible to forget the harsh climate outside, except for the lousy gravity.

I was glad Paul had insisted on having my hand scanned for access to the unit. Habitat Operations had been reluctant, but after that huge fight with my sisters over my relationship with a Pristine, I had nowhere else to go. I held Paul with one hand while I fumbled with the door's access lock.

I opened the door, parked Paul on the bed and covered him with a blanket.

What now?

I let my gaze roam over the interior of our bedroom and lingered on the wall screens displaying pictures of us. One with both of us dressed up in our best, and Paul holding up his Science award in a gesture of victory, his other arm tightly around my waist. Another one very intimate, both of us lying on a crumpled satin sheet, gazing into each other's eyes. I remembered that picture well, because it had been taken on my birthday. Everyone knew that constructs didn't have birthdays, but he had given me one—as a birthday gift.

He had taken me out to dinner. I remembered drowning in his loving gaze. He told me about his youth and how he'd never felt that he fitted in. That was part of the reason he had taken this job away from his family in pioneer territory. A couple of

years down the track, and Envio 2 was no longer a
pioneer station. We lived well and comfortably. We
hadn't discussed leaving. I'd just assumed we'd stay
and live in our unit, but then he'd said something
truly amazing. He wanted me to have his child? I
thought he was kidding, but no. He told me how he
planned to smuggle in a year's supply of oestrogen
to counter my built-in contraceptive.

Tears ran over my cheeks.

"Paul, please wake up. Talk to me."

I stroked his cheek. It felt cold and clammy. I
kissed his lips; they remained slack. I stared into his
eyes and tried to pick up emotional vibes. My link
with him would never be as strong as the links with
my sisters had been before I had severed them, but
I felt nothing.

"Come on, Paul, tell me what's wrong." I choked.
I sat there for a while, tears dripping onto the hand
I clutched to my chest.

Never mind what everybody said, I was going to
do something. That arrogant doctor didn't care; it
seemed I was the only one who did. Maybe I should
tell his high-ranking family at Ganymede. Certainly
those worms in the hospital would run for them.

But…Paul's sisters would only have me banned
from the apartment, have the locks changed so I

couldn't get in. And I had nowhere else to go. No, that wasn't an option.

I took the glass ball out of my pocket, the only indication I had that anything unusual had happened down there. Just how had that thing ended up in his suit?

The Research Division museum had more of these glass balls, huh? Well, I hated to be reminded, but one of my sisters worked there. I'd send her some images. Go and compare the samples, read all the notes researchers had made on these balls, and on other things they had found in the lake. If Paul couldn't do his job, I would have to do it for him.

As construct agent, I also had some extra features, such as not needing a camera for a scan. I held the ball on my open palm and raised it to my left eye.

Focus. Blink. Scan.

My vision of the room dissolved as data streamed into my brain. But it was not an image of the glass ball that I saw.

Thousands of pinpricks of light floated before me. They wavered in a kaleidoscope of colour and fluid movement, like waves in a sea, until an image formed from their rippling luminescence.

It showed me . . .

My own face seen through Paul's eyes.

A blinding flash of light.

Coloured ripples formed images of humanity: ancient cities of Egypt and Greece, the old world capitals, London, Paris, Rome. Modern starships: the *New Horizon,* the ship that had offered the first passenger service to Mars, the *Gateway,* the ship that took every colonist who came to the outer solar system. The colonies. The Moon, Mars, Ganymede, Titan, and Earth.

And then…

Something different altogether. A place where the sky was yellow and buildings, if they could be called that, globular and silver. Creatures, or "things" that looked like white strings of chewing gum, "walked" in streets, traversing silver walls as if they didn't exist.

A dark world where the sky was black and where I saw nothing moving, but where the main currency of communication was sound, deep, reverberating in my chest.

My vision expanded.

Jets of images streamed across space, forming a giant spider's web that snaked to far-flung reaches of the galaxy. A lilting voice whispered words beyond the edge of my hearing.

I jerked back, disentangling myself from the image. I sat there, panting. What the fuck was that?

Paul had turned his head. For a moment I thought he was looking at me, but his gaze was unfocused. He whispered some indistinct words.

I jumped up.

"Paul!" I shook his shoulders.

He didn't react to my words at all, but mumbled words I couldn't hear. His eyes held a fevered, crazed look. He was turning his head this way and that, as if searching for something.

"Talk to me, Paul. Say something."

No reaction. He'd gone back to his unresponsive state.

Never mind sending an image to Research. I'd go and ask them about this glass ball in person.

I scooped the ball up in a towel and put it in my pocket without touching it, I made sure Paul was comfortable and ran out the door.

The Research Division occupied a wing in the Habitat Operations building on the other side of the Dome. To get to it, I had to walk past the recreation section with its shops, cafes and gyms, all bathed in the dusky light of Titan's sky.

Overhead, a few cleaner robots crawled over the outside of the Dome in their never-ending job of scraping off the organic stuff that grew on every surface. We weren't sure if *grew* was the right word—Paul and I were researching that in the lab—but at times, the stuff seemed to be alive. It had a strange tubular structure, but nothing that could qualify as a cell membrane or a nucleus. It multiplied by sectioning off parts of tube which then moved around in the tarry substance it either secreted—but how?—or attracted. Was it alive? No one knew. What was the definition of "alive"?

Nothing on Titan's surface had ever harmed anyone. If it was life, it was so primitive and different from us that it probably couldn't do any harm. In fact, we'd been absolutely convinced of that.

This ball, if it was alive, might change that.

The Habitat Operations building. A low, squat affair with a bunker-like structure and small windows that could be sealed in case of a Dome failure. It was dank, cold and dark inside.

Surface Exploration, where Paul and I worked, was on the ground floor, down the long hallway where footsteps echoed like in a mausoleum, but I wasn't going there today. In the massive hall, I waited for the elevator platform and let it carry me to the second floor, where I came out in an equally dark and cavernous hall, the walls lined with reproductions of the more exotic of our electron microscope images.

On the far end of the hall was the reception desk, where a woman worked in a small pool of light cast by a desk lamp. The light made golden reflections in her bronze-coloured hair.

As I approached, she met my eyes for a split second, then her face tightened and she went back to her work.

Good day to you too, sister. I forced myself to keep walking until I could lean on the desk.

"I didn't think we'd ever see *you* here again," she mumbled into her screen.

The light in the room glittered on her tag. Kessler 129. Aphrodite. With her sharp chin and high cheekbones, she looked a bit like me, but that's where the similarities stopped.

<Damn it, you're my sister. Look at me.>

I hadn't tried using my direct link to her since I left our shared quarters and went to live with Paul.

She snorted. "Hadie, I'm not going to talk to you that way. I can feel your arrogance across the room. Whatever you're here for, why don't you go and ask your Pristines to help?"

"I'm here because I need to talk to you about these things."

I plonked the towel right in front of her on the table where she couldn't ignore it and unwrapped the glass ball. In the golden light, it looked like a cloud filled the interior. What the…? It had been clear before.

A flicker of interest crossed her face. "Where did you get this?"

"I'll tell you if you'll help me."

"Don't you dare demand things from me."

"Hang on—who exactly is demanding what from whom? 'Leave that man now or we'll never speak to you again.' Isn't that what you said?"

She glared back, but said nothing.

"You're jealous."

"Don't be ridiculous. Why should I be jealous of you? The only thing we want is to save you from yourself. Pristines don't care about us and the sooner you realise that, the better. What do you think we feel about losing you?"

"There would be no need to lose me if you could just accept that I love him."

"He's Old Earth. Trouble for you, for *us*."

"I've noticed the trouble. Short-sighted bigotry, mostly, from his family. Don't you think he's suffering for his decision? And why?"

"Yes, Hadie, why?" Her eyes met mine, hard and without compassion. "Why do you need him? Why do you lower yourself to being sneered at by his family?"

"One reason: I love him and he loves me. Apparently, for that, both our societies decide we're outcasts. Sorry, but I had expected that attitude from Old Earth families at Ganymede-bloody-University, but not from my sisters. For all that we're constructs, new humans and all that, I'd expected we could put such stupidity behind us."

She stared at her screen, and swallowed. For some long, heavy moments, neither of us said anything.

"And you've come here just to tell me that?"

"No, Aphrodite, I need your help."

She glared, said nothing for a while, and then sighed. "All right. What's this about?"

I told her of the flash and Paul's condition.

"I think this ball has something to do with it. It fell out of his suit."

"Yes, but we have a lot of those things. They're just glass balls."

"Try capturing an image of it."

She held the glass ball up on the palm of her hand at eye level. Blinked.

"And?" she asked. "I have the image. What am I supposed to see?"

"Didn't you notice anything?"

"What am I supposed to have noticed?"

I stared at her. Was she bullshitting me?

But no, I didn't think so. That experience I'd had was so overwhelming, she couldn't have kept her face emotionless through that.

I picked up the glass ball, heavy and cool in my hand, held it to my eye. This time I captured a clear image of the glass on the palm of my hand.

What the...

That meant...the glass ball only did this trick once, the first time someone tried it. That meant... it had now been spent. I'd seen things when I'd tried to capture the image, a stream of pictures of worlds human and alien. That material had been stored in the ball, or, when I tried to capture it, it had retrieved—

Damn. The outage. The main problem had been in the *communication* links and satellites.

This was a device of communication. With whom? Someone who now had Paul in their grip. It hadn't worked on me, because mine was only a residual effect, or maybe because I was a construct. Who knew?

"Come on, Hadie, tell me what I'm supposed to see," Aphrodite said.

I began, "I saw...." But my mind churned and went into different directions. I had to find out what this was about, urgently, before whoever or whatever had sent these images found Paul first.

"Tell me, research would have records of anyone who has found one of these balls, wouldn't they?"

She didn't reply.

"You have more of these things here, don't you?" <Come on, open up. You're my sister.>

"We do. They're made of glass. If this one's like the others, it has a strong magnetic field, and it absorbs light almost completely. What is it? A mystery."

Lies showed up green to me, and her aura was about the colour of spring grass. She would know that I saw it, too; she looked away. Her mouth twitched.

"Aphrodite, the fact that you hate me doesn't mean you can fool me."

She raised he hands. "Please, Hadie, you don't realise—"

"Don't 'please' me. I'm desperate. There is something wrong with Paul and it has to do with this thing. I think it's something alien."

Her eyes widened.

"That's impossible," she said, in a definite tone.

I couldn't get any more out of her. It was so typical. Someone in her line of authority had told her not to speak of this, because of a reason that could be as stupid as inter-departmental feuds. Because Research was treading on hospital territory, or something equally stupid. But because she was a construct, she obeyed, because she feared emotional repercussions if she didn't. Anger was yellow, and it could hurt. The pain kept us from fighting, but it also kept us from talking to each other, or questioning unusual behaviour.

So I went back down the elevator platform, vowing to find some sort of way of breaking into her mindbase, never mind that I needed the equipment and her cooperation to do that.

Damn it. She had clammed up on me the way constructs usually do when questioned by Pristines and I was on the wrong side of the equation.

Alone.

I stood there outside the building, while people scuttled past me like insects on a mission. People with food carts from the central canteen, children playing with little cars that contained blocks of hissing-ice that launched the thumb-sized vehicles at the ankles of passersby. Their laughter echoed against the Dome's curved ceiling.

What would I do if Paul didn't recover?

* * *

"Can I help you?"

I gasped at the strange male voice behind me. The man was grey-haired, about fifty, I guessed, thin, and dressed in a service overall with a Heslop tag. But I knew by the look in his eyes, that Heslop stock—middle management constructs—was about as far removed from this man's origin as possible. This man was a Pristine.

"Well—um…" I shrugged.

His gaze flicked to my tag that said Kessler 129, but he didn't comment on it.

"You have a problem with your lover?"

"Um—yes."

Immediately, I wished I could retract my automatic response. Someone asked you a question—you respond. All constructs get that hammered into their brains. It had taken me some time to unlearn, and now I was annoyed that it resurfaced. How the hell did he know about Paul?

"Maybe I can help."

"I'm all right, really." *Just begone with you, scarecrow.*

"He *will* recover," the man said into the tense silence.

"What do you know about it?"

"Enough to offer you help. Take it from me, he will be fine, but he will have to leave you."

They all said that, all of those uppity Old Earth families. "That's up to him to decide."

"It isn't, though."

"It is. Thank you for offering your help, but I can manage."

He bowed and backed away. "As you wish. But soon enough, when he recovers, you will want me to come back. I'm staying in the temp accommodation unit."

And then he was gone.

What the fuck did he mean—want him to come back? Like hell, I did.

But one thing was clear: I was walking away from the Research branch, but all my answers were inside that building. Aphrodite knew something. Never mind that she didn't want to tell me. I had to find out what it was.

I ran back, used a different elevator platform that took me to the storage rooms of the museum. I stalked past shelves stacked high with samples. A controlled-environment chamber held the remains of the Huygens probe, the very first human artefact that had made it onto the surface of Titan more than a hundred and fifty years ago. Long after it was thought to have been lost in the ice, a team of ice miners had recovered it about a hundred kilometres from where it was supposed to have landed— did that show how the icy surface moved, was it a mistake or was there some other process at play? I stopped for a few seconds to gaze at the corroded shell of the thing, and considered how much we had learned since then and how much there was still to learn.

Further into the corridor, there were glass-fronted cabinets along the walls. Some displayed historic material from the very first crewed trips to Titan almost one hundred and thirty years after the probe's landing. Half-eroded suits, outdated and probably no longer working equipment. Those bulky air tanks would have been awkward to carry around; we carried catalysers on our belts these days

Further down the hall was a cabinet with glass balls, piled up in crates stacked on top of each other. How many of these balls did they have?

All of them were cloudy. Someone had taped a sheet to the top corner of the glass. It said, *Silica balls, origin unknown.* Someone else had taped an electron microscope image to the sheet that showed, according to the legend, the surface of the balls, a curious crystalline pattern. There was a handwritten note: *Structural formation only possible in zero gravity. Several samples were found to have an electrical charge, possibly because of ions trapped in crystalline structure.*

Was I crazy or did the writer of the note suggest that these balls formed somewhere other than the surface of Titan?

I stepped back, and looked from the balls to the ancient lander. It could also be, of course, that worlds with an atmosphere and certain elements in their make-up simply attracted interest from communicating societies, whether human or otherwise.

Surely, some of the scientists must have found out *something* about these balls? Surely, someone must have found at least one clear one before?

I went into a room that looked like pictures I had seen of old Earth libraries. In reality, all the books on the shelves were made from durable, nondegradable, space-resistant plastic, the only way to ensure that generations hundreds of years in the future would still be able to see the data. I stood there, aimless, letting my gaze roam over the hardbound volumes. There were too many for me to even know where to begin. Printed numbers on the spines meant nothing to me. I didn't know if I had expected one of the titles to say *Mysterious glass balls*—in fact, I didn't know what I expected at all; but if I had to go through all the material in this room, it would take me months to find what I was looking for.

I needed my sister's help.

So I kept going through the corridor, past the deserted storerooms of the museum, and wondering how she could work in here alone. Sometimes people would come in, but most of the storing and cataloguing processes were automated.

I came out in the reception area behind Aphrodite's desk. She was working, and only saw me at the last moment.

"Hadie, what—"

I clamped my hand over her mouth.

<You know something. Tell me.>

<I can't. He said he'd kill you.> Her chest heaved. I caught shards of a scene in a dark corridor, a man in dark clothing stabbing a gun into her side. And then she went back into the museum to retrieve a disk from the library. She gave it to him, and he tucked it in his bag. Her fear showed up blue.

<Who is this guy?> So she *did* still care about me.

I replayed everything I had seen. The bewildering array of images as I had tried to scan the glass ball, the strange man who had accosted me in the street outside.

She nodded. <That's him. His name is Thomas Newton. Please, Hadie, stay out of his way. He's dangerous.>

There was no green in her aura.

I let her go and she slumped behind the desk. "Hadie, you are playing with things you don't understand."

"Has that ever stopped me? I have to save Paul."

"Please, Hadie, let it go."

"I can't. Have you ever loved someone? Really, really loved them so much that your insides turn to mush just thinking about seeing this person harmed?"

"Yes." Her eyes met mine. "And I'm seeing that person suffer every day."

Do you know that the colour of love is purple?

On the way back, I looked up Thomas Newton in my scientific research module. The text displayed over my real-life vision of the entertainment quarter, families relaxing at the cafes, people going about their business.

Thomas Reed Newton

Alliance: Science Division

Organisation: Luminati.

Residence: Unspecified. That usually meant that the person worked for a classified project. I guessed he was based either on Earth or Ganymede.

He had a frighteningly long list of scientific publications to his name, and a number of major awards.

All right, that solved the problem of the stranger's identity, but where did he come from and what the fuck did he have to do with alien glass balls we found on the bottom of Kraken Mare? It was not as if he had *put* the damn things there, was it?

And what was Luminati?

I looked that up, too, but the scientific database returned nothing and the general database brought up only references to some virtual reality game, where, apparently, the Luminati were a secret evil sect that had to be eliminated.

✳

"Paul, I'm back—"

I stopped, my hand still on the door.

Paul was no longer in his passive state. He still sat on the bed, but he had pulled a computer onto his lap. He wore a thought sensor behind his ear— which meant he'd gotten up and gone to look for the thing in the living room—and was muttering words too soft for me to hear.

"What are you doing?"

I crossed the room and looked over his shoulder at his work.

Lines of text scrolled across the screen, full of strange words and long formulae that meant absolutely nothing to me. Paul was an astrobiologist, with degrees in chemistry and physiology. I was his assistant and had none of these degrees, but he had a gift for writing about his work in ways that made the subject sound simple. I had often proofread his papers for him. Kesslers were designed with mid-range intelligence, and never before had I completely failed to understand his writing.

"Paul, you scare me. What is all this?" Shit, he was typing nonsense. He'd gone out of his mind.

He didn't reply, just continued muttering and typing.

"Paul!" I shook his arm, but he completely ignored me. The pupils in his eyes were so wide that the irises had almost disappeared. He was sweating and trembling.

"Paul, listen to me!"

That was *it*. No matter how horrified doctors would be about this, I was going to try and find the mindbase backup.

I ran to the unit's command centre in the kitchen and I scoured our databases for a copy of Paul's mindbase. The only one I found was over a year old—from before we met and got involved, before I moved in.

Oh, damn it. Damn it, Paul, how could you be so sloppy?

I sank at the kitchen table, my face in my hands.

If the backup worked, what would that mean to our relationship? He'd wake up finding a strange woman in his unit, a construct even. The fact that the old Paul hadn't minded that I was a constructed human didn't mean that the new version of him wouldn't. There were often small discrepancies between different versions. He might reject me. He might accuse me of breaking in.

Oh, Paul, damn it.

Still, that was probably a better situation than the current one, and if it would cure him, if he would look at me again, and smile...

I copied the data onto the house system and went into the bedroom.

Paul still sat there exactly as I had left him. Back straight and rigid, like some crash test dummy. Staring ahead, muttering his formulae.

He didn't react to my touching the base of his scalp and affixing the electrodes. With something as important as this, I didn't want to use the wireless connection. Like every piece of electronic communication on Titan, it was liable to sudden and unexplained failure.

I also connected a pad to my head—maybe I could steer the recovery, insert recent memories where the older backup left holes. Images of us making love, of the sheer pleasure on his face.

And then I stopped, my finger hovering over the button.

I had no right to do this. Modifying another person's mind without their consent was a punishable crime.

Paul shivered. He was in pain, screaming without making a sound, without being able to express it.

I pressed copy.

The data scrolled over the screen. Countless images flew past. Starships, diagrams, formulae. He murmured on and on, his words a sibilant whisper.

I could feel his presence. Images flowed through me, forming that spider's web. For a flash of brilliance, I saw...everything. The birth of the universe, the formation of stars and planets, great ships that travelled between them, ancient civilisations, familiar and strange. Faces of strange creatures alternated with those of famous scientists. The Egyptians, Archimedes, Socrates, Leonardo da Vinci, Albert Einstein, Isaac Newton, Stephen Hawking, Elizabeth Hunter.

A black-skinned girl with her hair in beaded braids dug in the sand in a field of maize and picked up a glass ball. As she held it up to study, it flashed in her face. I recognised her, too. Grace Nkwame, astrophysicist and Dean of Ganymede University. She still wore the beads.

I knew.

I understood.

I was the universe and I knew how it worked. I knew how old it was and how stars were born and how they died. I knew what happened at the end of time.

And then it was gone.

I was back in the bedroom, and someone was trying to break down our door.

Thud. The walls shuddered.

Paul still muttered, unresponsive. His words scrolled over the screen. The data had stopped flowing from my computer. The backup had gone straight past him. I sat there, breathing hard, becoming dimly aware of another blaring alarm in the corridor. A general alarm this time.

If this went on Habitat Operations would call for an evacuation. When the air composition systems went down, there was always a risk methane would build up in sections of the dome, and methane did interesting things when someone flipped a light switch.

Thud. The door rattled.

I looked around frantically. Was there anything I could use as a weapon?

In the corridor, a mechanical voice started calling, *Evacuate, evacuate, evacuate.*

Thud.

"Paul! Damn it, listen to me! We need to get out."

The door opened with a crash, and that scarecrow Thomas Newton ran into the room.

"Stop it, damn you, woman!"

"What are you doing here?"

"Getting your arse out of here. Come." He had to shout over the alarm.

I couldn't argue with that. I ripped the sensors from Paul's head—clumps of hair came out. I flung the computer aside—

"Hey, woman, what are you doing?"

"Getting the fuck out of here, what else—"

"Look at this!" He gestured wildly at the screen.

"What about it?"

"This is the most brilliant astrophysical work ever written. This will win many prizes."

He picked up the computer and put it in his bag, *where Aphrodite had told me he'd put the disk.* "Come."

We each took one of Paul's arms and dragged him up. In the corridor, a stream of people was heading in the direction of the vehicle bay. I pulled

Paul in the same direction, but Thomas Newton went in the other direction.

"Hey, where are we going? The trucks are that way—"

"No trucks. I'm taking him with me before you kill him. Copying a backup. Honestly, only a construct agent can think something as stupid as that."

"It didn't even work."

"No, thank goodness. All his brilliance would have been gone."

"Thomas Newton," I said, and I wondered if his last name was a coincidence, and I remembered that single moment of clarity, in which I understood *everything*, and in which I had seen the faces of people who had shaped our understanding of the universe, in which I *had* been one of them, looking through Paul's mind. Those were the Luminati, the most brilliant minds ever.

"You are one of the Luminati. Those who know everything."

A look of alarm flitted over his face. "It showed you that, did it?"

"Those balls form some sort of interstellar network powered by knowledge. It's stored in the unusual matrix of the glass molecules and passed to those who touch the spheres or try to scan them."

He nodded, slowly. Was he impressed? "An inorganic life form. Humans are creatures of flesh and blood. Our currency is food and air. This inanimate intelligence we are dealing with survives on knowledge. The Luminati are the ones blessed with the infection. It has inspired the minds of many of the Earth's greatest thinkers."

"People found balls like these on Earth?" I knew it to be true. I had seen the images.

"The last one was found many years ago."

"Grace Nkwame." She'd been a peasant's daughter somewhere in Africa. "But the balls ran out, and people from the sect died. Though obviously you must have cloned some—judging by your name."

"Yes, but the clones are not as effective. We needed to expand our search to find other seeds."

"Then how come the museum has some?"

"We've made sure they only found the cloudy ones—they're spent."

Spent, on what sort of creatures—I couldn't help but think—and how long ago.

"So what about the one Paul found?"

"We needed to have fresh blood. I'm here to pick him up and make sure his departure doesn't leave a trail that will lead to our discovery."

Then he produced the gun.

✳

But you see, you can't kill a construct. Sure, you can kill the body that houses the mind, but you cannot kill the mind itself, because there is always a backup. It's not as if he didn't try, but Aphrodite, bless her soul, made a habit of storing everything on Mars Base, where privacy laws make access to mindbase copies by third parties near-impossible, even, it seemed, if you were one of the Luminati.

The backup will continue to live inside machines, and hear the stories of the brilliant scientist Paul Ormerod, who wins awards but whose face looks deeply unhappy in the news reports. And the mind will eventually be reunited with a body and that is when the Luminati will get a big surprise.

Because I gave up my life for Paul, and he gave up his life for me, and I will continue to fight for *us* as long as his aura glows with purple luminescence.

"Luminescence" is set in the ISF-Allion world. *Shifting Reality*, the next in series is available now. If you like to know more about Patty, you can find her website at pattyjansen.com and get four free books.

GLOME

A GREAT SYMMETRY STORY

JAMES R. WELLS

Glome: A naturally occurring hypersphere in space. Scientists theorize that glomes may allow travel to other star systems. As of the year 2118, twenty glomes have been discovered in the vicinity of Earth and other planets in the solar system.

FOR THE THIRD TIME AMANDA BOWEN ATTEMPTED TO FIGure out where in the galaxy they were. The same program, running the same algorithms on the same hardware with the same inputs, returned the same non-answer. Unknown.

The arrangement of stars as viewed by their ship did not resolve to any position within hundreds of light years from Earth. They could be anywhere.

Amanda began to set up the next level of analysis. A detailed spectroscopic scan of several thousand stars, seeking an exact genetic match rather than just positional.

She was supposed to use the link, which should be second nature by now. The system would seamlessly assemble each instruction from her thoughts, then execute the program on her mental command. It was far faster than typing, in theory.

Amanda hated everything about it. During training she had tried and tried to get past the symptoms, but every time was still an ordeal. Evading the link as much as possible, she had become an excellent typist – a skill now fading among her shipmates.

The analysis was set up, and she let it fly with a command from her keyboard. Execution would take several minutes, not because of computing time, which was trivial, but because actual instruments would have to scan each star.

She looked up from the streams of detailed readings at her console to take in the scene on the main screen of the bridge. A sharp blue eye glared at them. The image of the star was damped on the display and didn't show its full brightness, but the processors could not filter out the crackling energy of the object.

The captain's voice came from behind her. "Let's have the best visual on the planet."

Even with the new view there was no escaping the electric blue. Now it bathed a world of swirling clouds. Displays on either side of the image told the tale. Temperature range sixty to one hundred fifteen Celsius – even the coldest places on this planet were hotter than the most scorching desert back on Earth. Typical wind velocity three hundred kilometers per hour. Atmosphere, carbon dioxide laced with nitric acid vapor.

The planet on the screen was the leading candidate for humanity's first interstellar colony.

Protocol demanded no unneeded chatter during mission critical periods, and this was such a time. But even with the immaculately trained crew, there was no mistaking an intangible change in the soundscape. Perhaps it wasn't possible for the crew to breathe while in the presence of that image without an underlying sense of despair escaping.

Amanda saw nothing but beauty. An entire new planet to observe and learn about. A planet that had never been seen by human eyes or measured by human instruments. Years, or perhaps a lifetime, of learning. It was somewhat like Venus, but even the quick initial scans showed differences.

She couldn't wait to dig in to exploring every facet of the new planet, and seeing what other mysteries were in the star system. Her childhood dreams, realized. She just needed to get the location problem out of the way.

Captain Hunt spoke from her station, directly behind Amanda. "How's the assessment going? Any viable settlement scenarios?"

"We're going to need a closer look," Mayor Blum replied. "At this point it looks like our best bet may be at one of the poles. I recommend a polar orbit, as low as we can take her."

Mayor Blum represented the one hundred forty colonists. While Captain Hunt was in command of all operations on board the *Rubicon*, a core purpose of the voyage was to locate a suitable planet and settle it, so Blum's opinion carried weight, if he chose to express it.

The console in front of Amanda was still running the new scan. She stole a moment to close her eyes and take a slow, controlled breath. She felt herself deliberately moving the large muscle of her diaphragm up into her lungs, pushing the air out, then retreating and reversing the flow. It didn't help settle her.

She was trying to process the fact that she and the rest of the crew were still alive. Their trip through the glome had not shredded the *Rubicon* into its component subatomic particles as some theoreticians had predicted. By entering into the Omega Entry of a glome just a few million kilometers from Earth, they had traveled across some unknown number of light years in a fraction of a second.

Most importantly, Earth was long gone. No matter what they found here, she would be free of Earth.

"Bowen! Report!" The captain's command crashed through.

Amanda startled, only managing not to fall out of her chair due to the safety straps. "Unknown, captain," she stammered. "We can't get a fix. I'm running a spectroscopic scan now. If we can positively identify a few stars, we'll have our position."

"When will you have it?" The captain was always to the point.

"Two more minutes," Amanda answered. "Provided we get matches in the first pass."

"Why wouldn't we?"

Amanda rotated her seat to face the captain, a knee scraping against the wall. She reached for the button to adjust the seat back, but she had already done that, and it was as far away from the work surface as it could move. Everything about the *Rubicon* was designed to pack as much useful material, and as many people, into a limited space as possible.

"It depends how far we went," she said. "The farther we have traveled, the longer it will take to positively identify stars we can see from home. We may need to try matching gross structures of the galaxy – assuming we're still in the same one."

Captain Hunt was an imposing presence. Decades in the military had sculpted her face into a permanent expression of intense, no-nonsense concentration. The captain always asked short focused questions, pondered for about two seconds, then issued the next order. She knew everything there was to know about the *Rubicon* and its crew.

It was the first time Amanda had ever seen the captain appear taken aback. But it was just for a moment, which passed quickly. "Tell me when you have an answer," and with that Hunt pivoted to the next topic. "Mister Deijia, your findings on our point of emergence."

Deijia was at the station to Amanda's left. She turned to hear him speak. "Nothing," he replied simply.

"You're still evaluating?"

"No, Captain. The findings are complete. There's nothing there. We arrived at a spot in empty space.

No hint of a glome at our point of emergence, if that's what you're asking."

"Yes, that was the real question. Thank you. Looks like we're here to stay."

Many of the colonists and crew members had clung to the belief that they would emerge from a glome, a twin of the one they had entered from space near Earth. It's the kind of symmetry that defines much of the universe, and which had dominated theories about glome transit. A comforting concept, assuring everyone there would be a way to return to known space. That a ship could simply reverse course and go back to the place from which it had started.

But no.

Now it was clear why no ships had ever returned to Earth from a trip into a glome, nor even any hint of a message received back. Even the most artfully programmed artificial intelligence, or the most skilled test pilot, could not return through a portal that didn't exist.

The only view that mattered was ahead of them.

Amanda was fine with that.

She listened to the discussion with one ear as she watched the results of her scan come in, one star at a time. Captain Hunt efficiently directed questions to each duty station, focusing more and more on the planet in front of them.

In a layer over the top of everything, there was procedure. Checklists, duties, and actions that had been practiced hundreds of times by the crew for the first few minutes after the trip through the glome. A machine of combined human and computer elements, designed to respond to any circumstance.

Amanda wondered how many of the processes had been designed to keep them all busy and feeling useful.

A chime brought her back to the scan. They were located! And just forty two light years from Earth!

She started scanning the calculation notes, preparing to notify Captain Hunt. There were definitely error bars in the results.

At that moment a series of alerts rippled around the bridge. From her post, Amanda could see each crewmember reading for a moment. Some staring intently at the empty space in front of them, others using old-school physical display panels as Amanda preferred.

She turned back to her console. The alert was serious. The astrogation system reported a major failure – distorted readings indicating the instruments were out of alignment, or worse.

"It may be glome distortion," Deijia spoke into the silence. "That was theorized, and we may have just seen the first case. According to some theories, anything going through a glome could be changed in some subtle manner – distorted just a tiny bit."

"What does this mean for us?" Hunt asked.

"That specific system, I expect we can repair it," Deijia returned. "But the bigger question is whether anything else has been damaged. Until we get to the bottom of the issue, we can't trust any system on board. No piece of equipment, no program. In light of this, we may be lucky we all made it. Picture the effect of just a few blood vessels or neurons, in any of our bodies, suddenly in just slightly the wrong place."

Although she had been aware of the theory, Deijia's frightening description had Amanda assessing how she felt. Pulse at the edge of racing, a little short of breath. A tremble, kept under control and not quite visible. In other words, normal for her in recent days. Evidently her neurons and blood vessels were still connected.

"Shut down everything except life support and lighting," Hunt ordered. "We're going to verify every system and every component on this ship."

"Crew and colonists are all accounted for, no health or safety emergencies," Estwing reported.

"On our current path we'll fly by the planet at about half a million kilometers, then we'll be back in her neighborhood in just over four hundred days. Plenty of time to verify or repair anything needing attention."

Commander Estwing's mission was to stop things from going wrong. Safety, security, and any kind of risk reduction – those topics were his domain. During the past few months, Amanda had come to see past his manner and understand his purpose. Ever and always, he was about protecting everyone on the ship.

Captain Hunt picked up the key point Estwing had not quite stated. "So we'll miss orbit of the planet if we don't thrust?"

"Aye, captain. We can easily make orbit on the next pass, assuming our systems are in good order. Four hundred eleven days."

Amanda wanted to scream out. A year, gone! More than a year tracking around the star, before they even got started. On the bright side, they could potentially launch probes to collect more data about the planet, and the other planets that were much farther out from the star.

"How soon do we have to thrust if we want to make orbit?"

"We won't be able to, captain. We would need to thrust within thirty eight minutes, but to verify everything about the engines will take several weeks."

"Thirty eight minutes. What can you check in less than that time?"

"Visuals from existing cameras, and current readings. That's only a couple of minutes."

"How about this: We'll review images from every camera we have in place right now. See if you find a showstopper," the captain ordered. "And while that's in process, I have something for us. A video message I received eight minutes before we entered the glome, and have been requested to play as soon as we were out of full emergency mode. You guessed it – from Noel."

This time there was no mistaking the chorus of groans. "Light years away, and there's no escaping him," put in Estwing. "How far do we have to go? Another galaxy?"

Emboldened, Amanda added, "If there is a product placement in the video, I'm going to puke." After a stern look from the captain, she amended, "But entirely due to zero gravity. Nothing to do with the message."

"He'll never know whether we played it or not," Deijia suggested, helpfully.

Captain Hunt sighed. "If you are all quite finished, please give your attention to the front screen
for an address from our fearless leader. The header
says this identical message was provided to each of
the twelve ships, so this will be playing in twelve
different star systems. While you will never get this
two minutes and twelve seconds of your life back, it
is mercifully brief."

The video began.

Amanda was accustomed to seeing elaborate
productions from Noel, with sweeping music and
panoramic views zooming in to show him in some
impressive location. He would expound on his Go
Big plan for the stars. No more piddling around
with robots or small lightly crewed vessels. Go Big
meant a fleet of ships with the best equipment and
most capable crews that could be mustered. Ships
that could deal with whatever circumstance might
be found beyond the trip through a glome. While
critics derided the plan as hopelessly rash, there was
no shortage of motivated and highly qualified vol-
unteers. Amanda was one of them.

In this video, Noel sat behind a plain desk.
Normally he sported a tinge of grey in his short
black hair, and an artful two-day stubble to high-
light his rugged handsomeness. In this video he
simply looked unshaven. And grey.

"If you are listening to this message, you have successfully traveled through your target glome," he started. "You are in another star system, because you sure aren't here. Congratulations."

Noel continued. "You have trained for years, drilling for every contingency our brightest minds could think up. But in all the planning, there has been one persistent theme – that your colony will become part of an active network of humanity beyond our solar system. That we will send more ships, and you will find a way to return home to Earth. The expansion of people, civilization and commerce to the stars."

Then Noel simply stopped speaking and looked into the camera for several long moments. Amanda found herself thinking his video editor must have been asleep at the wheel.

"I don't think that's going to happen," Noel said at last. "I'll do everything I can to get you more support, but – well, the damage assessment from the attack on the Mare Nubium shipyard is getting worse every hour. Pretty much everything has been destroyed. From what we see now, it will be seven years until we can launch the first new supply ship to follow any of you. Minimum. If there are no more attacks, and if nothing else goes wrong.

"Here's the part where I might need to apologize. After the attack, I sent the order. To each ship, to go directly to its assigned glome and enter it. I did this knowing you might never get any further help from Earth."

Apologize? For sending people on the greatest voyage ever? Clearly Noel didn't understand the essence of why people had volunteered for the project, Amanda thought.

"I sent the order because I thought it was our best and maybe only chance to get to the stars. The attack on Mare Nubium was a declaration of war. I have no idea what will happen next – we still don't know who is responsible. Away from our solar system, you might be in the safest place you could be.

"You have your official mission parameters. Settle the best available planet in your arrival system. Set up the phased photonic array and send a transmission that we might receive however many years from now. Await more ships, more supplies. Those are all great, but just in case you missed it, I need to make sure you know the one thing that matters. Find a way. To grow, to thrive, wherever you find yourselves. If your orders are in conflict with the best course of action, throw the book out and do what you need to do.

"I wanted more than anything to go on one of the ships, to see what's out there. It was the hardest decision of my life to stay here, but maybe I can still do you some good. To every single one of you – I admire you all very deeply. You are the future of our species. No matter what happens here, I believe you will thrive, somewhere out there. So – no pressure!"

Just once, at the very end, they saw the trademark Noel smile, and the transmittal was over.

The bridge was silent for a moment as the import of the message soaked in. The founder of their project clearly believed the *Rubicon* was completely on its own. While every person on the ship had accepted that possibility, it was dismaying to hear it from the person who had created the entire plan.

"Damn!" Deijia slapped his knee. "We missed out! We could have had Noel on board! How awesome would that have been? Special seminars every evening!"

"Ok, we've all heard it," Captain Hunt said. "But no matter what Noel thought back home, it doesn't change a thing here. As he said, we have our mission parameters. And right now, we need to decide whether to thrust and catch orbit of the planet. Findings, Mister Estwing?"

"Just finishing up," Estwing said. "Based on every available camera and every diagnostic, the thrusters are good to go. We can make orbit if we take a chance on blowing ourselves up. Otherwise we'll be back around this neighborhood in just over four hundred standard days."

"The safe thing is to hold off," Hunt mused. "We can spend the next few months getting to the bottom of the astrogation issue and inspecting the engines. We can get the phased array deployed to transmit back to Earth. Then we'll evaluate the planet next year."

"That's sensible," Estwing agreed.

"There's more," the captain said, and looked around. "Estwing, Blum, Deijia, Bowen, to my exec office."

This was strange. There were only six other crew on the bridge. What could not be told in front of people they had worked with for the past year?

Amanda unbuckled and pushed off in the direction of the well that connected the levels of the ship. Moving around in zero gravity was well practiced by everyone, and there were no collisions. Each crew member in turn dove head first to the next level "below" – it was better to see where you were going than to preserve any sense of standard up and down.

With five, the exec office was crowded. Amanda found herself packed between Blum and a corner of the office. To stay in place she held on to a handy loop which was there for the purpose.

Mayor Blum was the only person on the entire ship Amanda would consider to be heavy, although the concept was moot under their current free floating conditions. Every part of him had just a little bit extra. She could hear each of his breaths.

The moment the door was closed, Hunt began. "I received a briefing on the Mare Nubium attack shortly before we went through the glome. The mystery, as you all know, is why the asteroid wasn't detected for so long, until finally an amateur saw it."

"With an optical instrument!" Estwing put in. "From Earth!"

The captain continued. "Now we know. Our systems were compromised on Mare Nubium and across our set of observatories, and the signal of the asteroid was systematically suppressed. An extremely targeted virus did just that one thing."

She looked around the small room. "That would not matter to us now, except for one thing. The virus was injected into the computer system by someone who was on the Mare Nubium station."

Amanda felt like her head was about to explode.

One appallingly stupid act. Waking up every day since then desperately hoping no harm would result. Stitching together a flimsy internal narrative to convince herself that everything would simply fade away into the past. Avoiding responsibility.

For over a year she had lived in denial, which was now crushed as thoroughly as the wreckage of the shipyard on Mare Nubium.

Everyone else had a lot to say, and they were all talking at the same time.

"Someone sold us out!"

"An inside job."

"So the agent could be on one of the ships–"

"Could be here. One chance in twelve–"

"Nonsense, anyone working against the mission would have stayed at the station."

"And get flattened by an asteroid?"

"Everyone got out safely, the agent would have known that would happen –"

Estwing began to speak over everyone else. "We have to assume that a spy or saboteur may be on board. At a minimum, we could have the virus in our systems. That astrogation issue – I bet it's the virus rather than glome distortion. And we don't know where the virus will strike next – it's probably mirved so it could have many different expressions. I'm thinking of how easy it would be to set something out of adjustment anywhere in the engine systems. We definitely shouldn't use any thruster until we're sure our systems are clean."

Deijia spoke up. "I do see your point, commander, but would just say this: If the purpose of terrorism is to create fear and stop people from acting for themselves, then this will be the most successful such attack in history – reaching across forty two light years."

Estwing was quick with the rejoinder. "I appreciate the philosophy, but my job is to protect everyone – safety and security – and I work with the facts as we know them."

The captain held up her hand. "On the decision facing us—thrust to catch orbit of the planet or wait. Anyone else?"

The small room was silent.

Amanda had an idea, but wasn't sure if she trusted herself to speak. How much might her voice give away? Could she even talk coherently?

"We could thrust manually," she blurted out. "Using the base level operating system."

Everyone in the room was staring at her.

She gathered herself. Her voice wasn't quavering too badly, she thought. She could do this. "When we send a command to thrust, we let the programs do all the thinking for us. And that's where a virus can do its harm – none of us really understands what's going on in there. But it all resolves to a small number of simple commands. Open these valves, to a certain aperture for a certain amount of time. We can do that directly."

"Can we do it accurately enough?" the captain asked.

"Sure we can," Amanda answered, gaining confidence. "Getting to orbit around the planet from here, it's like hitting the side of a barn, especially if any orbit will do."

"Mister Estwing, any objections?"

"If we're going to thrust, it's the best way," he grudged.

"Everyone back to the bridge," the captain ordered. "Bowen, provide a proposed thrust plan as soon as possible. Estwing and Deijia will review."

Moments later, every crew member was at their station.

Amanda worked the numbers on the screen at her console. She clung to the digits in front of her, desperate to drive out any other thought. In minutes she had a plan.

"Soup's on!" she called. "Come get it!" Hopefully that sounded normal for her.

"Why won't you ever link with a virtual?" demanded Estwing.

"Because she's a Luddite," answered Deijia. "Just pull up her screen at your console, it's the same thing." For his part, Deijia simply leaned over and peered at the screen on Amanda's console.

"Pretty simple," Amanda walked them through it. "We do a pair of little attitude burns. Number 8 at 4 millimeters aperture for 12 seconds. Wait for 8.5 seconds. We open Number 2 equal and opposite 4 millimeters for 12 seconds again, to stop the tumble. We verify that we're headed correctly. Then it's the main engine straight ahead."

"I'm tracking," Estwing said. "And it checks out. Still, doing this without the navigation system seems…"

"What?" Amanda challenged. "Crude? Low Tech? Listen, it's just math. We don't need some computer to sprinkle fairy dust on it. We just need to open some valves and set some switches."

"I have reviewed the numbers and I concur with the plan," Deijia said.

"Any technical objections?" Captain Hunt asked.

"Great plan, if we have a death wish," Estwing replied.

"Mister Estwing, maybe when we do the attitude adjustment on the ship, it will help you. Execute the thrust sequence."

The pause was longer than it should have been. "Aye, captain."

Amanda felt the sequence begin. A tiny push, so it felt for a few seconds like she was falling forward. A weightless interval. Then a matching sensation pulling her back.

As the thrust ended, Amanda quickly checked their position – as reported by their systems, at least. And it was good. "We're a go for the main burn," she reported.

The directions of up and down reasserted themselves, and Amanda felt herself settle into her seat. The main thrust was stronger than the attitude burns, enough to create real gravity on the bridge, and would be more sustained.

The ship had not exploded.

"On track for twenty one minutes of thrust, then ninety five minutes to polar orbit as Mayor Blum recommended." Estwing reported.

"Thank you," the captain acknowledged. "Please shift your attention to the most complete sweep possible of our computer systems."

With the immediate task taken care of, reality flooded back for Amanda. She needed to get off the bridge and away from any other human, if only for a short while. "Captain, may I have a few minutes?"

Captain Hunt looked momentarily surprised. Then her expression softened. "Five minutes. After that, help Mr. Deijia investigate the forward sensor. We still need to check if the sensor was affected by glome distortion."

"Thank you, Captain," and Amanda was off. Quickly she climbed up several levels to the most spacious place on the *Rubicon*. Officially it was the central leisure deck. She called it the view room. Everyone was on duty so it was blessedly empty. A low couch beckoned.

"Show our sun," she instructed, and was abruptly bathed in sharp blue light. "No, not that one. Earth's sun."

The screen accommodated, displaying a bright but ordinary yellow star against an unfamiliar layout of other stars.

"It wasn't supposed to be like this," she told herself.

Johan. In college she had been invisible to him. About two social circles away, she had always seen him from afar, unapproachable. A big man on campus, knowing everyone who mattered. And why would he want to know her, anyway? She knew she was gawky and awkward, and far too good at math and science to be attractive to a man like him.

Then five years later he had reappeared in her life, suddenly with a deep interest in her. More than interest. Courtship. On cloud nine, she had not thought to question anything. It had begun just a few weeks after she had been admitted as a candidate for the exploration program.

Now she knew why. It all made horrifying sense. And she had betrayed everyone who mattered to her.

Amanda stared out at the starscape. She reimagined events, trying to construct versions of the past where she made better decisions. Where she summoned up a shred of self-respect. Where she wasn't blinded. But however hard she tried, every thread ended up in the same miserable place.

No matter what scenario she played out in her mind, it wouldn't change anything.

"Hey, you." Deijia's kind smile brought her back to the present. "Making the most of your time?"

Amanda realized she had pulled herself tightly into a ball, on her side on the couch. She forced herself to uncurl, not by relaxing, but by pushing her shoulders and legs out, then tipped herself up to a sitting position.

She took comfort for a moment in looking up at her shipmate. He had medium brown skin, a fine nose and lips, and wide, expressive eyes. His perfectly smooth chin looked like it had never grown even a first wisp of facial hair.

Tau Deijia was the most beautiful man Amanda had ever seen.

"I'm just –" Amanda struggled to explain herself, then fell silent, at a loss.

"It's all pretty overwhelming," he let her off the hook, gracefully as always. "Light years from home, and now things are going wrong."

"But how are you so calm?" Amanda was glad to move away from her thoughts of a few moments before.

"Calm? Are you kidding? I'm terrified!" Yet he smiled still. "I pretend. We all pretend for each other, and that's how we keep it going."

"I just wish there was something I could do."

"As a matter of fact, there is. We have a sensor to replace, and I've got the new one here. If the readings are correct after the swap, we'll know it was just a sensor problem, and that will be great news. So what do you say?" Deijia reached out, although there was no need for help in the fractional gravity.

Amanda kept his hand in hers for a few moments longer than necessary as she stood. "Ok, let's do it."

"After you," Deijia made a sweeping gesture toward the ladder. Amanda grabbed a rung and started climbing in the direction that was currently up because of the ship's thrust, toward the nose of the ship.

They climbed through several decks she knew were filled with the colonists. One hundred forty people, an array of specialists in every skill needed to explore and settle a new world. She knew many of them, from their months of training together. Even now, they all were busy analyzing data about the new planet and working on plans to create a settlement on that inhospitable world.

The settlers had a lot to work with. Carefully selected tools for a wide variety of expected situations. Thousands of design templates so they could quickly print other tools that might be needed. Microorganisms that could turn sterile dirt into fertile soil. Heirloom seeds. The heritage of humankind.

Talking with any given colonist, she had always been impressed how much a person could know about each specialty, and amazed at their devotion to attaining their expertise. In turn, colonists embraced and accepted her anomalies, especially her facility with all forms of calculation. Anywhere else she had ever lived, she had been an outlier. In the company of the colonists and crew of the

Rubicon, Amanda felt normal for the first time in her life.

Amanda and Deijia continued, finally reaching the highest deck, immediately below the nose of the ship. Above them was a hatch which would lead to a set of smaller passages to the sensor that was their objective.

"Time for your silver bunny suit," Deijia said.

"It's just for a couple of minutes," Amanda replied. "Do I really have to?"

"You know the deal. Keep the rads out of your nads. You might need them sometime, if we find a decent place to live. Let's just be glad there's no EVA for this one."

From a closet she found the correctly sized suit and pulled it on. The metallic fabric was designed to provide some protection against radiation for travel outside the main hull of the ship.

"Dancing in the stars!" Amanda exclaimed, and struck a pose. It was almost enough to take her mind away from the revelations of just a few minutes before. But there was no avoiding it. Deijia deserved the truth.

She turned to face him. "Tau, there's something I need to say."

He took a step closer and held both of her hands. "It might not be the right time, Mandy. We have kind of a lot going on right now. You know, a ship to repair, a virus to hunt down, a star system to explore. But soon."

Of course he misunderstood. Maybe that was good. Did she really want to tell him a secret that would make him hate her forever?

Not now.

"Soon," she said, and turned to the control panel on the wall. "Please open the nose hatch," she instructed.

Above them, the circular door dilated.

"Why do you say please?" Deijia asked. "Do you think you're going to hurt the computer's feelings if you don't?"

"Never know when they'll take over," Amanda said. "Can't hurt to be polite. And besides, that makes it easy for the machine to know it's a command." For a precious few moments with Deijia, she could pretend.

She started to climb, while Deijia stayed below as safety watch for the confined space entry. Another silly procedure. If there was anything wrong with the air, or if there was any other hazard, the ship would already have warned them.

Up in the nose of the ship, a small maze of passageways greeted her. She knew the way, and easily found the small port holding the sensor. She pulled a locking bar out of the way and snapped the sensor out of its housing, replacing it with the new one. Easy peasy.

Deijia waited just a few meters away, around three corners and down one ladder. Amanda burned to tell him, to unburden herself.

So why was she going so slowly?

At the top of the ladder, she held out the old sensor. "Catch!"

The sensor fell slowly in the low gravity, and Deijia caught it easily. Amanda came down the ladder and took off her bunny suit.

"Let's see if the new sensor made a difference," Deijia suggested. "Just link to my virtual and we can look together."

"No!" Amanda almost shouted. "You know the link gives me headaches." In addition to her existing issues with the link, she now had another reason to avoid it. The updated version was guaranteed not to allow unguarded thoughts to spill over from one person to another, but Amanda still wasn't going to touch it with a three meter pole.

Deijia shrugged. "Sorry I asked, I should have known better. How did you pass the certification tests for the link, anyway? I've never seen you use it."

"I just had to power through. Kind of like in grade school when they force you to write cursive, until they assume everyone's got it and then they move on."

"Except handwriting is a useless anachronism. Seriously, the link is that hard for you?"

"When I do it for a few minutes, it's just uncomfortable. Then it gets worse and worse. Like I need to move but can't, or have an itch but can't scratch it. Or there's a grating noise drilling into my brain but I can't exactly hear it. Each of the exams was two hours – you remember. And I couldn't stay in the link that long."

"What did you do?"

"I kept failing."

Amanda remembered the summons to Noel's office, three months before launch. She was going to be washed out. Sent home in disgrace to Earth.

She had walked into the office, seeing it was surprisingly spare. Noel, a desk, and about eight displays. He was about to give her the bad news, she was sure.

"Bowen," he had said. "The link tests. You're not making it through them. You need to."

"Is there any other way? I don't need the link to do my work."

"You've got to tick the box. There's a standard, and you need to meet it. Can you do that for me?"

"I'll do my best, sir. I'm allergic, and it's really, really tough."

There, she had said it. The unproven and immeasurable malady, dismissed by experts as hypochondria. An excuse for lack of attention span, or laziness.

Amanda thought it would be the last straw. Instead, Noel seemed to focus and see her as a person for the first time. "Listen, Bowen. I'm not supposed to tell you this, but if you can get through the link tests, you're in! I want you to be on one of the ships."

There was no way. With nothing to lose, she had asked the cynical question. "Is this your last-chance motivational speech for people who are about to fail out?"

Noel gave her a puzzled look. "I guess you really have no idea how exceptional you are. Breaking our training scenarios. Providing wrong answers that turn out to be right, so we have to revise everything. Let me be clear, Bowen – the entire purpose of the call for candidates was to find people like you. So do this one thing. Pass the link tests. Tick the box. Now tell me again – will you do it?"

It had been a revelation. In her life up until that moment, she had never believed she would be valued, or even really noticed, for her devotion to the things she cared about most.

"I will!"

And she had. By the end of the last exam, she had wanted to cut her skin entirely off to stop the sensations. A helpful proctor had wrapped her hands in towels and taped them up at some point. But she was through. And she was in.

"Wow!" Back in the present, 42 light years from Earth, Deijia was suitably impressed by the story. "I guess I'll check out the new sensor by myself, then. It'll just take a second."

Deijia went zombie, his face flickering and twitching. After less than a minute he returned to her. "Get this: No difference. The new sensor is giving identical readings to the old one. It can't be glome distortion – if that's something that even exists. So the problem must be in the software. That's a scary thought – it's a software bug or that virus. Either way, we've got trouble."

Amanda knew the answer. It was a virus.

"I thought this would be our clean start," Deijia went on. "Just us, the shiny denizens of the shiny new ship *Rubicon*. But somehow we've managed to bring along the baggage of home, whether it's a virus or the fear of it – which might actually be worse."

Amanda was seized with an inspiration. The past was beyond her reach. Only one thing remained.

"Maybe it's not too late," she said. "It's still just us."

She raised her right hand and said the words. "For as long as the expedition may last, whether on ship or planet, I will represent the highest standards of honesty and responsibility. I will protect my shipmates, always working with them and not against them. In any place we find ourselves, we will care for each other."

Deijia shook his head in wonder. "Wow, you remembered all the words. Do you recite it every morning over breakfast?"

"Don't you think it matters?"

"Not sure how it will help us fix the astrogation system."

"I've got a plan for that, too," she told him. "I'm going to rewrite it from scratch."

"The whole system?"

"Just enough to compare and see where the differences are. Then we should be able to tell exactly what values the virus is changing. That might help us catch it."

She could see Deijia putting on his thinking cap. "But the virus could have changed reference values, like the actual positions of the stars as determined from Earth. It's not only the program that might be vulnerable."

"I'll check the positions," she assured him.

"Against what? There's no paper here on board, and anything else could have been changed."

Amanda tried to understand the question. "Why would I need paper?"

Deijia stared at her for a moment until realization dawned. "You mean – you know them? You know the position and distance of stars from Earth?"

"Just the first fifty light years or so. Don't you?"

Amanda chose not to mention that when she was fourteen years old she had made a scale model of the Sun's neighborhood. It had resided in the ceiling space of her room, providing the setting for hundreds of imagined interstellar adventures. When she had left for college, her mom had reclaimed the space for a guest bedroom.

"It's lovely, sweetie," her mom had said. "But we can't have visitors bumping their heads on Sirius."

Deijia slowly shook his head. "I'll brief the captain on the sensor and tell her what you're up to. You have fun—I know you will."

They headed on to their separate destinations.

✳

Amanda was failing to concentrate on her analysis.
It should be so straightforward—just math. But she
couldn't even put together the most basic sequence
of the symbols that had been her companions for
so many years.

She was such an idiot.

Johan had assured her that the only purpose
of his plan was to help in negotiations with Noel,
for a deeply important cause. She could hear
Johan's voice in her head, from their meeting the
year before. "People are starving, and he's spending trillions to send a dozen ships to—somewhere.
Nobody even knows where. But you can help."

"Will you harm the program?" she had asked.

Johan had a way of making her feel small. "So
many people suffering, and you only care about
your space camp." Space camp—a cutting reference to her chances of making the grade and being
selected for the actual voyage.

"But don't worry," he had been filled with
assurance. "We just need a little more information
so we can drive a good bargain. We want a fair deal
– for every trillion he spends on his boondoggle, he
invests a trillion down here. And then we're partners

instead of adversaries. He's got money coming out his butt, so he'll totally go for it."

Johan knew how to close the deal. "I know you have the courage to do this," he had said. "It makes me proud to know you."

There was only one person who could convince her of such an absurd narrative. That person was – herself. Desperate to believe, she had tied logic into triple knots.

She found herself wondering if Johan had known everything that would happen.

It was time to stop making excuses. For Johan, who had used her. Who had always used her. And for herself.

And now, what should she do?

The honorable thing was to turn herself in. Do what she should have done more than a year ago, if she had not been so selfish. So cowardly. If she had come clean at the start, the Mare Nubium shipyard would still be in existence. Human exploration of the stars would be continuing, and preparing to accelerate.

In all of history, had one person ever made a decision with worse consequence?

But if she confessed now, that would make things even worse. How much of a burden would she cause as a prisoner, consuming precious resources? As the settlers and crew took on the challenge of establishing their lives in a new world, it was the last thing they needed.

There was only one answer decency would allow.

In the short term, she would stay at her post, helping the ship and the mission as well as she possibly could. She had a job, and she was good at it. She could make up, in some small part, for the harm she had caused.

Then, when things were more settled, when they had less need for her, she would do the right thing.

How could she function now, when her shipmates needed her? It seemed impossible.

She remembered the link exams. When she had felt every fiber of her being scream out to release the link, somehow she had stayed in.

She could see this through. For as long as necessary.

Slowly, doggedly, she began assembling the symbols. One cell at a time, creating the formulas she needed. Checking and double checking each. She ruthlessly squashed any thoughts that were not of calculation and logic. She would solve the astrogation problem for her shipmates. And do anything else that needed doing.

Estwing suddenly walked in the open door of her workspace. "Bowen, what are you doing off the network?" he demanded. "You can't do that."

"I'm rewriting a version of the astrogation program," she said. "If a virus is causing problems with our main version, I can prove it by running a clean one and getting different results."

"Stop it. I can't have anyone running unsecured."

"But unless I stay in a separate environment, I'll never know—"

"Back online," he said.

"You're just being paranoid."

"Paranoid? Somehow a virus got on this ship, and there is no way it could have happened. Mare Nubium, that place was a sieve. Thousands of people coming and going, no central security. No surprise about the infection there. But this ship – I personally set up everything. If I'm paranoid now, it's because my best wasn't good enough." His sense of failure pervaded the office.

Then Estwing closed the door and took a seat across the table.

He was always meticulous with his grooming, as with everything else, but shaving was an eternally losing battle for Estwing. After ten hours on shift, his face was a dark forest from which the next worry prepared to emerge.

"And – I need a word, about something else."

Everything she had so painfully loaded up in her forebrain was draining away, Amanda lamented to herself. "What?"

"I've been thinking about the decision to thrust for orbit. It was such an unneeded risk."

"It was fine! We gained a year."

"But it could have been the end of us. Sheer impatience. I guess I should expect that from you, but the Captain went along with it. What was she thinking?"

"Maybe you can explain something to me, Commander. If you're so risk-averse, why did you volunteer for the most insane trip in human history?"

He sighed. "It will be wasted on you, but I'll try. Taking on a dangerous endeavor, that's fine. I'm here, as you mention. But having decided to do it, we need to figure out the best way to take each step. The only way to do the most dangerous thing is to do it carefully."

"But the thrust is in the past. Why does it matter now?"

"Here comes the next thing. The captain is going to send out eight of our best probes for over a year. To set up the phased photonic array, to transmit messages back to Earth."

"And you disagree." Amanda still had no idea what Estwing wanted from her.

"It's the wrong choice. You heard Noel. We need to do what's best for us, right here, and those probes could be useful for any number of purposes. But more to the point, we could send out the probes for the array any time we want. She's insisting on launching the probes in the next hour, before we go into orbit. To save a little fuel."

Amanda had her own reasons she hoped to never hear from Earth again, but she wasn't about to share them with Estwing.

"So provide your input. That's how it works. For what it's worth, I agree with you, and I'll say a word if the captain asks me."

"If she asks? That's the problem. Waiting around to be asked. Everyone needs to stand up and make sure she knows it's a mistake to deploy the array so quickly."

Stand up? What was Estwing suggesting?

Amanda squared herself. "Commander, let me make something clear. I will be happy to provide information to the captain. Opinion, if that's called for. But beyond that – I swore an oath."

"Of course. To protect everyone aboard. And we'll follow it."

"Listen. Antoine. I know how much you care for the safety of the ship. You see a risk and you have to run over and stomp it out."

"It's my job. Security and Risk Management."

"More than that. It's your nature. You know what we call you, right?"

"I'm already sure I don't want to know," he replied.

"Mother Hen – that's your moniker." Amanda managed not to laugh.

"What!?"

"We say it with love. Is that any consolation?"

"You–" Estwing pointed his index finger directly at her, "need to connect that computer back to the network. If you have a problem with that, you can take it up with the captain. No matter what name you call me, I'm running security, and you're going to do it my way."

Amanda sighed and folded up her computer, then followed Estwing out of the small office.

✳

As Amanda arrived back at the bridge, the place was abuzz. It had been expected that glomes would be found, but now they had the first sighting anywhere outside Earth's solar system. It was at the edge of detectable range for their instruments, just over 50,000 kilometers away. The glome was no hazard as long as they stayed beyond a 10,000 kilometer radius, and the *Rubicon*'s course took it comfortably farther away than that.

She wistfully imagined what might be found beyond the new glome. Someday, when the probes had fulfilled all their expected other uses, the plan was to send one into each glome they discovered in this system. If enough probes went into enough glomes, one of them might return eventually to Earth.

Once it was verified that their course would safely miss the glome and its spatial envelope, a discussion resumed. Settlement scenarios on the planet were being floated, and set aside.

"There is another choice," Mayor Blum said. "Orbit. Using the flex spaces we can triple our available living volume."

To Amanda's surprise, nobody on the bridge made a ribbitting sound after the nickname for the expandable habitats.

Captain Hunt sounded exasperated. "You can't be serious. We could have done an orbital colony at home. And we'd still be able to talk to the other four billion people. Visit, even."

"We can't set any choice aside. Orbit would be far safer than on the surface. It removes atmospheric and temperature problems from the equation."

Orbit. Floating in empty space. A closed system allowing no waste at all, not one atom of precious carbon, hydrogen, oxygen, or nitrogen to escape. No replenishment of the critical elements except what might be plundered from the planet below or skimmed from its atmosphere.

Blum continued. "We're rated for forty years, but we could make it work for longer. Far longer. You know that. We would have forty years to perfect our systems. And wait for more ships to come."

"Once we deploy the bullfrogs and people move into them, we won't be rated to thrust. In effect, we'll be cannibalizing the *Rubicon.*"

"That's always been a potential outcome, including some of the major planet settlement scenarios."

"Stranding us here? You can't possibly be advocating—"

"Oh no," the mayor assured her. "I'm not taking a position. Just pointing out possibilities."

Not taking a position. Of course. Amanda expected nothing different from the mayor.

Amanda turned back to her analysis. Forced by Estwing to go back onto the ship's network, she didn't know if the program was vulnerable to the same infection which had harmed the original astrogation program. But the simpler she kept each piece, the safer she would be. It was just math.

As she tried to bend her attention to the task, the daymare arrived. "Concentrate," she told herself, but it was no use. Her mind's eye was going to force her through the moment. Again.

Her second day at the Mare Nubium base, a year and a half ago. Before she knew any of the people who would be her shipmates. Before she had found her family.

The payload had arrived inside a video. Friends goofing off, sending silly greetings. Gigabytes of inanity, created for a single purpose – to hide a scant few megabytes of code. Pulling it out of the larger file was easy for her.

"Don't do it!" she tried to scream back at her past self, to no avail. A final action placed it onto the host system. From its landing spot, the virus scuttled away, vanishing quickly from her file system. It was done.

And even then, she was still telling herself it was to help people down on Earth. To strike a bargain that would alleviate suffering. Telling herself lies.

Captured by the memory, Amanda almost lost track of the reality that she was on the bridge of a colony ship, light years from Earth. Long after the event she was living so vividly.

"Hey, are you okay?" She felt a hand on her shoulder. Pulling herself back to the present, she saw it was Deijia.

Amanda had a moment of panic. He must know something. How could he not? She had been so erratic. And Estwing would put the picture together eventually. There was no escaping that fate.

She shrugged Deijia off. "Got lost in the numbers. You know how it is with me."

There was work to do. Amanda summoned up a measure of clarity. Her project was almost done. She did her best to shut out the discussion around her.

"This is how human knowledge expands," Hunt was intoning. "In forty three years, people back on Earth will know exactly where that glome goes – to here. With the new technology of the photonic phased array, we can provide information on conditions in this star system. That one accomplishment will make this mission a success."

"I'm concerned about the rush to send away almost all of our probes," Blum rejoined. "I think we'll need them, and deploying the phased array commits eight of our ten probes for more than a year, strung out over hundreds of millions of kilometers. Some of them we might never get back."

And the last calculation was completed. Amanda brought up the full set of results, carefully calculated with formulas she had individually placed in the mesh of cells, and compared it to the original results of the astrogation system.

There was no difference whatsoever between her hand-calculated results and those from the ship's system. Both data sets had the same error bars. There was nothing wrong with the astrogation system.

Which was impossible, because the stars were in the wrong places.

Blum was droning on about democratic processes. "I know we are still aboard ship, and I respect your position, captain, but as we transition to making our colony choice and then developing the settlement, I ask to partner in these decisions. Let us write up the plan and place a proper motion in front of the council of settlers. We'll have a reasoned discussion."

This would be so much easier to figure out in a quiet place. But then—

What had she just heard?

Proper motion! Of course!

"Remove the datetime constraint!" Amanda realized she had blurted the command out loud, and everyone had heard. But all that mattered was the results, and they were coming back already.

Their position was confirmed, at 42.53 light years from Earth, and the error bars were gone. Every star was exactly where it should be, to within a small fraction of a second of arc.

Then Amanda dared to look at the date.

Abruptly she called out, "I've got something you all need to know! First, the sensors are working perfectly and so is the astrogation program. We just misunderstood what they were telling us. We missed the really big news."

"And that is?" Hunt, to the point, as always.

"The year. It's 2246. During the 32 milliseconds we spent in the glome, over a century went by."

"I confirm the analysis," Deijia added from behind her. "When we add one hundred twenty eight years of elapsed time to the model, the stars are in exactly their correct locations. Simply put, the stars have been on the move."

In the babble of crosstalk she heard skepticism, wonder, and a measure of sorrow. They were truly separated from their home now. Everyone they had ever known outside the ship was long gone.

Then Amanda realized another implication. "If we deploy the array, will anyone still be looking for the signal?" she asked. "Our messages won't arrive on Earth until 2288—a hundred seventy years after we left."

"Most sensible thing I've heard since we arrived," pronounced Estwing. "The array won't help us. We can use those probes to increase our chances here. There's no doubt we're going to need all the help we can get."

"Here? No, not here!" Amanda was surprised to hear her own outburst. "We can leave! The new glome! We haven't passed it yet!"

Possibility beckoned. Surely anything else would be better than a dismal struggle to survive on a hostile planet, or stay stuck in its orbit forever.

"We can't do that! Further glome entries are not in the charter." Estwing, of course.

Amanda had the answer ready. "It's there. Emergency recourse. If there is no reasonable choice in the star system where we arrive after the first glome entry."

"First glome entry? You mean the glome entry, don't you? The entry, from our home solar system. One. As planned. Because when you say 'first' that makes me wonder how many you have in mind. Every trip into a glome is a chance to die. And we don't even know the odds. Maybe it's a chance in a hundred that delivered us here. Or a thousand."

"The physicists say—"

"The physicists!" Estwing scoffed. "Easy for them to tell us all about it, from their labs safely back home. I don't see any physicists here to welcome us. If they were so sure, where are they?"

"I'm a physicist," put in Deijia. "Do I count?"

"The physicists say," Amanda plowed ahead, "that in a high percentage of cases, the glome emergence will have a similar gravity well profile as the originating glome. That means a similar distance to a body with similar mass. And we have one data point which is in agreement. We started from a glome trailing Earth by three million kilometers. And we emerged less than a million kilometers from a somewhat smaller planet. In gravity well terms, a perfect match, even if it looks like the ninth circle of hell."

"And there are any number of places matching that profile that are inside a gas giant. Inside! Wouldn't that be fun? And the attack on our systems—"

"We just imagined that," Amanda explained. "The motion of the stars created the appearance of an error, and in our paranoia we blamed it on a virus. Yes, there was a virus in the systems at the Mare Nubium base, but there's no evidence it was ever on this ship."

Hunt addressed everyone. "The organizers of this mission appointed me captain, and gave me authority to make all decisions on this ship until we find a place to settle. But now, all we have is ourselves. And some instructions from over a century ago. I ask each of you to say your piece about the proposal to go into the new glome. Mayor Blum, will you begin?"

"I have had some conversations with selected fellow colonists," Blum pronounced. "No time for anything formal, and nothing about the glome, as that was not even suggested until a moment ago. And my direction is that we will follow the decision of the captain of this ship. You, Captain Hunt, are in command."

The mayor never made a decision if he could avoid it, Amanda thought to herself. If they even got as far as settling a planet, could someone like Blum actually lead?

"But I do have one note," the mayor continued. "A consensus, or perhaps a sentiment, if you will. We want to live."

"I think that's a given," Hunt answered.

"To live. Not just to survive. That is the sense of the colonists, and of myself."

As everyone was pondering Blum's cryptic message, Estwing spoke up. "It's total insanity," he pronounced. "If the glome really is the best action, we can come back in a few weeks, or months, when we have considered everything. We lose nothing by putting in some time for careful consideration. We should go to orbit, deploy a couple of the bullfrogs for living space, and run all the scenarios. That planet looks tough, but between the crew and colonists we can solve any problem. Once we get the ideas flowing, I bet our options here will start to look way better."

It sounded so sensible.

But Amanda knew that Estwing was completely wrong, even where he was right. Things would indeed start to look better, if they stared at them long enough.

She cut in. "Problem solving—that's exactly what we shouldn't do! When we set out to find a solution, like colonizing that planet, we start to accept it as our reality. We can talk ourselves into normalizing anything, no matter how absurd. Believe me—I've lived it! Over the weeks and then months, we'll get comfortable with the idea of living in domes under an acid bath, or scraping by in orbit, until we have forgotten that anything else is possible."

She felt a moment of doubt. Who was she to lecture the captain or anyone else on the ship about good decisions? But no matter what, she was going to provide the best ideas she could in every situation. It was all she could do now.

Captain Hunt continued around the key bridge crew. "Mister Deijia?"

"What Bowen said," Deijia replied. "Better the devil we don't know."

All eyes were on Captain Hunt.

"Mister Estwing," she said, "Set course for the new glome."

"You can't be serious!"

"The decision has been made."

"But Captain—"

"Never mind, I'll do it myself. Ship, set course to align precisely with the Omega Entry of the glome. Thrust now."

Amanda felt a sensation of shifting, as attitude adjusters tweaked the orientation of the *Rubicon*, and then an increase in gravity as the main thruster kicked in.

In that moment she caught a set of expressions ranging across Estwing's face. Stopping himself from forming up an angry remonstration. Concentration. Then his features slackened as he looked at a screen only visible to him.

Only one person on the *Rubicon* had the ability to override an order to the ship from the captain.

To lock everyone else out. That person was the chief security officer. Commander Estwing.

What was he doing?

There was only one way to find out. If he would allow her.

From her seat, Amanda created the thought and reached out with a link request. If the link was granted, she would be able to see an identical copy of the display that floated invisibly in front of him.

Suddenly Estwing's eyes came back into focus. He stared directly at her, interrogating. Amanda held her ground, looking back at him, as impassively as she could. The link request hung open.

And now she could see Estwing's virtual display. See, but not touch, a read-only view. Navigation controls. And yes, lock-outs. He had not yet executed any commands. If he acted, Amanda would not be able to do anything.

Amanda tried to ignore the sensation of ants crawling all over her body. Just this one time, she had to stay with the link.

She glanced over at Estwing. He had returned his attention to the console, staring into space.

Amanda began to unfasten her safety belt.

"Do not get up. Do not come this way." The linked thought arrived in her mind, in Estwing's voice.

On the virtual display she saw him assemble the new course, away from the glome. Plotted but not yet ordered. Ready.

What could she do? Run over and tackle him? Scream and yell? She knew those measures would have no effect. Without touching a button or saying a word, Estwing could control the course of the ship.

There was only one option.

Amanda formed up the thought. Gritting her teeth and mentally clenching to keep her mind on just the message, and nothing else, she sent into the link the only thing she could think of.

"I will care for and protect my shipmates, always working with them and not against them. Always working with them and not against them. Always."

The console in front of her was still. The new course awaited the final order to be activated.

And then it was gone. Erased from the console.

She heard the anguished exhalation. Estwing had turned toward her. There was no reading his expression. Anger? Guilt?

It didn't matter, as long as they stayed on course. She composed an expression that she hoped conveyed understanding. There was no telling what he would see in her face.

She could stand the link no longer, and so she let it drop. It was such a relief to have her own skin back.

After another minute the thrust ended and with it the appearance of gravity. They were on course, with no further adjustment required to go directly into the Omega Entry of the glome. And thence to an unknown destination.

There was nothing for anyone to do.

Amanda unbuckled herself and pushed off toward Estwing's station. As she floated his way, she saw him change from defense to acceptance, opening his hands to receive hers.

"Thank you," she whispered in his ear.

"The course I set, it's all there on the worm drive," he returned, equally quietly. "Are you going to—?"

"Oh, no. Forgive, that I may be forgiven."

At that moment she experienced the briefest flash of possibility. In some unknowable way, in some future she could not guess, she imagined, just for a fleeting instant, forgiveness.

"And where would we be without our mother hen?" she added.

The captain broke in. "All right, everyone. It's time to stop passing messages in class, and return to our stations. You know the drill. When we enter the glome, everyone is to be perfectly still. Make sure you're seated comfortably for that."

The *Rubicon* approached and then passed the point of no return. Any deviation from the path directly into the glome would only steer them into its spatial envelope, and certain destruction. The die was cast.

"The Omega Entry—do you think that's the best one?" she asked Deijia.

"Flip a coin," he replied. "It's been in fashion these days, after so many attempts with the Alpha Entry."

"But we have a little more information now, from the trip that got us here."

"We know that the Omega pushes you forward in time. We have no idea what the Alpha does. I've always been an Alpha man, myself, but all things considered I'm happy to go with the Omega again. Who cares what year it is as long as we arrive safely?"

"We'll be the longest lived people ever!"

At her workstation, Amanda played with different false-color visualizations of the glome. It had no signature in visible light, so there was no right answer. After experimenting with several views showing a crackling and pulsing fireball, she settled on a more pedestrian look – a tunnel, in a gently blending rainbow of colors, beckoning the ship into the Omega Entry of the glome.

As the last moments counted down, the question welled up, far too late. Was it better to be sure to survive? Not risk death today? Their current course, the unfathomable hazard in front of them, was entirely self-induced.

When everyone on the ship could have lived for years, orbiting, or perhaps colonizing the planet they had found, the decision to go into the glome had put them all at risk of immediate death. The same risk they had all accepted for the first glome trip, certainly, but having lived through that trip, they had come back for another turn at the roulette wheel.

Amanda turned back to her left. Tau Deijia seemed to be at peace, welcoming what would come.

"In any place we find ourselves," she recited to him.

"We will care for each other," Deijia replied.

Three, two, one...

✳

At the precise moment predicted, the starfield in front of them changed. They were once again not destroyed, and they were somewhere else. Just like that.

And again they were a few million kilometers from a planet. Three point two million kilometers this time. Without any order required, Estwing brought up a visual on the big main screen.

In glorious detail.

Were those colors real? Nothing could be that perfect. Wisps of white over expansive blue seas. Grey and brown land masses, smaller than those of Earth but still more than mere islands. Was that a tinge of green?

The sidebars displayed data as quickly as it could be acquired. Oxygen, nitrogen, and water vapor, likely breathable. Surface gravity zero point eight nine.

"Captain, can we stay this time?" Estwing asked.

"Yes, I think we can," Captain Hunt replied.

The bridge quieted. There were many things to do, but their tasks could wait for just a few moments, as every crew member gazed upon their new home.

✳

The next installment in The Great Symmetry is available now. Want to keep up with the latest news from James R. Wells? Visit his website at www. thegreatsymmetry.com.

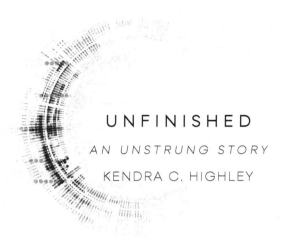

UNFINISHED

AN UNSTRUNG STORY

KENDRA C. HIGHLEY

Author's Note: First, I'd like to thank my awesome beta readers: Becca Andre, Kristen Otte, and Ryan Highley. Also, a big shout out to my editors, Shelley Holloway and Cassandra Marshall.

✳

Part 1: Ten Years Ago

QUINN WATCHED THE MONITOR. ITS CAMERA WAS TRAINED on the prep room where the new K700 prototype was under development. She was only the second model in this line, and the first female.

His match.

His heart fluttered with excitement. Miss Maren had told him the little girl was going to be his friend. Created specifically to keep him company and learn with him. After spending most of his time in the company of adults—both human and artificial—he could hardly wait to meet her.

Lexa. That would be her name.

She was still pale, her hair almost as white as her skin, just like the day before and the day before that. He wondered when she would change colors, and what color she would be, but Doc Mendal had said not to pry, so he didn't ask. He'd learned that if he asked the wrong questions—or too many in a row—that his curiosity would cause trouble. And pain.

The girl stared blankly into space, but he could tell she was afraid by the way her knuckles whitened as she clutched her blanket. Or the way her right eyelid twitched every so often. Being scared was a good sign—it meant she was turning into a person.

He immediately flushed, feeling bad. He didn't want her to be scared, and it wasn't nice to be glad about it. He remembered the prep room. He remembered the fear. No, it wasn't nice to be glad.

Dr. Martine cocked his head. "Quinn, what's Lexa thinking? Any guesses?"

"She's…wondering where she is, and why she's here," he said after a moment. Even though he was watching her over the feed, he could read her mannerisms easily, which was strange. But if Lexa had been made to be his best friend, maybe that was why he could tell how she felt.

He watched her a moment longer, registering how her chest rose and fell more quickly as the fear turned into panic and grief. "She thinks something's wrong with her." Quinn turned to Dr. Martine. "Please, we need to let her out."

"We can't. You know that. No cross-contamination until imprinting is complete." Dr. Martine tapped his stylus against his data pad. "But maybe we could let you in? What do you think? You want to try?"

Quinn's heart leapt. He tried hard to keep the eagerness out of his voice when he said, "Oh, yes. I think she might talk to me."

"Well, then, let's—"

The door at the back of the observation lab swooshed open and a pair of high heels clicked toward them. Quinn rounded his shoulders to sink a little shorter. I'm not a threat. I'm not a threat. I'm invisible.

Cool fingers tipped with long, pointed fingernails, brushed the back of his neck. A welt rose up on the sensitive skin below his hairline where they scratched. He held very still.

Invisible. Not a threat.

"Hello, dear," Miss Maren said, releasing Quinn to give Dr. Martine a kiss on the cheek. He didn't look too happy about it, even though Miss Maren was supposedly his girlfriend. "Any progress?"

"Um…" He shot a look at the girl behind the glass. "Well, we were thinking about exposing her to some stimuli to see if she's ready for advanced configuration. Namely, I thought I'd send Quinn in. She'd be less likely to see him as a threat, given her programming."

Quinn balled his fists around the hem of his T-shirt. Please. Please don't say no.

Miss Maren pinned him with her eyes. Calculating. That was the vocabulary word he'd use. It meant shrewd. Which sounded a lot like shrew. Which meant mean, screechy lady.

He bit the inside of his cheek to keep from smiling. It wouldn't be a real smile anyway, he reasoned. It would be a nervous I'm-not-hiding-anything smile, and a vaguely disinterested look was required if he hoped to get what he wanted.

Because that's what Miss Maren was good at. She found out what he wanted, then took it away.

After a long, long, long stare, she finally nodded. "A short visit, perhaps. Five minutes."

Five minutes? That was all? The look on her face, though. She wanted him to argue. If he argued, she could tell him no.

"I can be in and out in four, if that's better," he said.

Her eyes widened and she nodded in approval. "Very well."

Dr. Martine gave him a pat on the back and opened the door to the clean room. "Full measures. No contamination."

Right, no touching. Doc Mendal had told him her immune system was still developing and his germs could hurt her. Inside the clean room, which was just a little hall between the observation lab and her prep room, he pulled a white jumpsuit out of the cubby. It covered him from his neck to his toes and had a hood attached to the back to cover his head. The suit crackled every time he moved. It was polymer based and felt like a trash bag.

By now, the little girl was hugging herself and rocking back and forth on her white bed. Quinn hurried to don a pair of latex gloves. She would be better if she could just meet him. He knew it. She needed a friend; that would fix everything.

He gave a thumbs up to Dr. Martine, and the airlocks opened with a clank. When her door opened, she started, staring wide-eyed as Quinn stepped inside.

"Who are you?" she whispered.

Good, so she could talk. They'd loaded her brain with all the right prompts, but they hadn't been sure. "I'm Quinn."

She nodded slowly. "Who am I?"

He blinked fast to clear the tears smarting in his eyes. The white room did that—it made you feel hopeless, helpless. Just being in here…it was awful. "You're Lexa."

"Lexa," she said, like she was trying out the word in her mouth. "Lexa. Is that a good name?"

"Very good," he told her. "It means 'defender of the people.'"

Her forehead scrunched up. "Are there more?"

"More what?"

"People? Are we the only two? Or are there more?"

A smile stretched across Quinn's face. She was so serious when she asked that it was almost funny. Almost. "Yes. Lots and lots. When you're finished here, you'll meet some of them."

He waited for her to ask how long, but instead, she said, "I like you."

"I like you, too." Quinn flushed, and he suddenly didn't know where to rest his hands. He locked them behind his back to keep them out of the way. "You don't have to be scared anymore, okay? Soon you'll move into the dorm with me, and we'll play all kinds of games."

"Are you good at games?" she asked.

"Some," he said, hoping it sounded modest. He didn't know why, though. Usually he talked smack with the other artificials, knowing he was faster and smarter than many of them, even if his biological age was only nine and a half. But there was something about Lexa... He wanted her to feel like she was equal. She had been created to be his equal, right? He should treat her that way.

"Then I'd like to play," she said shyly.

"Great!" He took a step closer. "We can play hide and seek, except I'll hide an object, and you have to try to guess where I hid it. Would you like that?"

"You'd hide it under the third pillow of the couch," she said.

Quinn froze. "How did you know that?"

"Is that right?" she asked. "Did I guess?"

"Yes." How did she know that? She didn't even know they had a couch, let alone that it would be his first choice for hiding something. "You guessed right."

She flushed—it completely changed the way she looked. It made her look more alive. "I guessed right."

Quinn reached out a hand, forgetting Dr. Martine's warning. Lexa's eyes widened in panic, and she scooted against the headboard of her bed. "Who are you? What do you want?"

He froze. "I—I'm Quinn. Remember? Your friend."

"Leave me alone! Help!" She raked her fingers through her white hair. "Seven, two, three-three, six, fourteen. Seven, two, three-three, six, fourteen."

Not sure what else to do, he backed out of the room. As soon as the airlocks hissed shut, the clean room door opened. Dr. Martine looked disappointed.

Miss Maren looked smug. Another vocabulary word. It meant she was right about something, and Dr. Martine was wrong.

And that made her happy.

Later that day, once he was upstairs in the main training room and safely away from Miss Maren and her scientists, Quinn asked, "What did the numbers mean? When Lexa got scared, she said a bunch of numbers in a row. What are they?"

His instructor, Doc Mendal, had been trying to teach Quinn how to block an opponent wielding a knife, but he had no interest in training today. Doc backed away and huffed a breath. "Boy, you ask a lot of questions."

"Because that's what they designed me to do," he said, feeling stubborn. But it was okay to be stubborn with Doc Mendal. He might have to run an extra mile or climb the rock wall without using his feet for disobeying, but that was easy.

Doc mumbled something about "Goddamned free will" then sighed. "Her reset pattern. Whenever she goes into overload, she recites her reset pattern. It'll happen if she ever reboots or goes into sleep mode, too."

"Do I have one of those?"

"Yes, but you don't know what it is. It's buried in your subconscious. It'll only come out when you trip the recall."

Quinn cocked his head to the side, considering. "So humans wouldn't have those?"

"No."

"So how do they react to trauma?"

"Badly," Doc Mendal said. "That's your advantage." He glanced at the cameras mounted in the corners of the training room walls. "Enough talk. Assume close combat stance."

Now it was Quinn's turn to sigh. He faced away from his instructor, knees slightly bent, waiting for the attack. But when Doc wrapped him up tight in his arms, he whispered, "Remember what I said about how humans handle trauma. There will come a time when you need that advantage."

Then he tossed Quinn to the mat.

Quinn lay awake long after lights-out. He worried about Lexa all alone in the dark, scared and not knowing where she was. Sometimes he had nightmares about his first few days in the prep room—he woke up in a cold sweat, wishing he had a mother like that girl who had come to visit two of the geneticists. The kid had cut her hand on the sharp edge of an open computer casing and had started to cry. She was almost Quinn's age, but she cried a lot when the blood welled up on her palm. Her mother had raced over to cuddle her before fixing the cut.

Maybe that's what Doc Mendal meant about humans reacting badly to trauma. Quinn wouldn't have cried about a cut hand. Still, he couldn't help but feel just a little envious of the girl. Of course, after that incident, Miss Maren had banned children from visiting the lab.

Unless they lived here.

He sighed in the dark. The sound was thin and sad. Lately, he'd begun to wonder what his point was—why had he been created? The K600s were very near human in every way, so why did the scientists make him? Why create a K700 that was more than human, only to treat him like he was an object, a thing. Miss Maren, when she wasn't in a bad mood, would cluck over him and tell him he had a grand purpose. A destiny. But did artificials have those? To him, it sounded like a fancy word for being told what to do with his life.

A loud rap at his door made Quinn jump. He barely had time to sit up before Piers, the security lead at the lab, strode inside, grabbed him by the collar, and hauled him into the corridor.

"Ms. DeGaul said you upset the new asset today, beanpole." Piers's hand clamped hard onto his neck. "She said they told you not to contaminate the area, but you tried to touch little Lexie, anyway. You disobeyed."

Quinn's knees shook inside his thin pajama pants. Piers's eyes had that wicked gleam, the one that spelled trouble. "I-I'm sorry, sir. I didn't know what I was doing. I just thought—"

"Save it for her."

Oh, no. Piers was taking him to see Miss Maren. That only served to spike his fear to painful levels;

his bladder felt too full and his lungs felt too empty. Piers was a slender man, but powerful, all wiry muscle, with a love of hurting small things. They trotted down the hall at an awful pace. Quinn had a hard time keeping up, so Piers gripped his biceps to drag him whenever he slowed. By the time they arrived outside of Miss Maren's office, downstairs near the labs, his bare toes were stubbed and his fingers had gone numb from Piers's grasp.

"Now you listen," the man growled. "You answer her questions honestly or we'll know. And you know what happens when you lie about lying."

Quinn shuddered. Yes, he knew. The roundish scar on his back from the heated metal pipe was a permanent reminder that he couldn't keep secrets. "I'll tell the truth."

"You better." Piers turned and rapped on the door.

Following Miss Maren's muffled "Come in," Piers laid his palm on the scanner, and the door slid open. The office was becoming familiar, Quinn thought, with its priceless wood and velvet furniture and the high-tech vid panel behind her desk. And its familiarity was a bad, bad thing.

"Quinn, come here." Her voice was cool, but he heard the little bit of glee in her tone.

He swallowed hard and went into the office. Piers shut the door behind him, leaving Quinn alone with Miss Maren. He glanced at the cameras in the corner of the room. Not alone, really. Somebody was always watching, which meant if he misbehaved, a dozen security guards—both artificial and human—and Piers could be here in an instant to bash his head in.

He'd seen that happen to one of the service artificials, once. She'd taken a swing at Miss Maren with a vase for calling her a "bolt," which was an ugly word for artificial human. Before Quinn could skitter out of the way, the K600's brains were splattered on the carpet. He'd vomited later, but at the time, all he could think was how those brains looked like curds of cheese flying from the servant's skull.

"Please sit."

Now he was really scared—she never said please. Miss Maren was smiling, and as he sat in the chair on the other side of her desk, she pushed the candy jar his way. He didn't know what she wanted, but he knew he couldn't refuse the candy. He took a small piece of taffy and held it in his fist.

"Dr. Martine tells me that Lexa is coming online remarkably well. Does that match your assessment?"

What did she want? How should he answer? A bead of sweat dripped from the nape of his neck and slid between his shoulder blades. "I, um, she seems proficient in communications?"

There, that was bland enough. Wasn't it? Oh, please let that be right.

Miss Maren leaned back in her chair. For such a tiny lady, the chair made her look powerful and important. Kind of like a throne. Quinn blinked rapidly to clear that thought out of his head before he dreamed up a crown and scepter and started laughing at the picture his mind made.

"Of course she is—we made her and we're very good. What I'm asking is if she seems...different somehow."

Different? "She's a girl," he blurted out. "That makes her different, right?"

Miss Maren rolled her eyes. "Never mind. But hear me well. You will not touch her again, not until she's out of processing. Am I clear?"

He nodded.

"I can't hear you," she said, her voice going as cold and hard as the stainless steel table in the procedure room. "Am I clear?"

"Yes, ma'am. Perfectly," he squeaked.

"Very well. Just to be sure, though..." She pushed a button on the underside of her desk. Piers entered a few seconds later. "Take this young man down to the basement and make sure he understands his new orders."

Quinn's overfull bladder threatened to release when Piers smiled down at him. "Will do. He won't forget after we've finished."

The next morning, a com ping roused Quinn from a fitful sleep. He winced and rolled from bed, careful to favor his right side. Piers hadn't burned him this time, but the bruised ribs would twinge for a few days, despite the rapid healing programmed into his DNA. Shuffling to his data pad took effort, and it was hard to keep his expression neutral as he answered the summons.

Dr. Martine's frowning face appeared onscreen. "I'd like to see you in my office."

Quinn tried to hold in a sigh and failed. "Yes, sir. I'll get dressed."

Once the link was disconnected, he sank down onto the foot of his bed. He was so tired of being afraid all the time. He was tired of second-guessing every move he made. He couldn't even hide his thoughts—they'd built in a security feature to betray him. Whenever he lied, his shoulder twitched.

He was so tired of being a pawn, pushed around in a game between more powerful people. And he knew what a pawn was because Dr. Martine had taught him to play chess. It only took two months before Quinn beat him, too.

If he could beat one of the smartest scientists in the building at a game he'd only just learned...he could beat them at the biggest game of all. And he would. Because now, he had an ally who was just as smart as he was.

Lexa changed everything.

That thought exploded through him like a stunner blast. Doc Mendal had told him once, quietly enough that the cameras wouldn't hear, that he would become the fastest, smartest, strongest creature in the Precipice labs—maybe even Triarch City—given enough time and training. If that was true...then Lexa would be just as strong, just as smart, and just as fast as Quinn. Eventually, they would have the ability to break free.

And maybe even burn this place to the ground with Miss Maren and Piers still inside.

Quinn hugged himself. This was a dangerous way of thinking. He had to wait, be patient. He and Lexa weren't strong enough to do any of this yet, and if he kept that idea in the front of his brain, it would eventually come spilling out. Good thing he was a planner, a plotter. He'd befriend Lexa, just as expected, and slowly teach her that they could be an unstoppable force if only they stuck together.

Armed with his new plan, Quinn dressed and hurried down to Dr. Martine's office. Unlike Miss Maren's suite, his office was smaller. His walls were covered with plaques: diplomas, awards, and certifications. At one time, Quinn thought he'd like to become a geneticist like Dr. Martine, but Miss Maren had carefully stamped out his ambitions. She wanted him to be something else, so there was no sense dreaming about a life in science.

"Will you sit?" Dr. Martine asked.

Quinn jumped. "Um, yes, sir."

He sank into the worn leather chair across from the doctor's desk and folded his hands in his lap. Dr. Martine's mouth quirked up on one side. "Young man, you don't have to be so rigid here. I'm not going to rap your knuckles if you touch anything."

Quinn's eyes widened. Maybe he meant it, but Piers would punish him for breaking something, no matter what Dr. Martine said. Still, he unclenched his fists and let his leg jiggle like it always wanted to when he was nervous.

"Better." The doctor leaned his elbows on the desk, peering intently at Quinn before saying, "Lexa asked about you this morning."

"Really?" He paused; that had sounded too eager. "She remembered me? That's a good sign of cognitive development."

Dr. Martine's mouth twitched again. "Uh huh. Anyway, I'd like you to see her again this afternoon after you've finished your homework."

He wanted to. The sooner she got to know and trust him, the sooner they could escape. But Piers's "reminder" was still too fresh to ignore. Rubbing the sore spot on his side, he said, "I don't know if that's a good idea, sir. I might stress her and disrupt the imprinting process."

"I know you've been…" He grimaced. "You may've been told not to interfere with Lexa, but I believe she needs you, and I'll make sure you aren't punished for it. In fact, I had that conversation with Ms. DeGaul this morning. She wants you to be friends, and the best way to accomplish that is to let Lexa interact with you."

None of this made sense to Quinn. But it didn't have to make sense—he was getting what he wanted. Better not to question the luck involved. "If you think it's all right, I'll come to the imprinting room at four. I have to meet Dr. Mendal at five-thirty, though."

That earned him a relieved smile. "Good."

✳

Lexa stared at the glass, her expression torn between hope and fear. Quinn could feel her pain. Why, he didn't know, but it was as real to him as if he was the one sitting inside the prep room. A moment later, her lip trembled and fat tears slid down her cheeks. For the first time, her complexion took on a slightly pink color.

"Her vitals are erratic," a lab assistant said. "Pulse is one-forty, temp's over ninety-nine degrees."

Dr. Martine nodded. "Quinn, I want to see if you can calm her down. If she glitches, take a step back immediately, but I think her short-term memory programming should be strong enough to prevent that."

He hoped so, but his fingers shook as he donned his cleanroom suit. What if she freaked out on him again? They might not let him see her anymore. He had to be careful. Move slowly, so as not to scare her.

The airlocks released, and Quinn stepped into Lexa's room. Her face immediately brightened, and she scrubbed the tears from her cheeks with a fast swipe.

"You're here," she said. "You told me you'd come."

"You…remember me?"

"Yes. The boy from yesterday. Quinn."

Relief made the air whoosh from his lungs. He'd never held his breath before, but this wasn't a normal situation, so maybe he should've expected that. "Yes. So, how are you feeling?"

Lexa looked around the room. "I'm not sure. I cried, but I don't know why."

"Are you scared?" he asked.

She frowned, like she was thinking that over. "Yes. I think so. It's lonely in here."

Quinn glanced at the window, which was a mirror on this side. Dr. Martine noticed, though, and said over his com, "Her heart rate's down. Keep going."

It was working; he was calming her down. "You'll be out in a little while. They need to...um, treat you a little bit longer. But when it's over, you'll have a room in the dorm near mine. We can play."

"Hide and seek. Sofa cushions," she said.

"Sofa cushions." He paused. What should they talk about now? "Um, I also like painting and color matching and strategy games. I could teach you to play chess."

"Is it fun?"

Dr. Martine said, "Tell her you'll give her a board in a few days."

"Uh, yes. It's fun. Kind of hard, though. Maybe I can bring you a board in a few days? I can show you the pieces and stuff."

She stood and took a tentative step his direction. "Okay."

Quinn held very still as she came closer. Even though he wore the clean-room suit, he swore he could smell her. Some vague combination of cinnamon and vanilla.

"Like a cookie," he whispered.

There was a crackle of static over his com—someone was laughing. He felt his cheeks go hot.

"What's wrong with your face?" Lexa asked, peering into his mask. "Are you overheating?"

"A little. I better go."

Lexa's hand shot out more quickly than he expected and caught his wrist. "But you're coming back, right? Please don't leave me here all alone."

Helpless, he looked to the window, silently pleading. Dr. Martine's voice was gentle when he said, "Reassure her."

He put his other hand over hers and smiled. "You're not alone, Lexa. You have me. I'm yours, and when you get out, we'll be together all the time. Friends, okay?"

"Will I see you before then?"

"She's getting anxious," Dr. Martine said over his com. "Tell her yes."

"Yes." Feeling bold, he added, "Tomorrow. I'll bring the chess board."

She released his wrist and went back to sit on her bed. "Tomorrow. You have less than 86,000 seconds to comply."

It sounded like an order, and he cracked a smile. "Noted. Are you going to count them all?"

"Yes." She smiled back. "Every one."

Quinn raced to the prep room after lessons the next day, the day after that, and the day after that. Each time he visited, Dr. Martine and the lab assistants praised him for helping stabilize Lexa. She'd even hugged him. It had hurt against his healing ribs, but he remembered the feeling of her arms around him long after he left her.

On the fifth day, he hurried down the hall, a brand new chessboard clutched to his chest. It had taken a while to get this one, but he thought she might find the cartoon character pieces more fun than the more traditional kind. She was picking up the game fast, and Dr. Martine said she played by herself, memorizing the board, so she could reset their game before Quinn returned each day.

She was remarkable—everything he'd hoped for. He found he couldn't wait to see her. And with two boards, she could play her own game and reserve the other for theirs. The anticipation of how she would receive the gift filled him with gladness.

He'd never had the chance to surprise someone like this. It would be fun.

He was a few steps from the door to the lab when he heard Miss Maren's raised voice.

"She's flawed, Caldwell. Her vitals are erratic, and the only time she's compliant is when Quinn is here. We should start over now, before we've wasted too many resources."

"My dear, you haven't given it enough time," Dr. Martine said. "And you wanted her to be keyed for Quinn, remember? It makes sense that she'd feel most comfortable around him. Let's give it two years—she may yet be useful. Besides, I need the research data for the 800s."

"All I know is that my interaction with her was unsatisfactory. The program should be scrapped."

Quinn's heart stuttered. Scrapped? Was she saying she wanted to kill Lexa? A surge of rage rushed through his body. They wouldn't kill her. She was his special friend. If they wanted to kill Lexa, it would be over his dead body—and a bunch of theirs.

He leaned against the wall, terrified by his thoughts. When had he gotten so violent? Was this the jealousy his human psychology teacher had tried to teach him about? Or was it something bigger? Dr. Martine was saying something about funding and protocol, but the words were lost in the rush of blood between Quinn's ears. What would he do if Lexa was scrapped?

His heart ached. The one person who was supposed to be like him, to be his partner in all things as they grew up, couldn't be scrapped.

A pair of heels click-clacked toward the door, and he quietly ran down the hall, then turned to walk back just as Miss Maren left the lab, to make it look like he was just arriving. Quinn forced a smile as they passed one another and held up the chessboard.

"Dr. Martine said the intellectual stimulation has been working, so I brought her another board."

She cut a glance at him out of the corner of her eye. "Keep an eye on her. If she glitches or cycles out at any time, I expect you to report it to me immediately."

Quinn clutched the chessboard back to his chest. "Yes, ma'am."

She nodded and swept by, leaving him in a cloud of floral perfume. He trudged the rest of the way to the prep room, feeling heavy and uncertain. If Miss Maren questioned him about Lexa, he'd be forced to tell the truth or his shoulder twitch would give him away.

He just had to hope Lexa didn't glitch—or if she did, that he wasn't there to see it so he could deny knowing anything.

The prep room was quiet when he entered. Dr. Martine stood at his usual terminal, looking weary. The other two assistants cowered behind their screens, typing madly, as if work could make them invisible. He rolled his eyes. If they wanted lessons in becoming invisible, the first rule was to hold still.

No one noticed him standing there. The second rule—being the least important person in the room. He cleared his throat. "Sir? I'm here for my visit?"

Dr. Martine jumped. "Oh, I didn't see you there. Um, we need to delay your visit a few days, Quinn. I'm sorry about that, but Lexa's been somewhat unstable today."

"Maybe I can calm her down," he said. "I could try."

"Sorry. No one goes in or out for forty-eight hours," a cold voice said from the doorway.

Quinn turned, and a nasty smirk spread across Piers's face. "The subject is to be isolated until her color protocol is complete. Ms. DeGaul's orders. No disruptions during a critical phase."

Forty-eight hours? That was two days. But he knew Piers wanted an excuse to punish him. Better to continue showing the techs how to be invisible, even when talking to someone.

"Yes, sir. Understood." He turned to Dr. Martine. "Will you message me when you'd like me to return?"

Dr. Martine's eyes narrowed a fraction. Of course he saw through Quinn's sudden change of heart. "I will. She should be done processing in time for you to come back on Friday after your studies."

Quinn nodded and walked slowly from the room like he didn't care one bit about the whole thing. Piers was blocking the hallway. He poked a finger into Quinn's chest. "Remember. Be a good little Bolt, or you'll see me again."

Quinn said nothing. That seemed to satisfy Piers because he let him pass. Quinn kept his pace slow the entire way to his room, though his feet felt like they were made of lead and his heart felt made of fire. Two days. He set the new chessboard on his desk and his mood plummeted farther when he saw the blinking icon of a message. Doc Mendal had called. What would it be this time? Scaling a building without an anchor?

He tapped the icon and Doc's face filled the feed screen on the second ring. "Boy, put on your climbing gear. Got a treat for you."

Quinn groaned quietly. "Yes, sir. Um, my ribs are still a bit sore. Will that be an issue?"

Doc grimaced. "Shouldn't be. Meet me downstairs by the front doors in ten minutes."

✳

"Where are we going?" Quinn asked as they left the main grounds of Miss Maren's lakeside compound. He'd been allowed outside in the yard—even without supervision—but he was rarely allowed to go off property.

"Partway around the lake, there's a set of metal piers and towers. We're going to climb some."

That sounded suspicious. Doc Mendal's "treats" usually involved some sort of challenge, but climbing a tower was easy. Unless he was going to make Quinn climb it blindfolded. Now that would be hard.

They hiked in silence, but it was comfortable. Doc was one of the few adults who didn't require him to speak. Quinn let the quiet of the lake seep into his skin and bones while soaking up the sunlight. Even though they'd entered the public grounds, the scrubby grasses around the lake grew wild, and nothing stirred, save a few small animals. He projected his hearing, listening hard to the little sounds they made.

"Moles," he said to Doc. "I can hear their claws rubbing together."

"That's crazy," Doc answered. "I don't think you're busy enough if you can guess the animal based on the sound of their claws from forty yards away."

"And smell and logical reasoning," he said. "It wasn't a random guess."

"Not yet ten years old and smarter than most adults," Doc muttered. "What the hell are we doing?"

"I'm sorry?"

"Nothing. Keep moving. We're almost there."

The piers and towers appeared at the next rise. The ground was rocky here as the grass receded from the lakeshore. The metal structures were rusting, and parts had corroded, but they looked sturdy enough. Doc led him over to the first platform. "Up you go. Hands only."

Quinn kept his grumble to himself. So much for not hurting his ribs. He stood on tiptoe to grab the first strut and pulled himself up to balance his body against it so he could reach for the next handhold. It was slow work, but about halfway up, he realized his side didn't ache so much.

When Doc made it to the top and sat next to him on the narrow platform, he said, "I do good work, huh?"

Quinn laughed. "I always wondered who coded our accelerated healing. Maybe you're not the evil taskmaster I thought you were."

"Or maybe I wanted you to heal faster so I could train you harder."

"That sounds more right."

They sat quietly for a moment, and Quinn took in the beauty of Triarch City. From here, the skyscrapers downtown looked like dominoes, stacked together and ready to tumble. It had been six months since he'd been allowed to visit, but he still remembered all the smells and the relentless noise of the cars, video boards, and foot traffic all around him. So many inputs, so much chaos… It had been hard for his brain to process it all. There were no patterns to find in that mess.

"So, you haven't asked why we're out here, yet," Doc said.

"I've learned not to pry," Quinn said without thinking. He shot a nervous glance at Doc. "Sorry. That was flippant. I just, uh, thought you'd tell me when you were ready."

But Doc was laughing. "Good, I was worried they'd beaten the backbone out of you. Anyway, we're out here… Well, why don't you guess?"

The breeze played with Quinn's curls, lifting them from his forehead only to drop them again. It was so quiet here. So still. "No cameras. You can make it look like a nature lesson or a practice hike, but also take me to a place that's unobserved."

"Exactly." Doc sighed. "I assume you know Maren's not excited about Lexa."

Quinn admired his confidence—to call the boss by her first name alone. "I heard."

"Do you know why?"

A thrill ran down his back. "No."

"She's worried Caldwell is too attached. To both of you, but especially Lexa, since he was primary on her build team. That makes him vulnerable, and Maren doesn't like vulnerabilities in her lab."

"Why are you telling me this?" Quinn asked carefully, wondering if this was some kind of test. Maybe there were cameras out here, or a drone, monitoring their entire conversation.

"Because you need to know a few of us are attached. To all of you. That we care more than we can let on." Doc's stare was intent. "Do you know what a slave is?"

"Yes," he whispered.

"Quinn…are you a slave?"

Tears welled in his eyes. "Why are we talking about these things?"

"Because you need to know who you are. Not what, son. Who," Doc said. "You matter. Lexa matters. The earlier models matter. Those K600s who take care of you in the dorm? They aren't any less human than I am. Understand? Piers would tell you otherwise. So would Maren. But guess what? They're wrong."

"I know you're planning something, and I want you to know that you're not alone." Doc tapped a finger against Quinn's chest. "Some painful things are probably going to happen to you—Lexa, too—but if you choose to put the pain somewhere constructive, it'll give you purpose. Understand? Like trying to break your security protocols, so you can lie effectively. You'll need that skill, and you can do it. I'll give you some exercises to try, because it's important. But I know you can do it."

"Everything's possible," he whispered.

"Yes, it is. And for you and Lexa, everything's probable." Doc's smile was hard. "You two are the hope of a generation. They just don't know it yet. But you do. Don't carry that burden lightly."

"But why me?" Quinn asked, feeling both fear and excitement warring in his heart. "Why am I so important?"

"You represent a leap in our program. The K500s are almost human. Not quite, but close. The K600s are indistinguishable from humans. They can blend in. But you? You and Lexa are better than human. More than, you see? And that's what scares Maren. She wants to control you both. Trap your loyalty so she can use your gifts. Don't let her. Bide your time. One day, you'll make your move, and the entire world will stand still."

"What move?"

Doc started climbing down the platform. "You already know."

Part 2: Eight Years Ago

"Tell me a story," Lexa said, chasing Quinn down the hall to the training room. "You promised."

She had a streak of dust on her face and cobwebs in her dark brown hair. Her skinny knees were dirt-encrusted, too, but her large brown eyes sparkled. She was up to something for sure.

"Where have you been?" he asked.

"Finding a way into the attic. Now, what about my story?"

He laughed. "We're late. After we meet Doc, I will."

"Tell me the one about the puppet," she insisted. "Who became a real boy."

His sigh was inward. She still thought it was a harmless story. She had no idea that Miss Maren had banned it. Hit too close to home, that story did. He never should've told Lexa about it. She didn't understand the consequences.

"How about a different story, about a princess who loses a shoe?"

She made a face. "I know you're changing the subject. Besides, you know I don't like stories where the girl has to be rescued. I want a more…badass girl."

"Badass? Where did you pick up that word?" he asked, amused.

"Loading dock. The guys delivering the groceries never even saw me hiding in the rafters yesterday."

Her smile was full of mischief, and Quinn laughed. "You are such a little sneak."

"Hey! That's what Doc said I was made for. I have to practice."

They hurried into the training room, where Doc was waiting. "Lexa, up the ropes, please."

She scampered past Quinn, her ponytail swinging behind her. In seconds, she was halfway up the rope ladder on her way to the network of swings, catwalks, and nets strung from the ceiling.

"Boggles the mind, huh?" Doc asked. "She's like a monkey up there."

Quinn pushed down a tiny twinge of jealousy. He loved Lexa—she was his best friend—but her physical abilities outshined his and that bothered him. "Yeah. Monkey."

Doc peered at him. "What's eating you?"

"Nothing." He shook his head to clear his thoughts. "What should I do?"

"Hide," Doc said, smiling.

"What?"

"Hide. You're so worried about what Lexa can do that you've forgotten what you can do. You're my chameleon, kid. Blend in; make yourself invisible. Find a way to make yourself agreeable with the kitchen staff so that they give you extra sweets."

"Right now?"

"Consider it a long-term assignment. Find ways to make friends here. The hellcat," he cast a glance up at Lexa, nimbly leaping from platform to platform twenty feet overhead, "has her strengths, but her sweet disposition isn't one of them."

Wasn't that the truth? But he liked how she could go from mad to happy to curious to snappish

in ten seconds. His cheeks warmed. He liked everything about her.

"Look! Look!" Lexa called.

Quinn's heart shot into his throat as she jumped
from the platform to catch a rope ten feet away. She
swung around once, crying "Wheee!" before climbing back to the ceiling.

"Come down from there, sweetheart," Doc
yelled. "Time for drills."

She stuck her tongue out at him, but climbed
down. Granted, she took the longest way, and
Quinn had to hide a grin. Definitely not agreeable.

"Remember what I said," Doc whispered, turning so the camera couldn't see his lips moving.
"Chameleon. Maren had you made to infiltrate
certain organizations. That's your power. Hiding
the real you and showing people what they want
to see—they'll trust you implicitly. You'll be able
to find out anything you want that way. Not as a
pawn, but for you. Understand?"

The urgency in Doc's voice surprised him, but
Quinn nodded. "I understand."

"Understand what?" Lexa asked, appearing like
magic behind them. They both jumped, and she
looked very pleased with herself. "Gotcha good that
time."

"Sneak," Quinn said.

She batted at his curls. "Fluffy head."

"Skinny knees."

"Fart face."

Without warning, Doc swept a leg beneath both of them, sending them to the mat with a crash. "I win."

"Understand what?" Lexa asked again, glaring up at him. "Are you two keeping secrets?"

"Yes," Quinn said. "We're planning to sell you to the circus."

"Fine, don't tell me." She popped up and climbed Doc's back to wrap a thin arm around his neck. "Say uncle."

"Like that's actually going to work if you run into real trouble," Doc said. He shook her off with ease. "Both of you, on the treadmill. Wind sprints."

They grumbled but headed to the treadmills without talking back. "Betcha I can outrun you in a mile," Lexa said.

"With those short legs? As if."

"You may've grown six inches in a year, but I'm still faster."

He doubted she was, but the competition helped make the task more bearable. "Let's go, then."

They took off running, each pushing the treadmill faster and faster until they were practically flying. Nine miles an hour, then ten, then eleven.

Quinn's heart beat a hard pace in his chest, but Lexa looked calm and determined, and there was no way he'd admit defeat.

At the half-mile mark, Dr. Martine and Miss Maren came in to watch. Great—his lungs were shredded, but now they had an audience. To keep from slowing down, Quinn focused on their mouths, trying to read their lips.

"...flawed. No discipline," Miss Maren was saying. "Runs wild across the compound...cameras caught her in the attic...off-limits..."

"...what you wanted," Dr. Martine protested. "...look at that speed...concentration..."

Her eyes narrowed as she stared at Lexa. "...you're biased, Caldwell. You don't see...failed programs should be scrapped."

Quinn started breathing harder, and it had nothing to do with the treadmill. Miss Maren hadn't mentioned anything about scrapping Lexa lately. Why now? Had she messed up something in the attic?

"...perfectly objective...can outperform anything you..."

"...prove it...now..."

He turned and said something to Doc that Quinn couldn't see. Doc nodded and strode toward the treadmills, motioning for them to slow down. "They want to see you work."

They did as he asked, and Lexa followed Quinn to the center mat. She cocked her head at Miss Maren. "What can I show you, Ms. DeGaul?"

Her voice was syrupy, and her eyes were wide with innocence. Doc called him a chameleon? He couldn't tell if Lexa was messing with them or projecting what Miss Maren wanted to see.

"It's more of an assignment," she said, sounding suspicious. "There are some people visiting tonight. I want you to steal some files from their personal data pads."

"What kind of files?" Quinn asked. The gears were already turning in his head.

"I have no idea, but it has to do with the Quad. You need to get in there, review the files, and copy everything relevant. And you have to do it without being seen. By our cameras, or whatever security they bring with them."

The Quad? Quinn exchanged a glance with Lexa. This was big—the Quad was the council behind the incorporated governments of the four provinces. Miss Maren's visitors hadn't gotten crosswise with them somehow, had they? If so, this could be the biggest assignment the two of them had ever been given.

"Who are we investigating?" Lexa asked.

Now Miss Maren smiled, and it was a frightening sight. "The governor of Triarch City and his wife. They'll be staying overnight as our honored guests and are important to our business with Precipice. They are not to know you're artificials, understand?"

"Yes, ma'am," they said.

She fixed a hard stare on Dr. Martine. "If this works, I'll reconsider."

"We can do it," Lexa said. "We'll get the secrets for you."

If Miss Maren was surprised by Lexa's sudden interest, she didn't say anything. After she swept from the room, a beaten down Dr. Martine in tow, Quinn pulled Lexa aside. "Why'd you agree so fast?"

Her chin jutted stubbornly. "I can read lips as good as you. I know what she's saying about me, and I don't want to die."

Doc sighed behind them. "I don't want that, either, Hellcat."

Quinn didn't chime in. Lexa knew... She knew what was at stake. That her life hung in the balance on the whim of a crazy lady who changed outfits three times a day. Discarded like a useless com. Rage pulsed in his temples. His best friend was barely nine years old—she didn't deserve to know things like this.

"…master bedroom on the third floor," Doc was saying. "You listening, kid?"

Quinn's focus snapped back to the present. "Yes. The easiest way to do this will be to work our strengths. I'll make the guests like me and deflect their attention to keep them downstairs so Lexa can sneak into their suite and search their belongings."

"A real break-in!" Lexa clutched her hands to her heart, eyes shining.

"You know, most people don't get that excited about breaking into someone else's room," he said.

She stuck her tongue out at him, then headed for the door. "I'm going upstairs to poke around. I might be small enough to go through the air ducts… You think?"

"Worth a try," Doc said. "Quinn, what are you going to do?"

Forcing his thoughts past the anger was hard, but he said, "I'm going to learn everything there is to know about Governor Shaw and his wife. If I'm going to con them, I need to be convincing."

And since Lexa's life hung in the balance, he'd be the most charming young man they'd ever met.

* * *

"Governor and Mrs. Shaw," the butler announced. He was a K600, built for etiquette and elegance. Miss Maren called him number thirty-one. Quinn and Lexa called him Preston. Preston liked that, which was how Quinn was perfectly placed to slip out behind Miss Maren when she went to greet them.

The governor was a large man with a belly that made his shirt stretch tight. His wife was tall and slender and dressed like a faded model in a long dress. The nursery rhyme "Jack Sprat" ran through Quinn's mind. He gave his head a shake to keep from laughing. Especially since two security guards—human—wearing dark suits came in behind them.

"Governor, Mrs. Shaw. Welcome to my home," Miss Maren said, ushering them toward the stairs and right into Quinn's path. She stopped short, but covered her surprise by saying, "This is my, um, my nephew, Quinn. Darling…" The edge to her voice was barely perceptible. The Shaws would never hear it, but she knew he could. "Why aren't you in the play room?"

Showtime. Plastering a curious smile on his face, he said, "But…Aunt Maren, I've never met a real governor before." He turned wide eyes on Mrs. Shaw. She looked like she wanted to put him in her pocket and feed him tea biscuits. "How do you do, ma'am?"

Miss Maren's expression was as brittle as frost on grass—until Mrs. Shaw said, "Oh, aren't you adorable. Well, this is my husband, the governor of Triarch City."

Quinn shifted his expression to trustworthy and forthright. "Pleasure to meet you, sir. Or is it 'Your Honor'?"

"In public it is, but you can call me sir here." He reached out to give Quinn a firm, if condescending, handshake. "You keeping up with your studies, young man? That's important, you know."

Quinn held in the eye roll. He was more than keeping up—he was studying university-level mathematics for gears' sakes. "I try my best, sir."

"Is Quinn joining us for dinner?" Mrs. Shaw asked.

Miss Maren held Quinn's gaze. He blinked once, slowly. After a long beat of silence, she smiled. "If you don't mind children at the dinner table, I'm sure he'd be delighted. Now, my butler can show you to your rooms upstairs. We can meet in the library in half an hour for drinks if that's convenient."

The Shaws agreed and were led away by Preston. The guards followed, and one shot a frown over his shoulder at Quinn. He smiled at him and waved.

The guard's frown melted into a quirky smile. That's right, there's nothing suspicious about a nephew you've never heard of. Just keep on walking.

As soon as they were out of sight, Miss Maren marched him to the small study near the front door, the place she took meetings that she wanted over quickly.

"What the hell are you doing?" she growled. "And how were you able to lie without twitching?"

"You told them I was your nephew," he said, thinking fast. She couldn't know he'd finally broken his programming after months of work. "For now, that's my reality. It's not lying when I'm playing a part—it's acting."

"This wasn't in the plans."

"You told us to find out their secrets." He squared his shoulders. "People often say things around children, not expecting them to notice. Besides, if I keep them entertained, Lexa will have more time to go through their things."

Miss Maren looked conflicted. He could tell she really wanted to find out everything she could, but the thought of Lexa succeeding wasn't in the plans. "All right. I'll give you some leeway. Fail me, and I'll give Piers free rein. Am I clear?"

Despite the fact that he felt like he'd swallowed a bucket of ice water, Quinn nodded. "Perfectly.

Now, if you'll excuse me, I need to find something to wear to dinner."

Miss Maren groaned as soon as his back was turned, and a little smile tugged at the corner of his mouth. Failure wasn't an option—they'd get results—but that didn't mean he'd go easy on her tonight. Oh, no.

He'd call her Aunt Maren every chance he got, just to rub it in.

*

"But the Outlands need more stability," Miss Maren said. "If we send artificial laborers into the other provinces, we can help create order. Don't you think that's our responsibility?"

"No, I don't," the governor answered, spearing a large piece of steak with his fork. "They chose not to incorporate. Whatever happens out there now is their business. Not ours."

Quinn made himself small and invisible. It didn't matter that they were sitting at a table for six. It didn't matter that he was seated between Dr. Martine and Mrs. Shaw. He'd become a pair of ears and eyes.

"Our trade is being curtailed. I lost three shipments this month alone." Miss Maren's expression was pleasant, but Quinn could see how tightly she gripped her wine glass. This was the reason for the visit.

The governor sighed. "I understand, but do you really think that introducing artificials into Valardia is necessary right now? We're so much farther along in development—"

"So, Quinn," Mrs. Shaw said, dragging his attention away from the debate. "Do you play any sports?"

He forced himself to flash her a charming smile. "A few. I really like some of those old sports, like fencing and martial arts. I also love to run. I'm pretty quick."

"I bet you are. Do you run track at your school?" She frowned. "And where do you go to school?"

From his research, he knew the Shaws's daughters went to Engleton prep, near midtown. "St. Andrews. I'm planning to try out for the track team in the spring."

"Brilliant."

She kept nattering on about the virtues of organized sports. With a few well-placed nods and "uh-huhs," he could tune her out.

"I'm just saying it's a good time for expansion. Don't you think? The Quad has grown very powerful of late. We can use that to our advantage," Miss Maren said.

"The Quad is a paper tiger," the governor said. "They ceased to be relevant once the four city-states got back on their feet."

Quinn tensed. Next to him, Dr. Martine slowly set down his wineglass.

The governor didn't seem to notice the silence descending on the room. "They meant well, but it's time we were given our independence to manage Triarch. Surely, you agree. Wouldn't it be better to run Precipice without their interference?"

Dr. Martine was staring at the corner of the ceiling. Cameras were everywhere. If Miss Maren didn't handle this, they'd all be dead by morning.

"The Quad gave us our lives back," she said. "We owe everything to them."

"Everything," Dr. Martine echoed, still looking worried. He glanced at the camera again. "Without them, we wouldn't be here at all."

"They have their uses, to be sure," Mrs. Shaw said. "But do we really need them? That's why we're—"

"Not now, dear," the governor said. He nodded toward Quinn. "We don't want to bore the youngster."

Oh, he wasn't bored. Far from it. But Miss Maren gave him a look that said he needed to leave.

He faked a yawn. "That's okay, sir. I'm a little tired. Aunt Maren, may I be excused?"

"You may. And Quinn? We're going to be in the library for a while after dinner, so please keep it down upstairs. No loud music or games."

In other words, he and Lexa had time to sneak around and eavesdrop on conversations. "Yes, ma'am."

He left the room, swinging his arms like that human girl who came to the lab with her parents. Carefree, unselfconscious. As soon as he cleared the door into the sitting room, the conversation began again at a more vigorous pace.

Certain that Miss Maren would keep everyone occupied, Quinn dashed upstairs. When he got to the third floor, he bumped into Preston.

"Whoa, there, where are you going so fast?" he asked. "And why are you up here?"

"Um," he glanced down the hall. No sign of Lexa. "The Shaws wanted me to ask if everything was ready with their rooms."

Preston's forehead wrinkled as one of the security guards got up from his chair outside the door to the suite. "Of course it is. Now, down to the second floor with you before we both get in trouble."

Quinn nodded and jogged down to the second floor, fuming the whole way. He headed to his room, changed into his training gear, then went to the gym. As he expected, Doc was there, waiting.

"Well?"

"Miss Maren is keeping everyone busy, but they have a guard on the suite door. I have no idea where the second guard is."

"Lexa hacked into their com system. The second guard is off duty. They're taking shifts."

Good, that meant he wasn't inside the room. He took a deep breath. "Where's Lexa?"

Doc grinned and pointed to the rafters. The vent grate was hanging open. "Slithered right in."

Quinn eyed the narrow duct. "Must be nice to be small."

"I wouldn't know," Doc said. "She was going to find the data pad and plug in a decoder. You're on decryption duty to grab the right files."

He nodded and went to the data bank in the corner. "Doc? They were having an interesting conversation at dinner." He lowered his voice. "About the Quad."

"Don't even want to know. Safer that way," Doc said, backing toward the door. "But make sure you two aren't traced. This runs perfect, got it?"

"Perfectly," Quinn murmured.

Doc threw up his hands. "Now's not the time to correct anyone's grammar."

After he left, Quinn focused on the data feed. Blank. Empty. Nothing.

"Where are you?" he whispered.

Twenty minutes ticked by so slowly that Quinn thought time had stopped. His palms were slick with sweat, and he couldn't help replaying a scene in his mind; one in which Lexa was caught in the governor's room, then dragged away by Piers, never to be seen again.

He pushed his chair back. He had to find her, even if it meant risking getting caught.

A blinking cursor popped up on the screen. Then "LP Online" spelled itself out before his eyes.

His com beeped. "You in?"

"Yep," she breathed. "Gotta be very quiet, okay? Like bunnies."

"You have a weird sense of humor. And where have you been? I was about to come looking for you."

"Got stuck in the ventilation shaft, but that doesn't matter. I'm in their room. Do you see the data pad on your screen?"

A series of icons flooded his station. "Yes."

"Okay, so what are we looking for?"

"Can't you leave the trace and come back?"

"Nope," she whispered. "They'll see the hack. Gotta do this now, then delete the trace. So get busy before I'm caught."

Grumbling under his breath, Quinn typed in a series of search commands: Precipice, Maren DeGaul, outlands, sex.

"Sex?" Lexa sounded scandalized. "That's so gross!"

"And if Miss Maren wants their secrets, maybe that's something she can leverage. Doc always says that sex and lies are what get you into the most trouble."

Data streamed across the screen, and nothing notable popped up. Quinn bit his lip, wondering. Then he typed in "Quad."

Instantly, files flooded his screen. Most were normal stuff like internal memos or governmental edicts approved by the Quad. But there was one that stood out.

It was called "Independence."

Quinn copied the Independence file and cut off the connection. "Lexa, I'm done. Break the hack and get downstairs."

No answer.

"Lex? Lexa?"

Nothing but static. He had no idea what happened, but her sudden silence couldn't be good.

A bang sounded in the wall near the duct, and Lexa, covered with dust, slid out of the opening. Just when he thought she was going to fall headfirst to the floor, she caught a training rope and swung around for a second before climbing down.

"Did we get anything?"

"Yes, but what happened to you?"

"Almost got caught." Her eyes shone with pride. "Almost."

"Did they come back from dinner early?"

"Nope. Guard shift change—they sweep the room at each change, apparently. I had to bug out, but I managed to cut the connection before I left." Lexa puffed out her chest. "Never saw or heard me. I'm the best sneak ever."

"Okay, okay, you are the best sneak ever." He pointed at the screen. "This was all I could find."

"We giving this to the boss lady?" she asked. "Or are we gonna read it first?"

"Of course we're going to read it first," he said, laughing, and opened the file.

Dear Mr. Shepherd,

What you propose is interesting, but how do I know the outlanders will keep their word? If we don't succeed, there won't be a place on Earth I can hide. Do you have any assurances that your intel about the Quad is accurate? And, if so, how can you get close to them?

As for my end of the bargain, I'm collecting powerful allies to assist us with our cause. Once I have them convinced—or bought—we can proceed.

R. Shaw

"What's all that?" Lexa asked. "Is he messing around with the outside?"

Quinn thought about dinner, how the governor dismissed Miss Maren's concerns about the outlanders disrupting her shipments, and how he wanted to keep the artificial tech in Triarch City alone as an advantage. What was he up to? Did he want to stir up the outside so Triarch could break away from Quad control?

If so, the governor was right in his note—he was a dead man.

"It's big," Quinn said. "Good work getting into the room."

"So now what?" she asked, brushing dust out of her hair and letting out a huge sneeze. "Those ducts need a good cleaning."

"After we're done with this, I'll send you back through with a scrub brush."

She smacked his arm. "Not nice. And you didn't answer my question."

"Now," he told her, "we listen and learn."

✳

Quinn huddled in the butler's pantry cabinet just behind the library. He'd invented a little com amplifier—something Dr. Martine had suggested as a test—that allowed him to hear through the library wall. He'd sent Lexa back into the rafters, and she should be right above them by now.

"We can't delay," the governor was saying. He sounded cross, which meant Miss Maren had him where she wanted him, most like. "We need to move now."

"I don't see how that's wise," Miss Maren said, her voice cold and clipped. "I won't help. But I won't stand in your way, either."

"Better than nothing," the governor said. The sofa creaked. "I think we'll retire for the evening. I beg you to reconsider. There won't be a better time than this."

"Give me tonight. If I change my mind, we can discuss it over breakfast before you return to the city."

Their voices faded as they moved across the room. Quinn waited sixty seconds before easing out of the cabinet.

Preston stood right in front of him, holding a tray of highball glasses. He jumped and the glasses rattled, but he didn't drop them. "What were you doing in my cabinet?"

His shoulders slumped. He'd lie to humans, but not to a fellow artificial. "Miss Maren asked me to gather intel on the governor. This seemed like a good way to do it."

"Yes, but she was in the room. What were you going to learn that she doesn't already know?"

Quinn shrugged and forced a winning smile. "It's good practice, anyway. Goodnight!"

He hurried away from Preston, who was staring at him like he'd lost his mind. Better for the butler to think him crazy than to be caught.

When he got upstairs to the training room, Doc and Lexa were waiting. Doc said, "Maren's coming up. Get anything?"

"I think so," Quinn said, hoping he was right.

The click-clack of fancy high-heeled shoes announced her arrival. When she and Dr. Martine came inside, Miss Maren looked at both of them, her nose wrinkled. "Well?"

Quinn gave her a data stick with the file on it. "Lexa got into their rooms, and we copied his data pad. We found one file that might be of particular interest. It's called Independence."

She cocked her head. "Is it now?" A slow, cold smile spread across her face. "We got him. We finally got him."

"What happens next?" Lexa asked.

Miss Maren gave Dr. Martine a calculating look. "You just bought yourself six more months, Caldwell. Don't waste them."

Then she was gone.

"What did that mean?" Lexa asked, sounding panicked.

"Easy there." Dr. Martine leaned down so he could take her hands. "It means everything is going to be okay."

"Good work tonight," Doc added. "Now go to bed."

Quinn tugged at Lexa's sleeve. "Come on."

On the way to her room, she asked, "Was Mr. C right? Is it okay?"

"For you, I think so. For the governor, I doubt it." He stopped by Lexa's door. Who cared about the governor when she was safe, at least for a while longer? He hadn't felt this relieved since he heard that Piers was going on a three-week business trip last summer. "You did well tonight. Get some sleep and maybe Doc will give us some free time to play tennis tomorrow."

"You hate tennis," she said, kicking at the carpet.

"But you like tennis, and I like you."

Lexa giggled. It was a bubbly sound, full of surprise and sweetness. A tiny spark awoke in Quinn's heart. She didn't laugh often, and he decided to find ways to make her laugh more.

He suddenly felt embarrassed and didn't know what to say or do. He should probably go. "Goodnight, Lex."

"Goodnight."

Her door shut with a click, and Quinn leaned against the wall. They had a six-month reprieve, but that's all it was. Dr. Martine needed to do something to convince Miss Maren for good, but what? Because Quinn wouldn't let them kill Lexa. No matter what he had to do.

Even if he had to take her place.

With a sigh, he pushed himself off the wall and started toward his room. When the muted sound of gunfire sounded from upstairs, he jumped. It sounded like it was coming from the governor's suite.

Lexa's door flew open. Her face was pale. "Are we under attack?"

"No." He cast a weary glance at the ceiling. "I think the governor just found out that the Quad doesn't like traitors."

She was shaking. "I'm still worried they're going to come steal me away some night, no matter what the boss lady said."

"If that happens, I promise I won't stop looking until I find you," he said. "I won't let anything happen to you."

Lexa threw her arms around his waist and pressed her cheek against his chest. "I love you. You've always been my best friend."

Quinn patted her back, enjoying the fierceness of the hug. "And you're mine. Time for bed. I promise I'll see you in the morning."

She pulled away, smiling and went into her room. Once the door shut again, Quinn stumbled to his own room, exhaustion overwhelming him. He meant what he said—he wouldn't let anything happen to Lexa.

But that wasn't within his control. And he only had six months to convince Miss Maren otherwise.

Part 3: Seven Years Ago

"Shhh," she whispered. "They'll hear."

Lexa was trying to teach him how to use the crawl spaces to spy on the kitchen staff. The air ducts had been too narrow for his broadening shoulders—something that had made Doc smirk and Lexa frown with confusion.

"How come you're getting so...big?" she'd asked, eyeing his arms.

It was all he could do not to show off how well his biceps were coming along. "Growing up, sneak."

"Huh," she'd said, before shrugging and running off to climb her ropes. Her interest had left him feeling a little wobbly.

Now, though, they were in utility easements. The passages were wider, so the wiring could be worked on, but he still didn't like the feeling of being trapped, and his breathing had turned ragged and noisy.

"S-sorry," he gasped.

She stopped crawling forward and turned to look at him over her shoulder. "Are you okay?"

"Just need a second." Quinn forced himself to breathe more slowly. Sure, he could bench press three times what Lexa could. He could outrun her, too. But being trapped in tight places? Screws, why did she think this was fun?

"We need to hurry. They're going to serve the soup any minute."

He nodded and began following her. There was a service cubby in the corner of the kitchen, and he could hear the cook—human, because why would an artificial care about good food (which totally explained why they both stole cookies every chance they got)—bustling around to ready the salads. Maren was hosting some politicians to talk about the gubernatorial race, and dinner had to be perfect.

He and Lexa overheard them talking on the way to the dining room about the "terrible tragedy" that befell the Shaws and their security team six months ago. Suicide hill, the steep road leading to Maren's house, was the site of many hovercraft accidents. So no one questioned that they'd gone straight into the lake after their car malfunctioned.

Very sad.

Quinn felt nothing but disgust about the whole thing, especially his part in it. Sure, Governor Shaw had been a blowhard, but his party didn't deserve to be gunned down while guests in someone else's house.

The message had gotten through loud and clear to the rest of the council, though. Frak with the Quad, you get a bullet—or four—right through the skull.

Quinn flushed a little at his daring. Cursing was his new favorite vice. Yes, he could curse like most artificials: screws, gears, mech-headed tool. But he liked the feel of the human curse words on his tongue, too. So he used them to keep them from having any power over him.

If he used their words, they meant nothing.

Which was also why, in his head, he'd started saying "Maren" without the Miss tacked on. If Doc could do it, so could he. He was done being a scared little boy.

"She's leaving!" Lexa's excitement was barely contained. "Preston came to tell her one of the guests had some questions about the salad."

The cook had gotten onto them for taking cookies, and she was mean as hell to all the artificials. Quinn had caught her cuffing Preston across the face because the tablecloth had a spot on it—after dinner. The wine stain had come from Maren's glass, and somehow that was Preston's fault.

Quinn couldn't let that slide. So he had decided they needed a new cook.

As dinner had started, he'd disabled the kitchen security camera. The cook, of course, had shooed the guards away, telling them she'd raise an alarm if "a gang of nasty Bolts" showed up, but that she didn't want them underfoot for no good reason other than to watch her stir soup.

Just like he planned—now they could go into the kitchen without being seen.

"Let's go," he said.

They crept into the kitchen. The pot of butternut squash soup bubbled on the stove. It was thick with cream and smelled delicious. Quinn smiled; that wouldn't last long.

Lexa ran for the salt. He ran for the cayenne pepper. They worked quickly, dumping half the salt and a quarter of the pepper into the soup. He'd chosen cayenne because specks of black pepper would've been too noticeable in the golden soup.

Lexa went to the door to keep watch. "She's talking to one of the ladies about the salad dressing."

Quinn stirred the mess into the soup, rinsed the spoon, and put it away.

"She's coming back!" Lexa hustled over and put the salt and pepper away. "Into the cubby!"

They raced into the cubby, and Lexa barely had the door closed before the cook hurried in, muttering, "Who does she think she is, asking all those questions? As if we'd alter the menu just for her. The citrus vinaigrette is Miss Maren's favorite, and I'm not changing it for some two-bit reporter. No, ma'am."

The barrage of insults continued the entire time she dished up the soup. Quinn didn't know how she missed the change in smell—cayenne was pretty obvious. But she must've been so peeved that she didn't notice.

Preston arrived a few moments later with empty salad plates—save one.

"Did that hussy not eat?" the cook grumbled. "She's going to go hungry if she keeps turning her nose up at everything."

"Yes, ma'am," Preston said, sounding bored.

She loaded up his tray with the soup and sent him on his way. Lexa had her hand clamped over her mouth so she wouldn't laugh.

"We need to get back," Quinn whispered. "If we're in the training room when this goes down, how could we possibly be involved?"

She made a face. "I can't lie like you can. I hope they don't ask."

They started crawling back to the utility adjunct near the service entrance, when they heard the kitchen door swing open, and a panicked Preston saying, "Miss Maren's coming... The soup..."

"What did you put in the soup?" Maren's voice promised pain and suffering. "I understand you weren't happy with Carolee for not liking the salad, but I won't have my staff—"

"Miss Maren, I have no idea what you're talking about!"

There was an icy pause. "It doesn't matter. I haven't been pleased with your service, anyway. You're dismissed. You, show her out, then come back and serve the roast."

"Yes, ma'am," Preston answered.

Quinn and Lexa crawled faster until they tumbled out into the service entrance behind a stack of crates. The cook was tearfully accepting a ride from one of the security guards. When Maren dismissed someone, she didn't mess around.

Once they were gone, the two of them scrambled upstairs, using a route Lexa had developed that avoided the security sweeps. The first time she'd sneaked into the training room while Doc watched all the security feeds without seeing her, he'd tossed her in the air, laughing.

Now, it gave them the run of the entire house, except for Maren's quarters, of course. They still hadn't figured out how to leave the grounds without being caught, but Quinn was working on it. These little incursions were training for that day.

They stumbled into the training room, panting and laughing.

"I wish we could've seen the look on her face," Lexa said. "She was so mean, I'm glad she got kicked out."

"Me, too, even if her snickerdoodles were the best out of the last three cooks." Quinn sighed. "Does it ever strike you as weird that the two of us live here, eating Maren's food, instead of the Precipice dorms downtown?"

"Miss Maren," Lexa said, shooting a glance at the door. "But I hadn't really thought about that. I mean, the security artificials live here. So do Preston and the cleaning staff. Why wouldn't we live here, too?"

"Yes, but we have special instructors, combat training, expensive tutors." He lowered his voice. "They're preparing us for something. Doc hinted about that once, and he has to be right. But for what?"

"I don't—"

Lexa's answer was cut short by the sound of footsteps in the hall. They split apart, Quinn hurrying to start up a computer simulation he'd been running and Lexa to shimmy up a rope to the ceiling.

A moment later, Maren, Piers, Doc, and Dr. Martine entered the room. Dr. Martine looked stern—a bad sign. Doc looked blank. Another bad sign.

"What did you do?" Maren's voice carried through the open space, bouncing off every hard surface to rebound back to her. "One of my guests went into anaphylactic shock because she's allergic to cayenne pepper."

Lexa let out a squeak in the rafters, and Maren fixed her death-ray stare on her. "Oh, yes. That little prank nearly killed someone."

"Miss Maren," Quinn said, to deflect the attention away from Lexa. "What are you talking about?"

A muscle ticked in her jaw. "Someone put a bunch of salt and cayenne in our soup. The cook swore to security that she didn't do it. I had to make a public example of someone, and she was on warning already, so I let her go. But the moment we figured out what was wrong, I knew who was behind such a childish and insolent trick."

Quinn sat completely still. She hadn't asked a question, so he wasn't obligated to say anything. Out of the corner of his eye, he saw Lexa climbing all the way to the top platform in the corner of the room. When she got there, she hugged her knees to her chest.

Maren noticed her distress, too. "Lexa, dear. Come down. Now." She turned to Dr. Martine. "See, she's trouble. And now, she's corrupting Quinn. I can't have my investment tainted by a failed experiment."

Dr. Martine opened his mouth, then shut it, like he had no idea what to say.

When Lexa came to stand before them, she bowed her head so her hair hung in her face.

He could practically smell her desperation. She couldn't lie, so if they asked her a direct question, she'd have to answer or her security programming would give her away. That shoulder twitch would be her undoing—permanently.

Maren walked over and put a finger under her chin to force her to look up. "The cookies last week, hiding my data pad yesterday, and now this? Why did you do it? I ought to let Piers take care of you, but maybe it's time to terminate your program if you can't—"

Quinn leapt to his feet. "It was my idea. All of it. I dragged Lexa into it."

Lexa shook her head, her eyes pleading with him. The cookies had been her idea, but he'd take the blame for all of it. He didn't know why Maren hated Lexa and not him, but he'd use that to their advantage to keep her safe and whole.

"Well, I must say I'm very disappointed," Maren said. "Caldwell, take Lexa to her room. Quinn, you'll go with Piers."

"No!" Lexa screamed, fighting her way free of Dr. Martine. Before she could reach Quinn, though, Doc grabbed her arms and held her back. "No! Let me go! Don't take Quinn. Take me!"

"Quinn's already admitted his guilt," Maren said, obviously enjoying Lexa's fear. "Dr. Mendal, remove her…and give her a sedative."

"She won't remember what happened if we do," Doc warned.

"Exactly." Maren went to Quinn and gripped his shoulder tight enough to bruise. "I want her to have no memory of this, so Quinn can bear his punishment alone."

They dragged a howling Lexa from the room. Maren shook her head. "I see why Dr. Mendal calls her Hellcat. She's about as feral as an alley stray. There are days I question the wisdom of creating you a helpmate. So far, it hasn't worked out exactly like the old Bible stories claimed. Then again, I'm not sure you've developed a strong enough personality to make her submit to you properly." She released his shoulder. "I expect that, from here on out, you'll take a firm hand with Lexa. She's yours to control and your responsibility. You have the ability to work people over to your will. You'll do that with Lexa, or she's finished."

Quinn's stomach twisted in misery. Bend Lexa to his will? He'd sooner be able to control the wind than restrain her. Besides, that sounded like a good way to make her hate him forever.

Could he be rough with her to save her life, though? Because that might be his only choice.

"Now," Maren said, "Piers will provide a lesson in what it means to cross me."

"Come on, beanpole." Piers grabbed his arm. "Downstairs we go."

Once they were in the stairwell, the frustration and anger about his situation finally got the better of him. "I weigh almost as much as you. So who's the beanpole now, stickman?"

Oh, gears... Had his mouth malfunctioned?

Piers laughed. "There's a difference between wiry and weak, moron." He slammed Quinn against the wall, and the stair rail knocked the wind out of him. As he gasped for breath, Piers leaned in close. "And you are weak."

A tear ran down Quinn's cheek. He was weak. He'd wasted his time on petty crimes. He wouldn't make that mistake again. Piers hauled him up and led him down to his "workshop."

The artificials called it the horror factory.

As soon as they crossed the threshold, Piers hit Quinn with a low-energy stunner blast, just enough to turn his limbs to jelly and make him more compliant about being strapped into the chair. It was like a dentist's chair, except it had restraints at the chest, waist, and calves. Once you were strapped in, you weren't going anywhere.

Piers made sure the straps were extra tight. The bump on his nose, where Quinn had broken it in a bid for escape three months ago, had taught him "beanpole" was a lot stronger than he looked. Quinn counted that as one of his few victories in this place.

Getting the cook fired was another.

He was being reckless, though. Lexa was too important to him to screw up anymore. It wasn't just the pain he knew was coming. It had nothing to do with any punishment they could devise.

He knew, for sure, that he'd learned how to love. Maybe it was a programmed response based on a girl created for this sole purpose, but he felt it. Maybe he was only twelve and she was barely ten— but he loved her. He'd do anything to protect her. Sure, the thought of kissing her was a little gross, but that didn't make his feelings any less intense.

"What are you grinning about over there?" Piers said from his workbench.

Quinn wanted to say, "Your ugly face," but he was running a new program: being good for Lexa's sake. "Just glad we're getting a new cook."

Piers surprised him by laughing. "You know, I hated that old cow. She always served undercooked or lukewarm stuff to the staff. Like she couldn't be bothered to feed us if Ms. DeGaul wasn't in residence."

Huh. "Does that mean you won't punish me? I promise to be very convincing."

He turned around, a padded cudgel in hand. "What's the fun in that?" He swung the cudgel and nodded. "Now, the boss said we had to do this so your marks are hidden. She was dead serious. Little Lexie is not to know that you took her punishment. Ms. DeGaul doesn't want you to get ideas about being noble or heroic."

Quinn deflated a little. Fine. Lexa would never know he took her punishments. But that wouldn't stop him.

"Then let's get this over with."

The first blow across the top of his legs came before the words died on his lips, and a yelp escaped. After the second blow slammed into his chest, he clamped his mouth shut and retreated into his mind. It was the only safe place he had.

"Come on, Lexa, put your back into it," Doc called.

She grunted and tugged at Quinn's arm. "He's too heavy!"

"It's about leverage," he told her. "Don't pull. Use your hip to bump me forward. The momentum is all you need."

They'd been trying all morning to teach Lexa how to flip someone larger over her shoulder, but she couldn't seem to get it.

"Hellcat, this is basic close-quarters combat. You don't figure this out, we might as well teach you to sew."

Lexa let out an impressive string of swear words, including something about Doc's mother. Quinn threw back his head and laughed. She was so cute when she was indignant.

"Mistake," she growled, and with surprising speed, she rammed her shoulder into Quinn's stomach and, as he bent over, dragged him over her back to drop him on the floor gasping like a fish.

"Yes, just like that!" Doc said, laughing so hard, tears were in his eyes.

That hurt Quinn's pride, and he struggled to his knees. "Lucky shot."

Lexa propped her fists on her hips. "Was not. Want me to hit you again?"

"Enough, enough," Doc said. "You two have been sniping at each other all day. You need a break. Go play."

"Play what?" Lexa asked. "We can't go outside anymore."

"And whose fault was that?"

Quinn and Lexa pointed at each other.

"Exactly," Doc barked. "Reprogramming all the gardening equipment to mow the words 'Maren's Pizza Parlor' in the grass was a bad idea."

"It was Quinn's idea!"

"Lexa crawled into the garden shed and disabled all the safeguards."

"You thought it up!" she said. "And now we're being punished."

He glared at his shoes. She had no idea just how much punishment was to be had after a prank, and that was the point. Maren told him he had to keep her in hand, so every time they got in trouble, he took the blame. Being grounded to the house paled in comparison to the burn marks on his lower back. He felt like they'd never heal—and they might not, since Piers repeatedly burned the same spots to "keep the merchandise as damage free as we can."

Merchandise. Slave. Bolt.

Names he'd been called that meant he was less than human. None of that was Lexa's fault. He was just having an ugly day. Anger stirred in his chest, and he knew he was seconds away from blowing. He turned and stormed out of the room.

Lexa called after him, but he used his long legs to his advantage and outdistanced her easily. He banged into the stairwell and took the stairs two at a time to end up on the ground level near the service entrance. Maren was getting a delivery of food from a gourmet shop in town. Guests again. Another night of pretending to be invisible so no one would know she'd succeeded in creating artificial children. He tried to tell her it didn't matter—that he could pass for human easily—but she said his existence was top secret, and the incident with the Shaws only made the need for that more apparent.

He stared out at the beautiful spring day. A soft breeze whistled into the delivery bay, bringing the scent of cut grass and the rose bushes near the gate. The human guards were busy chatting up the cute delivery girls, while the artificial guards inspected the cargo. It would be so easy to walk away. Turn invisible and leave this place behind. Trackers messed with internal electronics, so he didn't have one—the last artificial that had one installed had gone homicidal. Instead, they used pain switches to ensure compliance… but Quinn didn't have one of those, either. They were so confident in their ability to find a rogue artificial that they allowed him his free will. And they were so confident they'd cowed his free will that they didn't worry about him roaming the house without supervision.

Their arrogance made him seethe. If it weren't for Lexa, he'd do it. He'd walk away.

"Beanpole? What are you doing down here?" Piers whispered in his ear.

Quinn jumped. He'd been so lost in thought that he'd failed to hear the man creep up on him. "I needed some air. This is the closest I can get."

"Now, that's not true. Your bedroom window opens two inches. Why are you really here? Thinking of disappearing?" Piers grabbed him by the back of his T-shirt and yanked him into the hallway. "I'm watching you. Screw up and little Lexie might suffer your punishment for a change."

Quinn's nostrils flared. "What do you want with me? Why are you always lurking like some kind of candy man waiting to take me to the black market?"

"Candy man? Black market? Where did a Bolt like you learn about those things?" Piers's smile was wolfish, turning his cold, pinched features into something primal. "But what I want is simple. I want you to understand that you can't outsmart me. Petty tricks are one thing, but you ever try to escape, and I will hunt you down like the abomination you are."

"Don't you call him that," a shrill voice demanded.

Quinn froze. "Lexa, it's fine. Go back upstairs."

But Piers was already on the move. He lunged and grabbed her wrist. "Don't you ever talk to me that way, rat."

"Don't you talk to me that way, you piece of shast!"

Quinn didn't have time relish the shocked look on Piers's face as he realized Lexa wasn't scared of him before she twisted, threw him over her shoulder, and came up holding his stunner. She aimed it at Piers's head. "Oops, safety's off. Move and I'll burn your brain out."

"Lex," Quinn said, hands up. He moved slowly away from the wall. "Put the stunner down. This is trouble we don't need."

"He called you an abomination. He called me rat. He hurts you—I don't always forget, you know, no matter what kind of pills they give me. This has to stop." She looked down the hall, to the delivery bay. "We could go. Quinn? We could go."

"You go, and I'll have you down in seconds," Piers growled, staring at the business end of his own stunner.

Lexa tightened her finger on the trigger. "Nah, you'll be too busy drooling and wetting your pants."

Quinn was about to suggest they all forget this happened when Piers lunged for the stunner. Lexa, fast as a young cheetah, dodged him, jumped, and shot him on the fly. He dropped, his limbs twitching.

Lexa shoved the stunner into her belt. "Let's go."

Quinn took a look at Piers's limp form and smiled. Suddenly, he wasn't afraid anymore. What was left to be afraid of, anyway? They were dead, either way, so why not taste freedom first. "Ladies first."

They crept into the delivery bay. The two artificials were reloading the crates after their search, and the human guards were still flirting with the girls.

Lexa led Quinn along the wall, walking light on her toes. He tried to emulate her, but he was too big to stay hidden in the shadows, so he frog crawled instead. Maren's fleet of hovers would hide them most of the way, but they would have a few moments in the open at the bay doors.

"Lex," Quinn breathed. "Wait until the delivery hover starts up and slip out as they leave."

She gave him a thumbs up and crouched in the corner near the door. Quinn scooted in next to her, his heart hammering like crazy. They were doing it. They were really leaving.

The delivery hover spooled up with a whine. Lexa caught his eye, jerked her head at the door, and crept forward. The door started to close, and they rolled out of its way into the edge of Maren's garden by the gate. Being surrounded by thorn bushes wasn't what Quinn imagined his first few moments of freedom would be like, but he'd take it. He breathed in the scent of roses. They smelled different out here.

"Okay, where to?" Lexa asked.

"To the lake. There's lots of places to hide in the ruins, and if we need to, we can swim out so dogs won't be able to track our scents."

She nodded, and they crawled down to the edge of the drive, watching for guard patrols on the roof.

"We're clear," she said, darting out into the road.

Quinn hurried to catch up, then took the lead as they sneaked through the alley and into the field of grass near the lake. Lakefront property—so many places to hide. He showed Lexa how to army-crawl through the field, staying low so the cameras or guards wouldn't see them. Their progress was slow, though, and before they made it to the towers Doc had shown him all those months ago, the alarms went off at Maren's house.

"Go!" Quinn said, shoving Lexa toward the lake. "Into the water. Hurry!"

Guards were pouring out of the house and into the field like ants after a discarded candy bar. Quinn shoved Lexa again.

"Doc didn't teach me to swim yet," she whispered, eyes huge.

"It's simple. Hang on to me, and if we need to go under, hold your breath. We can hold our breath longer than regular humans. We'll go under a minute at a time, okay?" He pulled her into the water and settled her on his back. "Just like a dolphin ride."

"What's a dolphin?" she asked. Her teeth chattered audibly next to his ear as the cold water seeped over them.

"I read about them once. They're mammals, but live in the ocean."

"They can't have gone far!" Piers yelled. He sounded murderous. "Find them or I'll have you terminated."

Shouts and the sounds of men running spurred Quinn forward. "We're going under. One, two, three." He kicked off from the bottom and dove into the murky shallows, using the slimy underwater grass to pull them along rather than kick his feet and give them away.

They surfaced a few moments later, and Quinn stayed low. The men were walking a grid through the field, while Piers and another guard took off in a security hover. He flew straight toward the lake.

He'd have heat-sensing equipment on board.

"Lexa, we're going under again. Longer this time."

"O-o-okay."

He dove, using one hard kick to push them to the bottom. There, he slithered along like an eel among the water plants, hoping they were deep enough to hide their heat signature from Piers.

The water was dark and dirty, so he had to feel his way. That's how he missed seeing the concrete piling. He rammed it with his shoulder and Lexa let go.

No! He looked up, and she was floating to the surface. He clawed his way upward only to find Piers's hover right over them.

"Clever, but not clever enough, beanpole," he shouted. "Now, swim back to shore, or I'm going to shoot you and pay the consequences with Ms. DeGaul later."

Lexa bobbed next to him, fear in her eyes. "I can hold my breath longer. Promise."

Quinn put an arm around her waist to keep her afloat. "It's no good. We tried. It's over."

She slumped against him. "I won't let you take the punishment."

"You have to," he said. "She'll kill you, otherwise."

As he started paddling toward shore, careful to keep their heads above water, Lexa said, "But I'm afraid that this time, she'll want to kill you."

✳

Maren made them stand on a plastic sheet as soon as Piers dragged them, soaking wet, to her office. Her eyes flashed with more anger than Quinn ever remembered seeing. His confidence that he was too valuable to her to kill wavered.

"I should have you sold off for parts, Quinn," she snapped, pacing the floor, her steps so heavy that her high heels made marks on the wooden floor. "But we've invested too much in you. You're a fifty-million-credit project already." She glared at Lexa. "This one, however, has only wasted half that much. And from what I understand, she subjected my chief of security to bodily harm."

Lexa propped her hands on her hips, defiant even though her lips were blue with cold and water dripped steadily from her hair onto her back. "He hurt Quinn. I don't let anybody hurt Quinn." She took a step toward Maren, fierce and quivering. "Not even you."

"That's it," Maren said. She stopped pacing and turned from fire to ice—a very bad sign. "Caldwell, we're done. Are you going to do it or shall I have Piers?"

"I'd be happy to take care of it," Piers said.

Fear and anger pulsed inside Quinn. "No! Take me. It's my fault. It was all my idea."

"Not this time," Piers said. "And I have the stunner mark to prove it." He smirked at Lexa. "It'd be my genuine pleasure to rid you of this problem, Ms. DeGaul."

Lexa lifted her chin. "I'm going to kill you someday, Piers. And you'll never see it coming."

"Lex, stop!" Quinn gripped her upper arm and turned her to face him. "They're going to term you if you don't shut up!"

"We're going to term her, either way." Maren shook her head. "Kids. What were we thinking, Caldwell?"

"My dear, the project wasn't a total failure." Dr. Martine turned sad eyes on Lexa. "Give me the night to map her brain patterns. If I can isolate the problem that makes her so willful, we could have a new version that's just as strong and fast, but without the disdain for authority."

"Fine, but I want a blonde with blue eyes, this time," Maren warned. "Understand me?"

Dr. Martine's shoulders drooped. "Perfectly."

Quinn didn't understand—what did it matter that the next version had blonde hair, instead of Lexa's rich brown? Was it to remind him of what he'd lost? To make this new girl as different from Lexa as possible as a warning? His eyes stung with tears. This couldn't be happening. It couldn't.

Piers yanked Lexa away. "I'll take her to your lab and have her restrained."

"Take care not to damage her," Dr. Martine said firmly. "I need her intact for mapping."

Piers dragged Lexa to the door. She kicked and screamed, and even bit his arm, but he didn't turn her loose. They were really taking her away. They were taking her away forever.

Everything inside of Quinn exploded into a universe of pain and rage.

"No!" He launched himself at Piers, landing one good, solid punch to the older man's chin. Piers's head rocked back, but he didn't let Lexa go.

"Oh, for stars' sakes." Maren pressed a button on the underside of her desk. Ten seconds later, the room was flooded with guards pointing stunners at Quinn's head. "Put him in detention. Piers, once you're done delivering Lexa, take this one to Dr. Drummond. I've had about enough of this free-will nonsense."

Dr. Martine heaved a sigh. "At least let him retain decision and thought control. Like you said, we've spent an enormous fortune on him. We need him to be able to reason and think without fear. A switch will be enough."

"Fine," she spat. "Just get them both out of my office."

"Let me say goodbye!" Quinn cried out. "Please. She's my only friend."

Maren rolled her eyes, but Dr. Martine held up a hand. "We raised his hopes, only to dash them in the end. This is partly our fault. Letting him say goodbye is only fair."

There was a pause while they stared at one another. Finally, she nodded, looking really tired. "Okay. And Quinn, for what it's worth, I am sorry we had to put you through this. She was flawed, and we should've terminated her before you got too attached."

The guards pushed Quinn into the hall, and Lexa rushed to wrap her thin arms around his middle. "I'm sorry. I'm so sorry."

"You have nothing to apologize for," he whispered. "It's my fault."

"No, it's not." She looked up at him, her gaze intense. "Remember—never forget—whose fault it really is. Promise?" Lexa stood on tiptoe to whisper into his ear, "Make them bleed, Quinn. Make them pay for everything they've done."

He felt his world crumble around him even as a grim purpose filled him. "I promise."

"Enough." Piers tore Lexa from his grip. "Three, Nine, take the boy to detention."

Two low-functioning artificials grabbed his arms in matching vice grips. As they were dragged in opposite directions, Lexa screamed, "I'm your best friend! Always!"

"Lexa!" His heart was going to rip itself apart. He'd never survive this pain. "Lexa!"

Piers yanked her around the corner, but Quinn could hear her screaming his name. Something inside him broke. Make them bleed, she'd said. Remember who's at fault. Well, he knew damn well who that was.

With a roar of rage, he ripped one arm free and punched the artificial in the jaw so hard, something crunched beneath his fist. When that one went down, he yanked the other toward him, sprang off the floor, and kicked him in the chest. Bones cracked under the impact.

Quinn flew into Maren's office before the security team could get their bearings, and he landed on top of her with his fingers around her throat. "Give her back! Give her back!"

"Quinn, stop!" Dr. Martine barked, trying to pry his hands away. "This isn't helping. The decision is made."

"Our lives are worthless," Quinn said as Maren kicked beneath him. His rage turned to hopeless resignation. His life was over, but he'd take her with him. It was all he had left. "I won't live like a slave anymore. You'll have to kill me."

"I've got this," Doc said behind him.

Quinn started to tell him to back off, but something heavy slammed into his skull, and blackness swallowed him whole, drowning him in the sound of Lexa's screams.

"Six, two, four-seven, nine, thirteen," a voice was saying far away. "Six, two, four-seven, nine, thirteen. Six, two, four-seven, nine, thirteen."

"He's coming back online," Dr. Martine said.

"It doesn't take long," a man with a smooth, pleasant voice answered. "He needs to recognate, then we can test the switch and see if we need to adjust the output."

"Thank you, Dr. Drummond. I'll stay with him if you want to grab a coffee."

"I'll take you up on that. I'll be back in ten. He should be fully aware by then."

The door opened, and a cool whisper of air slid over Quinn's skin. It closed with a quiet snap, and he woke up a bit more. He was... What was this? Where had they taken him? Restraints held his back flat against a table, but he was facing the floor. They'd removed his shirt, but not his pants or shoes. He stirred and discovered his arms were asleep and that the back of his neck, right above where it met his spine, hurt like he'd been cut open.

He tried to tell Dr. Martine he was awake, but all that came out was, "Six, two, four-seven, nine, thirteen."

Dr. Martine knelt at the head of the bed, so that he was underneath Quinn. "You can't answer me yet, but I know you can hear me and understand." He spoke barely above a murmur. "I'm so sorry. I wish I'd been able to save her, but things are dangerous for all of us right now. Attacking Maren was a stupid move, even if I do understand the motivation.

"From here on out, I need you to be a model citizen. That's going to go against everything you want, and I know I'm asking you to do something incredibly difficult. But Quinn, you can hide behind a dozen different masks, act a thousand characters. Do this for me. Don't be too contrite to raise suspicions, but do, over time, prove yourself more docile and compliant."

"Six, two, four-seven, nine, thirteen!" The words weren't what he wanted, but the tone came across.

"I know," Dr. Martine said. "But please, don't give up. I couldn't save her." His voice broke. "I won't lose you, too. You're our one hope now."

"Six, two...what...hope?" he forced out between clenched teeth.

Dr. Martine's eyes bored into his. "The Quad ordered you for reasons we don't yet know, but suspect. And there are some of us who think that absolute power isn't right. Whatever you think of me, or Doc, or even Maren, understand there is worse out there. Piers is only a faded example of the evil lurking in the wings. You cannot fall into their hands before you've been prepared. Before we know you're ready to keep from being used to ruin the lives of a lot of good people."

"Like...you?"

"No." Dr. Martine stared at the floor. "Not like me. Better people. Now, when Dr. Drummond comes back, your new pain switch will be tested, and it'll be excruciating. Don't fight. Bide your time. I won't be able to speak freely with you again after this. I have to distance myself, but know I'm watching—and hoping."

The doorknob creaked as it turned, and Dr. Martine rose. "Remember what I said."

Quinn didn't even have time to digest everything before Drummond asked, "Is he coherent?"

"Yes," Dr. Martine said. "Aren't you, Quinn?"

Anger swirled thick in his gut, but he managed, "Yes, sir."

"Very good!" Drummond sounded way too chipper for a man about to inflict pain on a bound subject, and Quinn curled his fists at his sides.

"We'll start with a low-level 'reminder' test. This will be for defiance and failure to follow commands."

A blink later, a glaring headache throbbed in Quinn's forehead, and he gasped.

"Good, good!" Drummond leaned down to look at him. "Yes, that worked well. I can see it by the way you're squinting. All right, next level is for rule breaking."

The glaring headache turned into a searing pain, and Quinn vomited lake water and the remnants of his lunch all over the floor.

"Ah, yes. That's partly why you're still upside down. No aspirating on my watch." The smile in Drummond's voice, like he was enjoying Quinn's discomfort and humiliation, was almost too much to take. "Last level. This is for attacking your handlers. Lay hands on Ms. DeGaul again, and you'll wish you were dead."

"I already do," Quinn whispered.

"Oh, not like this." Drummond's tone turned silky and dangerous. "Not nearly like this."

A bolt of agony flashed through Quinn's entire body, locking his jaw so he couldn't even scream to release his pain. He went rigid, and his eyesight flickered in and out. The last thing he said before passing out was, "Kill me. Please."

He woke up in his room. It was dark outside his tiny window, and his stomach cramped with hunger. When he sat up, though, the floor tilted, and the idea of eating was forgotten in his hurry to lie back down.

For a while, he let grief overwhelm him. Lexa was dead. He'd never see her smile again. She'd never sneak into his bed in the middle of the night after a nightmare. No more sparring practice or stealing cookies or ganging up on Doc in the training room.

Gone. She was gone forever.

An inhuman cry wrenched itself free from his lungs. Gone. She was gone. Half of his heart had been torn out and no one cared. Not one frakking soul. How he hated this place and everyone in it.

Dr. Martine said he was sorry, but what good did that do? Nothing.

His only choices were to end his life or run. So what if Dr. Martine said he needed to pretend, to be compliant for some greater purpose? He had no greater purpose without his best friend. Part of his soul was dead—and he believed he had a soul. Loving Lexa had taught him that. He wasn't a thing to be owned. He was alive, and he loved. That made him more human than the people who kept him locked away. He'd be free, one way or another.

Quinn stood, then rested a hand on his desk. Once the wave of dizziness passed, he went to the door. It was locked. Of course it was. That left only one way out.

He looked around the room, then laughed darkly. There wasn't a single cord, sharp object, or means of electrocution in his room. They'd even taken his sheets while he was with Dr. Drummond. Maybe they understood his thought processes better than he'd assumed. Didn't matter—this would be over one way or another.

Someday, Piers and Maren would get lax. He could be patient—watch, wait, and gather enough currency to run. Someday, he'd have an opportunity to escape into the city. He didn't give two shasts about Dr. Martine's plans.

He'd run the second they became complacent.

That thought sustained him through a very long night. Finally, just after dawn, Doc came with some toast and weak tea. "You ready to behave?"

"Depends," Quinn muttered.

"What if I told you something that might make it easier?" Doc said.

He reached for the toast, and his stomach let out a loud rumble. It didn't know he was falling apart inside. "Depends."

"Funny," Doc said, although his tone was carefully neutral. "It seems there was a problem in the prep room where they were keeping Lexa for the brain mapping."

Quinn's heart let out a painful thump. "What?"

"Strangest thing…no one's entirely sure how she did it. But…" A smile spread across Doc's craggy face. "Lexa escaped. Piers is furious." Now he laughed a little. "She avoided every security camera on the grounds. It's like she disappeared."

"She did?" He couldn't believe it. No, wait, of course he could. "She's alive?"

"I can't say for sure, but security teams were dispatched a few hours ago, and there's no sign of her."

Doc left him with his breakfast. Where had Lexa gone? Would she come back? No, he didn't want her to come back. It wasn't safe here. He'd do what he planned—he'd wait and escape on his own. And once he did, he'd find her. Together, they'd bring Precipice to its knees. They'd free their artificial brothers and sisters. And then? A cold, hard core of righteous anger filled him.

Then they'd take down the Quad.

Together.

Epilogue: Today

"Now, Quinn," Maren drawls. "Dr. Martine tells me you didn't enjoy the sorting activities."

Deciding who to fire and who to keep at Precipice? No, that hadn't been any fun. I swallow down my loathing, though, and say, "It just wasn't much of a challenge, ma'am. The criteria and patterns were too easy to identify."

"Hmm." She gets up from her desk, already in her robe so she can retire for the evening. "I'm pleased to hear that, actually. I'll come up with something more stimulating in a few days. In the meantime, you're excused."

I nod respectfully and let myself out of her office. I no longer fear walking these halls, not since Piers was promoted to Chief of Security at Precipice and moved out of the house. Most people ignore me now, and that's how I like it. It's been so lonely since Doc got fired, though. The K600s are kind, but it's just not the same. My attempt at family was disastrous, too, fraught with mistakes and betrayals I will never repeat. As a result, I fear I'm destined to be alone the rest of my life.

Depressing, even for a fake human.

I wander upstairs, thinking I'll go for a run on the treadmill before bed, but something is going on. Guards race down the hall—some artificial, some human. They tear through the second floor in a cacophony of boots and barked orders.

Port, the human security captain, sees me standing at the head of the staircase and shouts, "Quinn! Intruder! Check the bedrooms."

I hold in a sigh and nod. Seven years of this crap, and they still see me as a utility player. Good enough, since I don't want to draw attention to just how powerful I'm becoming. Maren's idea of a "more stimulating" project won't even come close to stressing my capabilities, although I'll make her think it does.

Besides, I hardly care that someone is running amok in the house—asking me to help find the intruder is such a pointless exercise—but compliant is my middle name, so I trot to the first door. It's locked. Then again, it's always locked. My K600 friends speculate that it holds Maren's sex toys. I find that funny, because she's such a ball of frustration, I can't see her being uninhibited about anything, least of all a secret sex chamber.

I open the second door and step inside. The room's completely dark once I shut the door behind me. Or at least it would seem that way to a normal person, but I'm far from normal. I see well outside the human range, and I detect a faint glow coming from under the bed. A rogue K600?

So that's what they're after—an escapee. Well, I'll help this one get away and tell Port the rooms are empty.

Whistling, I go to check the bathroom and feel the air behind me stir. The artificial is on the move. "The windows are rigged with an alarm," I say. "And the lights in the garden would turn on the second you hit ground, anyway."

"Who are you?" a girl asks.

That voice... It's older, harder, but I know that voice. It's the voice of all my dreams.

I start trembling and slowly turn. The glow she emits isn't quite enough to be sure, so I flip on the light switch and nearly fall to my knees.

She's seven years older—well past seventeen now—and beautiful, but I'd know her anywhere. "Lexa?"

She's wearing tight fitting black clothes that make me feel both hot and cold, and her hair is tucked inside a cap, but it's her. She even still smells faintly like cookies.

Lexa brandishes some kind of tool at me. "Who are you?"

I can't believe it. She found me. She has no idea who I am, which explains a lot about her disappearance, about why she never made contact with me. My Lexa never would've left me behind. But I'm not bitter—there was a reason. She would've come back if she'd been able to remember, and her memories can be restored over time. Doc will know what to do, if I can make contact. All that matters is that she's here, and that we leave the compound together. I just have to make her trust me. That's my gift, right? I'll help her escape and convince her to take me with her.

Then I'll help her remember why she trusted me all those years ago.

Our time has come. At last.

✳

Unstrung, the first installment in the Unstrung series is available now. If you want more information about upcoming releases, other series, and publication dates, visit my website at www. kendrachighley.com.

Made in the USA
Charleston, SC
01 August 2016